A LITTLE SOMETHING TO HIDE

CRAIG BROWN

A Little Something To Hide

Copyright © Craig Brown 2024.
All rights reserved.

The right of Craig Brown to be identified as the author of this work has been asserted by him in accordance with the Copyright, Designs and Patents Act 1988.

The characters and events portrayed in this book are fictitious. Any similarity to real persons, living or dead, is coincidental and not intended by the author.

No part of this book may be reproduced, or stored in a retrieval system, or transmitted in any form or by any means, electronic, mechanical, photocopying, recording, or otherwise; nor used or reproduced in any manner for the purpose of training artificial intelligence technologies or systems without express written permission of the author.

To keep up to date with the work of Craig Brown, sign up to his mailing list at craigbrownauthor.com

Paperback ISBN: 978-1-0685513-0-7
eBook ISBN: 978-1-0685513-1-4
Cover design by: Jason Heffer, Disrupt Media

PROLOGUE	1
SAN FRANCISCO BUS STATION	3
BOBBIE – SAN FRANCISCO	7
SAN JOSE DIRIDON STATION	33
SANDRA & BABY GEORGE – SAN JOSE	37
SALINAS TRANSIT CENTER	67
ROSA – SALINAS	71
CANAL / BASSETT STREET, KING CITY	105
MICHAEL – KING CITY	107
MTD TRANSIT CENTER, SANTA BARBARA	131
TIM & BRIONY – SANTA BARBARA	135
LOS ANGELES BUS AND COACH STATION	165
TOBY – LOS ANGELES	169
W WELLS ST / S LOVEKIN BLVD, BLYTHE	207
GRANNY MAC – BLYTHE	211
PHOENIX BUS STATION	231
JEANNIE – PHOENIX	235
FLAGSTAFF BUS STOP	261
SIMON – FLAGSTAFF	263
GALLUP TRAVEL CENTER	277
JIMMY – GALLUP	285
EL FUGITIVO	303
FELIPE – LOS ALPES	309
NEARING ALBUQUERQUE	339

PROLOGUE

PROLOGUE

Somewhere between San Francisco and Albuquerque, a lone woman steps onto the battered Briscola coach that will take her to where her life will be different. As she steps onto the bus, the first passenger she passes gives her a shy smile. His smile says *Hello*, but his eyes say, *Please don't sit next to me*. The unspoken message doesn't bother her, she's comfortable with travelling alone, she has much to consider.

She is neither troubled by his look, or that which she is leaving behind. In many respects, the only regret that she carries is that she didn't act sooner, but she's a patient woman, pleased with what she's done. There are others on the bus who, in their way, harbour similar sentiments.

A calm settles over her when she sits, rummaging through her bag, taking from it the photos that she carries with her wherever she goes. She spends time looking at each of the images, those that she loves, lamenting that which she has lost by leaving things for too long. *Still,* she thinks. *It's done now.*

Restoring the photos to her bag, she burrows further, equipping herself for the journey, a woman content, believing herself to be ready for whatever comes next.

To look at her, you wouldn't know that lying in the basement of the house she left that morning is a man whose head is twisted at an impossible angle, wearing a rictus smile that suggests he might have enjoyed his final moments. The woman doesn't look like your average murderer, but then, does anyone really know what a typical murderer looks like? I am better placed than most to provide an opinion, and what I can tell you, is that they don't all look the same. No one on the coach is likely to suspect her, nor would most of them know, that she's not the only killer travelling to Albuquerque.

A LITTLE SOMETHING TO HIDE

SAN FRANCISCO BUS STATION

```
Departures
Time      Destination              Expected
20:00     San Jose                 On time
```

SAN FRANCISCO BUS STATION

The Briscola coach to Albuquerque delivers a rancid belch of midnight-blue exhaust as it departs the San Francisco Bus Station along the broad boulevard of Folsom Street. The coach carries those that can't afford to fly, or don't want to, to distant locales, far from the waters of San Francisco Bay, across the thousands of miles of asphalt veins that criss-cross the country.

Those keen to guard their money forego the sleek, air-conditioned luxury of a Greyhound Bus, opting for a nastier alternative, suffering a ride with Briscola Coach Services, on a bus that will mash through its gears on leaving the station, its toxins poisoning the air.

Briscola Coach Services isn't concerned about California's emission standards; the owner of the noisome coach, Anthony Briscola, has friends in the California Air Resources Board, biddable officials that he ensures look the other way. Each is one of many such people sitting on a clandestine payroll providing ancillary services. Anthony Briscola encourages his Management Accountant to record the expenses as grease.

'Put it down as grease,' he says. 'We gotta keep the axles greased for the wheels to turn.' It might have seemed funny the first time he said it, he still thinks it does, but the refrain hasn't aged well, neither has his fleet.

His manner, as well as his accent, are gruff Brooklyn, both affectations. He believes the brashness signals strength, that his corrosive approach lends authority to his business endeavours, cultivating fear in his competitors and his workers. He wants people to think he is dangerous, like a mafia Don, the patriarch of a dynasty built with disdain for convention and the law.

A LITTLE SOMETHING TO HIDE

The bluster masks his background, a West Coast privilege stemming from the wealth created by two preceding generations. He has control of the business his grandfather and father built. They both died young, leaving him to inherit a thriving organisation that is steadily crumbling under his stewardship. His father's attempts to impart commercial nous to his son were unsuccessful. The father knew he was dealing with an idiot; the lessons fell on arrogant ears. His father's dying wish, which he took to his grave, was that he hoped the company's success could survive his son's ignorance; it seems unlikely.

All manner of people ride a Briscola coach, not just those eschewing expense. Some travel toward dreams, others are escaping horrors, each carries their secrets and the belief that they harbour truths known only to themselves. Despite these beliefs, we're never entirely alone with our secrets, often they're there for others to see. Most are ill-equipped to conceal their darkest thoughts or outsized ambitions because they're worn in expressions, in movement, in tics and tells.

As they board, one can learn a great deal about a person from their choice of seat. The depth to which they enter the bus declares how much they want to hide from the world. The inquisitive occupy the front, soaking up the passing landscape, sharing the driver's perspective, marvelling at the changing topography, commenting on distances to go. They are gregarious, if at times, dull.

The timid hustle to the rear, although they're not brave enough to occupy the last row. They carry memories of school outings where the cooler kids evicted those having the temerity to occupy the rearmost seats. Even as adults they'd rather avoid the risk of the humiliation, but still they wander deep into the bus before tucking themselves against the cool glass, planting a bag in a vacant seat to thwart contact and hide from the world.

They'll reluctantly move their luggage if the bus should fill, finding themselves apologetic at requests to occupy spare seats, before sitting uncomfortably beneath their bag to the journey's end, declining their neighbour's invitation to place it in the overhead storage, a decision they will regret for the remainder of the ride.

The alpha-types, wearing their confidence as a mask to their deficiencies, choose the back rows or stake a mid-bus position, aisle seat, guarding the space by the window as an extension of their domain,

SAN FRANCISCO BUS STATION

freeing it only to impudent demands. If absolutely necessary, they'll yield their second seat with a grunt that accompanies the effort of twisting legs; they're too self-important to rise and allow an easier passing. They'll sit in quiet fulmination, bile developing, releasing it slowly, in a discourse that accords to societal norms, but contains niceties laced with jagged edges. No one should have the audacity to invade their space. The reward for invasion is a conversation stuffed with unvarnished and unwanted opinions that illuminate their prejudices.

The uncertain move deep into the sanctum, not by preference, but because they see faces that communicate unclear meanings; hostility, anger, hate – exaggerated expressions of malcontent. They'll often retrace their steps, retreating, seeking friendlier faces, ones they imagine to be less judgemental than others they have seen, reverting to a previously ignored position, where they'll sit in silent embarrassment for having spurned their new neighbour on the first pass.

Finding people easy to read comes with experience, a truth I know to be immutable. I'm endowed with an all-seeing eye, perhaps the only thing that I have in common with Briscola Coach Services.

Anthony Briscola convinced himself that an Eye of Providence should appear in the company's logo, unwittingly drawing comparison to the divine – his narcissism knows no limits.

He's unable to recognise it, but the Briscola eye speaks of distrust, a testament to the patriarch's nature. It signals a malevolence toward his employees and passengers and provides evidence of his paranoia.

While Briscola may want his employees and passengers to think that they are scrutinised when they are not, they are under surveillance. Not from him, from me. I am always watching, but not in a mistrustful way.

I only need a glimpse of a person to see their past. Their pallor paints their entire life, their gait tells a story. I gain insights into their lives as they search for a seat, and I understand more than they would wish.

Everyone wears a façade behind which they believe they can hide; it allows them to conceal their past and reveal only what they want others to know. It's a folly, it doesn't work. There are signs that can be read: movement, glances, the way they breathe. Everything intervenes to inform their narrative, unveiling those things they wish to keep hidden. None of them ever tells their whole story, but a close inspection reveals more than they might like.

Those that ride on a Briscola coach are far more interesting than a cursory glance reveals. As they tread the worn steps into the bus and peer into the gloom to search for an available seat, they enter a domain they believe to be secure, if only for the duration of their trip. They all step past me as though I don't exist, drifting, unsuspecting, to their seats, thinking their secrets are safe, unaware that I know their stories and can predict their future.

My voice, full of inflections, is influenced by others, by what they choose to reveal and the things they dare not say. Although they may be reticent to share, I am not. I don't pretend to speak with their voices, but I know their truths, the secrets they wish to conceal. I see all that they have hidden the moment they step on the bus. Telling their stories is what I enjoy most. They've all got a little something to say and everyone has a little something to hide.

BOBBIE – SAN FRANCISCO

Robert Jamieson has a secret that he is hiding from his parents. He thinks that makes him unique on the bus, but it's the only thing he has in common with everyone that boards. It's not even a particularly well-concealed secret. He moved to San Francisco to pursue a career in the performing arts. He could have gone to New York or Los Angeles, where the opportunities were greater, but as he explains to anyone that cares to listen, San Francisco feels like a better fit. Those listening nod knowingly.

He's leaving San Francisco but doesn't know for how long. It's his home now and may be forever, but that doesn't stop him taking a deep breath before placing his foot on the lowest step of the bus, feeling something that he hasn't felt for years ... uncertainty.

He is the first to climb aboard and the only passenger going all the way from San Francisco to Albuquerque. Others stepping onto the bus head for LA, where they'll see their dreams blossom, or more likely crushed, as they eke out pennies in restaurants and bars, failing at auditions, getting over-excited for call-backs that lead to more rejection, hoping for attention as extras in a blockbuster, yet predicting their scenes will find their way to the cutting room floor.

They'll catch the return bus in two or three years with tales of the *oh so close*, the *if onlys*. They'll speak of star-struck encounters; serving flat whites to Hollywood greats who hide beneath baseball caps and behind mirrored lenses; of snatched glimpses of the rich and famous dining *al fresco* at restaurants where the cost of the meal could feed the average family for a week. They'll recount their sightings, at first with enthusiasm, but that will diminish, along with the dreams they once fostered.

A LITTLE SOMETHING TO HIDE

Robert Jamieson is the name that his family and old school friends from Eldorado High School will recognise, but in San Francisco, she's better known as Bobbie James. It's the name that the patrons of Oasis on Eleventh Street know her by and it's where she's been performing for the six years that separate her from her hometown of Peppertree-Royal Oak in Albuquerque, NM.

Bobbie remains in San Francisco. It's Robert on the bus and he'll stay on board beyond LA, where other performers might step off to seek the bright lights. That's not for Robert, or Bobbie, the silver-screen is of no interest. Robert's passion (well, Bobbie's really) is for the stage.

From an early age, Robert liked to perform. He'd ferret in his mother's bedroom looking for boa scarves, diamante necklaces and heels that threatened to topple him. He'd stage burlesque cabaret routines for his mother who sat watching her son perform, wearing an indulgent smile. She knew. He was talented too; musical theatre would suit him. Singing, dancing, and acting came naturally. His passion for the arts carried him to Oasis and a niche form of fame on the San Francisco drag scene.

Dr Arnold Jamieson, Robert's father, had long since given up the hope that his son might follow in the family footsteps. A neurosurgeon, Arnold married his college sweetheart, Marjorie, an Orthopaedic specialist. Robert didn't show an aptitude for medicine, the sight of blood leaves him faint. Arnold saw his hopes of living a vicarious existence through his son disappear in the waft of a make-up brush. It didn't trouble him that Robert preferred the stage to the scalpel, he wanted only for his boy to be happy. What troubled him though, was that Robert rarely seemed to be.

Arnold found this to be an unsolvable conundrum. In his mind, it was impossible to provide their child with greater privilege. His belief is that his son's life, his very *existence*, comprises of nothing more than a series of continuous blessings. Robert is the Jamieson's only child, their *special* child. Their wait for his arrival was excruciating. They had multiple IVF treatments, with heart-breaking failures, before the successful conception and birth of their beloved boy. It brought an intensity to their love for him approaching the extreme, it manifested in the excessive. They doted, giving him gifts they thought that every young boy should have: remote controlled cars; tree-forts in the garden; footballs; scooters; bikes; cars.

The boys at Robert's elementary school never declined an invitation to one of his birthday parties. They fought over Robert's latest presents, arguing amongst themselves about the next turn on the *AFX* track or the *PlayStation*, never having to compete with a host who was content to yield the latest gifts from his parents, parents who didn't yet understand Robert's preferences.

While his friends played, Robert observed, and in the evening, following the flight of their guests, Robert performed for his parents, recreating the exchanges he'd witnessed. Arnold and Marjorie thought that Robert's re-enactments reflected his enjoyment of the day. Instead, they represented the storytelling of a boy genuinely bemused by his friends. What he wanted from his parents was not appreciation for his performance, but an explanation of the other boys' behaviour. It didn't reflect what Robert thought of as fun.

He did well in school, despite a propensity for daydreaming and escapism. He was above average in English, adequate in Maths and Science, but in the Arts, he excelled. On the stage, he came alive. The boy that seemed so shy and reticent to play with his friends, unfurled his talent.

People loved the performer, but the boy inside was lonely. Robert's popularity on the stage didn't translate to fresh friendships. He found it difficult to establish relationships beyond the group of friends that moved as a herd through his childhood. As he and his peers aged, the attraction of the toys at Robert's house on Taramac Trail waned.

At his mother's urging, Robert reluctantly invited friends to spend time around the pool on sultry afternoons in the heat haze of an Albuquerque summer. The invitations went to the same cohort that fought over his toys. It never occurred to Robert that his mother didn't care who he invited, she just wanted him to be happy with friends. Robert's invites always went to the same names; a constancy borne from familiarity. There were other friends that his mother hadn't met, so of course she never mentioned them when prompting Robert. Notwithstanding, he didn't think she would approve; they were *unconventional*. He thought, instead, that he should conform to her unspoken expectations.

Some of his friends came to swim and laze at the poolside, enjoying the luxury of a private pool and the largess of the Jamieson family, but the frequency of their visits diminished as their interests diverged from Robert's. Through middle school and into high school, Robert found himself in a twilight of loneliness, struggling to forge relationships in his hometown.

He knew he was different around the age of nine but didn't entirely understand why. There wasn't an inciting incident or a trauma that led to his discovery. He simply found the company of other boys dull. He wearied of their clamouring for attention, their robust play, their serial attempts to assert dominance. Their make-believe: of soldiers; of cowboys; of Indians; of battles and triumphs, was tiresome. At his parties, his playmates grew accustomed to Robert skulking in his room, gravitating to a quiet corner, harbouring his thoughts, watching their adventures. They didn't mind. The Jamieson house brought them together in a place where the milk and cookies seemed in endless supply. They were enjoying themselves. Robert was an unimposing host, owning the latest games and gadgets. He placed no demands on them and didn't complain when they broke his toys.

When he wasn't observing the boys at play, destroying his belongings, Robert would gaze out of his bedroom window. In his thoughts, he would colour the sky amber, turn the leaves on trees to shades of blue and paint the distant Sandia Peak russet red, far-off, burning. Robert wanted colour and life in his world, not the dusty desert hues that surrounded him.

Albuquerque was a cocoon that should have provided a place of safety, comfort, development, *evolution*. It didn't. It constrained and enveloped, binding him tightly, pinning and smothering him, an unyielding chrysalis. It was inevitable that time would see him change and break free. For Robert, Albuquerque was a shroud that held him tight, serving only to suppress him as he grew.

His parents were Stanford Alumni, so when he mentioned he wanted to go to college out West, they harboured hopes. He dashed them, quickly, disabusing their notions, but not their wallets, as he chose an under-graduate degree in Theatre Arts from San Francisco State University.

Bursting free of his bounds, he flourished. In his junior year, he was the first male to perform in the University's annual production of *The Vagina Monologues*. His parents sat in the front row, beaming at their son as he instructed the audience on Vagina Facts.

He introduced them to his friends, a mixed array of characters, *unconventional* characters. His mother found them adorable.

Undiagnosed misunderstandings existed in the Jamieson family. Robert's parents loved him unconditionally but were strangely reticent to voice their feelings. Robert believed they loved him, but remembered the flash of disappointment that crossed his father's face when he learnt that the number of medics in the family would remain at two. The look his father gave was fleeting, dashed vicariousness, but it stuck with Robert. It materialised as shame, in the idea that he couldn't be who his father wanted him to be. Robert carried the certain knowledge that anything that he chose to do would fall short of the ideal of which his father dreamt, yet Robert's opinion went unspoken.

If the elder Jamieson had known the effect on his son, he would have explained how natural it is for a father to have such thoughts, but that it was his issue to resolve, not Robert's. Arnold's view was that his son must be who he wants to be, and that he, as his dad, must accept that decision. Robert didn't know that, nor understand it to be an inalienable truth to Arnold Jamieson.

Robert's misconception of his father's disappointment meant that when he left for college, he spared Arnold other revelations; he didn't want to upset him any further. An aspiring actor, he considered it an easy deception and was grateful when he thought Arnold feigned acceptance of his college choices. In a misguided moment of magnanimity, he decided that carrying the hidden weight of his sexuality was preferable to making a declaration.

When he did come out to his parents, they were waiting for him backstage after a performance of *The Vagina Monologues*, his mother holding a bouquet of pale roses and his dad cradling her at his side, arm around her in a protective embrace. Robert hadn't planned to tell them, but the sight of the flowers, and the evidence of their love, triggered a whim that tonight should be the night, that *that* moment should be *the* moment.

He felt they did a passable job of masking their surprise. When he reflected later, he wondered whether adrenaline had fuelled his spontaneity and dulled his perception, diminishing his ability to properly assess their reaction. Robert was expecting disappointment, but on seeing none, admitted that perhaps some of his talent for the stage stemmed from genetics. He didn't entertain that they might have known or suspected that he was gay, or that to them, his sexuality was perfectly normal.

Instead, he believed that their near silence on the subject reflected ignorance. His need for acceptance, for them to articulate their comfort with his announcement, failed to appear. His mother blithely said, *Oh, we know*. His father smiled and dipped his head a fraction, a token nod acknowledging his son's pronouncement and his wife's response.

Is that it? thought Robert. *The most monumental declaration of my life and all I get is a 'We know' and an insipid smile from my father.*

Mistaking their ambivalence for shame, Robert demonstrated the universal ignorance that children have of their parents, which in Robert's case, stemmed from nearly twenty years of disinterest in their lives. He didn't know his parents well, failing to realise that his mother's three words were meant to convey everything they felt; that they were aware and entirely comfortable with his sexuality. He took some comfort when they said they had long known that he was gay. It was, he felt, kindness wrapped in a harmless lie. He didn't entirely believe them. He was grateful for their attempts to make him feel comfortable, but decided that he would spare them further discomfort or embarrassment by not revealing his closest relationship. *In time,* he thought.

If only he had known that back in Albuquerque, while their boy lay sleeping in his room, dreaming irreconcilable dreams, his parents lay in bed whispering their thoughts, exchanging opinions, and agreeing that they should give him time, allowing him to come to them on his terms.

When Robert was younger, they often witnessed a doleful child, it was what provoked Arnold's fears that happiness eluded his son, but what they most failed to appreciate, was quite how much of his misery their actor son was concealing. They didn't fully understand him and made the mistake of believing that he knew how they felt.

When it eventually came, they knew his announcement hadn't been easy. By avoiding an interrogation, they believed they were granting Robert the privacy he deserved. If only they'd known that what Robert wanted more than anything at that moment was for them to be inquisitive, probing, asking him to tell them about himself.

Not only did Robert not tell them about all his relationships, he also kept a secret of the role that he played in San Francisco's eclectic nightlife. Given their absence of interest, he wasn't sure they were ready to learn more. Although they were doing their best to appear accepting, he thought that telling them that he was supplementing his allowance with performances as a drag queen, might be a disclosure too far.

Had Robert understood his parents, he might have told them more about the part he plays in his community. He might have told them more about his friendships and his effect on others. While some feel his force from his appearances on stage, others perceive the light of his presence from the confines of a bed, beneath the milky phosphorescence of a hospital ward, where they take comfort from holding his hand and the serene assurance that they are not alone, their murmured conversations augmented by the quiet metronomic parp of a bedside monitor.

Those conditions were familiar to his parents. They'd have understood why he was there and what it meant to the people he met, but that didn't occur to Robert. His bias came from thinking his parents wouldn't approve of his secret life.

Ward 86 of the San Francisco General Hospital didn't feature in Robert's plans when he moved west in the late summer of 2015. He didn't know it existed, but as he developed new friends, friends different to those he abandoned in Peppertree-Royal Oak, he developed a familiarity with the ward.

Despite knowing the need for safeguards and precautions, for some of Robert's friends, a visit to Ward 86 had a depressing inevitability. Robert found himself an episodic caller, spending the occasional weekend visiting and caring for those that had provided him with the friendship and comradery missing in his previous life. Most of Robert's friends got to leave restored. Most, but not all.

Ironically, his willingness to spend time at the hospital, supporting those he knew, didn't trigger the thought in Robert that his caring nature, like some of his acting talent, might result from genetics. Neither did he consider it to be a nurtured quality, although his parents could arguably claim responsibility. The raising of their boy in a safe, secure and loving environment had led to the creation of a compassionate champion.

Robert's entrance into San Francisco's LGBTQ community was gradual. Albuquerque had not prepared him to face the world. Robert's pubescent angst was different to the other boys. He didn't participate in dramatic entreaties to the opposite sex; couldn't understand the rising passion and the accelerating pulses of those he knew best. He didn't join in the catcalls or express the fantasies that an attractive girl would elicit from a pack of hormonal boys. He stood witness to the spawning of puerile chauvinism. Robert observed the boys' posturing, their schoolyard strutting. He thought the peacocking moronic, unable to fully fathom why his interests were so different.

Time and talent led to his metamorphosis. The Eldorado High School Drama Club provided a refuge and gave him an outlet to express himself. Robert had been refining his performance skills by spending his adolescence concealing who he was. The drama club gave him the opportunity to be someone else and allow him to relax from the effort of playing the character he had become in life.

His Drama teacher, Mr Elgars, a man perpetually young (though in truth, close to retirement), dressed in Robert's image of a thespian. His was a ruffled chic, a uniform that never varied in the clothing articles but was alive with colours and patterns. His colour choices for chinos demonstrated an abhorrence for the bland – no muted khaki, beige or grey occupied Mr Elgars' wardrobe. His pigments, plucked from butterfly wings, vibrant and loud. In contrast, his shirts varied between bold and banal, always buttoned, always with cuffs, always open at the neck. On dreary days he wore brighter shirts, patterns of paisley and Picasso, on brighter days the shirts were duller, their muted colours offset with an endless supply of extravagant cravats, tied with precision. The sartorial ensemble was incomplete without a jacket: velveteen; casually creased linen; patched elbows; tawdry options and always with a pocket handkerchief that threatened to clash with his overall look, but somehow, grudgingly, managed to complement the whole.

Mr Elgars hadn't always been a teacher. Before the classroom, he travelled extensively, performing in the world's greatest cities. He infused his teaching with his experiences, using his tales of West End triumphs and Off-Broadway maladies to inspire and caution. Robert loved him but couldn't comprehend why Mr Elgars seemed content in Albuquerque. He never learnt why his drama teacher came to settle in such a godforsaken place, but he was willing to listen when Mr Elgars encouraged him to go West. When Robert asked why, his teacher looked at him with a mix of bemusement and curiosity, trying to establish if the boy before him was feigning ignorance. What he saw in front of him was not an insolent young man, but a lost soul seeking answers. Mr Elgars' reply was suitably enigmatic. *Because*, he said, *that's where you'll find yourself*.

Robert had an inkling of what his teacher meant. He'd gone through elementary, middle, and high school with the same stable of rutting boys and capricious girls. Few people arrived in his south-west corner of the country, fewer left; he thought the place dulled the imagination, left one hollow. He worried it was a life sentence. He escaped. At San Francisco State University, he landed in an altogether different peer group to the one he'd known back home. The Theatre Arts intake at SFSU for 2015 had a different complexion. Robert found the cocktail of fresh influences quietly reassuring.

He found himself on a mixed dormitory, surrounded by a group representing a broad diaspora, each of them eager to exceed the parental restrictions they'd left behind. Robert rarely went to parties in Albuquerque, his consumption of alcohol occurred at extended family gatherings for Thanksgiving, when his father would pour him a half-glass of wine over dinner or invite him to have a beer during the football. Robert slurped through the former, always hoping for more, which never came, and declined the latter. It wasn't that he didn't want to try the beer, it was just that if he accepted his father's offer, he would feel compelled to sit and watch the game. The prospect of three hours nursing a beer while watching a sport he disliked, held no appeal. Being alone in his room, headphones jammed over his ears to drown out the professionally inane commentary, was infinitely preferable.

Robert arrived on campus two days later than the Freshmen corps. His mother was insistent he stay in Albuquerque to celebrate his eighteenth birthday. She argued it was an important milestone to recognise. The party was notable for the small number of guests. Many invitees had already left to start their college careers, others dredged limp excuses to avoid the event. The Jamieson house was no longer an attractive destination. Those of Robert's age that came, did so under duress, the offspring of his parents' friends. Their children's opinions about attending were irrelevant. Protestations faced rebuke and insistence; they would be going to the party. The younger set, feeling awkward, sat together in the den, listening to *Imagine Dragons* and *American Authors*, turned too loud to enable conversation. The children mooched over handsets which cast pallid glows into their bepimpled faces, yearning for evening's end. The adults, ignoring their progeny, quaffed Prosecco in the kitchen, enjoying themselves.

Robert's late arrival at SFSU meant he missed the mutual embarrassment of the newly landed. Forcibly awkward introductions, when enjoyed collectively, are easier to bear. Robert didn't wish to suffer the experience on a solo basis. He slipped, unnoticed, into his room.

Lying on his bed, flicking through the course outline on his first night in the dormitory, a staccato rap on the door interrupted his browsing. He opened it to find an impossibly short Puerto Rican standing in front of him, as wide as he was tall, dressed in cargo shorts that met his ankles, and wearing a polo-shirt buttoned to the top, which accentuated the abundance of flesh it failed to conceal. In one hand he held a half-filled bottle of Tequila and in the other, a stack of red pint cups that swayed as he moved his arms. Somewhere distant, Robert could hear a deep base pounding from another of the rooms. The Puerto Rican introduced himself as Antonio and thrust the cups at Robert. Robert took one, moving it beneath the bottle that Antonio upended with little regard to whether there was anything to catch the offering. *Come to Mary-Beth's room for a party*, he said, indicating the direction from where the music was coming, his cadence high and effeminate. He leaned in before whispering to Robert, *she'll lay anyone and everyone, if you know what I mean. And if she's not your type,* he added wheezily, *I can help you find someone*. He winked at Robert, before mincing away without waiting for a reply and knocking on the next door.

Robert was unsure what to do. He sniffed at the acrid liquid in the cup and glanced down the hall in the direction of the music, uncertainty immobilising him. He searched for Antonio, who had already moved to another door and a girl, looking as bemused as Robert felt, stood standing at the threshold of her room holding another of the red cups and eyeing it suspiciously. She noticed Robert watching her. He half-waved. She returned the wave and started toward him. *Hi. I'm Amy*, she said when she drew closer. *Shall we go and see what obscenities Mary-Beth is performing?*

Robert consented, deciding in that moment, that he was going to like it in San Francisco.

Mary-Beth's room was on a different corridor to Robert's. As he and Amy turned the corner, they faced a Bacchanalian scene. Inert bodies lay across the floor, others slumped against walls. The carpet, irrevocably stained, doused with a blend of alcohols. Mary-Beth was an enthusiastic host. She weaved in and out of her room and along the hallway, dispensing spirits of unknown provenance and flirting with each huddle she encountered. As she moved, she flicked away groping hands, staring fiercely when she deemed the advance inappropriate, at other times smiling suggestively at her assailant, leaving some certain of her feelings and others curiously unsure.

She saw Robert and Amy standing tentatively on the fringe and greeted them with the familiarity one adopts for the resurrection of neglected friendships. She kissed them on the lips, leading them both to believe that Mary-Beth was already a close friend of the other. She corrected their assumption when she asked for their names. Mary-Beth immediately pronounced Amy, *the Aimster*, before pausing to assess Robert. When she spoke, it was with an English, Home Counties lilt. Robert couldn't discern whether it was real or affected.

Hmm, she said, evaluating him as one might judge an animal at a county fair. *Immaculately groomed, stylish, handsome*. She took his hand. *Manicured*, she squealed. *You're going to have to be Bobbie*, she said, before adding portentously, *I know someone that would just love to meet you.*

BOBBIE – SAN FRANCISCO

Robert never discovered the identity of the person who Mary-Beth thought would love to meet him. She didn't introduce him or Amy to anyone, but by the end of the party, the Aimster had stuck, and more than a few people were calling him Bobbie. He found himself surprisingly comfortable with the new moniker, and more at ease with the people surrounding him than any of those from his school years. The alcohol helped. Despite his best efforts to drain it, his pint cup was never empty as Mary-Beth, Antonio and other unknown beneficiaries kept it full throughout the evening. By the end of the night, Robert was grateful for the bathroom in his room.

Antonio and Mary-Beth took turns at hosting impromptu gatherings throughout the week. Robert and Amy developed Pavlovian tendencies in response to the heavy base beats that broke the early evening calm. By the end of the week, they were veteran attendees, adept at pouring communal alcohol into the cups of their fellow students, and both were more than familiar with the cooling properties of glazed porcelain.

With the anarchy of the first week behind them, Robert and Amy were two of the first to arrive in the auditorium for their opening lecture. They chose to sit in the middle of the room. Trickles of students followed, occupying seats randomly. Despite the activities of the preceding days, both were surprised at how few of the people entering the theatre they knew. They thought Mary-Beth and Antonio knew everyone and that they'd met most of their counterparts during the revelries. Unfamiliar faces filled the room, Robert and Amy silently considered each new person, forming unvoiced opinions of those that entered.

Mary-Beth joined the throng, followed by a waddling Antonio, quickly assessing the room. They were known to many, exchanging waves and smiles, politely spurning invitations to sit next to others as they climbed the steps into the auditorium. When they reached the row of seats containing Robert and Amy, they shuffled down the line towards them, Mary-Beth wriggling past to sit on Amy's right, while Antonio plopped himself heavily in the seat next to Robert, his short legs popping straight out, his sneakered feet scuffing the chair in front of him. The anxious looks of other students entering the room vanished when they exchanged glances with Antonio or Mary-Beth, relaxing at seeing friendly faces. Antonio threw a pudgy thumb at those catching his eye, assuring them it was safe to enter. Unlike Robert and Amy's silent assessment of those arriving, Antonio gave voice to his judgements, which Mary-Beth either challenged or affirmed.

Twink, said Antonio.

Definite twink, said Mary-Beth.

Antonio. *Bull Dyke*.

Mary-Beth. *Never*.

Packing, said Antonio with approval as a tall, muscular specimen walked in.

He is, said Mary-Beth, with more wisdom than just a glance at the boy's jeans would attest. They continued as the room filled, Robert and Amy equally bemused by the terms applied to those entering: *femme, gold-star, unicorn, straight, clone, closeted, bucket boy, future-breeder, stem, ac/dc*. Antonio's lascivious lexicon was inexhaustible. Occasionally, he would divert from an expression of their sexual orientation to comment on their resourcefulness: *fake ID, alcohol, weed*. He catalogued their usefulness based on their ability to obtain the illicit. The last to join the room was the lecturer. *100-footer*, squeaked Antonio.

Oh, yes, declared Mary-Beth.

They were packing their bags at the end of the lecture when Robert leaned across and asked Antonio to define him. Antonio smiled at him conspiratorially. *I think*, he said, *you're nearly a Baby Gay*. As bemused as he had been earlier, Robert understood the context and experienced an odd mix of doubt and hope.

Really? He looked to Antonio for confirmation, unaware that Amy and Mary-Beth were listening to their conversation. Mary-Beth, who despite evidencing earlier that she often thought otherwise regarding Antonio's observations, provided the affirmation.

BOBBIE – SAN FRANCISCO

Oh yes, honey, she said. *Antonio's gaydar is 20:20, you'll see.*

Antonio's prediction proved to be the catalyst for Robert's awakening, the realisation that he had been trying to conform to a norm that he was never able to meet. He began to understand that there was more to his nature. Cautiously, he emerged.

Antonio supported his observation by introducing Robert to a wider circle, chaperoning him through events and parties, procuring him a fake ID and taking him, Mary-Beth and Amy to his favourite bars and clubs across the city. He guarded Robert and the girls with a feral tenacity, fighting off suitors that he deemed unacceptable, sniffing out jeopardies, guiding them matronly through the San Franciscan nightlife, gradually softening his restrictions and allowing others to access his friends with grunts of approval. Antonio was especially protective of Robert and wanted him to be prepared for what awaited. Through the course of an evening, however, his protective entreaties steadily declined.

Antonio's alcohol intake and his attention span may have been subject to Newton's third law, the consumption of the former causing a corresponding deficit in the latter. More accurately, his attention shifted, his growing intoxication leading to a heightened libido and interests beyond his immediate circle of friends. Social management of Robert and the girls lost its appeal. *You're responsible for your own holes*, he'd say, before adding that it was time for him to fulfil a chubby chaser's fantasy.

When they allowed their studies to intrude on their social life, Robert and Antonio shared an affinity for performance. Robert displayed a versatility that made him difficult to pigeon-hole. He could play almost any role, whereas Antonio's everyday identity saw him irredeemably typecast. His complaint, in a simpering falsetto, that he was always second in the race for masculine roles, drew mirth from his friends. Antonio feigned annoyance at Robert's ability. *You keep taking my parts*, he'd say.

Rumour has it your 'parts' are always available, said Mary-Beth. *I could be a star if it wasn't for him.*

A LITTLE SOMETHING TO HIDE

Maybe, you could be stars together, said Amy.
Doing what? asked Robert.
Cabaret, darling, said Mary-Beth.

It led them to an open-mike evening at Oasis in the SoMa district, where Bobbie James and her cuboid sidekick, Zontally Challenged, debuted. Antonio cavorted; Robert captivated. The little Puerto Rican brought hilarity, upstaging her elegant partner at every opportunity, but the bellowing audience stilled for Bobbie James's spot-lit solo, her final note hanging in the air like a warming zephyr; explosive ovation followed. The manager invited them to return. Before long, they were a regular feature on the circuit. It widened their circle and introduced them to a raft of admirers with differing appetites. Antonio exploited his burgeoning popularity, discovering more enthusiasm for his physical attributes than he thought possible. Audiences loved them, Zontally Challenged for unrefined humour, Bobbie James for sophistry. Bobbie had everything: extensive range; a glorious vocal; elegance – her movement almost feline. Her grace attracted many. A diverse mix of suitors took interest, coaxing Bobbie from her shell, lending her an Epicurean confidence. The retiring boy that left Albuquerque emerged as a burlesque performer, almost brash, yet despite Bobbie's gregarious temperament, Robert relished calm. Peter provided it.

Peter was a regular at the club where they performed, *a Daddy,* as Antonio described him – an older man who had lived in San Francisco from the early nineties and who had lost more friends than he cared to think about. A gentle, loving soul, Peter's personality contrasted with Bobbie the extrovert, yet lent balance to Robert's needs.

They were opposites. Bobbie, the young drag-queen who lived for cabaret and wowing her audience; Peter, softly spoken, inconspicuous, inoffensive, kind. Peter always had warm words for the Oasis girls after their performances; always encouraging with an understated positivity. Peter's compliments were frequent and sincere, but in a room of people, he was easy to overlook.

BOBBIE – SAN FRANCISCO

He lectured at SFSU, but not in the Theatre and Dance faculty where Robert studied. Peter playfully argued that his courses offered more cerebral stimulus. He taught World History, a subject so broad that he claimed to know everything and nothing. Bobbie teased that Peter had the wrong order, that he knew nothing about everything.

Peter often winced when Bobbie spoke. Robert was more empathic, never tiring of listening to Peter. Peter spoke of the foundations of science, politics, law, artistic expression. He'd outline the context for wars, religious bigotry, and spiritual beliefs. The quietly spoken man drew Robert towards him.

They came together slowly, imperceptibly, and unaware, even to themselves, of a growing attraction. When Peter invited him to a touring exhibition of Persian antiquities, Robert was at first surprised and then intrigued. If felt like an invitation to a date, but the man was twice his age. He demurred. Peter smiled, reading the thoughts of the younger man, seeing the conflict, and left Robert to cogitate, saying the show was running for two months. If he wanted, they could go at any time. Peter never again mentioned the exhibition – *the date*, Robert had to find the courage to raise the subject the next time they spoke. They went on the third Saturday after his invitation.

Surprisingly, Robert enjoyed himself. He didn't need to read the display's descriptions, Peter delivered a private monologue as they strolled the museum, bringing each artifact to life, enriching the tour as Robert's personal guide. At the end of the visit, Robert excused himself, Oasis was beckoning. They parted, with a promise from Peter that he would be there later.

Bobbie flirted with him from the stage but couldn't find Peter at the end of the performance; the older man left before the night was over. Bobbie got the feeling that Peter was avoiding her. She didn't see him again for nearly two weeks.

When she did, it was on campus, as Robert. Robert was lounging with fellow students when Peter approached, lifting a hand to say *Hi*. Robert absconded from his friends. Peter offered no preamble, no acknowledgement of their last encounter, or lack of it, just another invitation to a visiting Professor's lecture on the French Revolution. Robert had no interest in the subject but agreed to go.

After, Peter asked Robert if he'd like to have coffee. They walked close, silent, comfortable in each other's company. They perched on stools at Sightglass Coffee, stepping lightly through their histories, a first tentative sharing. Peter asked about Robert's coming out, listening intently. Robert got the sense that Peter's was more traumatic.

Their relationship built with a slow, barely conspicuous intensity, occasionally setback by Peter's ambivalence towards Bobbie, who felt Peter was almost reticent to speak with her. The encouraging Peter was always present, complimenting Bobbie after her performances, but in the post-show banter, his interest waned. Bobbie at first thought it stemmed from his discomfort with the girls' language, that the risqué comments, spiked with *double entendre* and more explicit imagery, offended. As Bobbie's participation in the banter grew, Peter's discomfort rose. He'd quietly divorce proceedings, slipping from the room. Bobbie accepted his departures with good grace until he noticed the occasions where Peter and Zontally giggled their way through their recollections of the evening. When Bobbie joined them, Peter progressively fell quiet, his participation in the conversation tapering to silence. Zontally didn't notice, Bobbie did. It led to an argument. *Why won't you talk to me after a show?*

I don't like Bobbie, said Peter with disarming candour.

But you're okay with Zontally?

Uh, huh.

That's bullshit.

No. She's just Antonio in drag.

And Bobbie is me in drag.

No. Bobbie's someone else. Antonio and Zontally are the same person.

I'm the same person when I'm Bobbie.

No, you're not. You're someone else. You're not real.

Being someone he wasn't, came easily to Robert. He felt he was more real as Bobbie than he was as himself. She lent him the outlet to be what he thought he always wanted to be, an extravagant showgirl. Peter held to the belief that Bobbie was a form of therapy, a means for Robert to vent the frustration from his early years. Bobbie was an extreme counter to the boy from Albuquerque, she wasn't the person that Peter wanted to know. He was happy for Robert to have Bobbie as an outlet, but when her performances ended, Peter wanted Robert to return. It was Robert who attracted him. It was Robert whose time and attention he wanted to share. He knew the importance of Bobbie, but he didn't think she was who Robert needed to be. Peter was supportive of Robert the performer, not Bobbie the person.

It presented a dilemma for Robert. He thought he knew who he was, that Bobbie was an essential element to his character. Peter didn't disagree, he understood the need for a release, for Robert to perform as someone else. He just didn't want to get to know Bobbie any more than necessary. There was no ultimatum from him, but Peter treated Robert and Bobbie as different people. When Robert challenged him, Peter responded with his customary calm. *Look, Bobbie's okay, but it's you I love*.

Beyond his parents, it was the first time he could remember anyone telling him they loved him. He didn't know it, but it was all he'd ever wanted to hear. Adored on stage, Bobbie's audiences worshipped her, always telling her how brilliant she was, that they loved her performances. It was a narcotic; she could never have enough. It was artificial, it was a stimulus that was fleeting, superficial. The high didn't last. It took his relationship with Peter to understand that Bobbie wasn't a therapy for his previous life, she was a drug to hide from it. Bobbie engendered contrived love, Peter's love for Robert was real. Real and sustaining. Robert felt safe, secure, and loved with Peter. He didn't need to pretend to be someone else. It was an unexpected realisation that led to an unexpected romance.

As it grew, Peter shared more of his past, speaking of his early days in the Bay area, of a time when he was gregarious, less cautious, when he trusted those with whom he shared his bed. Now he was more circumspect. He sought *real* people. Honest people. He learnt too late that some of those he got closest to, often weren't who they professed to be, that they didn't always share the truth. Instead, someone shared something worse. The illness.

Peter shared his secret with Robert, the cloud under which he lived. Robert finally understood; his epiphany was manifold. He felt removed from the scene, seeing Peter and himself as strangers, not recognising either, but experiencing a vague certainty that he suddenly knew everything about them both, moving from knowledge to understanding. He understood Peter's patience, the kindness, the intellectual intimacy, the subdued passion, the foundation of his caring. He marvelled at the lack of cynicism, the absence of complaint, of never hearing the shrill cry of injustice. He was in awe of Peter's acceptance.

Robert knew enough to know the virus was not discerning, but also that science and medicine were better bedfellows, safeguarding against its foulest vagaries. He knew it wasn't the death sentence it once was, but his youth functioned as a shield to the past, casual ignorance provided false assurance, a diminished concern for the risks.

Peter's experience was different. Peter had his HIV under control. His illness taught him caution and it was a lesson he shared. The tales were harrowing, stories of vibrant, vivacious men wasting in hospital beds with a nebulous sickness ravaging them, taking them with casual ailments, weakened immune systems unable to cope, thin veneers of flesh hanging limp across prominent bones, the rattle of pneumonic lungs.

Peter's portrait of a time past, led to Robert spending more time on Ward 86. The stories sat heavily with Robert. Stories of the early sufferers' fear and loneliness, their designation as pariahs, modern-day lepers, lying in isolation – ignored, banished. It was a different type of history lesson from Peter, causing Robert to moderate his behaviour. His relationship with Peter served to mollify his more carnal desires. For Robert, although Peter and science assured him of safety, the intimacy of their relations always carried a trace of unease.

Despite his reservations, he had never been happier. Robert, it would seem, was in love.

Antonio, on the other hand, was boundless in his enthusiasm for sex and took little heed of Peter's warnings. The little Puerto Rican was an outrageous flirt and a cavalier lover. His enthusiasm for sexual encounters and unorthodox gratification led him to experiment widely. Peter and Robert cautioned him, he'd dismiss their concerns with a wave of his chubby arm, citing the precautions he took, reminding them that Peter was a walking example of the efficacy of antiretrovirals.

Every Monday afternoon, after their lectures, Antonio asked Mary-Beth the same question. *How was your weekend's sexperience?* He and Mary-Beth swapped stories of their exploits while a bemused Robert and Amy listened with growing disbelief as the testimonies became increasingly bizarre. They gambled with depravity; nothing was off limits. Each week they sought to outdo the other's conquests. The more outrageous their deeds, the greater the other perceived the challenge for the following week. Expressions of incredulity from Robert or Amy resulted in invitations to join them on their forthcoming adventures. They declined, maintaining a constant refrain for Antonio and Mary-Beth to be careful, which both routinely ignored. Robert and Amy feared for their friends; they marked time.

Time passed. They graduated, all four achieving their aims. Amy's was to graduate *summa cum laude* and begin planning her move to LA. Mary-Beth's goal was to earn a degree without falling pregnant. Given her proclivities, both outcomes seemed unlikely, but she surprised her parents. They thought her slovenly, that her application to her studies was inadequate. Thankfully for all concerned, they didn't know about her extracurricular activities. Her friends, who did, were surprised by her mastery of contraception.

From the day he arrived at SFSU, Robert's response to anyone that asked him to state his goals was always the same.

A LITTLE SOMETHING TO HIDE

I want to graduate and find a job doing something I like. He made no apology for the modesty of his ambition, adding by way of qualification, *I just want to be happy.* Most people who asked didn't understand the importance of happiness to Robert. They thought he lacked drive, not realising how lofty Robert considered his goal.

Much to the astonishment of his friends, Antonio also graduated. Like Mary-Beth, his appetite for sex exceeded his appetite for scholarship. There was much that it seemed impossible for Antonio to learn, such was his inability to pay attention and absorb the lessons. He surprised everyone by gaining his qualifications. He also surprised no one with the news he shared on graduation day – he was HIV positive.

Antonio dressed his announcement in a salacious wrapper, his attempts to shock and entertain forming the foundation of everything he said. The words tumbled from his mouth as though he was telling the story of a conquest, but instead of the laughter he typically elicited, he faced silence.

He couldn't keep the tears from his eyes as he elaborated, clinging to an airy blitheness as though he was regaling them with just another of his tales. His previous belief in the protections of the drug regime evaporated. Doubts laced his confidence in the effectiveness and efficacy of available treatments. He stood four feet, nine inches tall and weighed 230 pounds. Good health was an unexplored country.

Two years passed and Robert watched his friend change. He initially thought the worst that was happening was the fading, the embers of Antonio's enthusiasm cooling, the vitality quietly vanishing. It was like watching batteries run dry; the vivacious Antonio disappearing, subsumed by an imposter intent on stealing his vigour. Robert was seeing his friend's identity diminish, even before the illness seized him, his mental health deteriorated.

Those that knew and loved him were powerless to address his decline. It manifested in small beats. His outrageous flirting acquired a paler imitation. Rousing remarks, teasingly thrown his way, no longer elicited entertaining ripostes, instead he'd allow them to pass on the air. He'd smile, but it wouldn't reach his eyes. He became an easy mark, once famous for caustic responses, now allowing taunts to slide.

His appetite diminished: for food; for sex; for life. He'd remain after his shows, enjoying the company of others without contributing, gradually leaving earlier, always alone, not wanting to forge relationships lest he 'contaminate' someone else.

Antonio wouldn't listen to Robert or Peter, he considered their relationship unique, an outlier. He didn't believe he could find a similar love, saying that now that he had HIV, he too was quiet like Peter, that it was the illnesses way of maturing him, mellowing him. He also believed that no one would like the new Antonio, the *boring* Antonio, he said. What he meant was the *dying* Antonio. He was too frightened to meet others. Too scared to form a relationship because the illness was repressing his personality. He couldn't reconcile himself to the possibilities he faced. None of them appealed. He would never find love, only solitude. He faced his demons alone – and lost.

The little Puerto Rican didn't care for himself or for anyone else; he began to fade. His lack of care led to a lack of attention; he neglected his medication. His performances ebbed. People stopped watching him. His star had fallen. Antonio no longer entertained, his act was flat, the lights that once shone so brightly had faded. No longer craving attention, he soon stopped craving companionship. He withdrew and receded from the landscape.

Robert moved on; it wasn't intentional. He didn't plan to ignore Antonio or separate their lives, they simply drifted. They stopped swapping memes, no longer tagged each other in posts, message exchanges wilted.

After graduating, Robert moved in with Peter. He told his parents of his new address without mentioning his relationship. He found work in a post-production company, editing badly written commercials for KOFY-TV and gradually ceded the stage for a career. He enjoyed his work, despite the poor scripts and dreadful acting; he found contentment. He floated into a normality that saw him discard the group in which he had thrived. He discovered a preference for the gentle comfort that Peter provided. They allowed themselves to be themselves and with that, lost touch with many that had grown to be friends.

When the call came, Robert listened in silence, the words coming from a disembodied voice that he didn't know, but which his parents would have recognised. The voice was professional, medical, doing a job. It saddened him that Antonio designated him next-of-kin. He felt a profound guilt, the shame that came from knowing he had failed his friend. Robert said he would get there soon and hung up. Peter watched him disconnect the call. *Antonio?*

Robert nodded in confirmation.

Peter rose to collect his coat and keys, but Robert stopped him, he had calls to make and although he loved him, he wasn't sure he wanted Peter to join him.

Robert went alone and didn't recognise the person before him on the bed. Sallow, jaundiced, slight, 120 pounds less than the man he once knew. He looked shrivelled. Folds of flesh on once cherubic arms hung limply. His once stocky legs, like an elephant's they'd joked, were sticks. Antonio smiled at him as he entered the room. *They're coming*, Robert said. *The first flights they can.*

Make me up, he said. *I want to be Zontally for them. I want them to see the real me.*

Robert didn't argue. He painted the face of his friend, masking the undercoat of the aged-pine hues daubed by Antonio's failing liver. He rouged him, gave him dazzling eyes, lifted his cheeks, added glitter, made him sparkle. Antonio insisted on a wig, he wanted Dolly; bouffed, blonde, glamourous. A part of him returned during the transformation. He joked that Robert would have to have the mini orgy with the girls without him. *Though I can stroke you to attention if you need it,* he said, the twinkle shining briefly.

The girls arrived together; Amy waited at the airport for Mary-Beth's arrival from Colorado. They couldn't disguise their shock. They couldn't hide their concern, just as Robert's make-up, so lovingly applied, couldn't hide Antonio's illness.

You still banging anything that moves? Antonio asked Mary-Beth as she walked in, laughing at his own vulgarity, leading to a coughing fit that threatened never to end. His three friends looked on helplessly, Robert offering a glass of water which Antonio waved away, the hacking seizing him, unrelenting.

When eventually it ended, he looked quizzically at Mary-Beth. *Well?* he said.

Not now, she replied.

Robert wasn't sure if that meant now wasn't the time to ask those questions or whether she'd changed her behaviour.

Antonio took a deep breath, struggling to get the air into his depleted lungs and held out his hands. Amy and Mary-Beth, on opposite sides of the bed, each took one. *Thank you*, said Antonio. *It won't be long.*

None of his friends contested the claim, the evidence lay before them. They chatted for three hours, quietly reminiscing about the years that had passed. Antonio, his eyes closed, lids heavy with the toll exacted by the illness betraying his body, laughed sleepily when someone said something that tickled him, a faint smile brushing his lips.

The conversation was natural, unstilted, a mix of shared memories combined with individual stories as they brought each other up to speed with their lives, Antonio contributing his weary laugh and forced smile. Nurses entered to monitor. A glance at a chart, an adjusted drip, a concerned, knowing look.

Another hour passed, Amy sharing an anecdote about the Hollywood actor who caught his penis in a trailer door. It was funny. Antonio should have laughed, but he didn't. He had quietly left his friends behind. They weren't sure when, didn't know how long he hadn't been with them. He'd drifted from them, just as he had drifted from the life he used to lead.

The girls stayed with Robert and Peter that night, telling more stories of their outrageous friend, smiling, laughing, and crying at his memory. In the morning, Peter drove them all to the airport. There was silence in the car as they contemplated their thoughts, each keeping their counsel. They would gather again, for one last time, two weeks from that day, to say a final goodbye to their diminutive friend.

It was during that ride that Robert decided it was time to be honest with his parents, and with himself, about Peter. There would never be anything more to hide, they would come to know all about him, about all his loves. He is comfortable now with who he is, comforted and protected.

In watching his friend die, he saw a glimpse of a potential future awaiting him and didn't want to face it alone. Peter was in control of his HIV, he was well, but time's ravages, he knew, would one day play their part. Peter had twenty years on him. If the illness didn't get him, one day, time would. Robert didn't want his parents to not know him.

He climbs on the bus mildly ashamed with himself that he hasn't introduced his parents to Peter. They don't know of the happiness that he instils in their child, the boy who cared not for cowboys and Indians, who cared only to find the man that he would be. Robert knew he was in danger of further shaming himself by not being brave enough to share the joys that he felt, for fear of the judgement that would follow.

It is time for candour, to make his confession and, if he avoids rejection, to arrange an introduction. Deep down, in the recesses where he stores his truest feelings, sometimes inaccessibly, he knows that there will be no rejection. He admonishes himself for failing to know that those that he loves, and who love him, will not care that he has also found love with a man twice his age. They would only care, and be delighted, that he is happy.

He needs them now, needs to feel their love again, needs it to fill the emptiness created by Antonio's death. He is heading home to feel the embrace of those whose love is unconditional; in whose eyes, judgement never appears, where he will be safe, secure, and loved.

He collapses into the chair and feels a spring pop beneath him and considers that it might be uncomfortable for the next twelve hundred miles. He doesn't mind, he chuckles to himself as he remembers a time, long ago, when an impossibly small Puerto Rican fell into a chair next to him.

SAN JOSE DIRIDON STATION

Arrivals
Time	From	Expected
21:00	San Francisco	Expected: 21:06

Departures
Time	Destination	Expected
21:30	Salinas	Delayed: 21:36

SAN JOSE DIRIDON STATION

There is little difference between a look of quiet determination and one of absolute serenity on the face of Sandra Mayhew. She carries a patient conviction and an inconspicuous courage. She is unafraid of adversity, yet bears a shyness that she fights to overcome.

Few recognise her determination; most are surprised to learn of the dogmatism with which she tackles her challenges. They see a naivety in her, and they would be correct in their assessment, but they would be wrong to believe that her innocence is a frailty. She is anything but weak. Hers is a quiet strength. She will never be fierce; she will rarely be outspoken. She is unlikely to cause the conversation to pause when she enters a room. No one considers her imposing. Consequently, most underestimate her.

Her strength is a constant, like water quietly babbling across the bedrock schist of a brook, a perpetual flow, eking away the flaws, power behind the beauty. It's not a trait the casual observer sees, the unyielding desire to achieve her goals. Most fail to notice the relentless pursuit of what she wants. She's quiet, unobtrusive, inoffensive – nice. *She troubles no one with her concerns or her ambitions. It appears that she allows the world to happen, yet she is quietly in control of its course, and we can all be happy with that. Those that know her think of her as* steady. *It is neither a compliment nor an insult, but it is accurate.*

When she steps onto the bus, she gives a tight smile of greeting as she climbs the three worn steps at the entrance. Her journey is only just beginning, but she was weary long before reaching the starting point. She is tired of the effort that has led to this moment, to her discovery. It has taken her close to two years to be able to board this bus. Two years of searching, of not knowing, of never giving up.

A LITTLE SOMETHING TO HIDE

She has a duffel bag over her right shoulder. The seams are weak, the white stitching prominent, threatening to surrender the contents. It contains the paraphernalia with which mothers travel to maintain a semblance of comfort for their children, often at the expense of their own. On the pavement behind her is a child's car seat, empty, waiting to go on the bus. She's left it there in favour of the toddler that she is guiding up the stairs. George is too small to negotiate the height of the risers. He half-climbs as his mother hoists him up each step, his right arm yanked high, stretched in the socket as she helps him navigate to the top.

They stand at the front of the bus, uncertainty duplicated; he's his mother's child, though the ice-blue eyes and the unruly wave of reddish-brown hair (which his mother is never quite able to control), belong to his father. Seeking the security of his mother, he clings to her leg, hiding behind it and his ever-present blanket. His thumb, jammed in his mouth behind a balled fist, obscures the lower half of his face. He appears wary of what lies in the murk beyond the steps of the bus; he waits for his mother to act.

Peering down the aisle, Sandra casts glances along each row of seats, seeking an unoccupied pair. None are obviously free, and she gives her young son a delicate push to encourage him along, finding the only available pair, which overlook the stairwell to the coach's toilet. She sighs the sigh of a mother who knows her child will wake every time someone uses the bathroom.

She lifts her son into the seat by the window. 'I'll be back quicker than a rattlesnake's bite.' The words come out gently, to comfort, but the sinister nature of her promise leaves him unconvinced. She ruffles his hair to assure him, turning to go. His anxiety deepens as she exits the bus, disappearing from his view. A stifled wail emerges from the child, plaintive, yet poised to build. Baby George wriggles across to the aisle seat, preparing his pursuit, readying a wail that will be more than plaintive. Both his wriggling, and the drawing in of air to fuel his cry, subside as his mother reappears at the top of the steps with his car seat. A drop of snot swells beneath his nose, but quiet descends.

Mild disgust and reproach replaces her ambiguous look of determination. She's hoping to convey to the driver that his assistance would have been welcome. He looks at her impassively, his distended belly enfolding the base of the steering wheel. He contemplated shouting for his partner to help, but that would require an effort beyond which he was willing to make. He decides that she has done all that she needs, and his look segues to a 'hurry the fuck up'. Impassive to impatient. No one gets help from him, the salary from the Briscolas doesn't pay for favours.

The driver doesn't wait for her to sit down before the bus lurches forward. Her legs scramble to keep up with her torso as she stumbles down the aisle. George, thrown back into his seat by the advancing bus, alerts her to the need to secure him quickly before the driver arrives at a traffic light and finds a heavy foot for the brake. Sandra suspects, rightly, that he'd do it for sport.

Her son is in the seat that she plans to occupy, waiting expectantly, unruffled by his tussle with G-forces. She examines the seat by the window, searching for anchor points to fasten the car seat and is disappointed to find that no such safety mechanism exists. She wobbles to the front of the bus, shoulders colliding with the tops of the seats that line the aisle, like an air steward battling turbulence, trying to find the rhythm of the bus as she moves toward the driver. They see each other through the rear-view mirror, and Sandra knows before she has asked what his answer will be, that nothing on the bus will improve her child's safety. The driver greets her flash of anger with a shrug, as if she should expect anything else when she's booked the cheapest option available to get her to where she's going.

Should an accident occur, Sandra's son George will experience much stronger G-forces than those which threw him against his mother's seat. His Maxi-Cosi will undergo a transformation to a projectile, hurling him at high velocity into whatever lays in his path. At speed, his mother's instinct to throw her arm across his car seat will be futile, but that action is enough to keep Baby George beside her when the driver hits the brakes with too much enthusiasm at an approaching stop sign. The assurance she takes, that she can keep her baby safe, is false. The driver looks in the mirror to see what effect he might have had on his passengers and smiles. He loves that prank. He's the only one who enjoyed it.

A LITTLE SOMETHING TO HIDE

SANDRA & BABY GEORGE – SAN JOSE

Two years ago, Sandra didn't know that there was more than one San Jose in the United States. She had lived in San Jose, California all her life and it never occurred to her to check whether there were more. Her curiosity mostly lies inert, rarely aroused. She is content, in the main, that things are as they are and that she should let them be. It applies to her knowledge and understanding of the world. What she knows, she understands, and she is satisfied with the extent of her knowledge.

She doesn't thirst for greater understanding; her interest is seldom piqued. Yet she becomes a hound when curious, provoked to rampaging through the undergrowth in search of discovery, of flushing out the facts, however elusive. Once she has a scent of a subject that stirs her, she will apply her determination to reach her objective. She will be quiet, steady, unwavering. She will achieve her goal, and when she does, few will know it but her.

Before she met Daniel Butterfield she knew only of the San Jose of her youth. She knows now that there are at least six. In particular, she knows that one of them is only 97.8 miles from the Alvarado Transportation Center in Albuquerque. When she gets there, she is going to hire a car and drive the final miles herself, with Baby George securely fastened in his car seat behind her. It has taken her a long time to find Daniel and, like Robert Jamieson who sits nearby on the same bus, she too has an introduction to make.

The first time Sandra met Daniel was at San Jose's SAP Center. They were there for the Los Tigres del Norte and Alejandro Fernandez concert. Neither was a fan, they'd never heard of the performers, though they considered their music inoffensive. They were there because they needed the money that came from stewarding the gig. Daniel to live his student life, Sandra to save for a new car, a Toyota Prius, her half-hearted attempt to be environmentally responsible.

She doesn't consider herself to be a crusader for the planet; no one knows her views on the world's health. She wanted a car for no reason other than it seemed the fashionable thing to do, as is keeping carbon emissions low. It has never occurred to her that her thinking is counter-intuitive. She doesn't claim to be an eco-warrior; doesn't see the irony in an unneeded car. Leonardo DiCaprio influenced her choice. She's heard that he drives a Prius; she loves his films.

The money that she makes from directing people towards hotdogs, bathrooms, seats, and bars, goes into her ferret account; the place for savings that she tucks away whenever she wants something beyond the scope of her regular earnings. She doesn't like credit, it adds a complication to her life that she can do without. *Work hard and only spend the money you have.* It's a reminder she repeats often. She knows it's a dated view; a mantra instilled by parents who encouraged her to save from as early as she could remember.

When she was in high school, she worked weekends at the Dairy Queen, pulling *Blizzard Treats* for the kids from her school, resisting their pleas for free ice cream. She needed her job, and she wasn't about to let the imploring wheedle of a classmate interrupt her employment. It was enough that she had to work when she knew that her contemporaries could draw upon the Bank of Mom and Dad for the things she so stoically saved towards: the clothing, the concert tickets, the make-up, and music; the material detritus that rapacious marketers have coerced teenagers into believing is important.

Sandra is susceptible to external influences, easily convinced of the latest trend's importance, but not of a middle-class adolescent's claims of penury at a Dairy Queen counter. Sandra wasn't about to risk her job for an ice cream she knew they could afford. She wasn't afraid of being ruthless, but didn't need to be, no one ever took offence when she denied their requests. Most kids from her school didn't get free ice cream, no matter how much they begged, though close friends, and some of the more attractive boys, might have received a larger sized *Raspberry Fudge Bliss* – but only if the boys' flirting merited the reward.

High school is far behind now. Sandra spends her days in the law offices of Holloway and Shelby, where she works diligently as a paralegal, earning enough to pay for childcare and meet the rent her parents demand for the room that she and Baby George share. Her parents had wanted her to go to college, but she didn't know what to study and couldn't see the point of spending money on uncertainty.

Sandra is careful with her income, managing it well. She wasn't about to spend tens of thousands of her parents or her own savings on something that she wasn't sure she wanted. There was also a baby to raise.

The Prius was different though. That was before George. She wanted the Prius, and faster than her monthly cheque from Holloway and Shelby would allow; she took extra work at the SAP Center to achieve her goal.

On the night she met Daniel Butterfield, he was an undergraduate Chemical Engineer in his senior year at San Jose State University. He wasn't particularly focused on his job that night, paying little attention to the Los Tigres del Norte fans, but he showed a lot of interest in Sandra. He toyed with innuendo when they spoke, occasionally treading the wrong side of appropriate, but was sensitive enough to rein himself when he thought Sandra might take offence. She thought his charm could use some work but indulged his stories. Sometimes he made her laugh when he wasn't boring her about his college programme. When he spoke of normal things (and didn't stray into the lecherous), she contemplated that he might be worthy of a bigger *Blizzard*. She was prepared to give him a chance.

After their first encounter, Sandra found it coincidental that their schedules saw them together in the same section every time they were at work. Daniel wasn't surprised. Chemicals weren't the only things he engineered.

When events didn't appeal, being a steward was dreary. Helping those arriving late to scurry to their seats was the height of excitement, augmented with the intermittent need to call first aiders if visitors slipped on the concourse floors, made slick with the careless spills of Bud Light and Diet Coke from earlier arrivals.

If a band they liked performed, like the Foo Fighters or Fall Out Boy, prized stewarding positions were at the entrance doors to the main auditorium, providing the exquisite bonus of getting paid while being entertained. The price for such an opportunity was to stifle their enthusiasm in case a sanctimonious supervisor should come along demanding neutrality, as though they were marshalling a political rally.

They found the NHL especially tedious, having to suffer the wisecracks and opinions of fans who considered their mediocre performances in the Little Leagues as the foundation for greater wisdom than the game's professionals.

Sandra and Daniel also disliked concerts where they had to witness aged fans clinging to fragments of the past as washed-up, once super-bands, wrestled with a back-catalogue of pale hits, now wispier and tarnished by age-stressed vocals.

On those nights, it was often preferable to mooch on the concourse. They were stress-free evenings; middle-aged crowds handled their medicine better, theirs being a cocktail of beer and weed, procured from docile amateur growers. Chemically laced tabs, bearing cutesy pictures that belied their effect, were the purview of the younger set which popped them with an enthusiasm that ignored the risks.

Los Tigres del Norte and Alejandro Fernandez was a mooching concert. If the row behind didn't object, Dad dancers and flailing Cougar Moms shuffled their feet and cried out with an artificial zeal, attempting to revive a youth that had long since passed its best before date. By the end of the night, with adolescent arrogance suffusing their conversation, Sandra and Daniel had shared their mutual disdain for the music, swapped disparaging comments about the *oldies,* and agreed that the crowd should let it pass, move on with their lives, and do something more befitting their age – boat shows or home improvement conventions.

They weren't on the same entrance the following night; an exhibition game where the Sharks were destined to lose in a shootout to the Golden Knights, so they roamed, abandoning their partners at post, prowling the venue in the hope that they might find one another. They had the same idea and ghosted each other unintentionally before meeting near the end of the game. The early fleers, those that consider beating the traffic of greater importance to their wellbeing than witnessing the conclusion to a game, caused Sandra and Daniel to return to their posts before much of anything had passed between them. His frustration led Daniel to loiter at the roster sheets at the end of the night, waiting to find a colleague he could coerce into swapping stations with him for the next event.

They mooched again, not learning too much more about each other that third evening, but enough to cause Daniel to stalk his colleagues at the pin-board regularly. By the fourth night, they were making each other laugh. She teased him whenever his conversation wandered to Chemical Engineering, reminding him that he had an excellent line in dull. He allowed the slight, he had plans for Sandra which garnered a tolerance to her insults, he could let them slide until he got to know her better.

Sandra could see that her teasing irked him, but she liked the way he reacted; mock indignation, coupled with the faintest trace of genuine hurt. It suggested that he was human, that there was something decent about him. She tempered her slurs; she didn't want to put him off. He'd pretend offence, gently pushing her from him. Their comfort zones shrank, they allowed a closer proximity, she'd push him back, defining the limits. The emerging physicality of their relationship was a development they welcomed. Sandra remained cautious, taking her time to assess, to evaluate; she wouldn't rush, but she was slowly warming to him.

The casual observer of Sandra Mayhew would be unlikely to detect an intelligent and determined woman, a reflection of their deficiency. Most people see her as a gullible innocent. When she knows little of a subject, the curiosity that she mostly subverts, leads to a tendency to believe people who speak with certainty. Sandra is a willing believer, susceptible to deception – until she learns otherwise. If her knowledge conflicts with what she knows to be misleading, she initiates gentle debate, willing to stand her ground. She won't tolerate arrogance if it masks a blusterer's ignorance. She is willing to assassinate with a quiet assurance.

While Daniel finds her attractive and recognises her intelligence, he also wonders at how she willingly believes most things he says. He playfully tests her credulity, talking often about his degree, when he knows she has no obvious interest. Interspersed with his monologues about biocatalytic processes and diffusion models for porous solids, he weaves what he thinks are obvious idiocies to establish whether she is paying attention or has the nous to question him.

Occasionally she halts him with a *That's not true*, and he tries to argue, which led him to the discovery of her deeply embedded stubbornness. When Sandra knew something to be true, attempts to convince her otherwise ended in futility. Other times, she absorbed fallacies as fact without question. It led him to practical jokes. To begin, they were simple, mostly harmless, leaving her mildly embarrassed and a little wiser, always just between them, a subject that the two of them would laugh about in private remembrances.

On the night of a Fleetwood Mac concert, Sandra commented on the absence of footwear from some of the patrons. *You know why?* Daniel asked, receiving the expected negative response. *It makes it quicker for them to take their drugs*, he told her.

She held him with a suspicious stare, not knowing what he meant or fully believing what he said, but she was willing to learn.

They rub cannabis oil into the soles of their feet, he added. *It sends it straight into their nervous system. Get the right spot and they can stimulate* everything. *It's like reflexology, but with drugs. It adds a super concentrated high to all sorts of places.* He winked at her.

She wasn't entirely convinced.

SANDRA & BABY GEORGE – SAN JOSE

Go on, he said. *Follow them into the bathroom and peek under the door.*

It was enough to ignite her interest. She suspected he was teasing, that she should ignore his claims, but he stirred her latent curiosity. She wanted to know the truth. Two barefooted women went into the bathroom and Sandra followed.

Outside, Daniel caught the attention of a supervisor, telling her that he was worried about Sandra, that she might be trapped in the bathroom. The supervisor entered the facility to find Sandra on her hands and knees, peering under a cubicle door. *What are you doing?*

Sandra put a finger to her lips, whispering with an urgency to her supervisor, *I'm checking for drugs.*

It wasn't the response she was expecting. Bemused, she ushered Sandra onto the concourse, demanding an explanation. When they exited the bathroom, a grinning Daniel was waiting.

Oh, you asshole, said the supervisor when she saw him. *He's done you sweetie-pie.* She laughed as she left Sandra to draw her own realisation.

When the concert ended, Sandra and Daniel entered a full staff room to find the supervisor on her knees, head to the floor, backside elevated, mimicking Sandra's pose, recounting the incident to those around her. Sandra flushed with embarrassment. Daniel added an unfiltered version of his involvement, either oblivious to, or ignoring Sandra's agitation. She couldn't determine which, hoping for the former, willing to give him the benefit of the doubt. Sandra didn't like being drawn as a fool; it was a cruelty that she wouldn't tolerate. The sound of her colleagues' laughter followed her as she left the room. Daniel tailed her, offering to walk her home; she declined, taking the bus instead.

At the next event they were on the same doorway; she ignored him all evening, preferring to listen to a band they both knew she didn't like. At the end of the show, she headed for the staff room without speaking to him, still angry at her humiliation.

While they were removing their high-visibility jackets, he asked if he could speak with her. She was non-committal, looking at him in silence, allowing him to determine which way he should interpret her ambivalence. Daniel decided her silence gave him license to continue. The apology that Sandra anticipated didn't materialise. Sandra expected him to say sorry, but instead, he asked her for a date. She looked at him askance, trying to establish if this was the prelude to another practical joke. His expression carried sufficient weight of hope to induce her to accept, but not enough to agree to him walking her home. There was thinking to do, to ponder whether his lack of an apology bothered her.

It was two weeks before they could meet outside the confines of work; the first occasion that both of their schedules were clear. On the nights they worked together, Daniel did his best to ease the tension between them, aware that she was still annoyed. He took tentative steps to repairing their relationship, trying to fuel her anticipation of what their first date might be like. The chemistry between them was improving. Gradually she was forgiving him and forgetting that he hadn't shown any remorse for hurting her.

He took her to Original Joe's on 1st Street. They had drinks at the bar while they waited for their table. He had a beer, she checked that he was paying before ordering a Long Island Iced Tea. They started on another round of drinks before their table was available.

He didn't wait to see what she ordered before asking for a bottle of Malbec. She assumed he knew what he was doing. He did; he was planning on a rib steak. Sandra didn't know that the wine wasn't a great match for her fillet of sole. If she had known, she would have detected his selfishness. Instead, she was impressed that he seemed to know about wine; normally when she went out with friends, she ordered Chardonnay by the glass; it was a safe choice. It also made splitting the bill easier, she could keep tighter tabs on her spending. That wasn't a concern tonight, Daniel was paying; she decided to go with his choice. When the wine arrived, he ordered another beer, saying he'd wait for his steak before joining her on the red. He didn't ask whether she wanted something different, although he poured the Malbec generously.

Later, she felt his leg under the table against hers, the barest contact, yet it felt deliberate. She looked at him, waiting to see an acknowledgement. He continued to saw into his steak as though nothing had happened. *Had he noticed? Did she imagine it? Was she reading too much into that faint touch?* She moved her leg, increasing the contact. He looked up; she thought his smile was closer to a smirk. There was something unsettling in his look – presumption.

It didn't feel like a first date. They didn't have the awkward vibe that intrudes on an evening of getting to know one another. They didn't struggle with the uncomfortable silences that haunt an evening of grappling to find interesting subjects. He knew enough not to talk about Chemical Engineering; she was comfortable answering his questions, following each response with, *And you?* hoping to discover more about him.

After telling him she was a local girl, she was sceptical about his claim to San Jose origins. He didn't sound Californian, but people can move when they're younger, following their parents, shipping accents along with belongings. She figured that was his case; she didn't press him for an explanation. Instead, she asked him about his high school. He told her, honestly, that he went to Pecos. Sandra didn't know it; it didn't exist inside her bubble. She didn't know that Pecos High School wasn't in California. Daniel's school was considerably beyond the sphere of Sandra's knowledge.

The search to identify mutual friendships foundered, Sandra pressed, but Daniel didn't know anyone from her school. She explored connections from football; she was an avid fan of her team, the Bulldogs; she suggested he might know some of the players. He thought it unlikely; he wasn't a fan of jocks.

If she'd quizzed him further, she might have discovered something to make her subsequent search easier, but his high school's name didn't stick; she moved on too quickly for the memory to form. Conversation drifted, meandered elsewhere.

A LITTLE SOMETHING TO HIDE

Everywhere and nowhere. When she reflected later, riding on the bus to Albuquerque, Baby George asleep in his car seat, mouth agape, another viscous sliver drifting from a nostril, she realised that she didn't know anything about Daniel. She planned for that to change.

On the night of their first date, unusually high humidity delivered a warmth to the evening, wrapping them like a light pashmina, an atmospheric cuddle keeping the cool at bay. After their meal, they strolled together for a couple of blocks toward East William Street and his apartment. They brushed shoulders, neither feigning an attraction now. Somewhere, between the pressure of his leg and the second bottle of wine, she forgave him completely.

Daniel didn't seek forgiveness, nor recognise his wrongdoing. He had consigned his transgression to the past, which is where Sandra thought she should leave the humiliation and embarrassment. It was clear that he was never going to mention it again. She slipped her arm through his and they drew closer. She was quietly buzzing, she expected he was too. There was a comfortable silence between them, each lost in their own thoughts, each thinking of what might lie ahead that night.

She had a rule: *never have sex on a first date*. It wasn't a moral stance or influenced by what others might think. It was more fundamental; control was important. She needed to be able to assert herself, for her partners to understand that she was making the decisions. Sandra wanted to limit the opportunity to be a discarded plaything. She knew that could still happen at any time, but on the first night, she was going to be in command.

This didn't feel like a first date though. They hadn't met each other in a bar and sidled off. They'd known each other for nearly four weeks, seen each other on most days, and had enjoyed a grown-up meal in the cosseted booths of Original Joe's, rather than shrieking at each other above the cacophony of a squalid night-club. She was still in control, she was still making the decisions and she decided that, for Daniel Butterfield, she might just make an exception.

SANDRA & BABY GEORGE – SAN JOSE

Daniel's thoughts on the subject were more advanced. He'd been planning this evening for some time and was deliberately heavy with his wine-pouring, he wanted her to relax, to be accommodating. He wanted her to be *willing*. He had also spent more than he had planned or could afford. Joe's wasn't exactly fine dining, but there wasn't much left from a Benjamin Franklin after his steak and the first bottle of wine. God only knew what sort of hole her iced teas were going to punch in his wallet; it transpired to be a large one. He wanted repayment; she must have known he was expecting a return, although he considered himself a patient investor. If he didn't have her tonight, he would accept a deferral – for now.

Daniel didn't think he was like other guys on campus. He'd only fed her alcohol; others were more sinister. Some of the frat boys had offered him a supply of Rohypnol. They laughed when he baulked at the idea, suggesting that the only way he was going to get action was by using *roofies*. He had a point to prove. He'd show them that a nerd could get laid, even if it wasn't tonight. He'd let her decide when she was ready, but he thought that feeding her two-thirds of the wine might help her decision; he wasn't averse to a little external influence.

To Sandra, it was obvious that he was keen for her to stay the night, but also that he was doing his best to avoid pressuring her, offering his Uber account so she could return to her parents' house, although she could sense the reluctance in the gesture. She would have to return home to circumvent a parental conniption, even though she was twenty-two and understood more about the world than they believed. Her father remained insistent though; while she lived under his roof, she should respect his wishes. That didn't stop him from charging her rent, but she was a good girl, she observed his rules – mostly.

It was 11pm when they stood outside Daniel's apartment, a poor impersonation of luxury accommodation, an uninspiring concrete slab. Sandra thought about the time. When she went to nightclubs, she usually got home at 1am, it was enough to earn her a scowl from her father in the morning, but he mostly contained his criticism. He wasn't entirely prudish, her mother had softened his rough edges, demonstrating solidarity with her daughter, cajoling her husband into relaxing his opinions. It was still early; she could risk tomorrow's crease in her father's brow. As an alternative to the car, Daniel offered his apartment. Perhaps nothing would happen, maybe they'd just have coffee, and she could still get home before one. Maybe. It was her call; she was in command. She decided.

The apartment was neater than she thought, as Spartan inside as it was outside. He labelled it contemporary; she thought it bleak. She supposed it was easier to keep it tidy when it contained so little. The tidiness was a good sign. Other boys she knew hadn't entirely emerged from the shelter of their mothers' care. They discarded things, failed to clean, or if they did, it was cursory. Daniel was different; everything ordered and polished. There was a sterility to his apartment, as though they'd entered a hotel suite. The magazines on his coffee table lay in a neat arrangement, the kitchen surfaces were clear, soft lighting crept from a single floor lamp up the wall, feeding its light to a lone pot plant and Andy Warhol's obligatory Marilyn Diptych. He had prepared. She felt safer.

The music came on as he was reaching into the cupboard for the coffee, the guttural hum of a Nespresso machine gurgled over Barry White. The cliché wasn't unexpected. She smiled to herself, secretly pleased that she had him measured. He invited her to take a seat and she kicked off her shoes, curling herself onto the sofa, sitting at one end, not being too presumptuous to occupy the middle and all that that might mean.

Daniel joined her, both cups held in one hand, the other empty. A coaster magically appeared, a party trick. With performative deliberation, he slid the polished stainless-steel circle in front of her. A second appeared which he laid alongside with the same fluid motion. He waited for her compliment before handing her a coffee and sitting down. *Impressive*, she said, with enough disdain to suggest she thought otherwise. Undeterred, he sat close, facing Sandra. He leaned across, thanking her for a lovely night. The Uber driver got her home at 3am.

Sandra didn't lament her broken rule. They continued to meet, arranging their shift patterns so they'd have time off together. He showed no signs of discarding her, leading Sandra to arrange for Daniel to meet her parents.

The introduction proved underwhelming; her father didn't like him. *There's something not right*, was all he would offer by way of explanation. George Mayhew considered his instincts powerful enough to support the assertion. Sandra thought he was being overly protective. It would take time, but she would learn that her father had a well-defined ability to assess a man's character.

Sandra's understanding of Daniel's character might have improved if she recognised the two elements that failed to feature in their conversations: the possibility of a future together, and discussions that focused on Daniel's past. He was reticent to talk about himself, never elaborating about his youth, evasive about his hopes. His preference was to talk about actualities: constructs, mechanisms, the practical. He dismissed the ephemeral, disparaged fantasies; science and logic ruled, the present prevailed.

This contrasted with Sandra's outlook. She was always looking forward, setting goals, planning. Her vision of the future was predictably suburban. She didn't lack ambition; her ambition coalesced around her concept of societal norms; marriage, a house, children, summers on the shore, occasional winter breaks to Colorado, schussing the Rockies. She wanted a stable, steady career, interrupted by the advent of children, supplemented by school committees, charity work when the children grew, a long and happy retirement. She didn't find the prospect dull; she planned a life well-lived.

If someone argued her goals were indifferent, she countered that it was a matter of perspective. Although they never spoke of a future together, Sandra knew she could have a fulfilling life with Daniel. She felt pragmatism would steer them to her bliss, if not a spoken accord. If it didn't, she trusted in her equanimity, she would let him go. For now, their bond remained, everything was going to plan.

For their six-month anniversary, he met her at La Forêt on the outskirts of town. It made Original Joe's seem like a roadside diner. Her father moaned on the drive there. *What sort of kid doesn't pick up his girl for a date?* Sandra made an excuse for Daniel that sounded hollow even to her.

Daniel was waiting for her when she arrived, already a few drinks ahead. They had cocktails above the creek, its quiet babble filling the air while they soaked in the cool of the late afternoon. He didn't consult with her before ordering, opting for the tasting menu with wine pairing; small glasses of perfectly matched wines to enhance the food.

The sommelier was on Daniel's programme at college, he gave them larger glasses, filling them for each course. They drank more at the bar after their meal. Sandra thought it beyond generous that Daniel wanted to prolong their stay. He didn't tell her the real reasons; tucked in the sommelier's pocket were three fresh twenty-dollar bills that meant he was happy to fill their glasses at the restaurant's expense, and would be driving them home when he finished his shift.

The sixty-dollar friend dropped them a few blocks from Daniel's apartment. They supported each other on the walk home, propping one another, exchanging sniggers as they traded stumbles. It felt like part of a game – *fore*-foreplay. Before the door had closed behind them, they were tugging at each other's clothes. They lurched to the sofa, discarding items as they went.

Sandra steadied Daniel's pawing hand. *Condom first,* she said. Reluctantly he drew away, searching the floor for his jeans, fumbling in the pocket, seeking the Trojan that he always carried. He found the packet, empty, not replaced since their walk in the Japanese Friendship Garden. There they'd found a secluded section, the jeopardy of capture causing them to giggle their way through the surreptitious act. Daniel had forgotten to replace the empty packet. He kept a supply in his bedroom but didn't want to spoil the moment with a diversion.

SANDRA & BABY GEORGE – SAN JOSE

If Daniel had a moral compass, it disappeared when he pretended to fit a condom, sitting on the sofa's edge, his back to Sandra, concealing his movements. He climbed on her quickly so she wouldn't notice the absence of a safeguard. It was early November, six months before Daniel's final exams.

Sandra's menstrual cycle was erratic, resisting any form of pattern. On the morning of 3 December, she had the vague notion that her period was due. By the evening, the thought had faded. She had the same thought the following day, but the disquiet didn't dissolve. She flicked through her phone, trying to find an event that would remind her of the dates for her last period. She doubted her memory, she suspected over five weeks had passed.

Keeping her suspicions to herself, Sandra took a different route home from work that evening, a bus down East Santa Clara Street, stopping outside Walgreens. She stood beyond the sensors that activate the sliding doors, not yet ready to commit. She shook her head, laughing at herself with no hint of humour. The door opened as another customer left the store, converting the foreboding interior into a brightly lit cornucopia; piped music wafted into the street. Her uncertainty disappeared, replaced with a veil of serene determination; she took her next step.

The Pharmacist looked up as she entered. She felt the heat rising in her cheeks, not wanting to draw attention to her reason for being there. He smiled at her before looking back at the prescription papers that lay on the counter before him. He'd observed that same shy embarrassment many times over the years. He guessed that Sandra would stroll the aisles, walking past the item she wanted. Some customers did it accidentally, others deliberately, summoning bravery, it was the routine of many.

Teenage boys were the same with condoms. He encouraged his female colleagues to serve the boys, he liked them to feel the discomfort of a woman asking if they needed help. He had daughters; he wanted the boys to face a reminder of just what they were planning. Girls like Sandra were different though. Their anxiety was palpable, a fear of what their purchase might reveal. He never knew what outcomes they feared, and he always prayed for them, that they received the revelation they were seeking.

Sandra found what she was looking for, he knew she would, she placed the Clearblue box on the counter in front of him, already armed with her payment card, momentarily catching the Pharmacist's eye. He hoped to convey reassurance with his glance; she thought he looked demented. She restored the card to her wallet and tucked the box in her bag, leaving with a quiet *Thank you*. The door waited interminably to respond to her approach; she resisted the urge to wave her hand in front of it, anything to avoid additional attention.

She sat on the toilet disbelieving, underwear around her ankles, watching the vertical blue line materialise in the slender plastic shroud. She wanted to doubt the result, conduct a second test to disprove the first. It would be pointless; she now knew that her last period was six weeks ago. She couldn't fathom how the scream of that extra blue line came to be. They had been careful, always using protection. She didn't know what went wrong.

Sandra was unaware of time. Her mother knocked on the bathroom door to ask if she was okay. Time had vanished in the face of that blue cross, taking with it the prospect of rational thought. The metallic tap of her mother's wedding ring brought her back to a present that was seismically different to her immediate past.

She flushed the toilet and pulled up her underwear, still holding the accusatory plastic in her hand. She tucked it inside her waistband and flattened the cardboard box which she then wrestled under her bra strap. She washed her hands and left the bathroom. Her mother was on the landing outside, looking anxious as Sandra stepped through the door. *I'm fine,* said Sandra. Her mother knew two things instantly; that her daughter was lying, and that now was not the time to ask questions.

In her bedroom, Sandra set about the task of concealing the test, knowing that at best, it was a temporary step, the evidence of her pregnancy would soon be apparent to all. In the coming days, she would have to tell her family, dreading her father's disappointment, knowing he'd dramatise his response, making her feel sullied rather than supported – his daughter, the succubus. That conversation would happen later, much later if she could help it, but now it was 6pm and she had to be at the SAP Center by seven. She had to ready herself to tell Daniel. The minute hand on her bedroom clock meandered until she left.

Daniel no longer needed to engineer their postings together, he had convinced the roster supervisor to save him the trouble. Tonight's billing was the *Not So Silent Night* concert, and he was keen to spend his time inside the arena. Sandra wasn't sure she would enjoy the music, despite liking the line-up. He told her the concert would put him in the mood. It wouldn't do the same for Sandra; she wondered if she could ever be in the mood again. She felt nauseous, and not from the pregnancy. The idea of breaking the news to Daniel aggravated the queasiness she'd been experiencing in recent days. The pregnancy was unwelcome news to her, she doubted Daniel would feel any different. He smiled at her in the staff room as they wriggled free of their high-viz jackets and got ready for the journey to his house. He didn't notice her unease.

Sandra opted for silence as they walked, trying not to seem indifferent, her thoughts conflicting, shrill cries competing with rational voices, all hers, clamouring for prominence; she feared that he would hear her thinking.

He remained oblivious to her torment. He effused about the concert, about the benefits that came with their work, the chance to be together for special gigs, gigs that *touched* him, music he could *feel*. He was a different Daniel to the usual staid scientist, far more emotive, his words laced with expectation for the rest of their night. Sandra didn't share his perspective, not that Daniel noticed. She doubted he would be sensitive enough to know that it was time for him to stop talking, to listen.

A LITTLE SOMETHING TO HIDE

She sat away from him on the sofa, earnest, a new persona. *We need to talk.*

It annoyed him that she was stealing the mood. Sandra wouldn't let him get close, pushing him away when he tried to kiss her.

This is important, she said. She saw his irritation, transitory, followed with instant suppression, controlling his uglier impulses, composure restored. His veneer transformed when she spoke again.

He didn't say anything. She expected her revelation to provoke a reaction; her musings leading to a variety of outcomes. She hoped for joy: a prospect of support. She anticipated shock: the heft of responsibility. She thought too, that there was a chance of anger: a future derailed. His metamorphosis was unanticipated, unexpected: guilt.

It didn't settle; it flitted, licking at his eyes, then disappeared, replaced with whatever disguise he chose to conceal his deceit. Although fleeting, it was enough for Sandra to understand. She knew it was his fault. She didn't know how, but she felt the betrayal. There was a different Daniel opposite her now, no longer the person she thought she knew, she could see him calculating, conjuring what to say next. *How?* he said with bogus scepticism, staring at her blankly.

You tell me.

He didn't answer her.

She couldn't rage – not yet; it was too soon. Disbelief shaped her thinking, she doubted everything she knew about Daniel. She could feel tears building and she didn't want *this* Daniel; the one that she didn't know, to see her vulnerability. She stood to leave, he stayed on the sofa, impassive, offering nothing. Barry White crooned softly in the background. She left Daniel to the music.

When she got home, the tears had dried, but the sense of betrayal remained. As her Uber driver pulled away, she stood on the pavement, seeking the courage she needed.

Her mother watched her through the French window, the streetlights casting their sodium glare around her daughter. She watched Sandra mustering herself at the foot of the path, noting the subconscious stroke of her belly, guessing what it might signal. She was waiting at the door as Sandra turned the key. She prepared herself for Sandra's entrance, holding her arms wide. The welcome disarmed Sandra, her fortitude deserted her as she fell into her mother's arms, the sobbing drawing her father from his seat in front of the TV. Her mother brewed fresh coffee while they waited for her to share her news.

They didn't condemn her. Her mother lifted a hand to quiet George Mayhew before he said something that would damage the relationship with his daughter. He let his wife speak. *It's okay*, she said. *Don't worry. We love you. We'll love you both.*

Her father contained his anger as she told him what happened. He did his best to keep the *I told you so* inflections from his voice. Her mother attempted a more optimistic stance, invoking excuses for Daniel's reaction, attempting to justify his behaviour. She was hoping it was just shock. *He'll come around*, she said. She ignored her husband's derisive snort.

The initial signs were promising. In the days that followed Sandra's revelation, Daniel appeared to accept his impending fatherhood. After three days of moodiness, he smiled his first half-smile, lips twitching at the corners when she asked how he was feeling. It was a difficult smile to read. It didn't indicate joy, it was wry, but it was a smile, and that was an improvement over the frowning or the impassive stares that spoke of denial. The staring was the worst, it was like he wasn't with her, that neither she nor her developing baby existed.

There was a part of Sandra that still didn't believe what that pale blue cross revealed until the morning sickness began. She had risen for work at 7am, following her routine: bathroom, online Pilates, shower, make-up, clothes, hair, a banana that she ate while waiting for the bus that would get her to work by nine.

The interruption came during the application of her make-up. She paused, mascara brush quivering before her eyelash.

A LITTLE SOMETHING TO HIDE

Her stomach advertised its discontent with little time for evasive action. She filled the sink, the smell of butyric acid driving her to sickness again, this time, blessedly, she made the toilet. This was different from the last time she was ill; alcohol had fuelled that experience, dulling her sensations. This was worse, she was lucid, her senses heightened, the tastes and smells pronounced. From the other side of the door, a hesitant enquiry from her mother. She answered with a strangled, *Fine*. She was a terrible liar.

In the days that followed, hurried trips to the bathroom punctuated her routine; she sacrificed her Pilates. Breakfasts resembled the eccentric; her favourite, slices of fresh avocado combined with slick-syruped peaches and topped with mayonnaise. Mid-morning snacks featured tomato sauce-soaked sardines; a tin carried everywhere.

She limited her evening work at the SAP Center, the Prius having to yield to her pregnancy. She wanted to see more of Daniel. He was keen for more work. She alleviated her disappointment with the belief that his enthusiasm for work was a sign of him making provision, taking responsibility.

In a discovery that came with agreeable disbelief, she developed an amplified sexual appetite. It bemused Daniel to find that sex was still an option. She joked that it was fine, she was already pregnant. They shared a heightened fervency; the novelty led him to skip nights at work. She rationalised that it was because he wanted to spend more time with her.

She decided that contained excitement accounted for Daniel's indifference to her pregnancy. As her shape began to change, he'd stroke her growing tummy, tentatively at first, curious at the evolving bump. His brief focus on her belly ceded to other motivations, his hands sliding toward her breasts, his attention always a precursor to sex. Sandra didn't discourage his interest.

As their baby grew, Daniel's finals became his overriding focus, dominating his time. By April, work at the SAP Center yielded to study, which was also his excuse for limiting his time with Sandra. He had long stopped seeing her at her parents' home. To Sandra, the responsibility for that development lay at the feet of her father, with his unwillingness to make Daniel feel welcome. They only ever met at Daniel's apartment, and never for long. He had to hit the books, he said. His dedication to his studies pleased her, boding well for their future.

Sandra told Daniel she wanted to take him for a meal after his last exam on 20 May. It was a Wednesday night. Her plan was to celebrate the end of college and the start of their new life together. *I'll be too tired,* he said.
Friday?
Can't. Out with my buddies. Maybe Saturday?
Okay. My parents are looking forward to it.
Your parents? I'm not sure about that.
I thought …
He interrupted before she could finish. *Let's keep it to us, Babe.* He promised to go to her house on Sunday for brunch with her folks. She was happy to compromise, it was reasonable.

She booked a table for seven at Le Papillon on Saratoga Avenue. She figured that by nine they'd be on their way back to his place where she'd take control of the evening. Daniel phoned at six to say his choice of the 280 back from the Westfield Valley Fair was disastrous. A six-car pile-up lay in front of him. He thought he'd make it to the restaurant but was tight on time. He said he'd meet her there. Sandra loved that he'd been thoughtful enough to phone early to let her know.

At 7.15pm, she wasn't too concerned about him; imagining the hold-up, believing he'd arrive soon. She sipped on a tonic water at the bar. Left alone for fifteen minutes in the past, an itinerant man would have ventured to impose himself. She knew the type, could spot them lounging on a stool, or lurching across a room. They were there tonight, she saw them, they saw her too. She could feel the lechery, evaluating, calculating their approach, pausing at the sight of her swelling stomach, deciding, and sidling elsewhere in search of other prey.

A LITTLE SOMETHING TO HIDE

At 7.30, the maître-d' asked her for the second time if she'd like to make her way to the table. She glanced at her watch. *I'll wait a while longer.* He wore a hint of sadness at her answer. He was wrong to be wearing that look, but that didn't prevent Sandra experiencing a small thread of anxiety. She hesitated over Daniel's number on her phone, before setting it down. She'd wait just a little, there'd be a perfectly rational explanation.

His voicemail kicked-in when she called at 7.45. It was good to hear his voice, even if it was just his answer phone. She didn't leave a message, didn't want him to think she was panicking. At eight o'clock (when she did, and she was), she tried to sound casual. *Just checking you're okay. I hope you get here soon.*

At 8.15, there was more of an edge to her voice, imploring him to call her back. *I'm worried*, she added. *I'll meet you at your apartment.* Still there was no call. She asked for the cheque before flicking to her Uber app. The maître-d' smiled his sorrowful smile and told her that the drinks were on the house. She felt patronised but thanked him for the kindness.

The car stopped outside Daniel's at 8.45. From the street, there was no reassuring glow of light from his windows. She slipped into the block as another resident left. On the stairs to his apartment, she remembered she didn't have a key. She had opted for elegant tonight, taking a sparkling clutch bag, leaving her battered handbag at home. His apartment key sat in a pocket of the ragged bag; she knocked – repeatedly. The knocks went unanswered.

With growing apprehension, she took the stairs to the basement garage to see if his car was there. Her heals clacked against the polished concrete floor, disconcerting clatter, increasing her anxiety. His designated spot was empty. She walked down the slip to the street outside, rebuking herself for worrying, but still searching for the number of the local Police. She asked about the accident on the 280. A gravelly voice, tired from some unknown abuse, answered. *There are no problems on the Interstate tonight, Ma'am.*

SANDRA & BABY GEORGE – SAN JOSE

What about the accident between the Burbank and Downtown intersection earlier?

Hold on a minute ma'am. Let me check.

Please check again, she said, when he told her there were no major accidents that day.

The Uber driver asked if she was okay when he dropped her home an hour later. She told him she was fine as she once more tried Daniel's number. It rang repeatedly, voicemail. *I'm scared Daniel. Please call.*

He didn't. Not that night, nor the following day in response to any of the four calls that she made to him before 9am. *Can I borrow your car, Daddy?*

Only if I can come with you.

I'll be fine, honestly.

Do you want my car? She relented, she had no choice, it was worth the trouble to know that Daniel was safe. Her rational explanations for his absence were increasingly tremulous.

Her father's Hush Puppies belied their name, each step he took, echoing off the bare walls. The usually sterile surfaces in Daniel's minimalist apartment, held traces of dust where it had settled beneath now vanished appliances. Crumbs from the toaster remained on the counter; there was a wispy grey outline of filth on the floor in the living area, a template of grime, recording the sofa's position. The sofa, on which they conceived their baby, was gone, along with everything else.

Sandra let out a thin guttural moan as she surveyed the room, vocal cords constricting, robbing her of voice. *Fucker,* said her father. She was twenty-two years old; it was the first time she'd heard him swear. He wrapped his arms around his daughter, apologising. She didn't know if it was for his language or her situation, either way, it didn't make a difference. She let him hold her tight, engulfing her. It had been a long time since she'd cried in her father's arms. The last time it happened, he held her for as long as it took for the hurt to fade. This time, she wasn't so sure he could do the same.

A LITTLE SOMETHING TO HIDE

After two weeks of trying to reach him, Daniel's recorded message disappeared from his voicemail; a female automaton cheerlessly told her the service was no longer active. Her emails went unanswered. She discovered too, that he had surprisingly few friends. The buddies from Friday's drink were a myth. The names weaved into conversation, the subjects of mirth, of boyish shenanigans, all were ethereal. The one she knew, La Forêt's sommelier, didn't know he'd gone. There was no new number, no forwarding address. Daniel had disappeared.

The baby's kicking was a welcome distraction from the likelihood of Daniel's desertion. It anchored her to a certainty; they would be okay. Each tympani beat from within cast her doubts, she kept faith, the belief that motherhood was a fitting destiny, her noble cause. The pressure of heel against womb, of shape altering leg stretches, kept her from the darkness, stayed her from languishing in desolation. George and Cynthia Mayhew assured her. *You are not alone.* She would keep her baby safe, love him, she would provide. Her OB-GYN was pleased with how well Sandra's pregnancy was progressing. In a few weeks, she expected a much loved and healthy baby to emerge.

Sandra's father was at her side when the baby was born, her mother jealously pacing the corridor. There was space in the delivery room for one other, Cynthia masked her disappointment when Sandra chose her father, his disgust at Daniel's flight easing with the prospect of supplanting him at the hospital. He said it was the only good thing that came from the butthole disappearing into the ether (George didn't consider 'butthole' a profanity).

Before Daniel bolted, Sandra knew that she was having a boy. She and Daniel agreed to keep the baby's gender a secret. She loved that he could be discreet. They had tossed names around before he disappeared. She didn't like his choices, but he clung to his suggestions. He was opting for names that attached to Greek mythology: Apollo, Artemis, Dionysus, Hermes, Zeus. He defended his choices, solemnly arguing that

SANDRA & BABY GEORGE – SAN JOSE

Sandra should choose from his list, treating her alternatives with disdain. She knew now that the names were just another of his practical jokes, one that he was willing to inflict upon their new-born son.

Now that he was gone, she decided Daniel's choices were idiotic. She would choose the name of her baby, she liked Leonardo, but thought it pretentious, she didn't want him to carry a name through life that might attract bullies; a *regular* name would be better. When her father, dressed in his hospital scrubs, held her son, beholding him with wonder, she changed her mind; the name she planned didn't feel right. He wouldn't be Ares or Poseidon, wouldn't be Leonardo, Michelangelo, Donatello, or Raphael. She had a much better name in mind. Her baby would be George, just like her dad.

As predicted by the OB-GYN, Baby George was much loved, with doting carers. George senior demonstrated a talent for changing diapers. Cynthia complained that the skill was missing during Sandra's earliest years. *Grandma's bleating again Georgie-boy*, he'd whisper to the child lying on the changing table before him, before raspberrying his grandson's belly to illicit a high-pitched squeal that pleased them both.

Cynthia bossed his bath time, asserting the highest qualifications for the role; CPR and mouth-to-mouth training from the '70s. That the extent of her knowledge came from the girl-guide troop of her youth goes unspoken, an irrelevance; her claim was steadfast. Sandra allowed, if not entirely welcomed, her parents' intrusions to the nurture of her child. She was resolute in the raising of Baby George, determined to map his path, he would learn things her way: purposefully, lovingly, beautifully. Where peril threatened, she guarded; if fear invaded, she comforted; where joy was absent, she created happiness. Her boy was the centre of her world, and with him she was almost whole. She had only one lament.

There were prominent features from his father: piercing eyes; the wave in his auburn hair; his serious countenance when concentrating. In other features and mannerisms, he was his mother's child. Diminutive, quick to smile, constantly chattering when confident, but the features of his father were a constant reminder of George's origin and what was missing from their life.

She began her search in the evenings when Baby George lay asleep in his crib. She started with the Butterfields of San Jose. She identified twelve families. Six had publicly available details; she phoned them all. One had a Daniel in the family; he was still in elementary school. She stalked others through social media, interrogating Facebook, Instagram, Twitter, LinkedIn – a relentless pursuit. After two months, twelve contacts gave her a variation of the same form of nothing. She widened her search, discovering that San Joses existed beyond California. It served as an epiphany, she increased her effort, as Baby George suckled, her fingers raced across her phone as she tracked and traced.

Daniel Butterfield had a remarkably clear digital footprint. The University alumni website revealed nothing she didn't already know. She turned search engines into verbs, she Googled, she Binged, Yahooed, and DuckDuckGoed, hoping to find something that would reveal his location. She dredged her memory, frustration mounting, unable to recreate the conversations with Daniel that she knew held the illusive remnant. She dug and dug.

Her obsession with finding him troubled her parents. *You're better off without him,* her father said.

We'll give Baby George all the love he needs, Cynthia added.

He abandoned you honey.

Sandra was convinced that if he met his son, Daniel would want to be involved in his upbringing. *He was frightened, Daddy.*

And now?

Embarrassed, I'm sure.

They argued that George senior didn't try to understand Daniel. *I may not know who he is, but I've got a pretty clear handle on what he is.*

She discovered a lot about the various Butterfield families; knew what their pages would reveal before following each link. She'd seen them hundreds of times, but kept clicking, hoping that the next tap of a mouse might uncover something that she hadn't learnt before. Social media's dynamics would reveal something, triggering his discovery, she knew she'd find him soon. Her parents were right, she obsessed.

They worried too, convincing her that they should take time out, go to the great outdoors, stretch their legs, enjoy the air; Yosemite National Park was only a short hop. *It'll do us good*, said Cynthia. They were right, it wasn't too far. According to Google, they could drive there in three and a half hours. Even Baby George, approaching 18 months, could survive the journey. *Let's rent a cabin, stay a few days. You'll feel better.*

Sandra studied the image of Yosemite she found online, her forefinger twitching above the scroll wheel. She ran her finger back and forth, zooming in and out above the landscape, drilling closer, establishing places to see, things to do, wondering if it was child friendly, wondering if bears ate toddlers. She glanced at the search window; a vibrant image of the park; a serene river flanked with conifers beneath the towering El Capitan. It looked magnificent, majestic, but not baby proof. She wondered where else they might go. The cursor flashed languidly in the search box, teasing, her fingers hesitating above the keyboard. Her thoughts drifted from vacations. She typed 'San Jose, AZ' into the search bar and hit return. She felt her disappointment rising, stealing over her, the familiar fabric of weary despair. The image grew before her, revealing the Arizona State Prison Complex at Safford. He wasn't there, she hoped; Safford wasn't what she sought. Fingers twitched, scrolled, searched. Besides the prison, the Gila River was the only thing of interest in an otherwise featureless 2D landscape. She had other options: Florida, Illinois, New Mexico, Puerto Rico, Texas.

Florida looked bustling, filling her with hope. She flicked between the satellite image and the map, back and forth, in and out, gazing at the page, aching to find a catalyst to release imprisoned memories. She burrowed using Street View, conducting virtual strolls down every street, a misguided hope that she would see his form emerging from a coffee shop, or a silhouette through a window of the houses she passed. Nothing.

San Jose, Illinois left her with the impression of a town plucked from elsewhere; a misplaced piece of jigsaw, a town deposited by an alien presence, or manufactured to create an elaborate set from a forgotten movie, a setting for an Ira Levin adaptation. She couldn't believe that anyone could escape from, or return to, such a place. She moved on, New Mexico. She saw the Pecos River and her breath caught; a memory stirred. *Gotcha*, she thought.

She found his high school, stanned alumni, discovered year books online, found his picture. She located his family, obtaining their number. Her mouse hovered over it, turning from an arrow to a hand, finger pointing, poised on the thin blue line below, a light tap separating her from a connection to his family home. It was a reminder of another blue line she'd seen more than two years before, leading to this moment. After all this time, all the searching and the promise of a resolution, she didn't know if she was ready to make the call.

A frail voice answered. His mother? His grandmother? *Is Daniel there?*

Not just now, Darling. He's away at work, back at the weekend. Shall I tell him who called?

That's okay, I'll call him later. He still lived at home – on weekends at least. She hung up. Excited. Frightened.

She stared at the number for two days before dialling again, waiting until Saturday. She hoped he'd be home, doubting that he would be out with friends; that wasn't in his playbook. The same reedy voice answered when she called. *I'll just get him*, she said.

Sandra hung up when he said, *Hello?*

Found him, finally. It had taken the best part of two years; their baby boy was now a toddler, scooting around his grandparents', reaching for the bric-a-brac raised beyond his grasp.

She researched. It took longer than she thought, but she discovered where he worked. Daniel was a tutor at New Mexico Tech. She ordered a copy of the college's program brochure and saw him, dressed in a lab coat, peering into a glass beaker over a Bunsen burner. He'd made the college's documentation, which meant a steady job. In Sandra's mind, it also meant that the college held him in considerable regard.

She is certain he will be thrilled to see her and meet Baby George. She hopes he likes their son's name. It's not one of his suggestions, but it is Greek in origin, georgos, a farmer, not a god. She doesn't want that for her boy, doesn't want him to be able to play with the lives of others, down that road lies cruelty.

She booked her ticket on the Briscola coach to Albuquerque on the day of her discovery. She had to pay three quarters of the adult fare for Baby George's seat. She considered having him on her lap for the journey but thought better of it. She wants her son, their son, to be as fresh as he can be when they arrive at Daniel's.

She can't wait to surprise him.

A LITTLE SOMETHING TO HIDE

SALINAS TRANSIT CENTER

Arrivals
Time	From	Expected
23:25	San Jose	Expected: 23:40

Departures
Time	Destination	Expected
00:00	King City	Delayed: 00:15

SALINAS TRANSIT CENTER

I like Rosa Fernandez. We've met before. She likes springing surprises, and she has two for her daughter Felicia. The first is that she's going to stay with her forever. Felicia knows Rosa is on her way to visit, but she doesn't know that her mother has a one-way ticket. When Rosa gets to Albuquerque, she will stretch out the first surprise, teasing her daughter until she guesses, ignoring Felicia's mock indignation. Her daughter will play the game, just as she did as a child. When she has guessed correctly, Rosa thinks Felicia will be pleased.

Felicia will inevitably ask the question that will lead to Rosa's second revelation. She won't play the game with Felicia when she does, there's too much gravity to her news. Felicia may not like the second surprise quite so much. Rosa suspects her daughter will be a little shocked, but quietly happy.

Felicia will understand too, why Rosa wants to stay forever. Rosa's escaping a nightmare. Going far from Salinas is the only way she can put it behind her. She is the last of her family to do it, to leave Salinas ... she had to be. No mother could take her action and knowingly leave others behind. That would be unspeakably cruel and Rosa is not a cruel woman. She is gentle and kind with an empathic nature, a quiet, modest woman who lets others have their say and drifts into the background unheeded, never one to cause a scene. She is the first to compromise, to support, to assist. It's what she has done for all her adult life.

There was a time, distant now, when she was a feisty girl, full of passion and fight; that time has passed. She is wiser now, more considered, humble. The burden of her wisdom shades her features, aging her, stealing her vitality, leaving a rumpled imposter in its place. Constant strain, unrelenting even in the quiet, does that. She doesn't complain, she doesn't want to argue for any more pain.

She wanted to be a nurse, but ... circumstances. *She became a mother. She wanted more, a career. Apparently, being a mother was enough. 'Make that your career, Bebita.'*

The surrender of her ambition upsets her, just as it distresses her to think that there were times, too many of them to count, when she failed to be a good mother.

Maybe he was right to say that she couldn't want more. She was perhaps fooling herself to think she could take care of others when she couldn't even take care of her family. She has reconciled herself to that view, acknowledging that although she hadn't always been good, she had always done her best. Her best, however, just wasn't good enough.

Those that join the bus along the route will witness a quiet woman, barely five-foot-tall, with a once pretty face, now worn thin by undisclosed business. What she carries, she carries unspoken. She worries that others will see through the veneer, beneath the creases that line her face, reading the stories they tell, like a palm-reader telling of a life from the etchings on a hand. She does not fear for the future, rather, she fears that the lines, which she has no choice but to wear, tell the truth of the past, of what she knows, of the secrets that she holds. She's not alone in knowing, she shares secrets with her daughters, although they're never admitted. They remain buried, where she thinks they are safe, where they can avoid the pain by denying the malevolence. Their silence operates as a collective denial, a means to avoid the hurt.

Rosa has conditioned them to believe that it is safer not to talk, that for their health, they must hide their knowledge. It has come at a cost; a price that Rosa has met. She believes it has bought them peace, which is why she can accept that they have left. By keeping their distance, they stay safe. She hopes her remaining children gain the peace that Theresa never found.

Rosa recognises the irony that stems from her actions. In allowing them to leave, she has sacrificed their love. She wonders how many other mothers could perform an act of love so profound, that by its nature, it will cause them to lose the love of their children. Rosa has lost them all, all that is, except Felicia. Felicia's love has never faltered. She is always there for her mother.

SALINAS TRANSIT CENTER

They never spoke of what happened, never; Rosa forbade it. To do so would cause more hurt. 'It's a woman's burden to endure the pain.' It's a lie she kept telling herself and her daughters. It made the accusatory looks from Felicia difficult to bear. It is the reason she can survive not seeing her other girls. They all wore the same expression, redolent with expectation; unrealistic expectations, Rosa thinks, for them to have of their mother. Those looks hurt, but Rosa will suffer them if they never speak of what happened. The sorrow they convey hurts, they carry a pain that has never diminished, is always endured.

When Rosa has settled in her seat, she will focus on her knitting. The needles will clack incessantly throughout the journey, flying, as each skein of wool diminishes in response to the activity. She has brought twelve with her, each the colour of a crimson horizon. It is more than enough to last the trip, more than enough for her needs. During the journey she will create a wardrobe of garments for her granddaughter, a six-year-old that she gets to see twice a year, once over Thanksgiving and again in March when the family extends a little to celebrate the girl's birthday.

Rosa would like to see her girls and their children more often, but it rarely happens. None of them come to stay. Rosa didn't realise it at first, but when each of them made the choice to leave the family home, their moves were permanent.

A LITTLE SOMETHING TO HIDE

ROSA – SALINAS

Arabella was the first of Rosa's children to leave, the moment she graduated high school she went to New York to seek her fortune. Rosa couldn't understand why she had to move to the East Coast when there were so many opportunities for her in California. San Francisco wasn't far and offered plenty of jobs. If the climate there wasn't right for her, she could drift down the coast to LA or even San Diego, but Arabella was insistent, only New York would do. Rosa tried to argue that the winters were brutal, but her daughter wouldn't listen. She wanted the bright lights, the chaos, the noise of New York. It was where she thought she would thrive, where it would be easier to forget.

Arabella found it easy to go. She promised her mother that she would come back often, that she would be a regular visitor to Salinas. It was a promise she didn't keep. She left in the summer of '98, returning only once. Before she left, she would tell her mother that New York wasn't that far, that it was just five hours on a plane. When Rosa pleaded with her to return, to have a break and visit the family, those five hours elongated, becoming too difficult to incorporate into Arabella's schedule. Rosa's husband vowed he would never step on a plane, so they were never going to travel East, and Rosa couldn't leave the other five children in his care while she went alone. She told people that he wouldn't manage, trying to minimise the disloyalty. Making him sound incapable was preferable to voicing her real fears.

Juanita went next. Arabella and she had been close. Rosa remembers how protective Arabella was of her younger sister. From the moment of Juanita's birth, Arabella watched every move that Rosa made with the new arrival, following her around whenever she was caring for the baby, helping wherever she could. By the age of three, Arabella was insisting that she and Juanita bathe together and that only she could wash her sister.

Although there were two years between them, they might have been twins. Always together, it was never clear which girl was mimicking the other's actions or moods. It didn't surprise Rosa that after one of Arabella's regular Sunday afternoon calls, where she would speak briefly with Rosa before monopolising Juanita, the younger sibling announced that she was going to join her sister in New York. She too said she would return, but Rosa recognised the absence of conviction from her statement; she'd heard it before. On the one occasion Juanita returned, she didn't visit the house. She and Arabella caught a taxi directly from the airport to a church, staying just long enough to hold their mother a final time as the family wept before a freshly dug hole in the churchyard.

Rosa knows why they left, but she is a dutiful wife. There are things she can't do, things she can't say. She knows the responsibilities a woman has toward her husband; she fights the weaknesses that threaten her vows. She is committed to her promises, it serves to exaggerate her disappointment in her two oldest daughters.

Rosa is all about family. She will do anything to keep the unit together, but they must follow his rules. He has always been clear about that. *He* is her husband, Jorge Fernandez. He too is about family; the family name is sacred. He doesn't care that two of his daughters have crossed the country. In his eyes, their behaviour was bringing shame to the family. It is better that they are far away, both for the family's reputation and for his wallet. He knows their absence makes Rosa unhappy, but he is pleased to see them gone, they were becoming disruptive. There are consequences if the family doesn't follow his rules.

Their children left them as soon as they could. Jorge believes that their children were an entrapment, the tool Rosa used to snare him, preventing him from being the man he was born to be. She saddled him with obligations in the form of her kids. Every two years, legs high, hitched in stirrups, squeezing out another mewling child, always a girl, never a boy, draining his resources, thwarting his ambition. Always she claimed it was an accident, but he knew it was part of her plan. Jorge thanks God for the miscarriages.

They were together because their families insisted it was the honourable thing. The elders colluded and gave them no choice; Jorge wasn't yet dominant enough to say no. He was close to eighteen, he answered his father back – for the first time; the aspirant seeking to assert himself.

His father frightened him; a man with a quick temper and a solid rage, prone to thrashing Jorge for innocent indiscretions. When his father demanded that he *Do the right thing*, the cub challenged for leadership, overestimating his status. Although Jorge was a fit and powerful young man, his father was a seasoned abuser; he lavished a beating. Jorge succumbed to his father's will. His father reminded him that the family's honour was more important than the boy's posturing.

Jorge and Rosa met at high school when she was a junior and he was in his senior year. He was handsome then, confident, always wearing his letter jacket, a large yellow S emblazoned on blue. His letter came from the pool. Latinos weren't renowned for their swimming, but he was the best; State championships beckoned. He loved the pool, was always there, always the first to hit the water. It gave him a vantage to watch the girls dive in, studying their form as they moved from changing room to poolside, admiring their developing shapes, imprinting their images for later – for private recollection.

His father considered swimming effeminate, forbidding Jorge to join the team. He wanted him to play soccer. Jorge reluctantly agreed, a reluctance that left him unable to sit comfortably for three days. He lacked the talent for the game, the skills eluded him, as did a starting place on the team. After three games, his father stopped coming to watch. *Why should I watch the useless sonofabitch carry the half-time oranges?*

A LITTLE SOMETHING TO HIDE

His absence suited Jorge, who maintained a charade of attending practices and matches, while secretly switching to the pool, where he discovered that he was not only good, but that the girls on the team liked the physique shaped by his hours of training.

He entertained the conceit that their focus was primarily on his swimsuit. He welcomed the attention, loving that he was the source of petty jealousies, exploiting them and fuelling them by being impossible to pin down. He allowed snagging, but never capture. He took advantage of their interest, more than some would allow, testing boundaries, seeing reluctance merely as a challenge to overcome; he had learnt the art of persuasion from his father.

He dumped them as quickly as they came, his interest extending only as far as conquest. He bored of them soon after he had his way, and he always got his way. He didn't care if they weren't ready or weren't interested in his *experiments*, their views were unimportant; another lesson he'd taken from his father. He knew to move on if their enthusiasm didn't match his; he didn't need the kind of trouble an unhappy woman could bring.

When Jorge and Rosa attended Salinas High, they were among a minority of Latinos. He knew her, vaguely, their ethnicity generating awareness if not solidarity; the younger Rosa of no interest to Jorge whose attentions were elsewhere. By her junior year, the pre-adolescent edges were gone, the slight, almost brittle child, yielding to age. He noticed her then. She wasn't a swimmer, which he thought a shame; he would like to see her in a swimsuit.

He was sure there was mutual interest; her glances lingered. It told him everything he needed to know. He felt her watching him, certain that she manufactured sidelong poses to accentuate her figure. He imagined a come-on smile too; leading him to wonder if she was happy to experiment. When he saw her in the bleachers at the next swim meet, he was convinced that she was there to watch him.

Jorge wasn't alone in noticing her. In the locker room she featured in the pubescent musings of hormonal boys who gained their knowledge of sexual relationships from clandestine glimpses of their fathers' pornography. A WASP boy explained in lurid detail what he would do to Rosa, piquing Jorge's jealousy. The boy couldn't have her, *she* was his, *he* would do those things to her, and other things the *gringo* couldn't begin to imagine.

Jorge was indignant that she might end up with him; the white privileged boy who wanted for nothing. He despised him for having everything. Jorge would get to Rosa first; the white boy could have her later, when there was nothing new for her to discover. Jorge wanted the satisfaction of knowing that he'd been the first to do everything to her. If the white boy was going to get Rosa, it would be after him, once Jorge had spoiled her.

It was the first time that Jorge felt the need to compete for a girl. Before, he'd always found it easy to attract those he wanted, but Rosa was different. To his surprise, he learnt that she hadn't come to the pool for him, she'd come to see Ryan Toogood, the *gringo*.

Rosa and Ryan were an item, but he knew the white boy's boasting was fantasy, locker room braggadocio that elevates imagination into conquest. Jorge smiled to know that he didn't have to pretend to boast of doing such things, everyone knew that he had been with most of the girls on the swim team, doing things to them the other boys could only dream. He knew the girls loved it, even when they said they didn't.

When Jorge next saw Rosa, she was waiting outside for Ryan. He slithered behind her, his breath warm on her neck. *Waiting for someone special?*

She started at his voice, pulling away, halted by the tight grip of his hand on her forearm.

He smiled, wolfish, releasing her arm when he spied Ryan coming towards them, allowing her to escape. *I can satisfy you more than the white boy*, he said, just loud enough for her to hear.

Jorge knew the idea would grow with Rosa; the prospect of intimacy too great to resist. The following day at the pool, he stood alongside Ryan, flicking his gaze between Rosa and his teammate's swimsuit. When he knew he had her attention, he gestured to his costume. She flushed, looking away. *She's pretending to be shy*, he thought. Jorge knew what that meant.

The relationship between Rosa and Ryan tested Jorge's patience. The white boy's money was surely the attraction. Having listened to Ryan's bullshit in the locker room, Jorge knew the *gringo's* only interest was her tits. He claimed erotic successes, but Jorge could tell from the subtext that none of it was true, he was lying to impress his friends. Jorge convinced himself that Rosa was holding out on Ryan; the white boy didn't have what it takes.

What Jorge didn't know was that Rosa and Ryan heeded their parents' obtuse euphemisms to exercise caution. They wrestled their sixteen-year-old's hormones, managing, sometimes only just, to curb their impulses. Rosa told Ryan he'd have to wait. He didn't attempt to conceal his frustration, she resisted his passive coercion, he didn't press too hard.

While Jorge remained ignorant of the couple's restraint, he believed he represented a growing attraction to Rosa. He caught her glances, the flirtatious smiles, always teasing. Her interest was obvious to him, but she clung to the white boy. Although he told himself that she had better come to him soon or she would miss her chance, his ambivalence masked a growing jealousy.

Ryan was unaware that he had competition for Rosa, thinking his rivalry with Jorge was limited to the pool. Their training swims assumed a competitive nuance, routine laps becoming races. They were always the last two in the pool. Their rivalry went unspoken, they didn't design to suggest to each other that every length was a race, it just happened. For Jorge, it fuelled his envy, intensifying the rivalry out of the pool, a rivalry of which Ryan remained ignorant.

The inseparability of Rosa and Ryan added to Jorge's frustration. He formulated a plan to isolate Rosa, and although basic, he thought it exceptionally cunning, almost sophisticated. It was neither. It served its purpose, but lacked finesse.

Having suffered Jorge, many of the girls on the team shunned him, preferring to avoid the danger that attached to his attention, unwilling to give voice to their encounters, burying the experience in the forlorn hope that the pain would disappear, unable to sever the memory of what he did.

Others fixated on him, inexplicably drawn to his sadism; he rewarded them with disdain. Some were willing to do what he wanted; Jorge saw them as vessels to satisfy his urges. They were too easy; he liked a challenge. He kept them hanging though, he had *needs*. Daisy Wallace was one of his turn-to girls. He didn't mind Daisy. She didn't resist when he demanded a blowjob. He boasted in the locker room. *She likes dick like a kid likes candy*.

Promising her a good time if she did him a favour, he held her hand against him and kissed her neck, swearing he'd make her squeal, a promise he wasn't troubled about keeping, making it only to recruit a co-conspirator.

As instructed, Daisy Wallace began flirting with Ryan at the end of training, sitting on the side of the pool, dangling her legs in his swimming lane. Alongside, Jorge allowed his rival to finish two body lengths ahead. *That's impressive*, said Daisy, as Ryan lifted his head from the water. *You killed him*.

Rosa appeared unconcerned when Daisy offered a jubilant Ryan help from the pool, until he fell into Daisy's arms when she hauled him toward her. They staggered together, Daisy wrapping her arms around Ryan as they restored their balance, finishing in an awkward embrace. Ryan disentangled himself, embarrassed, conscious of Rosa's scrutiny.

Studying the exchange between her boyfriend and the interloper from the bleachers, Rosa watched as they walked side-by-side toward the locker rooms, their shoulders touching, Daisy provocatively swinging her hips, an attempt to allure, too close for Rosa's liking. She didn't sense Ryan's discomfort or register that he couldn't move away from Daisy without falling into the pool. All she noticed was an intimacy that hinted at something more.

Ryan caught Rosa's eye as they passed, indicating he'd meet her outside.

Rosa acknowledged the unspoken message, but not before noting the triumphal smile of Daisy Wallace.

In the changing area, Jorge dressed quickly, ensuring he would leave the locker room before Ryan and Daisy. He knew too, that Daisy would be quick – if she knew what was good for her.

She heeded his warning, standing exactly where told, waiting for Ryan, hidden from Rosa's view, but with a clear line of sight to the boy's locker room.

Jorge smiled and said *Hi* as he passed Rosa, ostensibly heading home. After a hundred yards he paused, waiting in the shadows on the path that he knew Rosa would take, believing she would be alone after witnessing Daisy and Ryan.

To Rosa, it didn't seem coincidental that Daisy and Ryan were leaving together. She saw Daisy spring toward Ryan, taking his forearm, pulling his hand toward her, slipping him a piece of paper. They exchanged words before Daisy leaned forward to kiss him. It wasn't much of a kiss, a fleeting peck. Daisy let him go and moved away with a jaunty bounce, leaving Ryan to read the note that Jorge insisted Daisy write, angrily demanding revisions of drafts he didn't like, forcing multiple versions from her until he was satisfied.

Looking at him through the window from where she stood, Rosa couldn't see Ryan's expression, but his furtive glance, and the haste with which he stuffed the note in his pocket, spoke of ominous intent. She'd seen other girls flirt with Ryan, it was a frequent occurrence, but it never threatened their relationship, they were committed to each other – but that glance, looking for, but not seeing Rosa, troubled her.

Ryan couldn't see her in the early evening gloom through the window of the centre, but he knew she was there. He hoped she hadn't seen the exchange, feeling his guilt rise as he approached her. A solitary look confirmed she had.

What was that about?

Ryan tried to suggest it was nothing, gaining an arched eyebrow in return.

Show me the note.
It's nothing.
Show me.
Honestly, it's nothing, I'm not even going to do it, but there was no conviction in his voice.

Rosa held out her hand.

He implored her not to press, but she was adamant.

Meet me at Foster's Freeze after Saturday's meet. I'll show you something that'll blow your mind (and who knows what else I might blow). Come alone or don't come at all. D x. She added a heart with an arrow through it.

Tears formed as Rosa read the note, tearing it into fragments, flinging them to the ground. They fluttered, belying the force with which she threw them, their wispy flight infuriating, undermining her anger. Ryan tried to speak but she held up a hand to silence him. *Not now.* She wasn't going to speak with him, that would have to wait. She turned to leave, heading towards Jorge.

Had Ryan followed her, explaining that Daisy's message meant nothing, Rosa's life might have been vastly different. He watched her leave, disappearing around the corner. If he'd known that Jorge Fernandez loitered beyond view, he would have pursued her, but he didn't know that the predator lay waiting.

Thirty seconds after leaving Ryan, Rosa heard a whisper behind her. She hadn't seen him emerge from the shadows. *¿Como estas, Bebita?* She knew who it was.

Bebita. It was the pet name her father used. It should have been comforting, it felt sinister. He sounded like he cared, and he used the old tongue, but she couldn't shake the underlying menace.

I'm fine. She said it in English, she wasn't ready to be familiar. She continued walking.

He was unperturbed. *¿Estas segura?*

Si. He considered her use of Spanish a small success.

Okay, he said. *See you tomorrow?*

There was something implied in his question, a suggestion that he would let her be. Rosa's concern diminished, her immediate fear subsiding, but she remained anxious. She walked on, he didn't follow, she felt safer.

He let her go, watching her disappear, waiting, hoping.

She turned, looking back, wary.

He interpreted her movement as interest. *Ella es mía*, he thought. She's mine.

The next morning before class, Ryan implored her to understand. He had no idea why Daisy had given him the note, begging Rosa to believe that he had no intention of meeting her. He didn't know why she kissed him; he wasn't remotely interested.

Rosa allowed a little trust to seep in through her anger. She wanted to believe him, despite feeling cheated.

Interpreting her softening as forgiveness, Ryan tried to kiss her, but she pulled away. *Let's wait a bit*, she said.

Hovering nearby, Jorge hoped for a delay in their reconciliation, gambling that Rosa wasn't yet ready to pardon Ryan. He moved in when Ryan left to go to his class. *¿Como estas?* No Bebita this time. He smiled and won a smile back.

I'm okay.

Good, he said. *You know you're too good for him?*

Rosa stopped walking. *What do you mean?*

I've heard what he says about you. The things you do.

What does he say?

Everything.

Rosa waited for Jorge to elaborate but he stayed silent, leaving the last word hanging, pregnant with innuendo. She matched his silence, her look urging him to speak.

It's graphic.

What? she said, in a voice rising with indignation.

Jorge was hoping for the inflection. *Porno – graphic.*

The bell rang for class. Rosa didn't get to ask Jorge any more questions.

He was confident his words were landing.

Continuing to harbour her anger, she found Jorge at lunchtime. He pretended chivalry, refusing to repeat Ryan's words. He mused that a respectful man would never say such things to others. *Things like that should be private*, he said. *If you were my girl, no one would ever know what we did.*

Whatever he said we did; we didn't. I'm not like that.

He smiled at her; deciding to take a risk. *That's a shame*, he said. *I'd love to try some of those things with you.*

Watching her leave, he thought she pretended her shock, but he knew that secretly, she liked what she heard.

As base as it was, his plan was working; Rosa was arguing with Ryan again after school. Jorge figured that Rosa wouldn't be heading to the pool, he skipped practice, following her, maintaining a distance that she wouldn't find unsettling. If she noticed him, she would consider his presence normal, they lived in the same part of town. Jorge watched as she entered their local drugstore. On impulse, he followed, buying two milkshakes before waiting outside. *Bought you this*, he said as she emerged. *I thought you could do with some cheering up.*

He was right. What surprised her, was that he was able to do it. He made her laugh. She knew he was cocky and arrogant but hadn't expected him to be amusing. He mocked his Mexican parents, their beliefs and expectations, their desire to assimilate. She recognised her own family, giggling as he mimicked his mother; her mother was the same. She felt an affinity to Jorge that she didn't feel for Ryan. He sat close to her, their thighs touching. It was uncomfortable at first; it didn't feel right, but after a time, she relaxed. She was a little disappointed when he said he had to go. Before he stood, he kissed her. It was a longer kiss than the one Daisy planted on Ryan, lingering somewhere between goodbye and an invitation for more.

Jorge was sure she enjoyed the attention, loved that his focus was on her, that he was interested. He was going to stay close, keep the pressure on, creating tension in her relationship with Ryan. He would be clandestine, that made it more interesting. He'd take her from Ryan without him knowing.

He took every opportunity to infer Ryan's infidelity. He watched Ryan try to win her back, but Jorge's whispering in

A LITTLE SOMETHING TO HIDE

Rosa's ear made the task harder. Despite his efforts, despite their secret rendezvous on Thursdays for practice-skipping milkshakes, she still wouldn't break with the *gringo*. He had to ignite her passion, engender a split from the white boy. He needed Daisy.

Daisy reminded Jorge that he hadn't delivered on his earlier promise. He tried to convince her that he would, but she proved insistent, needy, grasping for validation. He was good at attracting the broken ones. Normally he would pity her, but he was angry now. She earned herself rougher handling, but he knew she'd still enjoy it.

Jorge wasn't surprised when she begged him to stop; some of the girls couldn't handle him. He made sure she agreed to do what he wanted before he did. He couldn't understand why one minute the girls wanted him so badly, the next they said it was too much. Women.

When Daisy demonstrated reluctance to play her part in the plan, Jorge supplemented his persuasion with a wave of one of her draft notes. *You don't want your parents to know about the blowjobs, do you?* He thought himself clever. *I'm guessing you wouldn't want them to see this?*

She snatched the note from him, jamming it in her mouth, chewing it like gum, masticating it to a pulp, as Jorge watched impassively. She spat it at his feet, triumphant.

He smiled at her. *You wrote a lot of notes, bitch. I've kept them all.*

Daisy's second performance with Ryan wasn't as convincing as the first. Jorge thought she would ruin the plan with her glances between Jorge and Rosa. Rosa didn't notice, all she saw was another brazen pass at her boyfriend.

Did you see that puta, Wallace? he asked Rosa when he joined her on her walk home. He put a comforting arm around her when she started to cry. *You can do better than him, Bebita.*

It never occurred to Rosa that their meetings were more than a coincidence. What wasn't a coincidence was that he asked her out before they reached the drugstore. He promised to buy her a milkshake if she said *Yes*. It wasn't the promise that earned him the answer he wanted; it was his smile. She knew he had a reputation, but he'd been so kind to her, so supportive. Maybe the stories weren't true.

He walked her home after their drinks, shoulder to shoulder. She thought of Daisy and Ryan walking by the pool in a similar fashion; it resolved her thinking. She didn't believe she was being disloyal to him; Ryan cheated first; he would get what he deserved. They were around the corner from her home when Jorge stopped her in the street. She looked at him quizzically. *I'm not sure your parents are ready to see this yet.*

To see what?

This. He pulled her towards him.

She briefly considered resisting; still not entirely sure, but he was intent. She let herself go with it.

When they parted, they agreed they would meet on Saturday. A date, *Grease* was playing at the drive-in. He told her he'd borrow his father's car, a 10-year-old Cadillac DeVille. It had a bench seat in the front, perfect for snuggling. Rosa had to admit she was a little excited at the idea. He was quite a kisser.

He arrived early; it was a condition of her parents. Her family had values, they wanted to meet the boy that would be dating their daughter. An approval process beckoned. He had a head start; like them, his family was Mexican. They believed his parents raised him well, projecting their strictures, a default belief he sustained; he charmed them all. Rosa remembers the smile her mother gave her as they were leaving, the one confirming her approval – such a nice boy.

He invited her to snuggle next to him when they parked at the back of the drive-in. She slid toward him, resting her head against his shoulder, he wrapped a protective arm around her. While watching the cartoons before the main feature, they giggled in the same places. When they finished, they kissed, filling the time while they waited for the main feature to start. Jorge knew Rosa enjoyed it. They paused when the movie started, Rosa resting her head on his chest, feeling more comfortable as he ran his hand slowly up and down her arm.

A LITTLE SOMETHING TO HIDE

She thought it an accidental brush initially, his hand slipped around her arm, she felt the back of his finger against her breast. The slow-motion movement continued, deliberate, the same light touch. He sensed Rosa stiffen. He moved his hand away slightly, a subtle gesture. She thought he got the message and understood. He stroked her arm a couple more times and his hand came to rest on her shoulder. Rosa was okay with that, he did understand.

He waited a couple of minutes before fondling her again. He opened his palm, brushing his fingers across her collar bone. His hand traced her shape, feeling more of her breast, cupping it. She tensed, trying to pull away, finding his arm tight around her, unyielding. *Relax. Go with it.*

No, Jorge. She moved his hand.

He put it back. *Chill.*

She pushed herself away, moving to the other side of the car.

He lifted his hands in surrender. *What's wrong?*

I'm not like that.

Okay. I'm sorry. My mistake. He smiled at her, that same winning smile, but she thought she saw something new in it – danger. *Let's forget that happened. Let's rewind.* He tapped the seat next to him, *C'mon.*

Rosa hesitated before moving back. She didn't lean in, sitting rigid, hands locked between her legs.

He tried to put his arm around her again and she flinched; he dropped it.

They watched the rest of the movie in silence. When the credits rolled, he turned to her, put a hand on her shoulder and said, *Sorry.* He moved to kiss her, and she leaned back.

Please take me home.

Whatever. He started the car and joined the queue of cars leaving the drive-in.

Rosa knew the route home; she'd been to the drive-in before, the route home was direct. Jorge should have turned right out of Simas Street onto East Market. He went left. *It's the other way.*

I know a shortcut. They both lived to the west of the city; there was no shortcut.
Where are you going?
Relax. You'll see.
They were moving too fast. Rosa wanted to get out. The throaty thrum of the engine the only sound as they sped down East Market, away from her home. Jorge took a flying right onto Quilla Street across the oncoming traffic. Approaching cars sounded horns as he turned in front of them. He blew through the intersection at Williams Road causing Rosa to scream. *Ssh, it's okay*, he said, the embodiment of calm. *Relax.*

He flung the car across East Alisal Street and into the car park at the Salinas Fairways Golf Course where he drove onto the course. He followed a buggy path and pulled up alongside a manicured lake. The light from the streetlamps on East Alisal Street cast no glow where they were; darkness abounds. *Look*, he said. *I just wanted to show you that I'm sorry.* Rosa was as far from him as she could be in the confines of the car.

It's okay, she said, not believing him. *Just take me home. Please.* She scrabbled for the door as he moved toward her. He reached over her and hammered down the lock.

Just relax. Go with it, Bebita. He was leaning over her now. She could feel the warmth of his breath against her neck. He nuzzled at her, his tongue darting, licking her. It should have been erotic. It felt reptilian.

Stop, she said, trying to push him away. He pinned her arms to her side and moved against her, the weight of his body holding her in place. She arched her head, pulling away, but there was nowhere to go. Her neck exposed; he moved closer; into the cavity she'd created. He nuzzled again, she could feel his tongue coursing along her chest, moving lower. She tried to wriggle free, earning a vicious slap. She froze, the pain in her cheek intense, her ear ringing, fear escalating. He looked at her, the smile still on his face. She realised the danger now. She was right, she'd seen it earlier. Now it was too late.

It'll be worse if you fight it. He came forward again.
She screamed.

He laughed at her. *No one can hear you out here. It's just you and me. Go with it. You might enjoy it.*

She screamed again and his smile vanished. He shoved a hand over her mouth and pinned his body against her, ripping her blouse open, rubbing his other hand over her breast.

Nice. He forced his hand beneath her bra. She tried to kick at him but there wasn't room to swing her legs. Attempts to buck him away earned a punch to the ribs, a short jab knocking the air from her, the pain far greater than the slap. *I don't want to hurt you, Bebita. But I will if you make me.*

She whimpered, which he took for pleasure. *That's it*, he said, forcing her bra over her breasts. *Nice*, he said again as he forced himself against her. She felt his hand move between her legs, moving inside her underwear.

Please, no, she whispered. *No.* She felt the violation of his fingers. She squeezed her legs together, but he forced his way between them. She tried to get him away by slapping at his hand, then he shifted, moving them both. He dragged her so she was lying beneath him, flat along the bench seat. He pinned her with his knees, loosening his belt, pulling it free from his jeans before tying Rosa's hands together and attaching the loose end to the door.

You'll love this, he said as he pulled her underwear down beneath her dress. *It's spicy.* His tongue traced what he thought was a provocative path across his top lip.

Still straddling her, he pulled down his jeans. Rosa wasn't looking, she tried to fling him off, but he wouldn't move. He slapped her again. *Stop it, Bebita. It's better for both of us if you don't struggle.* He lay across her, tongue teasing at her breasts and moved to be inside her. Rosa screamed as he entered, the pain of his entry intense; another slap, the hardest of all. He pumped at her, ignoring her pleas to stop. He kept at her, driving, driving, hurting, hurting, violating her further.

Rosa, head arched, too terrified to release the scream on her lips, looked out the car window at the dark sky above. The stars that she had once counted with her father, the only man she wanted to call her *Bebita*, poured scorn on her now. They weren't the haven of her father's stories, the place for storing dreams and keeping secrets, they were felonious, silent witnesses to Jorge's crime, accomplices to his actions. Between the pain and the stars, she found separation from herself, trying to shut down senses as he thrust at her, trying to escape her situation by closing out all feeling.

His grinding stopped, she felt him collapse, spent, felt his hand back on her breast and his tongue on her nipple, sucking at it. *Nice.* He wriggled off, sitting on the edge of the seat, hitching his jeans, content with himself. Rosa lay frightened, still tied, unable to free herself, terrified of what he might do next, unable to stem her quiet sobbing. *It's okay, Bebita. The first time is always the worst. You'll enjoy it next time.*

He drove her home, pausing before they reached her house to straighten her blouse and button it as high as it had started the day. He ran a hand through her hair, causing her to flinch. *Ssh. It's okay.* Rosa was too frightened to move or speak. He drove on, parking outside her house. He casually walked to her side of the car, opening the door before offering his hand, knowing that Rosa's mother was staring down at them from an upstairs window. He escorted Rosa to the door, the chivalrous young man that her mother believed him to be, planting a chaste kiss on Rosa's cheek, tasting her tears. He stepped away and smiled at her, conscious of the audience watching their performance, knowing they were beyond hearing. *You've got great tits, Bebita,* he said, smiling. *We should do this again soon.*

He left her on the stoop and returned to his car, waiting for her to go inside. She hesitated, frightened of the boy who had just left her, and scared of the shame that she was about to take inside. She looked to the stars, the taunting night sky whispering its knowledge, but promising to keep it a secret.

She didn't intend to see him again. He would be hard to avoid at school, he would be waiting for her, but she made sure she was never alone. She resurrected the friendships she'd allowed to lapse when she had started seeing Ryan, her friends welcomed her back, gossiping and keeping her company, castigating Ryan's infidelity, never knowing that after Ryan there had been Jorge, and never guessing at her secret. She was quieter, but they were too busy with their gossip-mongering to notice. Sometimes they mentioned Jorge, solicitously. They noticed him a little more, he was more of a presence. They wondered what he was like, whether the rumours about him were true or his reputation exaggerated. Rosa could have told them the truth. She didn't tell them what she knew.

When she missed her period, she didn't panic; she didn't do anything. The trauma it triggered saw her continue as though nothing had happened. It didn't prevent a well of tightness each time she thought about what was happening, the despair that came from knowing she would inevitably shame her family. Jorge moved on. He lost his interest in Rosa. He wouldn't trouble to resurrect it; he'd had his way.

After five months, she started to show. She had hidden her morning sickness from her family, but the physical manifestation of the life within her was more difficult to conceal. Her father noticed it first, which added to her shame. *You're getting fat, Bebita. You'll struggle to find a husband,* he teased. He had expected his daughter to snap back a feisty retort, he loved that about her, his *Bebita*. She had spirit. What he didn't expect were the tears. She lowered herself to her knees before him and started to wail.

He was surprised that his joke upset her. He felt the anguish a loving father feels when he realises he has hurt his child. His lovely *Bebita,* who he cherishes, in tears because of his crass joke. *Hey, Bebita. It's okay, I was only joking.*

She couldn't tell him. She didn't want him to know her secret, he would be ashamed of her, but she knew that she would not be able to hide her pregnancy for much longer. *I'm sorry, Papá.*

Why are you sorry? I was only teasing.

It's true, Papá. I am gaining weight.

Then maybe you should go easy on the tacos, he said, back to his gentle teasing.

It's not the tacos.

She was earnest now, her father sensed it. They held each other's gaze and Rosa could see her father's comprehension gradually painting itself. It was a mix of understanding clouded with doubt. He didn't want to think about the conclusion he was drawing, but the shame she wore confirmed his fears. Still, he didn't voice his thoughts. Articulating them, making them heard, would reinforce his fears and risk verification. He wanted to cast them far beyond the confines of their home, to find an alternative reality. *What are you saying, Bebita?*

The look of hope in his eyes was pitiful. She could feel his yearning for an explanation other than the one she was going to give, it was palpable, his hope for a different form of news. She was about to break his heart and bring shame to the family. *How could she do this to him? How could she have allowed herself to get into this position?*

Rosa couldn't see that it wasn't her fault; she hadn't told anyone of her rape. She had seen her mother's approval of Jorge when they met. She knew her mother wouldn't believe the nice young man could do something like that to her daughter. She would think Rosa mistaken, that she had sent the wrong signals. She would think it was Rosa trying to trap him. If she told her father what happened, he would believe her. He would trust his *Bebita*, but her account would transform her gentle, loving *Papá* into a monster, intent on a brutal vengeance. Rosa feared prison could follow for her father, that punishing Jorge's crime would lead to suffering for the rest of her family. She was sure of these things and knew that she must keep her thoughts to herself. Only she and Jorge would ever know what happened that night. While she could no longer keep a secret of the outcome of that evening, she could protect her family from the truth. *I'm pregnant, Papá.*

He fell back, staggering as though driven by an invisible blow to his chest. He hit their sofa, open mouthed, gaping like a catfish, trying to form his words. *Does your mother know?* he whispered.

Rosa shook her head. *Only you.*

Okay. He was silent while he considered the enormity of Rosa's confession. Resolute – *We must tell her now*. He called for Rosa's mother. The quiet whisper gone, replaced with a bellow for his wife. Rosa flinched at the shout. From a bedroom off the hallway, Rosa heard her mother coming, rushing, alarmed at the urgency of her husband's call. She entered the room to find Rosa still on her knees, eyes raw from tears; her husband stifling his anger. Mother's intuition emerged, partially, comprehending Rosa's condition, ignorant of the attack.

Oh, Rosa. How could you?

There it was. The blame that Rosa anticipated. She knew her mother would see it as her mistake. *I'm sorry, Mamá. I should have stopped him.* It was the closest Rosa came to telling them about her rape. She might have gone on to explain what happened that night, but her mother's words reinforced Rosa's assumptions, increasing the depth of her secret.

Was it that nice boy, Jorge?

Rosa nodded; she couldn't speak.

Does he know? her father asked.

Rosa shook her head.

He needs to, said her mother.

Agreed, said her father. They were having a conversation as though Rosa wasn't in the room. *I'll go and talk to the boy's father tomorrow. We'll fix it.*

Good, her mother said. *I'm sure they'll do the right thing.*

Rosa felt a rising panic about her parent's conversation. She had expected disappointment. She had anticipated shame, but she hadn't expected a resolution. Her parents were deciding her fate. *What do you mean?* she asked.

It's okay, Bebita. We'll sort it out. Don't you worry.

Her father was waiting for her at the school gates the next day, standing sentinel as the students of Salinas High School walked past on their way home. He smiled when he saw Rosa. It was a smile that attempted to convey reassurance to his daughter. Rosa felt dread. He put his arm around her shoulder when she reached him. *It's okay, Bebita*, he said. *Everything is arranged.*

They walked to his car where her mother sat in the front seat, handbag on her lap, impassive, looking ahead, ignoring their approach. Her father opened the back door, waiting for Rosa to enter before slamming it shut and taking his seat behind the wheel. He started the car. Neither he nor Rosa's mother spoke as they drove away. Rosa could feel the disappointment in them both, her father's occasional glances in the rear-view mirror carrying a wisp of the accusatory. They drove past their house, carrying on to Del Monte Avenue, stopping outside Jorge's.

What are we doing here?

C'mon, said her mother, curt, a directive. Rosa could tell that she didn't want to be there, but her daughter had given them no choice. Her father opened the door for her again.

We met with the Fernandez family earlier. It's agreed.

The 'what' of their agreement hung heavily between them. Rosa didn't want to ask and neither of her parents seemed inclined to clarify. They walked in silence up the path to the Fernandez house.

The door opened as they reached the bottom step and a severe looking woman stood in front of them, a thin, forced smile on her face. *Come in*, she said. Rosa's father entered first, followed by her mother. Mrs Fernandez let them through before saying, *It's nice to meet you, Rosa*. Rosa thought she had never heard anything less sincere in her life.

Inside the house, Jorge's father stood from the chair he was occupying. He heaved a heavy sigh as he did, groaning at the effort of moving his enormous frame. The physical characteristics of Mr and Mrs Fernandez couldn't have been more different. Though their clothing was formal, Jorge's father looked uncomfortable in his outfit, clearly, he rarely wore a suit and tie. Although he had recently dressed for the occasion, he had managed a heightened state of dishevelment. By contrast, his wife was immaculate. Her displeasure with her husband's appearance was obvious, but it was also clear that she was not going to pass comment. Instead, she asked if anyone wanted coffee. *Ay!* said Jorge's father. *Something stronger I think. This is a celebration.*

Perhaps when Jorge is home, said his wife. She was tentative with her suggestion, reticent to challenge her husband. A flash of anger crossed his face. Rosa had seen a younger version of

A LITTLE SOMETHING TO HIDE

that look before. He immediately masked it with a smile. The same smile his son had used on Rosa.

Of course. Where is that boy? He's late. His affability restored.

As if in answer, the front door opened, and Jorge stepped in. His mother beamed. His father smiled. So did her parents; that hurt. It was clear from his reaction that he knew why the guests were there. Only Rosa was oblivious, but she was speedily drawing conclusions. *Ah, here he is*, said his father. *Tequila!*

He waddled from the living room leaving his son looking awkward, unable to meet the eyes of Rosa or her parents. Rosa watched horrified as her father opened his arms to him, *Come here, Son.* Jorge moved to her father and fell into his embrace. Jorge's father returned with a tray holding a bottle of tequila and six shot glasses, already filled, spilling over the brim, swirling over the surface of the tray. He offered the first to Rosa's father, then his son before making his way around the room, ending at Rosa.

I'm not sure if you should drink in your condition, he said, winking as he handed her a glass. *Maybe just one for you, eh?* He set the tray aside and picked up the remaining glass. *To Jorge and Rosie*, he said, lifting the glass.

It's Rosa, Dad.

He shrugged as though the mistake wasn't worthy of comment. *To Jorge and Rosa.* He chugged his drink, the others in the room followed suit, all except Rosa.

What's going on? she said, looking at her mother, who looked at her feet, then at her husband.

We're here to celebrate, said her father, although the mood felt anything other than celebratory. *You two are getting married.*

Rosa wanted to scream. She wanted to tell the room what Jorge had done to her. She wanted to declare her innocence, but she didn't. She choked back her shame and tried unsuccessfully to find a smile.

The arrangements were hasty. Father Clemente of St Mary of the Nativity pronounced them husband and wife three weeks later. The dress maker did an exceptional job of concealing Rosa's pregnancy. On their wedding night, her parents paid for them to have their first night together in a hotel. Jorge liked what the pregnancy was doing to Rosa's figure. *You look much fuller,* he told her during the reception, his hand stroking her thigh. *I'm looking forward to seeing you naked, Bebita.*

Alone in their room later, he didn't wait for her to undress. He carried her over the threshold, ignoring Rosa's protestations and dropped her onto the bed, climbing on her and fumbling at the buttons of her dress. The elaborate sewing frustrated his efforts; he tore it open, buttons popping into the room. He moved the dress off her shoulders and lowered it, pulling it down and off at her feet. Rosa lay on the bed, cradling her stomach. Jorge admired her form, eyes resting on her swollen breasts. *Nice. Very nice.*

Rosa started to cry.

Jorge ignored her tears, lying down next to her, pawing, licking, kissing. He forced his hand into her panties and explored her. *Please, no*, she said. *The baby*, hoping that would deter him.

The baby won't care, he said, disregarding her protests, pulling her underwear down before climbing on top of her. *Besides*, he said, smiling his dangerous smile. *You don't get to decide.*

Rosa dropped out of school before her pregnancy was obvious to everyone. Jorge stayed until his graduation. Rosa's father was insistent that they live with them until Jorge found a job and they could find a place of their own. Rosa was grateful to her father. She thought that by being in the family home it would offer her some protection, some safety from Jorge. She believed that by being in her parent's house, it would moderate his behaviour, causing him to behave. She was wrong.

He raped her every night. In the last weeks of pregnancy, when her belly was so swollen that he couldn't lay on her comfortably, he forced her onto her knees and took her from behind. If she tried to stop him, he would pinch her, squeezing flesh and twisting skin, always in places he knew her clothing would conceal. She suffered in silence, too scared to

A LITTLE SOMETHING TO HIDE

complain to him in case he would do worse, too ashamed to tell her parents. She hoped it would change when the baby arrived. Mercifully, he granted her some respite when the baby was born. *I'm not keen on damaged goods*, he said. She wondered if he had found someone else. She hoped he had. That might keep him away from her.

He was still at school when Rosa gave birth to Arabella, he had a month to go. Both sets of parents agreed to keep the pregnancy and the marriage concealed from the school. It was important to keep the children's mistake private, hiding their shame; let them slip away without tarnishing either family name.

Jorge quit the swim team. His father insisted, initially incensed to discover his son's deception, quietening when Jorge reminded him that the life in Rosa's belly now made him a man. There were no heated exchanges this time, they agreed the terms of him pulling back man-to-man, over glasses of tequila, swapping spicy stories of their high school conquests. Jorge was disappointed that he wouldn't be able to accept the scholarship he knew he could earn.

He blamed Rosa for missing his opportunity to go to college. What made it worse was that the white boy got into Brown on a scholarship to join their swim team. He knew he was a better swimmer than Ryan Toogood. He might have stolen his girl, but the white boy stole his future. In the quiet of their room, when he knew her parents wouldn't hear, he let Rosa know that it was her fault.

He found a job after graduation, working as a mechanic in the local garage with his father. It didn't pay much, but there was enough to meet the rent on a studio apartment near his parents, and he could buy beer at the Alisal Club, where he and his father would go for a drink after work. He left Rosa to raise the baby but didn't provide her with money for food or clothing. He expected her to work to pay her share of the bills; part time at the grocery store, while her mother watched Arabella; taking in laundry and ironing; cleaning in the evenings, while the baby slept, and Jorge sat watching ESPN. He was tired from his work, he needed to relax.

Rosa didn't get to choose Arabella's name, Jorge's mother did, insisting they name her after Jorge's grandmother. He agreed with his mother before Rosa could express an opinion. When she did, he taught her it was disrespectful. The memory of his lesson meant she complied with the naming of Juanita, Theresa, Maria, and Silvana. All were legacy names from his family.

By the time of Felicia's conception, Rosa had solicited her mother's help to name their last child. They met for a party at Rosa's parents to celebrate Arabella's 10th birthday. Rosa had confided her latest pregnancy to her mother, explaining how she wanted the baby named after her mother's sister. Felicia was her favourite Aunt, the one who taught Rosa to knit and who shared contraband candy with her when she came to visit. If it was a girl, she wanted her to share Felicia's name. She knew she wouldn't have an input if it was a boy; during each pregnancy, Jorge had named their babies Jorge Jr. until the certainty of their gender was known, accusing Rosa of raising a coven against him with each subsequent child she produced.

They sat around the table when Rosa announced that they were having another baby. Her mother reacted with squeals of delight before any other response registered. *If it's a girl, can you call her Felicia after my sister?*

Sure, Mamá. Rosa hoped they'd settled naming rights in that moment. They both eyeballed Jorge's mother in a collective force of will, attempting to secure her concession. She moved to express her view, to announce the name of another of her relatives to honour. She stalled when she saw the determination of Rosa and her mother.

Felicia's a lovely name, she said, forming the tight, pursed-lip smile that Rosa had seen on the first occasion they met. Jorge ended the conversation.

Why don't you make sure this one's a boy? Then we wouldn't have to worry about this naming BS.

#

A LITTLE SOMETHING TO HIDE

Juanita joined her older sister in New York in April 2000. She didn't intend to return, she and Arabella shared that pledge, but they were back in Salinas five months later; Theresa made sure of it. Felicia was the one who found her. Her mother asked her to empty the dryer and the ever-dutiful daughter tipped the contents into a basket before turning around to find her sister hanging from a beam. Rosa, on the floor above, heard Felicia's scream. Even now she hears that scream; it echoes in her dreams.

They cut her down, tried to resuscitate her, but the life had long since departed Theresa Fernandez. She had become her father's new favourite when Juanita left, hating him for it. She despised him, feeling a primaeval terror in his presence; just thinking of him made her nauseous. She wanted the world to know exactly what he had done. She recorded it all.

Putting it on paper increased the burden, made her more desperate, made her feel that there was only one way out, only one way to expose her father. She knew she couldn't continue to be around him, or her family, once they knew the truth, but they needed to know; she had to find a way to reveal his evil.

Jorge engineered their moments alone together. He collected her from soccer practice and told her they were going to see Grandpa at work. Only, Grandpa wasn't there, he was already in Alisal's and on his third beer, having shut up shop earlier. Jorge flicked the switch to a single light in the entrance, casting a dim glow throughout the workshop. He called for his father, feigning surprise that he wasn't there. They made a circuit of the workshop, going through the customer's waiting area before entering the staff room, where the walls featured calendars of naked women and three-page spreads pulled from the centre of Playboy magazines. Theresa turned around to find her father in the doorway leaning against the frame. *Look at you, Bebita. You're all grown up. You're not a child anymore.* She didn't respond. She'd heard Juanita's whispers to Arabella over the phone. She knew what was coming. *I bet the boys at school are getting interested in you now*, he said, stepping closer and placing his hands on her shoulders. *Do you know what they want to do to you?*

No, Papá.

That's good. It's good that you don't know. But you should be ready.

Rosa would have recognised the way he ran his hands up and down Theresa's arms. *I'll help you get ready*, he said, smiling his perfidious, comfortless smile.

No, Papá. It's okay. You don't have to.

I do. It's what any good father would do. He drew down the zip on her tracksuit top and pushed it open. *They'll want to play with you*, he said. *Just here.*

No, Papá. Please.

Ssh, he said, leaning closer, reptilian tongue darting. *Relax. You don't need to tell anyone. Consider it our secret. My gift to you. Lessons in love.* He promised her he would be gentle; he was her father. If she didn't tell, he would make sure he never hurt her. On their drive home, he wondered why tears tasted salty.

She had written in her diary, revealing his abuse, hoping for discovery, hoping that someone would find it and understand his crimes, to act on her evidence. She included what she had heard Juanita and Arabella speak of; they would have to corroborate; it would save them all.

She left the diary in her locker at school. She thought the faculty would find it and learn what her father had done to her and to her sisters. She didn't consider that her father would collect her belongings from the school, that the janitor, who emptied her locker, would put everything in a brown cardboard box, handing it directly to the Principal, who passed it, unread, to her father. Jorge read her words, before using the pages of her diary to light a barbecue; they were having family and friends over to thank them for their support after the tragic and unexpected loss of Theresa.

In a refrain of Rosa's past, Maria fell pregnant when she was fifteen. Rosa insisted they send Maria and Silvana to live

A LITTLE SOMETHING TO HIDE

with their Aunt Felicia in Santa Cruz. Jorge argued that only Maria needed to go for bringing disgrace to the family. Rosa said it would look strange for just one of her girls to be leaving high school. She wanted to send Felicia too, but knew that was asking too much of her sister. It was also a fruitless argument; Jorge wouldn't allow it. She knew what that meant, feeling powerless to address her fears. She hoped he'd find Felicia too young.

Rosa was exceptional at deluding herself, but even better at managing Felicia's life. At first, Felicia thought her mother was overbearing. Rosa didn't care, she made sure her youngest was never alone.

When Maria gave birth, her grandmother was insistent the boy be Jorge Jr. Rosa felt the sting of accusation as her mother-in-law reminded everyone that the family had waited too long for a boy, arguing it was the least Maria could do to show respect to her father. Rosa balked; she wouldn't allow the child to carry her husband's name. Jorge laughed at her, humiliating her, but relented. *Alright*, said Jorge. *Maria can choose. We'll let her pretend she's important.* Later that night, Jorge reminded Rosa that she wasn't important either.

Jorge's mother wondered why her son had been so quick to allow Maria to name the boy. He'd been so desperate for a boy to bear his name; it was out of character. She dismissed the thoughts that followed, reminding herself it was disloyal to her son to think such things.

Maria refused to return from her aunt's; Rosa couldn't convince her to come home to Salinas. Silvana, resistant to the suggestion, didn't experience the same indulgence, she returned after her graduation in 2006, drawn tightly into the same protective realm that Rosa established for Felicia. During the day, the three of them found ways to avoid Jorge. When he was around, the girls remained together. If one was away from the house, the other was never far from her mother, terrified at the idea of time alone with him. He tried to isolate them with early finishes at the garage, knowing the girls would be home and Rosa still at work.

Felicia, go get me some cigarettes. Silvana, you need to do the dishes. With Felicia gone, he pretended pity, letting Silvana off her task, demanding repayment for his kindness. He found ways.

Rosa did what she could to protect them, but he excelled in his stealth. He was both gentle and brutal. He considered himself gentle with his girls, justifying to himself that his acts weren't harmful because he lessened their pain; he wanted his pleasure, he needed their collusion. To achieve both, he was careful not to hurt them, minimising their cause for complaint, while emphasising the risks of betrayal.

This must always be our secret, Bebita. I don't want to hurt you or your mother.

He saved his brutality for Rosa, fuelled by his time in Alisal's, convincing himself that she deserved what was coming her way. She needed punishing for not giving him a son, for disrespecting him by popping out girls, one after the other. He knew he could father boys, Maria had proved it, though he preserved her dignity by making sure they kept the intelligence between them.

Silvana simply left. The note to her mother read, *Sorry, I have to go. I love you.* She didn't say where, she just went. It was as though she vanished from existence. Rosa receives a birthday card from her every year; the postmark is never the same. Silvana wishes her mother a happy birthday, telling Rosa that she is fine before adding, *I love you.* There is never anything more to her message, no hint or suggestion of where she might be, or how Rosa could contact her. She provides nothing to cling to, but Rosa lives in hope of one day seeing Silvana again. None of her daughters confess to contact with Silvana, but Rosa hopes that she is in touch with at least one of them. She suspects it will be Maria who, along with the son she didn't name Jorge, still lives with her aunt.

Felicia met a boy in her senior year. She wanted to love him but found it difficult to commit. Fears, unable to fully present, shimmered in her thoughts when she considered their future. He was perfect for her; soft-spoken, kind, patient. Felicia wanted to take things slowly; he waited. They dated for three years, taking every opportunity to be together. Eventually his tenderness overcame the doubts that the life in the Fernandez house instilled in her. Rosa liked him; he reminded her of her father. He showed her daughter respect; she saw again the love and affection that she witnessed in her parent's marriage. She had forgotten what that looked like; she didn't mask her delight that Felicia had found a man that made her feel safe.

On Felicia's 22nd birthday, they announced that they were going to be married. *He knock you up?* asked Jorge.

Rosa laughed when Felicia told her father not to be an idiot, cringing when Felicia added that some people got married because they're in love.

Really? Then you're the idiot, he barked.

Rosa was proud that her daughter had the strength to answer back to her father, knowing she'd suffer later that night for her daughter's impertinence.

Rosa's heart broke when, three weeks after their wedding, Felicia told her that she and her new husband were moving to Albuquerque. Rosa marked the day in her diary, remembering it as the day Felicia fled to find happiness with a man bearing no resemblance to her father. Rosa's heart died a little that day, but it also filled with hope. Hope that now, all her girls, except darling Theresa, were happy and safe.

He got slower and fatter after Felicia left, but no less nasty. As the years unfurled, the physical abuse diminished, but his mental cruelty went unchecked. He came home drunk most nights, demanding food, falling asleep on the sofa with mid-mastication dribble and beer staining his shirt. He was too inebriated for rape, or at least, Rosa was more adept at avoiding him, but he would curse her, blaming her for driving his daughters away, for her failure to create a home in which they wanted to live. All of it was her fault – the shitty job, the lack of status, the penury, the broken family. He shouted obscenities, demanded conjugal rights that he couldn't fulfil, blamed her for ruining his life. *You fucked us all, Rosa. This crap is your fault.* She did it all. She was responsible.

Shortly after his father died, Jorge lost his job. His father functioned as a defence between their employer and Jorge's mediocre performance. With him gone, Jorge lost his shield, and his tenure. He didn't go to the bar, he was too angry; it reminded him too, of his father. He needed to find another way to direct his rage.

Rosa was in the basement when he returned. He was early. She heard the car door slam, reflexively looking at the spot where Theresa had taken her life. He crossed the floor to the top of the stairs, weariness in his trudge, while Rosa continued to fold the washing, musing that with her daughters gone, there was much less to do. Jorge shouted for her to get into the kitchen. She gathered the basket of laundered clothes, climbing towards him, each step heavy with the weight of a sour marriage.

It is eight years since Felicia left the house. Rosa has been the target of his attention and anger in that time, enduring it, telling herself that others have it worse, that the girls are now safe. She kids herself into believing that she has done her best to protect them, that she knows he can't do any more harm to her girls, that she will take his abuse to keep the rest of them safe.

She expected to find him in a rage. Instead, he is sitting in a corner crying, deep mournful sobs, releasing years of frustration and failure. Rosa felt an emotion that she had never felt for him before, pity. She expected him to launch a verbal assault or attempt to beat her, but he is small, shrinking into the chair, diminished; his fight gone. She can see that he is weak.

She crosses the room to be beside him and smothers the revulsion she feels towards him, wrapping her arms around him, pulling him towards her. His sobbing continues, muffled against her chest. *It's all over*, he said. *Everything's gone. My job, my girls, my father.* He sobs deeply at the mention of his father. *And my son.*

A LITTLE SOMETHING TO HIDE

Rosa releases him, stumbling back as if hit, catching herself on the kitchen counter. She knows what she has always known, the truth she suppressed, the truth hidden beneath the mantle of her guilt. His words reveal what he has done, announce what *she* has concealed; the vile, filthy certainty, brought to life. Shame overwhelms her pity; the common bedfellows, guilt and remorse, follow closely. He speaks of his failures, but she knows that they pale by comparison to hers. Her revulsion returns; she forgets her pity, resolving that she no longer wants to be near him. It is time for her to be cruel. *I'm going to Felicia's*, she says. *On my own. I could be there for a while.*

You can't go. I need you.

I have to go. Then echoing the words of Arabella and Juanita, she promised him she would come back.

A hint of the Jorge she fears returns, the man she vowed to obey. *You can't go. I won't allow it.* Rosa sees him differently now, her fear muted, rising in its place an emotion unfamiliar where Jorge's concerned. It starts as a giggle, causing him surprise. His reaction transforms her giggling to a fully throated laugh, how pathetic he now seems; she finds him hysterical.

His surprise morphs into anger, the transition fast; tears forgotten. He tries to stand, but stumbles, causing more laughter. He comes after her as she backs down the hallway. Little space exists between them as he stands at the threshold of the kitchen, balling his hands into the fists that have found Rosa's body so many times in the past. He snarls at her. *You're not going anywhere.*

The defiance rose more powerfully than the laughter. It was Rosa's turn to be angry. Forty-two years of suppressing her anger amplify in a single moment. *Fuck you*, she shouts. *I'll do whatever the fuck I want. You can't stop me.* He comes for her again, Rosa backing away to the top of the basement stairs, wondering where to go.

Rosa knits, a wispy smile dancing at the corners of her mouth as she recollects what followed. She is going to see Felicia, her youngest, her favourite. She's breaching parental protocols to think that way, she knows having a favourite is taboo, but she'll indulge herself. She's ignored other rules in recent days. All her girls know Felicia's her pet, but they're forgiving. Rosa and Felicia spent more time with him – *they deserve each other's love. Felicia stayed the longest, tolerating him for longer than her siblings, she earnt her mother's love. They stood fortified for as long as they could, until Felicia also needed to escape.*

Rosa's enjoying the freedom of the journey, the crafting she can do, uninterrupted. On other journeys, on those two times a year that they could visit Albuquerque, he wouldn't permit the noise. He said the click, click, click *of her knitting irritated him, so the balls of wool remained in San Francisco, coming out only when he was out of the house. She emits a disapproving snort at the thought. 'With the rattle of this bus,' she thinks, 'he wouldn't hear shit.'*

Rosa is glad they didn't have a son. Jorge said it was another of the dreams that she thwarted, denying him the opportunity to impart his wisdom, his prowess, to live vicariously through his boy, and enjoying the triumphs that he said Rosa prevented. Rosa's glad she denied him. Not having a boy for him to poison puts an end to his legacy.

The girls got away, all except Theresa. She wonders whether he could be guilty of her murder. He didn't tie the rope or kick away the chair, but he was responsible for her death. Theresa would never have killed herself if he hadn't given her cause. Of course, he blamed Rosa for Theresa's death, accusing her of many failings, but never the one of which she was guilty – denial. Denial of his intentions, denial of his actions, denial of his abuses.

Rosa wonders too, if she will ever be able to live with the guilt. She knows her denials make her complicit. As much as she knows this, her fear left her unable to protect her daughters, unable to keep her Bebitas *safe. She hopes they will forgive her one day. Forgive her for not speaking, for not listening, and for not giving them a voice.*

Rosa believes that it is time now for them to speak of the forbidden, that she will do whatever she must for her girls. It's a promise that she's made to herself; it's a promise she will make to her daughters when she gets them together again.

She smiles at her resolve, pleased to be in control, in charge of her future. Pleased to be knitting in peace. As the needles clack, she wonders if what she has done will finally meet her daughters' expectations. She wonders too, with her smile transforming to a grin, whether the pool of blood surrounding the lifeless form in her basement is already dry.

CANAL / BASSETT STREET, KING CITY

Arrivals
Time	From	Expected
01:27	Salinas	Expected: 01:47

Departures
Time	Destination	Expected
02:00	Santa Barbara	Delayed: 02:17

CANAL / BASSETT STREET, KING CITY

Michael Williams isn't like most boys heading to college. For a start, he doesn't want the hug from Momma to end. He has to stoop a long way for her embrace, but once inside, feeling her warmth, breathing in the hint of orange blossom from her perfume, he is happy to keep clinging. That suits Momma just fine. Momma excels at hugging and her boys know better than to wriggle free. She hugs on her terms; they end when she is ready. On this occasion, the longer she holds her son, the longer she keeps him from leaving.

Michael has already said goodbye to his father and brother. He still feels the mild ache of compression from his father's bear-hug. They squeezed each other tight, before his father held Michael by his shoulders, looking up with a warranted pride at the boy-turning-man. Raymond Williams is six feet six and a muscular 220 pounds, but he has to lift his head to his son.

When the ache in Michael's ribs subsided, he knelt in front of his brother's wheelchair. They held hands, Michael telling Stephen that he had to look after Momma while he was gone. Stephen let him know he'd have everything under control and brayed. His laugh, a rasp rising from a violent intake of air, carried to those on the bus, causing them to peer through the window. 'I love you, baby brother,' said Michael.

Stephen let him know he expected nothing less, hee-hawing at his own joke.

Most passengers took four steps to climb on the bus, Michael took two, lowering his head to avoid the door frame which has lost its protective padding.

A LITTLE SOMETHING TO HIDE

The Briscolas haven't replaced it, deciding that anyone tall enough to butt the frame will have experience of such hazards – they should know to duck.

Anthony Briscola pedals a vision of luxury that belies the experience. Expenditure that should go to safety and maintenance finds a different budget, one that underpins his deception. Those dollars go to ensuring that more reviews of a positive nature appear on TripAdvisor or Trustpilot than the genuine reviews of dissatisfied customers.

Briscola revels in the power of social media and knows that money poured into the coffers of a sophisticated bot farm is money well spent. He loves the gullible and the money they part with to ride on one of his buses, and he's not averse to a little technological trickery to influence their spending decisions, even though it might inadvertently lead to a passenger's headwound.

Although tall enough, Michael Williams avoids an injury. He is one inch shy of seven feet and, at eighteen, folks aren't sure if he has stopped growing. What they are sure about, is that he is heading for the NBA, and when he gets there, he is going to raise the average height a smidge. Some of those people think he should go there straight from high school, drawing parallels to LeBron James. Michael doesn't believe he is remotely close to being that good, a humility that keeps him grounded and masks his determination to succeed.

MICHAEL – KING CITY

Colleges from across the country pursued Michael Williams, banking on his humility to pave a conventional route to the NBA. For Michael, it would mean a three-year deferral of the riches that awaited him and, for whichever college he chose, the almost certain likelihood that he would bring glory to their school. Everyone wanted him, scouts had been following him for years. By the time he was thirteen, he no longer needed to buy his own basketball shoes. The company that kept him in footwear was already telling him that he'd have a shoe named after him when he got to *The Bigs*. He laughed it off as flattery.

Flattery found a way to Michael Williams. From the age of fifteen, there was at least one scout at every game he played. They threw praise at him like kids throwing bread to ducks, hoping their offering would be the one to attract Michael. Their fawning was stale. The scouts often huddled together, jealously guarding their plans for Michael, and exchanging moderated observations to hide their excitement at the young man's talent. The fact was, they didn't know whether he was going to be as good as LeBron or Michael Jordan. Most of them thought he'd be better, but each kept that silent assessment to himself, believing that only he had the foresight to recognise the wunderkind before him. The belief that they had a unique perspective on the boy's talent was less a reflection of their scouting ability and more an insight into their arrogance.

Two years before he was due to go to college, the scouts and coaches started to appear at his house. The ones he liked were kind to Momma and acknowledged his brother. They spent time talking to her and did their best not to ignore Stephen, confined to his wheelchair with cerebral palsy. Listeners not accustomed to Stephen's speech found him hard to comprehend, especially if they weren't inclined to try. His disfigured hands frequently spasmed, they distracted the uninitiated. When he spoke, it was at volume, which increased when he laughed, which he did often. It made some of the visitors uncomfortable. Some of them condescended to ruffle Stephen's hair after introductions, trying to hide their discomfort, and demonstrating their inability to differentiate between an intelligent boy with a disability and a domesticated puppy. Stephen would tell them they should wash their hands after touching him, laughing more uproariously the greater the level of disgust he provoked. The degree to which Michael indulged a person would hinge on how they reacted to that laughter; whether they had the modesty to appreciate that their ignorance was the cause of his brother's mirth.

Before they got to Michael, callers had to speak with Momma. Wiser guests were nearer to understanding his nature and ambition if they listened closely. The wisest understood they were dealing with a boy whose love for his family exceeded his passion for basketball. When she brought them into the room, or onto the porch on those days when the heat made the iced tea that little bit sweeter, Michael could tell from Momma's bearing if she approved of a visitor. Mother and son didn't need to exchange looks for Michael to know Momma's opinion. If she preceded the man, and they were always men, Michael knew the interview was worth his time. Momma would throw open the door, stroll in with arms wide to introduce the guest. If the coach entered first, Michael knew it hadn't gone well with Momma. She didn't deign to introduce those she didn't think were good enough for her son.

They all got time, that was the polite thing to do, some of them had travelled across the country, but some of them got less time than others. *Fifteen minutes, Mister Rowell,* Momma said to the man from the University of Illinois. He ignored Stephen and didn't ask after Momma's health, saying that he was tight on time, as though the outing was an imposition to him, that he was doing the Williams family a favour. Momma didn't intend to derail the schedule of a man who was too busy to be courteous, fifteen minutes would be more than enough time for him to spend with her son.

Mister Rowell might have travelled more than two thousand miles to represent the Fighting Illini, but he left his manners behind. That meant he'd suffered a long haul for just fifteen minutes with a boy who already knew the scout had wasted his journey. Which college Michael chose to attend was his decision, that's what his mother and father had always said, but some of his decisions had more than a little nudge of help from Momma.

The better the recruiters did their groundwork with his mother, the more time they had with Michael, the more seriously he considered what they had to say. The ones he tolerated did their best to sound sincere when they told him how good he was, how great he could become under their wings. He might have been humble, but Michael didn't lack self-belief. As brilliant as they believed they could make him, he knew that greatness sat within, that his efforts would bring it forth, his work would unveil the talent. *They* wouldn't be waking daily at 5.30am to run five miles before spending another hour alone on the court, shooting hoops, practicing fakes, improvising rebounds against imagined opposition. It was Michael investing the time, developing, honing, perfecting his skills and his speed on the court, before heading home to help Momma care for his brother.

Michael kept the water on the cool side as he showered, allowing it to wash away the morning's vigour, galvanising him for the day ahead. His routine saw him arrive at school before most of his peers, commandeering a quiet seat in the corner of the school's library where he'd pour over his books, giving as much attention to his grades as he did to his sport. He didn't want to disappoint Momma with anything less than straight As. None of the visiting dignitaries, with their misplaced perceptions and their entitled superiority, saw his activity, nor understood that he already had the mindset they promised to develop.

A LITTLE SOMETHING TO HIDE

The men he disliked forgot he was a person. Most projected, many assumed. The worst did both, believing that he was a deprived child from the projects who saw basketball as an escape from misery, whose only interest was in following the money. They promised immortality in the college pantheon, fame and protection from notoriety, greatness, and riches. Discreet riches. Riches, they promised, that wouldn't breach NCAA protocols.

The more principled among them knew they would flirt at the edge of propriety, others didn't care that they would disembowel the rules, trusting that the kid wasn't too stupid to advertise his rewards or their sources. They made offers they thought would be attractive to a deprived 18-year-old and his family. They made promises to take care of Momma. Some suggested that they could do something to fix his brother, hastily qualifying that he shouldn't consider it as charity when they misread his incredulity. Momma joked that she would flail him till he was six inches shorter if he even considered their *incentives*. He knew she was joking, but he also knew there'd be the crack of a wooden spoon against his upper arm if she thought the message required reinforcing.

The scouts didn't know him, they never would. They didn't know that Momma had raised him well, taught him right from wrong, instilled morals and ethics, but most of all, taught him the value of hard work and the reward for patience. She had belief in him, she knew what he could become, because she already knew that he was on his way. Momma told him that the money would follow, to be content to wait – that they had no need for illicit gifts.

He forgave the omissions and transgressions of the scouts that he disliked. It was a silent forgiveness that would surprise the men receiving it, not appreciating that it stemmed from their failure to conduct themselves in a Momma-approved manner. Michael knew they had a job to do, that they were trying to do their best. Most of them had been despatched by head coaches with a singular goal, to get his signature. The best head coaches came themselves, not entirely trusting their colleagues to land the exquisite prize that Michael Williams represented. The coaches were slicker and more convincing than their outriders, but few of them took the time to really understand him.

Greater than half of the ACC, PAC 12 and the Big East wooed him. He had visits from every team in the Big Ten and Big 12. Momma said she poured more iced tea to the men who called, than Starbucks served coffee. Michael could have gone wherever he wanted. The lesser colleges didn't chase him. They all knew, or thought they did, that he wouldn't consider attending their schools. One, however, was arrogant enough to suggest that Michael *had* to play for them. He was the only caller that Michael hated, even though Momma had taught him not to hate. The behaviour of the coach from San Jose State University managed to subvert Michael's Christian beliefs.

Richard Blair's players also found it difficult to be Christian when describing their coach. When they were being polite, they would adopt euphemisms such as blunt, direct, or outspoken to illustrate his manner. Coach Blair wanted people to think of him as a hard taskmaster. He didn't mind if they thought he was ornery; what coach wasn't? He was there to drive performance and instil excellence in the Spartan's basketball programme. If that meant crushing the sensibilities and fragile egos of the precious few beneath the stacked leather heels of his roper boots, then so be it. He was creating men and, frankly, if the boys on his team couldn't cope with a bit of spittle showering them when he was expressing his disappointment, then they were the wrong type of fellas to be in his team. He could cope with his boys telling folks that he was the embodiment of a combatant; he liked them referring to him as a man who didn't tolerate the slack-willed. That was a good thing to have people know about a man. It kept them honest and on guard; just where he wanted them.

Reality was a little divorced from the impression the coach wanted to give. While scattered euphemisms lay on the floor outside the locker room, the private language his players adopted when describing him took on a harsher vernacular.

In his hearing, they referred to him as *CB*. He thought that stood for Coach Blair. He was wrong about the *Coach*.

Blair arrived at the Williams household unannounced. As Michael's gatekeeper, every other visitor had the courtesy to make an appointment with Momma, but she opened the door to find Coach Blair standing on the deck of their house with a lit cigar dangling from the corner of his mouth. He looked her up and down, doubting that the short, fat woman before him could produce a figure as fine as her son. Momma had the feeling he considered her a nuisance, an obstacle to negotiate before moving on to her son. She was right. His regard of her was curious. He examined her as a cat might consider a stricken bird. Easy prey, but not worthy of the effort.

He wore a Spartans blazer and carried what he thought would be a Michael-sized Spartans hoodie. Wearing the blazer was a concession to the school. He'd gone there because he hadn't landed the job of coach at the Longhorns (or the Red Raiders, or the Horned Frogs, or any of the other Texas schools to which he'd applied). For him, the Spartans were an interim step. He knew that before long, the schools of the Lone Star State would be scrabbling to hire him, but in the meantime, he was willing to indulge the head of the Athletic department with his ridiculous demands to wear the school colours.

The rest of his attire was a caricature of the Texan he wanted people to see. Cowboy boots, denim jeans, a check shirt beneath the jacket and a Stetson which, if he'd been polite, he would have removed. He continued wearing it because Momma wasn't white. *I'm here to see Mike,* he told her.

She raised an eyebrow when he foreshortened her son's name, folding her arms across her ample chest. Nobody called him Mike, and if they did, they had better make sure it was out of Momma's earshot.

Coach Blair didn't recognise her pose as barring him from entrance to the house. Neither of them showed intent to move.

Who are you?

Coach Blair drawled that he was the man that Mikey was desperate to hear from.

MICHAEL – KING CITY

Is that so? Most people coming to see... Michael, she emphasised, *call ahead.*
Well, most people ain't me.

Momma remained unimpressed, but Coach Blair seemed untroubled by her reaction. He didn't expect her to know what a privilege it was for her and her son that he was standing on their doorstep. Momma mustered an *Mmm*.

Coach Blair took a deep draw on his cigar, blew some smoke in Momma's direction before turning from her while he waited for her to beckon her son.

From the shadows behind her, the lanky figure of Michael Williams appeared, features becoming clearer as he moved toward the door, not that Coach Blair noticed. He was surveying the neighbourhood, anticipating trouble to erupt from the street at any moment. He expected it did in places like this.

Michael stood behind his mother with a giant hand clasping her shoulder. *Who's this?* he asked.

The Texan turned at the sound of his voice and removed his cigar to affect a smile. It didn't sit naturally; his lips pursed, but his teeth didn't show. Smiling wasn't something he did often.

Neither mother nor son moved from the doorway; Coach Blair was unperturbed. He moved past them along the porch, his unhurried heels pounding conceit across the stripped boards. He sat on the hanging loveseat, indicating that Michael should take the chair alongside. *I could use a fresh lemonade,* he said to Momma.

Momma didn't respond, making no effort to accommodate the demand.

Just three cubes of ice.

Michael looked at Momma for permission to follow the arrogant man. They were good people, too polite to tell Coach Blair that his stay was unwelcome. Momma acceded with a shrug, allowing Michael to sit with the odious Texan.

As her son stooped to go through the door, she headed to the kitchen, opening the fridge to reveal a jug of the home-made iced tea that her boys loved so much. She moved to take it before hesitating, closing the door. *Fuck him*, she thought. The thought surprised her. It was a measure of her dislike for the man. Momma never swore and she felt disinclined to make him a lemonade.

Although Michael didn't know that the Spartans basketball team referred to their coach as CB, it was a conclusion he was beginning to draw himself. For the next ninety minutes he heard why he had to go to San Jose State. Coach Blair reminded Michael that it was the closest college with a decent basketball programme. *It's your dooty to be loyal to the school.*

Michael wondered what exactly it was that the school had done for him that would engender his loyalty, a thought he would have aired if Coach Blair had paused for any length of time. Instead, he told Michael he would be letting down the college and his community if he didn't go there.

Michael didn't believe the community was likely to express such disappointment, but kept the opinion to himself.

Coach Blair announced that no one could get more out of Michael than him. *I know how to get the best out of your type*, he said, leading Michael to wonder what *type* the coach thought he might be. He wouldn't have been surprised to learn that he was right with his first thought.

Kid, if I have to, I'll cut some lazy sonofabitch to make space for you on the programme.

The coach's cavalier disregard for his charges didn't sit well with Michael. The prospect that his presence might end someone's basketball dream didn't rest comfortably on the young man's broad shoulders. He knew his sport was a meritocracy, but he didn't want to associate himself with a man with so little consideration for his players. It told him most of everything that he wanted to know about Coach Blair. Michael had a clear read of the type of man that was sitting in front of him.

At the end of his monologue, Coach Blair adopted the noble air of a man about to make a profound declaration. *You know*, he said. *I could probably convince the head of faculty to give you a scholarship.* He leaned forward, placing a hand on Michael's knee, adopting what he believed to be an earnest

MICHAEL – KING CITY

frown, one that imparted a deep empathy. *I could be the father figure you need.*

Michael was more than happy with his father; he didn't harbour a need for another role model. If he did, he wouldn't adopt one in the shape of Coach Blair. Momma and his father had been happily married for 22 years, giving him daily servings of unconditional love. He doubted that Coach Blair could add anything to supplement his life. It was another opinion that Michael chose not to share.

Down the road, the heat shimmered above the tarmac. The Texan removed his hat, drawing an arm across his brow, looking distastefully at the darkened strip of moisture discolouring his sleeve. He shot an accusing look at the house. *Where's my lemonade?*

Michael lied, saying Momma was still making it. *She'll be sure to bring it out soon.* It wasn't an unintentional fib. He was almost certain that the coach was never going to see condensation sliding down the side of any glass that Momma produced.

Coach Blair tutted his disgust at the service Momma was providing.

The mean-hearted Texan reiterated his understanding of Michael's background. *I appreciate you got it tough kid,* he said. *No one's gonna be able to smooth the road ahead like me.* He also told him it was his job to break Michael's balls, on and off the court. *Call it tough love, kiddo. It'll make you a better player.* He was magnanimous. *I won't expect no gratitude neither. Just part of the job.* He paused for the first time, allowing Michael the opportunity to express the gratitude that he said he didn't need. Polite as always, Michael satisfied Coach Blair's silence with dutiful thanks.

Content that the boy understood him, Coach Blair reached inside his blazer and pulled out a sheaf of tightly typed pages that he unfolded and handed to Michael. Michael stared at the papers before him, seeing the Spartans logo in the top left corner and the words **AGREEMENT BETWEEN** resting above his name and that of the college.

A LITTLE SOMETHING TO HIDE

He heard a rapid-fire *click-click-click* as Coach Blair readied a pen, thrusting the thin silver barrel of a stainless-steel Parker between Michael's nose and the papers he held. Michael stood, looking down on the man sitting on the swinging chair before him, contemplating how to manage the situation. Momma had taught him always to be polite, to be tolerant, forgiving and kind. He leafed through the pages, turning each one slowly, not allowing himself enough time to read them, but ensuring that he turned them at a pace that would avoid stretching Coach Blair's patience. He could already see the man's leg twitching, hurried bounces, an urgent fidget signalling his desire to conclude his business. Michael reached the last page and saw his name typed in bold capital letters beneath a signature line. Above the name, **RICHARD BLAIR**, the coach had already added an indecipherable scrawl, a presumption that demonstrated his confidence in landing his man.

Michael smiled for a moment as a thought passed that would not have pleased Momma. He rested the contract on the table next to the swinging chair. It was the table where Momma would have left a chilled glass of iced tea for any other guest. He took the coach's pen, clicking it twice before turning the contract to the last page where his thought from moments earlier materialised on the page. He folded the agreement before handing it to Coach Blair who tucked it inside his blazer without looking at the signature. In Texas, a man's word was his bond, and even though this kid's background wasn't like his, he'd show him how men of honour behaved. It wasn't just brilliant coaching he provided; he gave life lessons too.

He stood, offering his hand to the young recruit. Michael, always polite, took it. Coach Blair had an iron grip and squeezed the boy's hand long and hard. He had to credit the young man; the boy looked him in the eye the whole time. He entertained the thought that it was unusual for a boy like Michael to know how to behave.

From inside the house, they heard Stephen's laughter. Michael smiled, he loved to hear his brother's laugh, it was his favourite sound, but the smile vanished quickly when Coach Blair recoiled, *What the fuck was that?*

Michael told him it was his brother, noting the expression of the coach, as though he was opening a refrigerator to the smell of rancid meat.

Blair moved on from his distaste, explaining that his secretary would contact Michael with details for the start of the semester. If he was lucky, Michael might hear from her soon. *If she did her damn job and stopped filing her nails. But don't worry,* he added. *I'll make her get in touch with you.*

Michael felt a surge of sympathy for the woman he was never going to meet.

Coach Blair was at the bottom of the steps when he remembered the hoodie. He held it up to the young man towering above him on the porch.

Michael looked at him, realising the older man had no intention of returning. Momma's ceaseless life-coaching bore the fruits it intended; Michael did the man the courtesy of retrieving the garment.

Richard Blair wore another nearly smile, *I wouldn't have given you this if ya didn't sign up.* Michael's thanks prompted the coach to marvel at the boy's behaviour. *There's an exception to every rule,* he thought as he drove away. If he'd paused to glance in his rear-view mirror, he would have seen the hoodie disappearing into the trash can that squatted next to the stairs.

Momma was standing inside the screen-door holding a tray bearing three iced teas. Thick droplets of water clung to the sides of the glasses; ice cubes sounded a soothing percussion in the dark translucence. She stood waiting for Michael to open the door for her as she had long ago taught him. He obliged, watching as she passed him wordlessly, his brother following in his wheelchair.

Momma placed the tray on the table before sinking into the swinging chair, a wearisome groan escaping her. She tapped the seat, beckoning Michael. He picked up the glass containing a straw, holding it for Stephen, who barked a thank you when he'd had enough. Momma smiled indulgently at her boys; they were fine young men.

A LITTLE SOMETHING TO HIDE

Michael sat next to his mother and the three of them stayed silent before Stephen's impatience intervened. *Well?* he shouted.

Michael assessed his mother, wondering if this was one of those rare occasions where she'd allow profanity.

She smiled, asking him what he had written in the contract.

He hoped for her indulgence; Momma didn't like people cursing, she said it highlighted a lack of learning and that cultured language existed to express the same sentiment. When Raymond Williams was present, he would chuckle, inducing a frown from his wife. *Sometimes,* he would say, *there's a time and place for a heartier choice of words.*

Michael figured this might be one of those moments. *I wrote FUCK YOU,* he said, smiling.

Stephen roared as Momma's eyes glinted with water droplets like those on the side of her glass.

The callers bored Michael and Momma. None of the coaches or scouts left them with an overwhelming desire to join their programmes. Michael was beginning to think that he should take the easy choice and sign with Duke. Momma reminded him about his values and his goals. He wanted to join a team that cared for all its players, where he could have influence. He knew he'd make a difference to any team that he joined. At some, it would be much more pronounced.

They debated whether to signal to the lesser colleges that he was still available, but the prospect of dozens more meetings with people like Coach Blair depressed them. The Texan had left an impression that wasn't healthy, their usually positive outlook blackened by his memory. They complained about him a lot and he featured disproportionately, dominating the conversation when the family sat for meals.

Where the subject of his son's prospects as a basketball player were concerned, Michael's father mostly kept his opinion to himself. It wasn't that he didn't have an opinion, he was just a quiet man, fully supporting the path that Momma and his son were taking. When they sought his advice, he gave it, but they rarely did. Everyone in the family was content with

MICHAEL – KING CITY

this arrangement, Raymond Williams would make his opinion known when he thought he should, otherwise, he was happy to let them plan Michael's future.

On the third night after Coach Blair's visit, when Michael and Momma were still complaining about the arrogance and ignorance of the man, Raymond came as close as he ever did to snapping. *Maybe you should go to a different school in Mountain West. Teach Coach Blair a lesson.* The family went quiet, considering Raymond's words. Stephen was the first to speak.

Fuck yeah, he bellowed.

Momma scolded him gently before joining the laughter.

It wasn't customary for the Williams family to leave anything to chance. Momma insisted that goal setting and making plans were the surest way to success, but they were weary of the recruitment process. The prospect of seeing scouts from another ten teams depressed them. They set aside their carefully formulated plans, folding slips of paper that they dropped into a bowl before Stephen. He extended his withered hand, swirling the mound of papers clumsily, before drawing one from the pile.

Coach Wilbur Hattermeyer inherited a failing basketball programme. As a softly spoken native of Wisconsin, with a lifelong passion for basketball, he'd grown up working on his father's dairy farm, fretting that he was too short to make a name for himself on the court.

He was into his third year as head coach of the New Mexico Lobos and had pushed them up one spot, to seventh, in the Mountain West divisional rankings. It wasn't a meteoric rise, barely a move at all, but he was happy that after three years, the team was moving in the right direction. He was at his desk, pondering the coming season, when the telephone rang. Cindy Rankin, his secretary, was on the end of the line sounding embarrassed. She explained that the caller was claiming to be Michael Williams' mother, wanting to invite Coach Hattermeyer to King City to meet her son. Cindy apologised. *It might be a prank call, but this woman is beyond adamant.*

A LITTLE SOMETHING TO HIDE

Wilbur Hattermeyer mumbled the occasional *Ah-yuh* as his assistant spoke, wondering at the same time, whether anyone would try to con the coach of a New Mexico college team into a random trip to California to meet Michael Williams. He decided they wouldn't. *Put Mrs Williams through please, Cindy.*

Momma didn't think anything unusual about her call to New Mexico. It was just one step more in doing the right thing for her boy. She explained about the bodies they'd seen, unable to check herself before recounting the visit from the obnoxious Texan. Wilbur Hattermeyer knew Coach Blair well; his team had twice lost to the Spartans since he'd joined the Lobos, and he'd found him to be the least gracious winner he'd encountered; Momma's recollection confirmed that the call was genuine.

They discussed when the Williams family might be able to see him. Coach Hattermeyer asked Momma to hold for one second, springing from his chair, adrenaline fuelling a childlike excitement, almost begging Cindy to book the first flight from Albuquerque to San Francisco. When he returned to the phone, he and Momma chatted chirpily about nothing to do with basketball, until his secretary put a flight reservation in front of him. *Is there a nearby restaurant where I could buy y'all dinner tomorrow night?*

That's kind of you Mr Hattermeyer, but it won't be necessary.

It was Wilbur Hattermeyer's turn to be insistent.

Well, my boys do love the pork sliders at The Cork & Plough on Broadway, and I guess Raymond and I are a little partial to their steak sandwiches – if that's not too extravagant.

You know, Mrs Williams, I think the college's budget might even stretch to a side of fries. He was the first coach to make Momma giggle.

Cindy was in the doorway tapping an impatient beat on her watch as Coach Hattermeyer said goodbye to Momma. The coach gave Momma no impression of urgency, but he was rising from his chair as he replaced the handset in its cradle, before racing home to pack an overnight bag.

He arrived at Keefer's Inn in King City at 9.45pm, tired from his journey across the country and his drive from San

MICHAEL – KING CITY

Francisco. He'd paused in Salinas and eaten at a Taco Bell just off the 101, less than a mile away from the spot where Jorge Fernandez would someday soon be lying in a pool of his own blood. The adrenaline that had powered his day was beginning to ebb. He'd made it to King City; for the first time since his conversation with Momma, he began to relax. He lay across the check-covered bedspread and was asleep before he'd removed his clothes.

When he woke the next morning, a 6 feet 11 inch teenager ran past his motel on his morning run. The teen was wondering into which preference category his family would drop Coach Hattermeyer. Momma had told him they were going to *The Cork* for dinner, which in Michael's mind, started the man in the 'like' column. Whether he could stay there remained unanswered.

By the time Michael arrived home to collect a ball for the courts at the Arts Magnet School, Wilbur Hattermeyer was stepping out of the shower, refreshed and grateful for the day ahead. The early part of his day was free, calling for a stroll through town. He didn't discover much, most of what describes King City is that it exists, dull suburban punctuation to the sumptuous fields and baked hills of the Salinas Valley. Coach Hattermeyer wondered what had brought the Williams family to town, one of the few black families that lived there, and wondered too whether they would stay when their son earned his fortune in the NBA.

He wandered down Canal, a road uninviting to pedestrians, turning right onto Division Street. Two hundred yards along, he stood at the intersection of Division and San Lorenzo Avenue, wondering which way to turn. In the still of the early morning, not too many folks in King City were stirring. Wilbur Hattermeyer sniffed the air, enjoying the solitude, listening to the morning's chorus, the hurried trill of Dark-eyed Juncos, broadcasting their availability, seeking mates among the stunted trees. He turned left to follow the avian call, missing the dusty bowl of the King City Stampede Ground, where rust-coated signs advertising spray shops, hydraulic pumps, and insurance for the rural community, would have confirmed his belief that not much of interest happened in the town. Instead, he wandered further down the road where he leaned against an eight-foot-high chain link fence, witnessing a sight that was far more impressive than an empty rodeo arena.

A sun-seared stretch of rye grass separated the coach from the basketball court on which Michael Williams was conducting his daily drills. He was forty yards from the coach, the drumming hammer-beat of the ball carried clearly across the space between them. Wilbur Hattermeyer found a gate that swung free and crossed the field. Michael sensed his approach, continued his workout, uninterested in the distraction the man represented. He focused on his programme.

The coach stood on the edge of the court, watching intently. Michael preferred to ignore his spectator, but Momma nibbled at his conscience; courtesy prevailed. He lifted a hand to acknowledge Coach Hattermeyer. Michael wasn't yet accustomed to strangers knowing him, despite 250,000 views on YouTube of a high school game where he scored seventy points, but he suffered middle-aged white men watching him shoot hoops, just not normally at 7.30 on a Thursday morning. It didn't surprise him when the guy called his name. He allowed that the man had the right person, a tick of annoyance surfacing as he watched him approach; he hated having his routine interrupted, it often laid the foundation for a disrupted day.

Wilbur Hattermeyer introduced himself and briefly moved from the *like* to the *dislike* column. He apologised for interrupting, at pains to explain the coincidence of his presence. *I don't wontcha to think I'm a stalker*, he laughed, unknowingly repositioning himself favourably in Michael's mind.

The coach asked if Michael had any objection to him hanging around. *I don't wanna wreck your practice. I'll take a hike if you want me to.*

Michael sanctioned his stay.

Coach Hattermeyer didn't interrupt him again but punctuated his viewing with barely audible admiration for

MICHAEL – KING CITY

Michael's skills. It was a monosyllabic commentary. *Nice. Shot. Wow.* Too often, people commented in Pavlovian tradition, like spectators on a golf course, shouting *Be the ball* at obviously wayward shots. If Michael did something skilled, yet routine, it garnered a *Nice*. The exceptional received a *Wow*. Michael liked that the coach knew the difference.

When he'd finished, Michael asked Coach Hattermeyer if he'd like to join the Williams family for breakfast.

I've disrupted your day already. I'd hate to be an imposition.
If I don't insist, Momma will whip me, Michael said, smiling.
Well, I wouldn't wanna upset Momma.

Momma heard the screen door slam when her son returned to the house. She shouted to Michael to help his brother finish dressing. She was surprised not to hear his customary agreement, turning from the poached eggs on the stove when she heard him enter the kitchen. She was even more surprised when she saw the small white man standing next to him.

Michael introduced Wilbur Hattermeyer to his mother, explaining about their chance meeting. Momma had experience of so many callers that nothing flustered her; she asked whether he preferred his eggs poached or scrambled. Hattermeyer saw the water in the pan and opted for poached. Momma noted his glance, approving of his thoughtfulness.

Michael left to help his brother, leaving the coach to ask Momma if there was anything he could do. Momma liked a man that offered to help. She pointed at a cupboard housing cups and glasses, telling him to pour two coffees and two iced teas. *And whatever you want to fix yourself.*

It was mildly dumbfounding to Raymond Williams to find a visitor when he entered the room. He was guilty of not paying close attention to his wife and son's schedule. Coach Hattermeyer offered Raymond his hand, watching it disappear into the bigger man's grasp. Raymond welcomed the upright hand and the firm grip; it made for a good first impression. Entering behind his father, Michael wheeled his younger brother into the kitchen. Stephen bellowed a *Hi* at the coach, lifting a hand in a wave.

A LITTLE SOMETHING TO HIDE

The coach surprised the family by walking over to the wheelchair-bound boy, offering an open hand to Stephen. *You must be Stephen.*

Momma had forgotten how long and how much they had talked the day before. He treated Stephen with respect; as a collective, the family moved Wilbur Hattermeyer to the top of their like column.

When breakfast ended, Raymond offered to run Michael to school, leaving Momma and Coach Hattermeyer to share another coffee, before she declared Stephen needed to work on his studies. Wilbur Hattermeyer said he'd be happy to clear the dishes while she tutored her son. Momma allowed her protest to die quietly as the little man began gathering the plates. She found it a pleasant change to have someone else clear the table.

Before Michael reached the driveway on his way home from school, he could hear Stephen's laughter from the porch. As he rounded the corner, he could see the shoulders of his mother jiggling as she chuckled at a story that Coach Hattermeyer was telling. Michael listened as his brother recounted the tale, with his mother and the coach smiling on. For the first time, Michael thought they might need a new column of categorisation for the coach.

They talked for another two hours, during which time, Raymond Williams arrived home, languidly climbing the stairs before leaning his heavy frame against a supporting pillar, listening to his family chat with their guest like they'd known each other forever. Nobody was talking about basketball. He guessed, rightly, that they hadn't talked about it much that day. He listened to them swapping stories for ten minutes before he uncharacteristically spoke. *Should we talk about the Lobos programme before we go to dinner?*

The small man from Wisconsin via New Mexico straightened, business-like. Raymond liked that the man didn't immediately launch into a prepared speech that aimed at selling the school to Michael. Instead, he looked to Momma. *Is it okay to change the subject?*

MICHAEL – KING CITY

Raymond was mightily impressed by the respect that Wilbur Hattermeyer showed to his family.

Momma gave her assent.

He started off by telling them about everything that the programme wasn't. That was different. He didn't boast of status, of greatness, of glory. He spoke of the importance of education, wanting to understand what major Michael would choose. No previous visitor had led with the learning. *Political Science,* said Michael. He had ambitions beyond his basketball career, knowing that he would have a voice at the end of his playing days. He wanted to use it for good.

Coach Hattermeyer apologised that he didn't have the school's prospectus with him, that it was back in his hotel room, but he knew the University had a strong POLS faculty. *I'll bring the catalogue over tomorrow morning. If that's okay?* he added.

He spoke of quiet ambition, of the team, of common goals. The goals, he admitted, were modest, but he assured the family that if Michael chose to join the programme, a review would follow. He didn't make false claims, but said he was massively excited to see where the team would go with Michael on board. Raymond thought the man shifted nervously, stifling a cough, signalling an intent to raise an uncomfortable subject.

May we talk about the funding of your son's education? he said.

Momma's eyes narrowed. She wondered if this was the moment when Wilbur Hattermeyer was about to undo all the good of the preceding hours. He didn't offer illicit sweeteners. He suggested that what New Mexico would be able to offer wouldn't seem as attractive as other colleges, but that he and the Dean had spoken on his drive to King City.

The Dean is supportive of a full scholarship, tuition and housing included.

The Williams family were silent.

Coach Hattermeyer interpreted the quiet as discontent. *You'll also get the same NCAA sanctioned allowances as the rest of the team, but that's all I'm able to offer.*

He didn't know that his offer, within the rules, was exactly what they wanted to hear.

A LITTLE SOMETHING TO HIDE

Hattermeyer promised that the college was able to offer wheelchair access accommodation should the family want to watch the Lobos play. *That offer's conditional though.*

As one, the family stiffened, waiting for the inevitable caveat.

It's contingent on Stephen sitting alongside me when Michael's playing.

Stephen wasn't one for maintaining a poker face during a negotiation. *FUCK YEAH.*

Momma apologised for her youngest son's foul mouth.

I've heard much worse in the locker room, Mrs Williams.

She gently chided his formality. *Please,* she said. *Call me Momma.*

Wilbur Hattermeyer didn't know how many other callers the Williams family had invited to visit. He suspected that he was up against some stiff competition from colleges able to promise much more. The modest man from Wisconsin, with quiet self-belief, a passion for basketball, and a belief in the potential of his young charges, opened his hands wide in supplication, shrugged apologetically and said, *That's it.*

There was no pressure from Coach Hattermeyer for a decision. It was an unusual position for the Williams family, an odd situation. It was easy to fend off advances, giving vague assurances to those that demanded answers or a commitment from Michael. Coach Hattermeyer showed no sign of forcing the issue. He had made his pitch, quietly and confidently, knowing that the family had better offers to consider.

He couldn't promise the prestige, the history, the fame, the accolades. Instead, he offered support, fellowship, security – a family. The Williams family expected him to demand a response. Other callers wanted instant feedback; a commitment from Michael that he was willing to pledge his future to their school. All felt that there was an urgency to tie the young man down, to secure his services, to add the name of Michael Williams to their roster and, with his name, an asset to the college's balance sheet. Michael would be box office. *Big* box office. The family from King City, California waited expectantly for the preordained demand. Uniquely, Wilbur

MICHAEL – KING CITY

Hattermeyer didn't oblige. Instead, he suggested that it might be time for some pork sliders and a steak sandwich.

The Williams family looked from one to another, a little bemused at what was transpiring. They were a close unit, almost able to read each other's thoughts. They each knew what the others were thinking, but none were bold enough to articulate the view. Momma asked if Coach Hattermeyer wouldn't mind giving them a moment. *Sure,* he said. *How about I go inside and get everyone some more of that delicious iced tea?* He was moving before anyone answered.

Momma looked at Raymond who nodded.

Stephen, recognising the need for discretion, beamed his biggest and best smile when Momma turned to him, choking back a squawk of excitement.

The last she looked at was Michael. They enjoyed a moment of mother and son telepathy as she gave him her blessing.

Michael may have been eighteen, but he had a maturity beyond his years. He rose as Coach Hattermeyer came back with the pitcher of tea, waiting for the coach to place it on the table. Michael thrust his hand toward him, offering Wilbur Hattermeyer his services.

The little man stood staring at the boy's hand, not certain that he was hearing the words correctly. He was about to sign a ball player who, in any year, would be a number one draft pick. The best high school player in the country was about to join the New Mexico Lobos – seventh ranked, of the unfancied Mountain West division. He waited for the family to start laughing at Michael's joke. Instead, he saw only a desire for him to accept the boy's offer. *Well,* he said. *I guess we should probably go to The Cork & Plough to celebrate.*

Raymond smiled at him, agreeing. *Only if you let me get the check.*

The University of New Mexico isn't in the Ivy League, it doesn't have a massive endowment on which to draw, but Coach Hattermeyer had agreed with the University's President that if he secured the services of Michael Williams, the largess of the college would be unlimited for dinner that

A LITTLE SOMETHING TO HIDE

evening. Hattermeyer began to dissent. *Oh no, tonight is definitely on me.*

Raymond adopted a disquieted look. Wilbur Hattermeyer saw it, understanding that if he pressed his case, if he showed a willingness to be frivolous with the college's money, he would insult the man before him. Raymond Williams held himself with dignity. He wasn't posturing, he wasn't being aggressive, but there was an underlying challenge in his look. He waited for the coach to decide whether he was going to demean or respect him.

As a black man in a largely white and Hispanic neighbourhood, he had seen his fair share of assholes; he was a great judge of people. The Williams family had decided; Michael was going to join Coach Hattermeyer at the University of New Mexico, but this was the final test, the one that would determine whether Raymond would trust this man completely or whether he would question his motives.

Coach Hattermeyer had seen that look from dozens of men over the brief time he'd been a head coach. Before then, he had seen it worn on the faces of men like his father, men who worked the livestock on the dairy farms of Wisconsin, men who earned their money from honest toil; guarded, but generous when it came to sharing. Men who, when offering generosity, expected acceptance and deemed any other response a quiet slur. Wilbur Hattermeyer knew what that look meant, and he was humble enough to know when one should yield to it. He smiled at Raymond Williams, thrust his tiny white hand toward the giant's massive paw and respectfully asked Mr Williams not to think badly of him if he added a prime New York steak to his Italian salad.

People below average height grumble about the legroom available on a Briscola coach, so for Michael, the journey ahead promised a prolonged period of discomfort as he wrestled with his too-long limbs whenever another passenger sought to pass him in the aisle. Within minutes of his departure, he was ruing his mode of transport.

Coach Hattermeyer had offered to fly him to Albuquerque at the end of the season to meet his future teammates. The coach didn't anticipate his boys would be competing in the post-season; March Madness was unlikely to be on their horizon until after Michael's arrival.

The Williams family agreed to the trip, but Momma overruled the flight – it felt like a stride toward inducement. Despite Hattermeyer's entreaties to convince her of the offer's legitimacy, Momma insisted the family pay for Michael's visit, booking their son on the cheapest form of transport they could find. Michael wasn't wealthy yet and Momma maintained a concentrated eye on everything that trickled from the family's purse. Extravagance could follow when Michael started meeting his own costs, which would be right about the time his first pay cheque from the NBA landed, more than likely eclipsing his father's lifetime earnings. Until then, a battered old Briscola coach would do to move their boy around the country.

Michael suffered his discomfort without complaint, but allowed an indulgence in what for most would be fantasy, but for him, a probable reality. It was one of the few times he permitted a divorce from his modesty. 'When I make it,' he thought, fidgeting into yet another position that provided no relief from his aches, 'It's a private jet or nothing.'

A LITTLE SOMETHING TO HIDE

MTD TRANSIT CENTER, SANTA BARBARA

Arrivals		
Time	From	Expected
05:44	King City	Expected: 06:16

Departures		
Time	Destination	Expected
06:15	Los Angeles	Delayed: 06:46

MTD TRANSIT CENTER, SANTA BARBARA

The I-405 was surprisingly clear when Tim Bovary returned to Santa Barbara eight months after his first visit. Briony, the woman he was heading toward, told him to arrive thirty minutes before the departure of their bus. The Briscola coach was scheduled to leave at 6.15am, but Tim didn't fancy leaving his home in San Diego at a time when most people enjoyed their slumber. He wanted daylight for company on the three and a half hour drive north.

Before he met Briony, he inhabited what he considered to be a normal and wholly dreary hemisphere, delivering himself to work according to strictures, behaving corporately, if unambitiously, existing inoffensively. This last was an easy state to occupy. Without friends, and sharing a home with parents who maintained an indifferent interest in his affairs, he had few enough interactions with others to generate controversy, finding a need to exercise composure only when his mother's observations on his lifestyle bordered on the irksome.

Despite his dull existence, Tim allowed his mind to dwell on the fantastic, cultivating thoughts born from an emersion in science fiction and horror, often curating visions of malignant forces with ill intent. It led to a wariness of travelling by night, at a time when he believed that the demons in his imagination were most likely to take form. To avoid a confrontation with a creature from the netherworld, he set off earlier than he might otherwise have needed – much earlier.

Stung by a near-miss on his first visit, he arrived at 4.15pm the day before the date of their trip, hoping that Briony wouldn't mind his early arrival. He needn't have worried, they made good use of their time.

While they waited at the station for their delayed bus, freshly showered from a night that knew no sleep and with twilight dancing on the horizon, Briony told Tim they would be travelling alone.

'What about the others?'

'They split. She caught him cheating.'

'Really? Is that possible with their lifestyle?'

Briony flared, offended by the question. 'Of course it's possible. He didn't tell her.'

Despite her irritation, Tim took comfort from her response, yet felt compelled to probe more, knowing that he risked provoking Briony and discovering unwanted intelligence. He wondered whether he was being unfair to ask Briony if she slept with others while he was in San Diego. The thought didn't stop him seeking confirmation. 'Have you ever done that to me?'

'No, of course not. I've always told you.'

Tim reflected on their long-distance conversations, failing to remember a time when she'd mentioned nights with others. He felt a hint of deceit, the quiet sting of betrayal. 'You told me you went out.'

'Exactly,' *she agreed.*

In Briony's world, going out and having sex weren't always mutually exclusive. As they climbed on the bus, he mused that he still had much to learn about her.

They walked past me, taking a free pair of seats toward the back. As they sat down, Briony folded down the seat table of the chair in front of Tim. It slapped into his lap, broken. 'That's a fucker,' *she said, clipping the table back into place.* 'That was supposed to hide the handjob.'

She looked about, finding a lecherous man watching them from across the aisle, his tongue darted, lizard-like, across his top lip. Whether he intended his action to be seductive or disquieting, he expected Briony to look away, cowed, unable to suffer his behaviour. She held his gaze, challenging with her own stare until he turned away discomfited. She leaned across Tim, still staring at their surveillant, unable to restore eye contact. 'Hey,' *she called.*

He pretended not to hear.

'Hey!'

He turned to face them to find Briony smiling.

MTD TRANSIT CENTER, SANTA BARBARA

'I'm gonna give him a blowjob,' she said. 'Do you want me to do it before or after you go to sleep?'

A LITTLE SOMETHING TO HIDE

TIM & BRIONY – SANTA BARBARA

When asked to spell his surname, Tim says, *Bovary, like the book*. If asked for clarification, he pretends a sophistication he doesn't feel, explaining the reference to Madame Bovary. It's an affectation inherited from his father, one that has irritated him since childhood. He thinks his father's a dick whenever he says it, yet finds himself repeating the mantra, barely suppressing his self-loathing.

Neither Tim, nor his father, has read Gustave Flaubert's book. If challenged, Tim is unable to name the author or relate the story's plot. When adopting his air of sophistry, he does so only with those he thinks are intellectually void, hating encounters with people familiar with the tale, dreading them wanting a discussion. When they do, his façade vanishes, replaced with his customary meekness and an admission of his ignorance; his preference is for Graphic novels.

The closest that Tim comes to resembling the novel's namesake is through pursuing infidelities and living beyond his means. Pursuing infidelities is a loose description. Before meeting Briony, he couldn't boast of trysts or romance. His erotic conquests, mostly imagined, are conjured during evenings spent in a darkened room with nothing more than a web browser, parental controls disabled, and himself for company. Pornhub informs his vision of carnal activity. His only experience of sex (a prostitute in Las Vegas whose number he found in a phone box), came when he visited the Consumer Electronics Show. She charged him six-hundred dollars for her services, they failed to meet his expectations. She might have done what he was hoping for if he'd asked, but he was fantastically awkward around women and couldn't bring himself to articulate what he would like her to do. She left him underwhelmed by the miserably orthodox nature of the event, wallowing in his self-disgust.

The prostitute insisted he pay for her services using Venmo, despite his pleas to pay in cash, leaving him to speculate how it would appear on his bank statement, wondering too, how he would explain it to his mother when she *accidentally* discovered the entry. It wouldn't be difficult to justify, it was just another example of his profligate spending, albeit anomalous. Typically, he reserves his frivolous excesses for beer, gadgets, and movie memorabilia. If he's indulged in the former, he often finds himself on a collectibles website, increasing his indebtedness.

Tim is on the Briscola coach with Briony, who doesn't discourage his enthusiasm for expensive trinkets; it was how they met. She encouraged him to buy a replica Kylo Ren light sabre, signed by Adam Driver, on the day they met at Comic-Con in San Diego. He didn't negotiate. *Plenty of money*, she thought, when he failed to bargain.

What she didn't know, was that his thousand dollars was courtesy of Mastercard, lending further weight to the heft of the monthly payments that he struggled to meet. Buying the item was a prelude to inviting her for a drink. He thought it would impress her. He could have saved himself the debt burden, Briony would have accepted the invitation, she was already formulating plans for him.

She noticed him on the first day of the convention, before he spotted her. His radioactive hair, dyed green, and the purple suit, were prominent even amongst the thousands of other cosplay dressers. His make-up: a luminous white face with disturbing red lips, enhanced his eyes, wrecked his smile. Despite the Joker's garish garb, he appealed to Briony. She didn't care that the seams of his suit fought with the frame they concealed, he looked fun.

She knew he'd seen her, hoping that eye-contact would lead to a connection, seeking his gaze whenever he passed, allowing the semblance of a smile to form, to flicker momentarily, coquettishly breaking the bond whenever she caught him stealing a look, growing frustrated with his inability to read her signals. Although his interest was obvious, he was slow on the uptake.

They got to speak on the second day, after his fourth pass of her stand. She was working the Star Wars booth, seeing no respite from the constant attention of convention guests; immediately she finished serving one, the next was upon her. She despised most of them, the young bringing arrogance and pimples, the old, halitosis which overwhelmed lame humour. She was always on the lookout for someone of interest, someone she could play with at the end of the day.

Briony's colleagues dubbed her *The Witch*; she had a way of influencing people. Knowing they were never going to meet if he kept sidling past, rifling through the same rack of shirts, pretending an interest where there was none, she willed him to join the line of customers.

While oblivious to Briony's will, Tim nevertheless adapted his garment fondling, lingering for longer than on previous visits. He appeared to sense scrutiny, looking about himself with nervous, surreptitious glances, searching for imagined adversaries. He spied her again, convincing himself that she offered him a smile. Inhaling deeply, a resolution making breath, he joined the snaking queue. Maybe her colleagues had a point.

Needing to juggle her customers so that she would be free when he reached the front, she allowed the wisp of a groan to escape as the elderly couple before her began doubting their choices for their grandson, soliciting her advice. Briony couldn't understand why the oldies had come to Comic-Con to get the kid's Christmas present in July; *hadn't they heard of Amazon?*

She did her best to encourage a choice, but they were incurably unsure of how their grandson would react. The old woman leaned forward, conspiratorial, the phenyl tang of her imperfect purple rinse drifting between them; wisdom beckoned. *It's so hard to buy for a sixteen-year-old.* Surplus wisdom.

A LITTLE SOMETHING TO HIDE

Give him cash; an incantation Briony wanted to scream, noting that her Joker lookalike had reached the front of the queue.

The assistant next to her rang up a sale. *Have a nice day*, he chirped to his departing customer with thoughts and prayers sincerity. He waited for Tim to move toward him, adopting the impatient slouch of a man with better, more important things to do. Tim was happy to let him do them, inspecting the ceiling of the centre, rather than acknowledging the opening. *Hey Joker. Do you want me to serve you or not?*

Not, thought Tim, feigning a startle, pretending surprise at his position in the line. He shuffled sideways, performing a charade, wrestling with pockets, trying to find his wallet, before adopting magnanimity to the person behind. *After you. I seem to have ...* he trailed, unconvincingly.

Briony knew she had him. With a level of exasperation that nearly caused her to explode, the elderly couple decided to try elsewhere. As they left, she looked up to see the Joker approaching, she smiled her perfect, wide smile. *Hello Sir. What can I do to you?*

The question disarmed him. He was sure he'd heard her correctly but didn't know how to respond. Having a character inverse to the Gotham villain's, Tim couldn't conjure a retort, despite his sustained attempts at developing a swagger.

Every morning, before heading to the convention centre, he stood in front of a mirror, mustering his best Heath Ledger, annoyed at his performative mediocrity. The plan was to deliver a killer line, to foster instant attraction. At home, he rehearsed for an audience of none – almost. His mother stood in his bedroom doorway, holding a laundry basket, watching his performance, wearing a vacant smile. Pink hues emerged from beneath Tim's pale visage when he realised that she was there. *Any washing, Dear?*

He shook his head, *No*.

Very good, Dear, she said, the way mother's do: part loving, mostly patronising.

Tim would like to tell his mother to *fuck off*, but he needed her money. He swallowed his response, waiting for the creak in the stairs that told him she was out of earshot, when he could resume practicing the lines he would deliver to the hot assistant on the Star Wars stand.

He'd been planning to approach her for more than a day. Now that they were face-to-face, primed to speak, his crafted words and choreographed nonchalance deserted him. A fine grit formed between his tongue and palate. He felt uncomfortably warm in the air-conditioned cavern, rational thought fled. *What had she said?* He looked at her blankly, willing her to speak again. To his relief, she did.

Can I help you?

He felt a jealous disappointment. That wasn't how she framed her question. There was something implicit, illicit, in what she said the first time. He still hadn't spoken.

Yes. The yes exploded, violent confirmation that she could help.

She waited for him to speak again.

Nothing followed. His thoughts squalled, simultaneous and incohesive, none of them forming fully, none of them congealing into words he could say. *Should I ask her out? Should I start some small talk? I can't do small talk. Should I ask about the show? Should I buy something? What idiot joins a queue with nothing to buy?* He was conscious of a broadening chasm between his last word and the next.

Good, she ventured, the word carrying a doubtful wariness. *So, what can I do to you?*

He fizzed inside. *That's what she said!* It didn't help. If he'd known Briony's thinking, he would have thrown an invitation across. He recovered his voice. *I'd like to buy something.*

Do you have anything in mind?

He had no idea what was available. He cast a look into the cabinet between them, saw the light sabre.

His inertia left him; his inner magpie asserting itself. His memorabilia collection was vast, but he didn't think he had anything as exquisite as the signed item lying before him, perched on a velvet cushion, a soft light casting its pall. To his collector's eye, it was a thing of beauty. He jabbed a gloved finger at the cabinet. *How much?* If he hadn't been standing in front of the woman he was trying to impress, he would have winced at the cost. *That's a bargain,* he managed to squeak, reaching for his wallet.

Great, she said.

Lovely smile. He felt his cheeks glow as he considered that he might have expressed the thought.

Her smile was lovely.

He approved of the reverence she gave to the light sabre, placing it delicately into a felt-lined box, along with a certificate of authenticity; a tightly rolled scroll tied with a red ribbon. A brass plate, proclaiming its provenance, lent further cachet to the cherished prize. He handed her his card, issuing a silent prayer for enough credit to make the payment.

Briony maintained a grip on the precious package as she handed it to him. They held it between them. She willed him to find his courage. If he couldn't, she'd end her interest. Tim took a breath, hoping she'd keep hold of the package, giving him an excuse to keep looking at her. That smile. Those eyes; lustrous coffee, almost indistinguishable from her pupils, losing him in their depth. *CANIBUYYOUDINNER?* The words (word) tumbled from him; he didn't want to pause in case his audacity fled.

Sure, she said. She waited for him to speak again. He didn't.

Tim was dumbstruck that she'd agreed. Ordinarily accustomed to rejection, his past entreaties regularly resulted in ridicule, often from some of the kinder girls. Others had been brutal, the humiliation a lasting scald. He didn't know what to say next, he hadn't planned as far as thinking she might accept his invitation. Briony filled the void. *Meet me here when my shift finishes. I'll be done by six.*

He bobbed away with the Joker's strut, happy, yet admonishing himself for not suggesting a drink; dinner would be much more expensive.

His mother was quick to notice the bounce when he returned home. She had no difficulty drawing an admission of the evening ahead. He had considered keeping it a secret, but her forensic exploration, and his ill-concealed excitement, led him to confession. If he could have read his mother's heart at that moment, he would have discovered a woman profoundly happy that her 26-year-old son was about to have his first date. His news, while imbuing her with joy, was also a moment of significant relief. It was a tiny step, but for a fleeting moment, she envisioned a house in which he was no longer a resident. Tim left his mother to her joy and the fanciful thought of him leaving home a married man.

He spent the next two hours riven with doubt. *Would she like him without his make-up? Would she recognise him, and if she did, would she find the unadulterated version repugnant?* He contemplated retaining the look for the evening, surmising that she might prefer him as a caricature. He was close to resolving that he would, when his mother popped her head through his door and queried why he was still in costume. When he explained, she called him an idiot, a momentary lapse in the otherwise unrelenting coddling she had afforded him since birth. The criticism stung; it was unusual from his mother, she always believed herself right, but rarely condemned. He took the rebuke well, reminding himself he'd soon be asking her for money.

The Old Spaghetti Factory was down Fifth Avenue, across from the Convention Center; he hoped she liked Italian food. He ordered the spaghetti with meat sauce, sighing inwardly when the plate of food arrived. Slim tendrils of pasta snaked around a viscous beef and tomato amalgam. Tim was a messy eater, his choice a critical mistake, a catastrophic first-date food. The first sauce hit his shirt before he had finished thinking that her spinach and cheese ravioli was a wiser choice.

He imagined an evening different to the one that was evolving. As each flick of sauce polka-dotted his shirt, he felt the chances of his fantasy outcome diminishing spot by spot. He tried cutting the spaghetti to avoid spatters from the dangling threads. Instead, worm-length strands fell from his fork, splashing into his dish, lending a Pollock-esque appearance to the tablecloth.

A LITTLE SOMETHING TO HIDE

On any other occasion, he'd have been wearing a dark t-shirt with anime cartoons or a science fiction theme. Tonight, he wore a freshly pressed white shirt with buttoned down collar; his mother insisted, saying it would be more appropriate. Despite his misgivings, he followed her bidding, regretting now that he didn't have the courage to tell her that she was clueless, as evidenced when Briony arrived, Comic-Con uniform gone, replaced with jeans and a t-shirt. A black Star Trek t-shirt. He cursed his mother; he'd planned to wear a parody shirt with the words 'Scott me up Beamy'; which would have been perfect. Instead, he had a pure white canvas for collecting bolognaise droplets. With each mouthful, ochre teardrops collided with his shirt. He hoped Briony wouldn't notice, conceding defeat when a portion of mince escaped his fork and rolled down his shirt. *Oh fuck*, he mumbled.

She heard, looked up, giggled.

Apologising profusely, he dabbed his napkin in a glass of water, before trying to clean his shirt, diluting the stain, spreading the mess. He sensed, rather than felt, his actions becoming more frantic as his shirt got wetter and the smearing worsened. She watched his endeavours, giggling again, telling him not to worry. She surprised him by saying, *We can take that off later*.

We. Did she say, We? He hoped he hadn't misheard her.

He relaxed a little, ordering two more beers without asking if she wanted one. He liked that she drank beer, he had no idea what to choose when it came to wine, beer was safer. She was drinking faster than him, he figured getting her another was a safe bet.

When the waiter returned to ask if they were having dessert, Tim let her order first. He fancied the Chocolate Mousse Cake, figuring that a little chocolate couldn't do much more damage to his shirt. He didn't get a choice. Briony chose the New York Cheesecake. *We'll share*, she instructed their server. There was an assurance to her, she was confident enough to order for him without consultation; his timidity allowed her decision to go unchallenged.

TIM & BRIONY – SANTA BARBARA

He masked his disappointment when the large slice of cake landed between them. She carved a piece, leaning forward, offering it to him, telling him it was going to be good. He forgot the Mousse Cake, expunged by the intimacy. They took turns at feeding each other until it was gone.

Irish Coffee. He wasn't sure if she were framing it as a question or an intention. She flicked her hand at the waiter, settling the matter. When they finished, he asked for the check before she could think of something more to add to the bill. He was quietly grateful to his mother for giving him fifty dollars more than he requested.

Outside the restaurant, they stood in the maritime warmth of the San Diego summer, uncertainty creeping upon him, leaving Tim wondering what to do. He needn't have worried, Briony made the decision for him, asking him to walk her back to her hotel.

It hadn't occurred to him that she wasn't from San Diego. He felt a faint regret with the realisation that she was a visitor to the city. He lamented his inability for small talk. *What idiot doesn't think to ask where someone lives?* he thought. She told him she was from Santa Barbara as they began wandering. *I've never been*, he said.

You'll have to come.

He liked that idea.

The Hilton San Diego Bayfront was ten minutes away. Peach slivers coloured the horizon, a distant mirage shimmering, belying the day's escaping heat. They walked side-by-side, close enough that the backs of their hands brushed occasionally. He apologised the first time, responding to the inadvertent touch by whipping his hand away as if jolted with electricity. She laughed, telling him not to worry. He wasn't sure if that was an implicit invitation to take her hand, but he wasn't bold enough to try. He walked her to the hotel's entrance, standing awkwardly when they arrived, shoving his hands in his pockets, shuffling on the spot.

His experience with women would take little to document; he felt acutely out of his depth. He neither knew what women wanted, nor how to behave. He was feeling the crush of indecision when she told him the hotel had a cool bar with some great beers. He said he preferred a great bar with some cool beers, cringing inwardly when she stared at him like he was a weirdo. He shrugged an apology for his feeble quip; she laughed again. *C'mon*, she said. *I'm buying, but only if your jokes improve.*

She ordered twenty-two-ounce glasses of Alesmith .394 Pale Ale; the pump clip proclaimed a six-percenter. *Girl knows how to drink*, he thought, and not for the first time. They took their drinks to the balcony at the Odysea restaurant. Before they were through their first, she'd summonsed the waiter for more.

He couldn't tell whether they were supporting each other or cuddling when she led him to her room later. In the elevator, she confirmed his hope. Bewildered by the speed of progression, Tim had neither the time, nor the faculty, to consider what he was doing. He allowed Briony's impulses to sweep him along; she guided and controlled him. He confessed to a lack of expertise, a self-protective strategy to guard against failings. She told him not to worry. *Just relax and follow my lead.*

He did, seeing many of his fantasies realised. *There's a woman in Vegas could learn a lot from you,* he thought later, as he fell into a gratified sleep.

She was breezy in the morning, waking at 8am. Bone white shards of light lanced through the blinds, causing him to wince. His head entertained a dull percussion, strings of pain accompanied his movements. Moisture evaded his mouth, evaporated on alcoholic fumes. He tried to summon a swallow, the crackle in his throat arguing against the action. He mumbled a complaint. Briony laughed at his discomfort, appearing to be suffering from no ill-effects of the night before. *Get up*, she said, with no trace of indulgence. *I'm on a later shift, let's get breakfast.*

He moaned, complaining that he and food were not necessarily going to get along.

She asked him what he could manage.

Coffee, he replied, failing to discern her invitation.

She rolled her eyes. *This guy really is clueless,* she thought, pulling him from the bed and into the bathroom where they showered.

He was feeling much better by the time she shut off the water.

Briony threw him a Force Awakens t-shirt to replace his food-stained shirt. It would have been loose fitting on her; he enlarged the typeface. She gave his belly a playful rub. *You can bring that back to me later tonight.*

Tim made a promise he was going to keep.

He spent the day at the conference beating a circular path around her stand, each circuit taking him thirty minutes. Sometimes she overlooked him, focusing on her work. Other times he caught her eye, giving her a bashful wave. He couldn't quite reconcile his new reality when she smiled back. It was a novel occurrence.

He was waiting ten minutes before her shift ended, like a puppy desperate for its master's return. She kissed him on the cheek before taking his hand as she started for the hotel. As they approached the lobby, he dredged his growing confidence, asking her if she wanted a drink.

No.

He felt bruised, unable to fathom her response. He scanned a mental catalogue of transgressions, searching for his wrongdoing. She read his expression, laughing at his hangdog look. *C'mon,* she said, leading him to the lift block. *I've got an early start and don't want to be up late.*

Tim was breathing heavily and sweating when she got up to use the bathroom. He checked his watch, 2am, amazed at her energy, undone by his exhaustion. Briony's stamina and desire seemed inexhaustible. When she returned to bed, she backed into him, feeling with her hand, squeezing him gently. He wondered what she would consider a late night.

She was gone by the time he woke; he didn't hear her leave. He'd woken content, the sun on his face serving as a warming comforter in the absence of an accompanying hangover. He resigned himself to the disappointment that they wouldn't reprise yesterday's shower. A hastily scribbled note told him her company was having an after-convention party and she'd text him the details.

At five, with the convention over and no message from her, he rationalised that she'd been too busy to send one. At six, he thought they'd still be breaking down their stand which explained why he hadn't heard from her. At seven, he decided he'd given her the wrong number. He opted to walk to the convention centre to see if she was there.

The security guard looked bored. Bored and ineffective. He stood at the entrance maintaining little interest in events around him. A fraction under six foot, he boasted an impressive girth. His fluorescent yellow jacket, wide open in the heat of the day, flapped loosely against an expansive belly, shaped as it was, from an affliction to fast food and pitchers of Sam Adams. His beard, scraggly and unkempt, crept high up his cheeks, morphing with his moustache to create a mass of hair that descended to the swell of his tummy. Beady eyes, dark and lustreless, peered from beneath a cap that concealed a polished dome which belied the profusion of hair that sprouted elsewhere.

Tim contemplated sneaking past, convincing himself that the rotund guard's attention was anywhere but on the job for which he was employed. He attempted the nonchalant stroll of belonging, aiming to exude the confident walk of one who fits. He was almost abreast of the security guard, thinking he was in, when a wedge of arm stopped him. *Accreditation*.

What? said Tim.

Accreditation, offered the guard, scanning Tim's body for the tell-tale lanyard of the legitimate.

I'm here for my girlfriend. The words surprised him. Not that he said them, but about their possibility. It wasn't a sentence he'd uttered before. It wasn't a prospect worthy of critical contemplation. A girlfriend. That neither he nor Briony had discussed the phenomenon was immaterial. Tim had just referred to another human in the possessive, something usually reserved for his parents. Here he was, claiming falsely, that he had a partner. *I promised her I'd help break down the stand.*

The beady eyes narrowed. Tim could see the guard wrestling with an authority that he wasn't sure he possessed. Earlier, with the convention in full swing, declining unauthorised entry was a simple decision. Now, with the show over, the centre contained naked Meccano sets of undressed stanchions and frames, the need for preventing entry appeared to have diminished. He weighed the decision, determining he needed more information, the kid would need interrogating. *Company?* he asked.

Star Wars, Tim replied, wondering if he should mention that it was a franchise rather than a company, deciding it was inopportune to demonstrate pedantry. It irked him that the guard didn't comment on the distinction.

Instead, the security man cogitated, evaluating the threat that Tim posed. Seemingly, the interrogation was over. Considering him mostly harmless, the big man straightened to demonstrate his authority, grunted a concession, and allowed Tim to pass.

The centre hummed with the sound of closure. Crews dismantled exhibition stands, others scurried: rolling cables, pushing trolleys, shouting warnings, clearing trash. Tim walked past unattended merchandise, products for which he lusted. He struggled to resist helping himself. At what remained of the Star Wars stand, he asked a black-shirted roadie if he knew where to find Briony. He received a blank stare and a shrug from the pony-tailed man. *I'm just a contractor.*

You'd also make a good security guard, thought Tim, looking around, seeing no one he recognised. He also noticed several boxes full of t-shirts, casually opening one to remove an item. The blood-shot eyes and intimidating scowl of Emperor Palpatine stared at him. The shirt looked large enough to contain him. *I'm just gonna grab this*, he shouted to the contractor, whose ambivalent shrug he took for consent.

Prior to meeting Briony, he wouldn't have considered stealing a shirt, but in the last 48-hours he'd gained a heightened confidence, a little daring. Taking it felt like something she'd condone. It didn't diminish his anxiety as he exited the building, tensed and ready to relinquish the contraband. He left unchallenged, the security guard casting nothing more than a suspicious glance. *They've already finished*, said Tim, desperate to run, striving to appear casual.

The call went to voicemail, her breezy message telling him that she was probably speaking to someone more important and to leave a message. It might have sounded funny if he wasn't beginning to think that she was avoiding him. Determining not to sound needy, he hung up without speaking. With no plan, he headed for the waterfront, thinking he might have been premature to consider Briony his girlfriend. The water offered him no comfort, allowing only the magnification of an inexplicable longing, which morphed into loss the longer he watched the lap of the tide. Sighing, he turned from the ocean's expanse, ordering a car to take him home.

At 8.45pm, she returned his call, a slur to her voice. Tim heard the hum of background conversation, thumping music masking her words; the party had started without him. *Sorry I didn't leave a messuge. Leff charger in hotel. Come join ush.*

Disney had arranged a private party in The Pool Club at the hotel. *The Margaritas are eggshellent.* She giggled at her blooper. His mood lifted, but self-doubt lingered.

What should I wear?

Dushent madder, she said, promising to get him out of whatever he was wearing once the party was over. He was on the pavement before he'd finished ordering the Uber and before his mother could tell him to change what he was wearing.

When he arrived, he was wearing his stolen shirt and he felt, for the first time, appropriately dressed. He suffered a disquieting guilt as he wandered the room searching for Briony, half expecting a condemning hand on his shoulder, dragging him away, incarcerating him for theft. Unchallenged, he navigated the room, finding Briony huddled in a wicker seat alongside a colleague.

TIM & BRIONY – SANTA BARBARA

They were halfway through large margaritas with another two waiting on the table. She saw him enter and jumped from her seat, grabbing a spare drink, sloshing it over his hand when giving it to him, licking it from where it spilt, before dragging him behind her. *Come meet my new girlfren,* she said, instilling in him another jealous pang.

Briony introduced her as Sandy, before collapsing next to her, pulling Tim to the other side, placing a hand on his leg, running it up the inside of his thigh. The contact stirred him – briefly. She leaned closer to Sandy, doing the same to her.

Alternating her attention between them, Briony's behaviour confused Tim, leaving him covetous, cheated of her time. She teased with the prospects of the night ahead, left him wondering what she was saying to Sandy, whether her words were equally arousing to the other woman. Whispers in Sandy's ear, leading to blushes, suggested promises made. Images from Pornhub sprang to mind, he paid closer attention to the woman garnering Briony's interest. He'd chosen not to notice her too much when introduced, but now he was beginning to think (hope?) he might get to know her a little better as the night progressed.

He excused himself to go to the bathroom, admonishing himself for the disloyalty to Briony and his quietly perverted thoughts. *What would his mother think?* He sniggered at his transition from unlikely lothario to a man entertaining a ménage à trois, just days after his first legitimate sexual experience. By the time he'd found the bathroom, his conservative upbringing asserted itself, invoking conventional thoughts of what might happen once Sandy had disappeared.

When he returned, the situation called for reassessment, with Briony and Sandy locked together, kissing. He stopped short, stunned, unable to draw closer, not knowing what he would do if he did. Another man slithered alongside him, spectating, voicing a lewd fantasy. Tim didn't comment, mentally indulging the man's ideas, experiencing an unfamiliar excitement at the possibility. Briony noticed him over Sandy's shoulder when they separated. She smiled, patting the seat next to her. *D'you wanna go upstairs?* she asked when he joined them. *Sandy's keen.*

Tim was unable to express an opinion, his mouth opening and closing to speak, his vocal cords uncooperative. Briony and Sandy decided for him, each taking one of his hands as they led him from the bar.

His imagination was lacking; fantasies falling short of the acts unfolding in Briony's room. Sandy's invention and willingness to experiment brought strident gasps, her moans intensifying the more she enjoyed herself. Alarmed at the volume, Tim voiced concern for the people in the neighbouring room. Briony told him not to give a fuck and embrace the moment. He tried following her advice.

In the space of three days, he had gone from having one, paid for, sexual encounter (which he now knew to be staggeringly conventional), to experiences that he believed were the preserve of the pornographer. Encumbered by embarrassment, he thought that what was happening to him could only occur inside the mind of a depraved script writer. Briony laughed at his timidity, goading him to be daring. *I'm not sure how,* he whined. The women showed him what to do.

In the morning, Tim woke to the sound of Briony and Sandy in the shower. He could hear their laughter through the bathroom door, followed by more evidence of Sandy's enjoyment. He dressed, making himself a coffee while waiting for them to appear. Sandy emerged, a towel around her midriff and another tied in a knot on her head. Drawing close to Tim, she gave him a lingering kiss. Despite last night's exploits, he felt guilty kissing her with Briony out of the room. It felt disloyal, a betrayal. They were still kissing when Briony appeared. She popped a capsule in the Nespresso machine, untroubled by their clinch, asking if they wanted coffee. Sandy broke away from Tim, saying *Yes please*, as she left the room to find her clothes.

Tim braced for a tirade.

Briony looked at him, smiling. *You okay for coffee?*

#

TIM & BRIONY – SANTA BARBARA

For the next hour they lounged, each scrolling through phones, giggling occasionally, sharing content they found amusing; a room of friends gathered to pass the morning. Tim hoped one of them would mention the night before, to lend normality to the situation. He didn't want to be the one to raise the subject, to reveal his naivety. The absence of conversation, of any sort, made him uncomfortable. He imagined that Briony and Sandy were sparing him their evaluations, saving him from shame.

Sandy stood, announcing she had to leave, making no ceremony of her departure, giving Tim and Briony kisses on the cheek, the parting of friends that will soon meet again. It was the last time that Tim saw her. He didn't know if Briony would see her again, she didn't comment on the prospect, letting Sandy leave with an elongated *By-eee*. Briony rose from the sofa, reminding Tim that she needed to check out before 11am as she disappeared from the room. *I'm not ignoring you,* she shouted from the bedroom. *I just gotta pack.*

He walked her to her car, watching her load her suitcase, feeling a profound sense of sadness, expecting this to be the last time he would see her. Melancholy descended, powered by the overwhelming belief in the restoration of his pre-Briony inadequacies, of days spent in the Geek Squad at Best Buy, working for an employer that simultaneously paid him and relieved him of his earnings, selling him gadgets that he didn't need, but couldn't resist. He foresaw evenings alone, sheltering in his room, gaming, or furtively browsing the web, ears finely tuned to the movements of his mother, anticipating her unannounced arrival at his door, knowing she would ignore his demands that she knock before entering. He suffered from the certainty that tedium stretched before him; long, continuous, stealing the aberration of his days with Briony.

Tim wanted to believe that Briony sensed his sadness. She gave him a hug, it seemed devoid of meaning, little comfort, no desire. He worried that if he tried to speak he would cry; he didn't want to reveal himself, to let her know of her effect. He said nothing.

A LITTLE SOMETHING TO HIDE

Speaking with her casual ease, she made it painless, confidently filling the silences with carefree conversation. *Come to Santa Barbara this weekend.* She knew he was free.

Without knowing why, he hesitated.

I'll move on quickly, she said, making his mind up for him. *It's this weekend or never.*

She was coolly dismissive. It was a take it or leave it option, hardly romantic. The realisation of what he meant to her flickered; it wasn't what he was hoping. The knowledge hurt, but the prospect of a weekend with her, extending the adventure, was too alluring to decline.

For the only time in his life, he attempted to play it cool. *We'll see*, he said. His response surprised her, placing a glint in her eye.

Will we? she said, sliding into her car, smiling, reasserting control.

He fretted at the sluggish hum of her lowering window.

I'll wait until 8pm on Friday. After that... She left the sentence hanging, pulling out of the car park, leaving him to wonder.

He tried matching her indifference, avoiding confirmation of his visit, thinking that was part of her rulebook, a behaviour that Briony would adopt, expecting the same from others, contemplating that to do anything other than arrive at her house on Friday evening would appear needy. Tim kept his plans to himself.

He also kept them from his mother, her influence on his weekend an unwelcome interference. She had been wrong about the shirt; she was unlikely to contribute anything that he might find useful. He also didn't want to give her the opportunity to suggest he should *Pack a condom,* the mortification of hearing his mother use that phrase too much to bear. Tim would allow her to sustain the allusion that he was joining a team building exercise with Best Buy. It was simpler, less awkward.

The feigned ambivalence didn't match his concern about arriving on time. The night before, he checked Google Maps, three times, reaffirming the length of his journey. He did it again in the morning, before his alarm sounded, and again, on entering and leaving the shower. Google was consistent, telling him each time he could expect a journey of three and a half hours. The midday check yielded the same result, but he decided to leave at 2pm – just in case, feeling a spike of anxiety before he left, when the predicted time shot to four hours. *Los Angeles traffic*, he surmised, trying to quash his growing unease, telling himself it would be okay. Notwithstanding, he hoisted his canvas tote, headed downstairs, barely pausing to say goodbye to his mother, ignoring the question on her lips, scrambling to avoid delay. If he were late, he predicted that Briony would be gone, along with any chance of resurrecting their ... what? Relationship?

He chose to go via the I-405 instead of the I-5, avoiding what he thought would be the worst of LA's traffic. According to Google, he'd travel three miles further but do it three minutes quicker. He regretted his decision north of Long Beach, when a tractor-trailer jack-knifed four hundred yards ahead of him, just after he'd passed the off-ramp. Six further cars concertinaed into the truck, blending their frames, making the scene impassable. Tim slowed to a stop, checking his watch. 4.15pm. He looked accusingly at the McDonald's wrappers beside him on the passenger seat, wishing he hadn't stopped, he wasn't even hungry, a Pavlovian reaction causing his pause at the golden arches.

After twenty minutes, the flashing blues of the emergency services arrived to assess the damage, to make sense of the carnage. Fire crews and ambulances jostled through the snaking backlog to join the Highway Patrol. An air-ambulance landed 30 minutes after the crash, remaining on the highway for another half-hour, waiting for those prised from their cars.

An hour into the delay, his extra-large Coke announced itself. He shifted uncomfortably, willing the emergency services to clear the road, to allow him to find relief at the next rest stop. Thirty minutes later, unmoving, the ache of discomfort mutated into pain. He eyed the empty cup beside him, deciding against the option it represented. Ahead, he saw another man spritzing the barrier at the side of the road.

A LITTLE SOMETHING TO HIDE

Unable to conceal the deed and embracing the ignominy, he duplicated the act. When he turned, zippering, a group of teenage girls peered at him from the car next to his, resentment cascading his way. Scurrying away, he sought the solace of his car, skulking low in the seat, conscious of their disapproval.

Cars inched around him, signs of progress, stilted movements promising more. The driver in front began thumping his steering wheel, his car's battery lifeless, drained by the unrelenting thrash metal that accompanied his wait. Before Tim could navigate beyond him, the driver sprang from his car, accosting him, begging assistance. He held cable leads and wore an imploring face above swirling blue-black tattoos, which to Tim's mind, lent an implied threat to the request. Tim checked his watch, 5.55pm. He still had close to one hundred miles ahead of him.

He wanted to say *No*, to leave the man to his misery, or to let him find someone else to help. A glance at the assailant's thick biceps and heavy hobnails resolved Tim to civic duty. By 6.05pm he was on his way. Google told him he would be in Santa Barbara by 7.58pm. He was getting close to the time when he might never see Briony again.

The option of sending her a text felt belated, having already resisted the courtesy of telling her he was coming, regretting his attempts to appear aloof. The idiocy of attempting to be someone other than himself weighed upon him. *Why didn't I just show her how keen I am?* he wondered. *I should have called.* If he'd gone a day earlier, he reflected, he might have enjoyed more rampant sex. He couldn't believe how much of a dick he had become.

When the traffic cleared, he sped ahead, grateful for his investment in the radar detector that he'd bought online. Where he could, he held a steady eighty-five miles per hour, slowing when traffic dictated, or the detector squealed its warnings. Issuing the wanton request of the unbeliever, he prayed that nothing else would slow him down. The minutes ticked away; Google remained resolutely stuck on a 7.58pm arrival.

TIM & BRIONY – SANTA BARBARA

The speeding gained him one minute; he arrived with three to spare. Briony was sitting on the front step drinking a beer. *You're early*, she said. Unable to discern the sarcasm, Tim contemplated telling her his plans for getting there sooner, conveying their missed opportunities, but held back in case she thought him presumptuous. She could make those choices; he wasn't sure that he could. Taking his bag, she threw it through the open door, before pulling it closed behind her. *C'mon*, she said. *The Uber man's coming*.

At the Wildcat Lounge, she seemed to know everyone, dancing with them all. Tim danced too, always close to her, trying to avoid separation, like an anxious child, knowing that if they parted, he'd spend the evening alone, leaning against a wall. Briony's attention varied, sometimes close and intimate, reminding him of her sexuality, other times there was more than just space between them, she allowed others to get equally close, leading him to wonder what promises she whispered.

They danced until closing. When the music stopped, it was just them. No interlopers, no rivals, no additions. So many had come and gone through the evening, he felt certain that Briony would be inviting at least one other to join them. Instead, she led him alone from the club. They clung to each other for the walk home, staying close, combatting the chill of the evening that their sweat-soaked clothes invited. *Shall we shower?* she asked when they were inside. Remembering Sandy's moans of pleasure from the Hilton, any attempt to appear casual disappeared with the indecent speed of his response.

Dawn was threatening the night sky when they separated, their exertion leading to a contented slumber. At eight, Briony woke, cheery, as though the night had gifted her plentiful sleep. She made him a breakfast of coffee and Pillsbury crescent rolls, the smells drifting to her room, waking him. He propped himself on the pillows, hands behind his head, scanning his surroundings. Adorned with posters, the walls demonstrated Briony's eclectic taste. Some were prints of old masters; nubile concubines, gossamer clad, lounging amorously in suggestive poses. Others were more contemporary, a challenge to the imagination; partial anatomies, abstracts, sleight-of-eye tricks, where images morphed from the obvious to the surreal, the sensual. On occasions, it took him a moment to appreciate the renderings, but a common theme was evident; gazing at her walls was a powerful stimulant.

It appeared that Briony also had a fondness for gadgets. A wall-length shelf held an array of pieces, many of which served an indeterminate function. Others, Tim noted without surprise, had a clear and obvious purpose. One such item sat on a purple cushion. Knowing instinctively it was the cushion that once held his light sabre, he entertained a wisp of hope that there was significance in the gesture. There were other items too, their utility recognisable, but he wondered, given the realm of her collection, what purpose Briony would find for them.

She walked into the room holding a tray, laying it between them as she sat on the edge of the bed. She passed him a coffee and a pastry, both valuing the silent communion as they ate. An object on the bedside table caught Tim's eye. When he finished his breakfast, he took it, turning it in his hands, trying, and failing, to guess its function. Intelligence eluded him, he felt a flush of embarrassment, Briony's look teasing an opinion. She let him simper, choosing not to relieve his angst, waiting for him to ask. His eyes pleaded, voicing the question, an unspoken query. It felt safer that way, less naïve, making it more difficult for her to ridicule if that's what she decided. She didn't. She moved the tray from the bed, joining him beneath the cover. *Let me show you*, she said, guiding the hands holding the object.

He wondered if there was ever a time when she wasn't keen.

In the afternoon, tide receding, they strolled along the packed sands of Leadbetter Beach, holding hands, comfortable with each other. *How had he got here; on the beach, with her?* He didn't entertain the question for long, allowing himself to just be, to enjoy. They'd had lunch at the Shoreline

Café, Briony telling him to order big, that he might be disappointed with dinner later that night at her friends. *Health freaks*, she added.

Arrangements were in place, made without consultation, his opinion redundant in the decision-making process. Admiring her confidence, Tim understood that time spent with Briony would be simpler by submitting to her plans. She seemed without fear, ever assured, untroubled by the perception of others, unafraid of consequences, the antithesis of Tim. Fun, in whatever hedonistic guise she could muster, was her motivation. Tim imagined that her enjoyment of life stemmed mostly from the pursuit of the carnal, his experiences to date, underscoring his opinions. *Who are we seeing?* he asked, hoping that her answer might suggest an agenda, or an outcome to the evening.

She took a bite of her burger, purring at the taste. *High school friend*, she said, mouth full, leaving him no wiser.

Mei Wong was the friend, a diminutive woman, almost fragile, veiled in delicacy. She glided when she moved, as though propelled by a sirocco. *Mei claims to be five feet tall*, Briony told Tim. *Give or take four inches*.

Hi, said Mei, immune to the taunt, her arm floating from her side, reaching toward Tim. Taking her hand, he expected a flaccid hold, not the power of her grip. She unnerved him with her scrutiny, a serene expression, her gaze announcing a critical evaluation. Tim sensed her immediate understanding of his flaws, the awareness passing between them. Perfect white teeth appeared, granting her approval, bringing him relief from a tension he didn't realise he felt. She let go of his hand, waving to the man beside her. *This is Deshaun*.

Just call me, D, said Mei's boyfriend. He joked that he'd borrowed Mei's missing inches, adding them to his original six feet. His words were unhurried, each deliberate, a sonorous drawl, betraying routes from the South, not quite masked by the West Coast confluence. He chuckled at his quip, deeply resonant, three metronomic *Huhs,* a droll cough.

A LITTLE SOMETHING TO HIDE

Tim offered a forced falsetto laugh in return, hoping not to offend.

Deshaun played college football and preserved the athleticism instilled by four years as a Defensive End at Notre Dame. A busted knee, in what turned out to be his final college game, saw the end of his NFL prospects, the evidence of MRI scans ending the interest of future employers. Even so, Tim felt intensely inadequate.

The differences between Mei and Deshaun were stark; delicacy contrasting brawn, mysticism allied to force. Mei ushered them in with a graceful movement, Deshaun welcomed them with a toothy grin and a bone-crunching handshake. Tim calculated deltas between them of twenty inches and one-hundred-and-fifty pounds, neither of them carrying excess weight.

Mei gestured to a jumble of oversized cushions, indicating they should sit, before she drifted to the kitchen, casually floating the idea that tonight's meal would be high on protein and low on carbs. Deshaun followed her, puppy-like.

Briony did nothing to conceal her *I told you so* face when Tim rolled his eyes. The mischief was new to him, he felt an unfamiliar thrill at the duplicity, followed by immediate guilt for the insinuation. Briony laughed. *This'll be the healthiest meal you'll ever have*, she said as Deshaun returned to the room.

Except for the beer, Deshaun said, his baritone undermining a conspiratorial whisper, handing bottles to his guests. *Gotta get your carbs from somewhere.* They clinked bottlenecks before Deshaun professed a need to help Mei.

Tim noticed that his help amounted to little more than molestation of the tiny woman, who kept sliding from his groping hands as she prepared their meal, granting Tim a sense of what the evening might hold.

It felt like a normal evening to Tim, or whatever shape Tim now perceived as normal. They sipped beers, ate desiccated rice crackers, chatting as Mei concocted, and Deshaun molested. They had egg drop soup and sesame chicken. Mei served the chicken with a tofu salad. Tim managed to add the salad to his plate without snaring a piece of tofu which he considered sub-edible. The wine, a Sauvignon Blanc, had Mei raving about its Kiwi provenance.

You just can't beat the grassiness and the minerality, said Deshaun, each word falling from his mouth, tinted with sardonic traces, leaving Tim unsure how to react. Mei slapped Deshaun's arm, Briony giggled. Tim had no idea why, but laughed anyway.

Who's for dessert? said Mei.

I'm in, said Tim. He didn't know why the others snickered at his response.

Who are you going to have first? Briony asked.

His epiphany was glacial. The taint of alcohol and the unfamiliar context hampered his comprehension, slowed his understanding. The expectation around the table triggered a realisation, the question's implication gradually forming, manifesting in indecision.

He wanted to state the obvious, the safe – Briony. *Was it safe?* he thought. *Would he be causing offence if he didn't say Mei? What would 250-pounds of former defensive-end do, if Tim expressed a preference for his girlfriend? What would Briony say?*

He felt the moisture leaving his mouth as he contemplated a third option, which having imagined it, he found impossible to clear from his mind. *Surely that wasn't one of the choices? Were there others? Should he only be thinking in the singular, and if not, how would the combinations unfold?* The silence rose around the table as they waited for him to answer.

Briony broke it, both rescuing him and plunging him into a fresh dilemma. *Why don't you get to know Mei better? We'll leave you to it.* She was standing before she finished speaking, leading Deshaun from the table and disappearing to another room.

Tim gaped, unable to conceal his panic. He felt Mei's hand on his thigh, she leaned close, *Briony tells me you're open to new bliss.* Her hand moved up his leg. *Have you experienced Asian Fusion before?* She stood, moving closer, pulling his head toward her breasts, nuzzling his hair, sensing his tension, his hesitancy. *I'm okay if you're okay*, she said. *We do this all the time.*

A LITTLE SOMETHING TO HIDE

Tim didn't know who, or how many *'We'* included, nor what *'This'* entailed. He was beginning to feel like one of Briony's sex toys, an object to play with, to share with her closest friends. *Relax*, said Mei. *It'll be fun.*

She stepped back, taking his hand, leading him toward the bedroom. The door was ajar; he could see Briony sitting on the edge of an enormous circular bed, obscured by Deshaun who was standing in front of her. His trousers were around his ankles; he purred his encouragement to Briony. Tim hesitated in the doorway, affronted at what he saw, his immediate thought a flash of anger. Mei dropped his hand, leaving him in the door frame, moving to sit next to Briony where she started stroking her hair. She looked over to Tim, who remained motionless, beckoning for him to join her.

As Deshaun voiced his pleasure, Briony ushered Tim in without breaking their union, urging him to enter. Hesitantly, he crossed the room, positioning himself in front of Mei, trying not to look at Briony, worried at what his expression might betray. Mei reached for his belt, deft hands unzipping his jeans, releasing him. He felt a slender hand, followed by her lips, then the unexpected, the pull of Deshaun, a powerful grip, taking him by the shoulders, turning him, drawing him close, kissing. Tim tensed, anxiety mixing with bewilderment. He felt another hand on him, he pulled away from Deshaun, finding Briony's hand on his belly. *Chill*, she said. *It gets even better.*

They were naked on the giant bed, carelessly entwined. Tim lay awake listening to the hum of slumber: the shrill whistle of air escaping Mei's pinched nose; Deshaun's snores, imperfectly formed, rasping glottal stops. Briony was mostly silent. Tim wondered whether she too was awake, but there was a resonance to her breathing that spoke of sleep.

Staring at the ceiling, he reflected on the previous two weeks. Prior to meeting Briony, there was the prostitute. He now considered her an 'experiment', as though his desperation to terminate his virginity was less sordid liaison and more research. Now, he was courting the idea that his ménage à trois with Briony and Sandy was passé, given that he had just practiced consensual sex with two women and a man. *A man!*

Struggling with emotional reconciliation, he worried that he'd enjoyed the encounter with Deshaun more than was appropriate, not knowing any longer where the boundaries lay. His mother's conditioning left him conflicted, wrestling with feelings of revulsion and the unadulterated pleasure he had taken from the acts. Two weeks earlier he would have fled the house, appalled at his bedfellow's suggestions, now he was willing to embrace every proposition. A thrill of excitement ran through him at the thought that there might be more to discover.

Slipping from the bed, he crept to the bathroom, appraising himself in the mirror, splashing his face with cold water to establish whether he was dreaming. The water ran across his chin, dripping onto his chest. The door opened and a naked Mei entered. *Hey*, she said, before sitting on the toilet. He listened to her fill the bowl, sneaking a look at her through the mirror. She exhibited no self-consciousness, completely ambivalent to his presence. When she finished, she casually bumped him from the sink so she could wash her hands. *Are you coming back to bed?* she asked, leaving the bathroom without waiting for an answer.

When he returned to bed, Briony and Deshaun were still sleeping, nestling with each other, a somnolent migration drawing them closer. Mei lay alongside, lifting the sheet for Tim to slide into the space next to her. She snuggled close, seeking only warmth, her breathing soon changing as sleep took her. Tim, dispensing with his thoughts, drifted somewhere comfortable.

In the morning, the smell of fresh bread and coffee filled the kitchen. Deshaun lined an array of cereal boxes on the counter. To Tim, they represented iterations of a dreary theme, the arid introduction of fibre into his diet. He craved a sugar fix, hiding his dismay at the absence of Froot Loops or Lucky Charms.

A LITTLE SOMETHING TO HIDE

Behind the closed bathroom door, Tim could hear the shower running. Briony was already at the table, studying her phone. Deshaun pointed to the coffee maker, *Help yourself.*

Briony looked up, *Hi.*

Tim felt removed from himself, other worldly, a participant in a surreal event in which he was the only abnormal person in the room, everyone else displaying archetypal normality. Mei emerged from the bathroom, naked, remnants of steam slipstreaming behind, long dark hair heavy with moisture. She traced a finger over Briony's shoulders as she passed, drifting into the bedroom, reminding Tim that what he considered to be normal two weeks earlier had shifted seismically. No one seemed inclined to mention their shared endeavour, it was as though nothing had happened. Tim was eager to talk to Briony about the previous night but felt uncomfortable in the company of his hosts.

Juice? Deshaun held up a carton of Tropicana. Tim nodded and watched as the hand that had once held him intimately poured him a glass of orange. *You going to Albuquerque?*

Really? It's eight months away, man. We haven't talked about it yet, said Briony before Tim could answer.

What's in Albuquerque? he asked.

Swing-Con, said Briony.

It was a matter-of-fact statement. She said it the same way she would have said Comic-Con, knowing that he understood the event. He weighed the odds of Swing-Con being something other than his first thought, considered those in the room, drew the logical conclusion. Briony didn't ask whether he wanted to attend, but he found himself asking for dates and checking his calendar. He knew without looking that he was rostered to work.

Yeah, I'll go. If Best Buy didn't grant his vacation request, he'd resign. Hell, maybe he'd do that anyway, move north. It was a thought he kept to himself. Too soon.

They agreed that Tim should come to Santa Barbara so they could all travel together. It was another discussion in which his opinions were irrelevant. Once more he found himself sucked into Briony's plans. He felt no resistance, only excitement at the possibilities.

Albuquerque. *What would people wear?* Cosplay at Comic-Con was often revealing. The Joker he could manage, but he doubted his wardrobe would contain anything suitable for Swing-Con.

With Tim back in San Diego, they maintained their relationship using WhatsApp. Briony made it clear that their absence shouldn't curtail their fun. Tim knew what that meant, fought the jealousy that instilled. Her stories involved bars and clubs, evenings with friends, elongated nights. Although she spared him the graphic detail, she couldn't still his imagination.

The pre-Briony status quo reverted for Tim, routine evenings, locked in his room, gaming, hiding from his mother. He didn't mention his web-browsing, some secrets he wanted to keep. Briony guessed. In her usual blunt manner, she asked him if he was doing anything more than jerking off. He admitted to a barren period, neglected to confess the masturbation. After their call, his phone buzzed with a message. *Maybe this will help.* He reacted by snatching the phone to his chest, concealing the image in case his mother had stolen into the room. She hadn't. He took a lingering look. Another message followed. *Show me yours.* He wasn't comfortable reciprocating, vestiges of his mother's morals asserting themselves. Briony was insistent, justifying her need. *If you're gonna do revenge porn, I'll need some insurance.* Before he could change his mind, he checked over his shoulder, freed himself, zoomed in for pride, snapped and hit send.

Just in case you're wondering, fellow travellers, the lecherous old man across the aisle of the coach never did get to see the show.

A LITTLE SOMETHING TO HIDE

LOS ANGELES BUS AND COACH STATION

> **Arrivals**
> Time   From   Expected
> 08:54   Santa Barbara   Expected: 09:36

> **Departures**
> Time   Destination   Expected
> 10:00   Blythe   Delayed: 10:36

LOS ANGELES BUS AND COACH STATION

When the bus reaches Los Angeles, it should be the end of the driver's journey. It isn't. Anthony Briscola wants to offer the fastest coach service in the country, a noble aim tackled through a concoction of dubious innovations.

His buses pause briefly when offloading and reloading passengers, the brevity of each stop a tactic for achieving his goal, but it is the pairing of drivers on longer journeys that represents a more questionable initiative. Rather than pausing for restful breaks, Briscola's drivers work in twos, one to sleep while the other drives. A fully rested crew conflicts with the family's financial goals; they view the cost of overnight accommodation as an unnecessary expense, avoiding the outlay through two-man teams on longer journeys. Briscola is content for each pair to negotiate their time at the wheel. It leads to an absence of universal suffrage – some driver's efforts are more pronounced than others.

The company guarantees it will make the journey from San Francisco to Albuquerque in 28 hours; four hours faster than a Greyhound Bus, and it promises to compensate passengers for missed service levels – conditionally, of course. Both claims are false. There are two certainties with Briscola Coach Services: its buses will run late, and it is impossible to trigger its guarantee criteria.

While deceiving his passengers consumes vast resource and energy, employee rights and healthy working practices are not something with which Anthony Briscola concerns himself. He is unwavering when it comes to the pursuit of union agitators within the workforce, taking hostile action against employee advocates, failing to appreciate that his behaviour is fostering the introduction of the very labour movements he is seeking to eliminate. He is destined never to recognise the paradoxical. He would rather settle his more egregious transgressions in court than meet the additional expense of addressing the root cause, eschewing an obvious irony, that it would save him money. He can admit to no wrongdoing.

The Briscolas also maintain a loose affiliation with the truth, which does little to mask their commercial motivation. The firm's recruitment pages make righteous claims which attempt to disguise the patriarch's parsimony. Its website suggests that its two-man crews expertly navigate the splendour of the US wilderness, adding that 'while one member of the crew unveils the glory of America's vistas, the other indulges in sumptuous rest'. It includes the equally outlandish claim that Briscola Coach Services is the only employer on the planet that encourages its workers to sleep on the job. It's an inconvenient irrelevance that the sleep is restless and that their drivers remain sleep-addled when they re-take the wheel.

Likewise, 'the splendour of the US wilderness', is a misrepresentation of the tarmacked tedium along which its vehicles trundle, following a visual morse code of thin white median stripes; zero, repeated infinitely.

The boasting continues with a video montage of stunning scenery, far from the routes that their buses traverse, and supplemented with a brazen declaration from a falsely magnanimous patriarch. 'Even when they're sleeping, they're getting paid. What other company pays its people to sleep? That's gotta be better than doing nothin' in a lousy hotel.'

It appears from the Briscola Coach Services website that new recruits will be joining an employees' nirvana. It doesn't take long to discover that the fecund marketing masks a barren experience.

The company refers to its snoozing employees as 'sleeping partners', inferring the benefit of equity where there is none. It should be no surprise that the firm amplifies its largess. Sleeping partners earn a quarter of that which they receive when behind the wheel.

Dissenting employees soon discover not to challenge Anthony Briscola's perspective. His retort, that sleeping isn't work, meets protestations of exploitation. It disappoints him that his employees aren't more grateful for what he considers to be a generous allowance. If an employee's complaint continues, the company serves to quiet the issue with a permanent invitation to remain at home, asleep if they like, where the family believe they will discover the true wages of rest.

While the drivers remain, weariness building, most of the passengers step off in Los Angeles. Bobbie James could tell you which of those leaving the bus are craving the Hollywood dream. They wear an air of trepidation that wrestles with contained excitement. It's one of the looks she'd associate with chasing the idyl. The other is determination. Those folks, the ones she'd see as driven, are the ones she knows will be less likely to make the return journey with egos bruised, hearts displaced, and a dull future beckoning.

Those that skulk home will be leaving their two-jobs-to-make-ends-meet lives, having wrestled timetables for auditions, or failed at call backs, adding little more to their palmarès *than uncredited bit parts as film extras. She knows they'll toil for two to three years before they quit, returning to their families, hopes ragged, searching for meaning that may remain elusive. The therapist's couch will replace the casting couch with small fortunes spent on restoring mental health.*

In years past, Bobbie might have stepped off to take a breath of that aspirational air. Some inhale the downtown Los Angeles smog, and it fills them with hope. Others detect the carcinogens of a dangerously hope-filled city.

There are those that fail but stay because they can't leave, their hopes decaying, eroded by failures that become habitual. Some discover demons. Their therapy will come from a bottle, quiet at first, a couple of beers to drown their sorrows, sorrows that deepen, as the liquor hardens. When that's not enough, other stimulants follow. Powders and tabs, pills and extracts, legal and illegal, somewhere in between. Over the counter drugs yield to more powerful tonics; slow drifts into illicit behaviour are as normalised as the normal life they disrupt. Model citizens find their morals softening, not recognising the drift from codified legality into forbidden dominions as the need for the next fix asserts.

A LITTLE SOMETHING TO HIDE

TOBY – LOS ANGELES

Hilary Ames was always telling her son, Toby, that he had big dreams. It wasn't a statement consistent with his thinking. Mostly, he was content just to be, happy with his popularity at high school. A good-looking boy, his mother didn't disabuse him of the belief that he was impossibly handsome. It was a notion that she promoted, one of the few opinions on which they agreed, although he remained modest on the subject. She would speak of it with her friends as though Toby's good looks came from a celestial intervention, as a burden to carry. *It's his eyes,* his mother explained. *They melt hearts.*

When his pale peach fuzz of hair became lustrous and wavy, darkening to an autumnal auburn, Hilary likened him to Samson. She opined that his olive skin, an inheritance from her Greek father, was the sign of Adonis. His cut figure, moulded from unrelenting sessions she commanded as his personal trainer, resembled David. Her son was everything she wanted him to be: sculpted, envied, desired.

Hilary clothed him in designer brands, curating a look, tailoring his image, attempting to push him to the forefront of trends with hasty imitations of magazine fashions. She placed him on a pedestal, cultivating his career, mapping a path. She commissioned photography, headshots galore; enrolled him with agencies, badgering them for assignments where he would pose: cute and gorgeous, cheeky and gorgeous, brooding and gorgeous; just gorgeous. Those genes. *It's so fortunate that my side of the family tree dominates.*

She pushed him, and others. Him forward, others out of the way, ignoring the principles of the Catholic school he attended. Always pushing: onto the stage, out front, shining. Joseph in the Nativity, Charlie in the Chocolate Factory, her boy putting the light into limelight. Hilary kept busy, encouraging his talent, promoting, advocating, selling; getting him noticed.

She never saw what was obvious to others, the wooden performances, teachers whispering prompts from the side of the stage, Toby straining to hear the words that he'd forgotten, Hilary blaming the Director for undermining her boy's talent. The other mothers nodded in agreement to escape her ire, hiding their eye-rolling, deferring their gossip for coffees around kitchen tables where she was too overbearing to receive an invite.

One line; asking for a room, that's all he had to do. He bungled Joseph's line in the school's Nativity. *Can we have a manger please?* The Innkeeper, flustered into improvisation, offered Mary and Joseph a room, cheeks blossoming rosé at his mistake as the school's moms and dads laughed at the faux pas.

The Innkeeper hissed at Joseph after the show, calling him a dummy for getting it wrong and ruining his part. Toby didn't interpret the audience's reaction as good-natured chuckling, feeling the rising heat of humiliation at the Innkeeper's justified outburst. He launched himself at his mother, tears streaming. She subverted his anguish by telling him how great he had been, how his brilliance had lightened the mood. Even as a five-year-old, Toby knew that Joseph's part wasn't a comic role.

His mother's belief was undiminished. She enrolled him in drama clubs, appointed a voice coach, pushed him into ballet. Ballet led to complaints of bullying, she conceded – partially. She moved him to a contemporary dance group. Dance, she told him, was important to his development as a performer. The bullies didn't make a distinction, the taunts continued.

In his final year at middle school, he auditioned for Charlie and the Chocolate Factory, pleasing himself that his performance earned him the role of Mike TV. It didn't matter that only four boys auditioned, or that Kiara Abrahams, the young teacher producing the show, debated whether it might be better to rename the character Michelle, giving the part to a more promising actress. Toby was unaware of her deliberations and wouldn't have been surprised, or too upset, to learn he'd only just avoided the baked orange make-up of an Oompa Loompa. He was content to play Mike TV; he could stroll the stage for much of the play, looking good, avoiding the pressure that came from holding the spotlight. He thought that would satisfy his mother. It didn't. She lobbied the school, badgering Miss Abrahams to elevate her son to the starring role. A weary Miss Abrahams refused to make the change, patiently explaining that it wouldn't be fair to Andy Miller – to Charlie.

Hilary's pursed lips and raised eyebrows signalled her disbelief at the junior teacher's temerity. She considered the girl naïve, finding her obstinacy an irritant to circumnavigate. She noted the slight, spawned a grudge for future churning, and chose to ignore Kiara Abrahams' opinion.

Loitering in the corridor of the administrative block, she manufactured a coincidental meeting with Gloria Armitage, the school's principal.

It's looking tired, don't you think? she said, indicating the school's trophy cabinet. *The school's achievements deserve something a little more ... sophisticated.*

Gloria had been in her position long enough to recognise a conditional offer, wondering whether it would require a harmless intervention or offend her sensibilities, knowing too, that harmless intervention rarely sufficed. She listened attentively as Hilary painted a lavish picture of how resplendent a new cabinet would look in the foyer. Gloria indulged her, waiting for her to raise her point and reveal the motivation for her generosity.

When it appeared, it didn't take her long to reflect on Hilary's offer. She studied the old cabinet and the bruises it carried: the cracked glass panel, its chipped woodwork, the scuffed exterior. She thought about the impact of her decision and how an impressive new cabinet would improve the image of the school.

Gloria Armitage was a pragmatist and an excellent manager. Despite budgetary constraints, she ran her school

A LITTLE SOMETHING TO HIDE

well. It was a generous offer. She knew too, that Hilary had a powerful voice on the school's Parent Association, with a proven ability to rally a caustic consensus when provoked. But Principal Armitage was also an educator, with a career established on the bedrock of a fundamental and unwavering principle, that of putting the children first. She agreed with Mrs Ames; a new cabinet would be a magnificent addition to the school's foyer. Toby's mother felt a transitory flush of triumph, which faded quickly when Gloria Armitage added her *But*.

There were many memories tied to the existing cabinet and the trophies that sat within. The scars it bore each told a tale; Larry Pinkerton, winner of a skateboarding trophy, was responsible for the gouged woodwork, his proficiency deserting him when his nonchalant flick of the board ended not in his hands but clattered into the side of the cabinet. The crack in the glass occurred as Jodi Lorenzo, the captain of the soccer team, lifted her team's prize high for the local newspaper to snatch a picture, only for the base to separate from the polished trophy and canon into the glass. The incidents, worrying at the time, but soon remembered fondly, flashed through Gloria's mind and she politely declined Hilary's offer. *The cabinet's got character*, she suggested. *It would be a shame to see it go*.

Chastened, but unperturbed, Hilary directed her offensive to Andy Miller's mother, inviting her to coffee, where she talked of Toby's distress. She invented his tears, his crippling insomnia, and her concerns about his mental health. She begged Andy's mother to intervene, appealing to her humanity.

Lori Miller's empathy for Toby's plight was genuine, even if the facts surrounding it were not. She knew Hilary was manipulating her, exploiting her nurturing instinct. Lori was genuinely concerned that the casting of the school play was distressing Toby, but she was not about to tear the tightly threaded weave that binds a mother to her son. She was justifiably proud that Andy had secured the lead and wasn't about to undermine him for the sake of Hilary Ames, a woman actively disliked, yet tolerated by the community in the interests of harmony.

Lori cooed in the right places, knowing Hilary regarded her as prey. There was no subtlety to Hilary, no stealth, Lori could see the attack coming. *Can't Andy help? Toby's desperate,* Hilary claimed. *I'm worried about what might happen if he doesn't get the role.*

At the mention of her son's name, Lori's resolve stiffened. She didn't harbour vicarious ambitions for her son, she wanted what most parents declare they want for their children – happiness; that sentiment that parents universally express when they're hiding their ambitions, too embarrassed or reticent to speak their minds. Happiness is safe. Impossible to challenge or dismiss. An admission of anything less would be deficient. In Lori's case, however, wanting happiness for her son was profoundly true.

Hilary sensed the hardening of Lori's resolve and felt the chances of the role she coveted for her son slipping away. The nativist school-mom, with unchecked ambition, was a playground guerrilla. If a simple plea wasn't working, she would sink lower, drawing on guilt and pride, manipulating the desired outcome, not caring that Lori would loathe herself or that it would be corrosive to the relationship that Lori enjoyed with her son.

Hilary didn't contemplate the consequences for the Millers; they were irrelevant to her aims. She didn't consider her actions as scheming, the impulses governing her behaviour were entirely natural. *What mother,* she reasoned to herself, *wouldn't do the same for the well-being of her son?* By her reckoning, her actions were both normal and justified.

She feigned embarrassment, a reluctance to speak, apologising for nearly saying too much, for straying too close to an ancient situation that was damaging to both their boys. *No,* she decided out loud, *it's best not to go there.*

Lori Miller knew she shouldn't speak. She knew the tactics, knew that she should let an uncomfortable silence develop between them and avoid being the one to break it; she should let Hilary be the one to concede the advantage by speaking first. But Lori wasn't like Hilary. Hilary was content to sit blowing the heat from her coffee, peering above the rim of her cup, waiting for the silence to break, focused on Lori, and waiting for her to wilt under the expectation of her stare. She knew Lori would crack, because Lori suffered the very ailment on which Hilary planned to prevail. An ailment not remotely afflicting her, a weakness she didn't suffer. Lori Miller was *nice*. The words fell from Lori's mouth before she could stop them. *Go where?*

When she thought about it later, wracked with the guilt from what she had done, Lori suffered a grudging admiration for the depths to which Hilary Ames was prepared to mine on behalf of her son. It pained her to think about the manipulation, how easily it occurred and worse, how she had succumbed.

Hilary exploited Lori's weaknesses, knowing she'd be susceptible, knowing that her guilt, combined with her *niceness* would see her yielding, righting a perceived wrong that Hilary claimed had left an indelible mark on Toby. Hilary also knew that Lori cared about what other people thought. She wasn't going to leave it to guilt alone.

Where her son lacked performance skills, Hilary excelled. She sighed the sigh of the reticent, bracing herself for the unwilling testimony that she was about to deliver. She laid a foundation that what she was about to betray would be painful for them both, inviting Lori to stop her, knowing the moment had already passed when Lori could escape the unfolding narrative. *I know I shouldn't dredge the past*, she said, *but it haunts him.*

Knowing the question would implicate her son but unable to stop, Lori asked, *What?*

The taunting.

There was more than a hint of melodrama. Hilary revealed her pain, as well as her son's, from the time when Andy teased Toby about his dancing. *I know he didn't mean to bully him, but, well ... Wouldn't it be awful for your family if others knew what happened? Perhaps Andy could help him now.*

TOBY – LOS ANGELES

Lori Miller bristled. Her son wasn't a bully, just easily led. Even in the gilded light with which mothers see their sons, she could envisage Andy's participation. Worse than the implied bullying, was Hilary's not so veiled threat. *Wouldn't it be awful for your family if others knew?* If she didn't get her way, Lori knew that Hilary would broadcast a malevolent version of the incident, fortifying a scandal that some might choose to believe.

The instinct to protect her son withered under the veiled threat. The threat sat between them, pregnant with malice. Fighting to control her seething, Lori said nothing, knowing that anything she voiced would risk an escalation. This time, Hilary was happy to break the silence, knowing she had won. *More coffee?* An innocent offer laden with the heavy notes of a woman bearing an impossible load. It carried the weight of managing her child's fabricated anxiety, as though the effort of making another cup was as burdensome as the care she'd provided to her broken child.

No thanks, said Lori. She'd had enough of listening to the woman's lament.

Ignoring the remains of her coffee, Lori made excuses to leave, offering a pre-emptive apology in case Andy was too upset to change, promising an intervention, knowing that only one outcome would gratify Hilary. She pounded the driveway to her car, defeated, accelerating from the house with the heavy footedness of the angry.

Watching the oversized SUV until it disappeared, Hilary allowed a satisfied smirk to play on her lips; there was always a button she could push. She knew that Lori would be wrestling with her dilemma on the way home, agonising over the words to justify her request.

The boy would suffer hurt, which Hilary considered appropriate penance for the pain he had caused from long forgotten taunts. It didn't matter to her that she exaggerated her claims, possibly even constructed them. It was enough for her to believe that Andy Miller *might* have been involved; his mother would have to pay the price for her son's transgressions.

The dredging of a long-held grudge, with details of the incident lost to the past, would bear fruit. It was why quarrels should fester, never forgiven. There was always a dividend to collect. *That'll teach her,* she thought, and without the slightest hint of self-reflection, *It's always the mother's fault.* She almost allowed a flicker of compassion to pass for Andy, to hope that his heart would mend, but she was crueller than that.

On the drive home, Lori ran through scenarios, each one more uncomfortable. The slender hands gripping the SUV's steering wheel manifested tension, knuckles threatening to penetrate pale skin. Her jaw ached from clenching, angst building as she contemplated the relationship she was about to damage. Even if Andy remained oblivious to her intent, unsuspecting of her motives, *she* would always know. She was about to undermine her son's confidence by persuading him that the lead role might be too big for him. Despite her anger and self-loathing, she would do what Hilary wanted, encouraging Andy to speak with Miss Abrahams, to ask her if he could play Mike TV.

His reaction surprised her. She'd convinced herself that he would be distraught. Instead, he was concerned only for Toby, explaining that he seemed happy to be Mike TV. Andy worried that the switch might upset him. The boy, alleged to have been a bully, was showing considerable compassion for his former victim.

That should have triggered Lori, but Hilary's deception subsumed rational thought. Her son was right, but still she pressed. Disgust would follow later, borne of the knowledge that her insistence was self-serving, that her arguments weren't to improve Toby's welfare, but to avoid Hilary's wrath.

That conclusion lay some way off, waiting until after she spoke with her son. The whisper of sense that nibbled at her conscience went unheeded, too faint to hear. Any doubts she had were growing too slowly to still her argument, floating beyond reach. She continued, knowingly damaging their bond, telling her son that the role of Charlie might take too much time from his studies, that his focus should be on attaining good grades. She appealed to his inherent goodness, leveraged their love, told him he should do it for her.

She could see his confusion when she suggested that he was less of a boy than she once believed, saw the flash of hurt when invoking their love as a tool to persuade. They both knew he would do it because he loved her. She could almost hear the rupture in their relationship. *Talk to Miss Abrahams*, she implored. *She will understand*, hating herself as she said it; Hilary Ames could do that to a person.

By the time he found Miss Abrahams, the remnants of his tears had disappeared, long since seeping into his mother's cashmere sweater when she tried to hug away his pain. Her hugs usually made him feel better, although the last one didn't seem to come from the same source as others. It ended too soon, an action that bemused him in much the same way as her insistence on swapping roles with Toby.

Andy outlined his reasoning with Kiara Abrahams who assured the boy of her confidence in him, restoring a fragment of the self-esteem that his mother had unintentionally eroded. Miss Abrahams convinced him that he would be perfect in the role, a boy made for the stage. Her words were comforting, so was her hug, in a way his mother's wasn't, but he maintained his certainty, trying to convince her that Toby Ames would make a better Charlie.

Still holding the boy tight, Kiara recognised the intercession of Toby's mother and marvelled at the meanness, the callous calculation that led one mother to manipulate another into betraying her son, caring nothing for the aftermath.

Kiara liked Toby; he had a gentleness that his mother's ruthlessness failed to spoil; the soft eyes of the child remained despite his mother's toxicity. Kiara wasn't as naïve as Hilary believed, she understood the machinations of the playground, appreciating that Hilary would be relentless in pursuing the change; the inevitable rested heavily on her shoulders.

She wasn't surprised when Toby paled at the prospect of taking on the bigger role. In addition to the heightened attention and the extra dialogue, he dreaded 'The Candy Man', Charlie's musical solo. He was happy as Mike TV, warming to the part. His good looks and noble stature lent itself to playing a spoilt, wealthy child. Kiara couldn't overlook the irony that she hadn't typecast him, despite the influence of his mother.

She admired the dignity of Andy as he encouraged Toby to take the part, telling him how much better he would be as Charlie. They both knew it was untrue, but both had the good sense not to argue. Toby checked that Andy was sure. Andy convinced him the change was best for everyone. Hilary was thrilled that, finally, someone recognised her son's talent.

Several mothers in the audience cast glances at Hilary who sat enraptured as she watched her son perform. Many of them thought, unkindly, that she should seek a refund for her son's vocal training. She didn't notice their scornful looks, transfixed as she was on her boy, but she did notice how they congratulated Lori on Andy's performance as Mike TV rather than marvelling at Toby's.

Hilary wouldn't allow her son to be despondent with his performance. He felt he had let his friends down, felt that the rest of the cast had performed better than him. She told him that it was normal for an *artiste* to feel that way, reminding him that it was innate to be harsh in self-reflection. *It demonstrates genius,* she said, reassuring him of his brilliance, telling him how he had carried the others. They embraced, his mother administering her usual half a hug, before reminding him of his greatness.

It was the same when he got to high school. She manipulated and schemed, hounding talent agencies until they found him assignments. They too yielded to her pressure, grateful that her son's appearance allowed them to find assignments to satisfy some of her whims. They found work that drew on his smile and good looks; dialogue never featured. Her embellishments didn't mask the truth; that he was a good-looking boy with an overbearing mother. She pushed and pushed, they yielded, as Toby yielded, to satisfy her vicarious need for fame.

She rationalised the absence of speaking parts, believing that Toby had outpaced the local scene. He was destined for greatness, he needed more powerful representation, a chance to pursue his career in the place where his fame came with a guarantee. Hilary focused her efforts on finding West Coast opportunities. The agents were more cynical, harder to break down. But she was formidable, she knew she would prevail.

The Toby Ames shaped by his mother stepped off a United Airlines flight at LAX. He didn't sniff the air for inspiration or hope, there was no need. His mother believes that a star on Hollywood Boulevard is an inevitability, preordained. He has the looks, the background, the training, the pedigree. It is his destiny. Toby will be everything that she has told him he will be. She has shaped him for success, it is in the stars; he will be a star.

If Bobbie James saw him when he arrived, she wouldn't have seen either of the looks she expects from LA's hopeful migrants. Determination didn't harden Toby's features when he stepped off the plane, neither did excited trepidation. Toby Ames looked anxious. He'd had 21 years of his mother telling him how great he will be, and he knew that for 21 years, she'd been lying to him. His motivation to step off the plane stemmed not from a desire to succeed in Hollywood, but from a fear of disappointing her. From his earliest days he had bent to her will.

There were no agents waiting for Toby when he stepped off the plane; no polished limo ready to whisk him to a luxury hotel. The paparazzi missed the memo. The screaming fans were crying themselves hoarse at someone else's party. He waited for his suitcase at the baggage carousel with other bored passengers, all mustering the energy to find their way to hotels or Airbnbs where they could ease their weariness.

He'd noticed a long-limbed slender woman at the front of the plane when he boarded; they exchanged knowing smiles. Hers gave him something to think about for the journey, he wondered if he'd had the same effect on her. She was the only passenger paying for the privilege of additional legroom, it bought her a hastier exit. He searched for her. She wasn't waiting with the other tired souls for their luggage. She had vanished, along with her laptop and handbag, scurrying to whatever business awaited her. Toby imagined that she was off to a studio to negotiate on behalf of one of her clients. He hoped his agent would look like her. He hoped he had an agent.

He scouted the terminal for celebrities, wanting to glimpse an A-lister travelling the concourse, suffering disappointment. He imagined that people would one day be searching the building, just as he was now, and spot him, nudging their travelling companions, asking, *Is that Toby Ames?* The likelihood felt remote.

His mother had tapped the address for his accommodation into his Uber app, ready for his transfer to what she had told everyone was his Hollywood apartment. She neglected to mention the *LAX-it* pickup point at the airport, his driver impatiently telling him that's where he was waiting. By the time he'd found it, he was feeling considerably less like the Hollywood star his mother had boosted him to be.

The car meandered along the 405. Bored commuters surrounded him, casting glances before turning away, disinterested. The traffic stalled frequently; irritated drivers glared boreholes in the heads of the drivers ahead of them. He reflected on the opening sequence of *LA LA LAND*, wondering whether a spontaneous song and dance routine would break out. An angry looking Latino in a battered Chevy scowled at him. He didn't look the singing type, more of a fighter than a dancer, Toby looked away before he could discover which. The Uber driver's console suggested they still had 30 minutes of driving ahead of them. They inched forward. The next time Toby looked, the read-out said 32 minutes.

Any feeling of self-importance vanished when the driver dropped him on the roadside outside his accommodation. The quarters were different to the image his mother had painted. It was a pokey cabin, assembled in the corner of a residential yard, costing sixty dollars a night. Hilary had found it in North Hollywood on Airbnb, not admitting to Toby or herself that it was far from the glamour of the Hollywood she would have people believe was his new home. *It's just for a week, until your agent finds you something more appropriate.*

Toby negotiated his suitcase into the tiny building, little more than a shed in his landlord's backyard. He took a tour of his new home; it didn't take long to explore the 160 square feet. A Valencia orange door, garishly luminescent, opened into a narrow kitchenette containing a small table. He looked about the tiny room and noted the presence of a single chair. A table for one. To the back of the room was a sink resting above two cupboards that occupied most of the space. To the right was a small free-standing fridge, tucked under a bench on which stood a microwave oven. There were no other facilities for cooking or heating water. Toby's culinary development would stall.

A door off the kitchen led into the bedroom which contained a single bed and a bedside table hosting a shadeless lamp. A transparent bulb, cloaked in a crust of burnt dust, poked into the air; it taunted of long lonely nights. When he wheeled his suitcase into the room, he couldn't access the table without first climbing onto the bed. He flicked the switch of the lamp; a faint pop followed a flash of illumination as the bulb shone its last. He sighed and opened the drawer beneath, hoping to find a spare. There was none. He glanced around the room for other sources of light, the walls and ceiling were bare.

Continuing his exploration, he entered the last of the cabin's rooms, a slender space created by the addition of a thin partition wall to form a bathroom. The entrance frame held no door. A faded fabric curtain, displaying images of migrating geese, hung from a wooden rail, falling a foot short of the floor, and affording the extent of the bathroom's privacy. For a lone occupant, the privacy was adequate, albeit the smell of the room would follow him to bed. Another curtain, vinyl, with a cosmic print of purples, blues, and shades of black, hung across a miniscule cubicle housing a large showerhead, green with algae. The curtain, he knew, would cling to him whenever he showered, leaving a slimy film each time he peeled it away.

Alongside the toilet pedestal stood a slim-profiled sink, positioned beneath a mirrored wall-cabinet, with little space between the two. When he brushed his teeth later, his head hit the cabinet, gouging a small notch from his forehead. An alarming level of blood seeped from the wound, panicking Toby into thinking the injury was serious. Divining the futility of his effort, he clamped a hand to his head and searched the tiny house for first aid provisions. Finding none, he opted for folded sheets of toilet paper and formed a compress to staunch the flow. When eventually it subsided, he examined himself in the mirror. Fragments of bloodied paper clung to the wound. *There goes my first audition,* he thought.

His host's opinion, that the rooms provided a cosy sanctuary from the glamour and glitz of Hollywood, wasn't one he shared. Nor did he think that being two miles from North Hollywood's underground Metro was a feature worth promoting. He considered the thirty-minute walk to the station a chore that would blight his mornings.

The information provided by his host also noted that there was a supermarket within two blocks, a fortunate point, having nearly exhausted the supply of toilet paper on his head-wound. He searched unsuccessfully for a spare roll before deciding to go in search of supplies and something to eat. Given the hyperbolic description of the cabin, he doubted the area would be awash with the claimed plethora of multi-ethnic restaurants.

Finding a Rite Aid on Victory Boulevard, he bought a noodle bowl, a lightbulb, and the provisions he needed for his bathroom. Across the road, a large red sign with white lettering read *LIQUOR*. Beneath it, another proclaimed *ADULT BOOKS ARCADE*, promising toys, DVDs, lotions, and potions. The store, Jason's Adult, carried a name that posed more questions than it answered, conjuring images of a vaguely paedophilic guardian standing watch over the eponymous youngster.

TOBY – LOS ANGELES

He crossed the road to enter the liquor store. Two men looking passably vagrant stood outside, waving fingers at each other, passing a brown paper bag back and forth, taking turns to drink whatever livener dwelt within. They watched him enter the shop, keeping their thoughts to themselves, but their eyes fixed. Was it watchful wariness or were they measuring malice, Toby couldn't tell, he scurried past, head lowered, oozing passivity. The bag exchanged hands again.

Daylight was receding. Before long, neon lights would be punching a glow into a doleful Los Angeles evening. The night promised to bring creatures to the street that were likely to cast more than just suspicious glances. The sanctuary of his compact lodgings suddenly appealed; he figured it was going to be a long week.

The following day, Toby discovered what constituted a plethora of restaurants when he walked in the opposite direction on Victory Boulevard. The outlets of a grubby strip mall included Lam's Thai & Chinese and Mi Carbonero, a restaurant boasting authentic Salvadorean cuisine, an assertion that meant nothing to Toby. The claim was the only thing written in English. Toby eyed the pictures of the food beneath the Spanish descriptions with suspicion, reflecting that the marketing image of a Big Mac bears little resemblance to the product served. If the picture of the Tamales was the personification of the product, the actuality was not something he was willing to face. He took down the phone number above Lam's and hoped that they delivered.

He sidled further down the strip to see what food the Iglesia Restauracion Palabra Viva might offer, only to discover that his Spanish language skills were wanting. *Food for the soul*, he later thought, wandering back to his cabin, and wondering what might be happening to his.

His mother had told him that she had booked the accommodation in North Hollywood because it was close to his agent. He questioned her research methods and the credentials of any agent that chose this location to establish their business. The area didn't pulse with the vibrancy she promised. Toby suspected she was a long way down her list of agents before finding one willing to add him to their roster; he wasn't hoping for much at their scheduled meeting the following day.

Standing outside 5636 Tujunga Ave, sweltering from the humid bake off the street, Toby felt overdressed in a navy-blue checked suit with a too tight floral tie. Hilary insisted that he make a good impression, stressing her certainty that agents worked harder for clients who cared about appearances. She'd selected his clothes, saying the suit embodied power, telegraphed confidence, attracted attention. A fly buzzed close, persistent, avoiding his languid swipe, skirting his forehead. Attention, yes, but not in the form his mother had hoped.

He arrived fifteen minutes early, dread roiling his stomach. A stretched vinyl banner fixed to the wall of a grey and blue building announced the Actors' Equity Association – a union. At one end, in block capitals were the words *MEMBERSHIP & RECEPTION*. *AUDITION CENTER* appeared at the other. He rang the bell marked reception and a disembodied voice asked if it could help. He tried to sound casual as he introduced himself, but a whine of tension elevated his pitch, betraying his anxiety. A metallic buzz released the door lock, signalling his invitation to enter. He stepped into a room with an open plan reception, plush furnishings and the cheery woman belonging to the disembodied voice. She smiled as he approached the desk, adjusting a camera that sat on a large monitor, preparing to take a picture for his security pass.

He stole a glance at his phone for surety before asking to see Marcia Rodriguez. The receptionist indicated the camera, *tsk-ing* at the resulting photo. *You can do better. I need your best red-carpet smile*, she said, winking.

Reflexively, he smiled with a sensuality that he didn't feel. His mother had trained him to pout.

Ooh, much better. She printed his pass, telling him to take a seat. Clipping the pass to his jacket, he noticed the misspelling of his name, *TOBIE AIMS*. His hope for a fruitful appointment ebbed further.

TOBY – LOS ANGELES

Marcia Rodriguez entered the reception, extending an arm as she walked across the room. Toby stood to greet her, shaking her hand. His earlier misgivings vanished. She looked formidable, exquisitely tailored in a burgundy A-line dress, cinched tight at the waist, every inch the professional. For the first time since he'd landed in California, his anxiety eased. He made a mental note to thank his mother, chiding himself for the prejudice that had coloured his thinking. Marcia invited him to follow her to her office, down a corridor with headshots adorning the walls, faces that he recognised, stars of television and cinema. He began to think his mother had succeeded in finding a prolific agent. His self-doubt began to fade, allowing a trickle of hope to flow.

Marcia Rodriguez' nameplate proclaimed her as Senior Business Representative. She invited him to take one of the chairs that surrounded a large table in a corner of the room. She poured herself a coffee before offering him a cup. He accepted, his mood lightening; his optimism growing.

It vanished quickly when she asked him to tell her about the trouble he was having with his agent. She referred to her notes, casually flicking through the pages of a notebook to the day when she'd taken the call from Hilary. His hopes wilted with each flick of the page, knowing that he was about to discover his mother's failure to discern Marcia Rodriguez' role. He could almost hear his mother's voice as Marcia parroted the phrases that he had so often heard her use down the phone. He noted the omission of *'finding'* between the words *'trouble with'* and *'your agent'*.

He massaged his eyebrows with thumb and forefinger as Marcia recounted the discussion with his mother, noting its one-dimensional nature. Mumbling an apology, he grew increasingly mortified as he explained the misunderstanding. Marcia was kind, taking neither umbrage nor finding humour in Hilary's mistake. Her sympathy made it worse. It felt as though she was making a concession to someone with a retarded capacity to comprehend simple concepts. He could feel his cheeks reddening the more she allowed for the error.

A LITTLE SOMETHING TO HIDE

The futility of his situation began to percolate. There was no representation, no auditions, no roles to fill. He had arrived to nowhere and found nothing. He asked some hopeful questions: fielded, answered, despatched. None led him to opportunities. The pity in Marcia's eyes stung as he implored her for help. It was her turn to apologise, there was little that she could do.

She sat quietly, waiting for him to appreciate that their interview was at an end, too kind to press him to leave, not wanting to add to his hurt. Averting his gaze before she could see that he was on the verge of tears, he thanked her, rising as she stood, allowing her to escort him to reception. When they got there, the receptionist handed her a note. She read it as Toby was reaching for the door. *Wait a minute, Toby. I need to make a quick call.* She disappeared into the heart of the building without waiting for his response, returning fifteen minutes later to pass him a handwritten note. *Call the number. They may have something in the morning.*

The number put him through to Ricky Stevens, whose office was off Sunset Boulevard. The agent gushed positivity; his every word delivered with a zealot's passion. He invited Toby to visit him the next day. *Bring your head shots. There's a strong chance we'll have something for you.* Toby allowed himself the barest wave of optimism, tempered by the experience from earlier in the day. He went home via Metros Beer and Wine on Victory Boulevard, grabbing a six-pack of Coors Light. A celebration seemed in order.

The LA evening was oppressive, his cabin lacked air-conditioning or windows that opened. Stripping to his underwear was the simplest way to keep cool, that and another can of chilled beer. The accommodation had no TV but offered a flaky WiFi connection from the main house. He sat on the bed, ear buds in, buffering his way through early episodes of House of Cards. He considered Frank Underwood a lucky bastard to be married to a woman relaxed about him having a piece on the side. He wondered if success in Hollywood would look anything like a career in fictional DC.

TOBY – LOS ANGELES

He hoped so, draining the last of his beers as an episode came to an end, before taking his imagination with him to the shower.

In the morning, he shook off a mild hangover. Toby was still young and fit enough to do that easily, congratulating himself on how well he could manage the booze, and how liberating it was to be able to drink without his mother's constant nagging. He contemplated his freedom from her, deciding that having a drink later would be an acceptable way of celebrating his escape. He wondered whether there might be a store selling decent wine on Sunset Boulevard, the selection at Metros targeted the less discerning.

Ricky Stevens had boundless enthusiasm and a fashion sense anchored to the 80s. His white linen suit and blue collarless shirt held echoes of Miami Vice. He effected a Crockett swagger as he ushered Toby into his office, greeting him as though they were great friends, previously separated by eons and continents. He wrapped an arm around Toby, guiding him through the door. Toby surveyed the room; it was smaller than the one he had been in yesterday. Ricky sensed a flash of doubt in his new client, promising him that although it looked modest, the rent was not.

Toby hadn't suffered the perceived doubt. Instead, he was trying to appear unimpressed. Not for the first time, his performance skills failed him. He suspected that Ricky was good at his work; the furnishing in the office was sleek, contemporary, and expensive. An iMac sat on the corner of a glass-topped table with polished chrome legs. There were no traces of cables, the only other items Toby could see were a mouse and a keyboard. No drawers or paperwork cluttered the office. To the side of the room stood a smaller table of the same design, which held a slender crystal decanter, the condensation indicating iced water within. Two highball glasses stood alongside the decanter, Ricky pointed a finger at the table, implying Toby should help himself. He declined, sitting opposite the agent. The chill from the air-conditioning had purged the heat from the room, leaving him cold and uncomfortable under the critical gaze of Ricky Stevens.

For an hour he grilled Toby about his capabilities, exploring every detail, understanding his past performances, challenging his motivations, delving into his methods, questioning his passion. He poured over the portfolio of images that Toby brought with him, cooing over his physique, sharing his love of Toby's image, convincing Toby that he certainly had *something*, not *someone*, with which he could work.

Toby didn't once mention his mother, but for the entire time that he was with Ricky Stevens, it felt as though she was in the room.

The agent gushed that Toby had massive potential. *With Ricky Stevens you're in great hands,* the agent said, devoid of all humility. They shook hands on the promise that Ricky would call him the following day. *Hopefully*, he added, *with something to think about*. It was a parting shot that encouraged Toby to go in search of a wine shop. He chose a Chardonnay. The sun was up, the evening warm, he had no facility to barbecue and justify a Zinfandel.

When he returned to North Hollywood, he put the wine in the fridge and changed to go for a run. *Just a short one, a few blocks*, he thought, planning a route past the Actors' Equity Association in the hope of bumping into Marcia Rodriguez. *I'll offer to buy her a drink if I see her*. It was an audacious thought – and ineffective; he didn't spot her. Instead of continuing up Tujunga Avenue, he ran a few times around the block on which the Association's building stood. It was just after 5pm and the doors to the Association opened from time to time, disgorging its employees. Marcia wasn't among them; he decided that someone in her position probably wouldn't watch the clock before leaving. He settled on a plan to run later the next time. He returned to his cabin, via the liquor store, where he reached for the emergency twenty-dollar bill he had tucked in his phone holder. He grabbed a few beers, something to have while he waited for Lam's to deliver and before opening the wine. Things were looking up.

TOBY – LOS ANGELES

He woke later the next day, sunlight invading the room through his blindless windows, radiating, heating him to a state of muddled wakefulness. Lids heavy, he opened his eyes to admit the day before covering them with a forearm to lessen the glare, moving his tongue, seeking moisture where there was none, feeling the sting of dehydration. Massaging the grit from his eyes, he turned himself out of bed, feet resting on the floor. A cockroach scuttled beneath the bed. He didn't react, watching instead with a glum curiosity. His head was thicker this morning, which he attributed to the heat rather than the beer and wine. A shower would help.

Still dripping, he checked his phone and was surprised to see that it was already 11am. He had missed three calls, all from his mother. He didn't have the energy to call her. He'd wait until he'd spoken with Ricky so he could share the great news. It would lessen the inevitable skirmish that would follow when he told her of her mistake with Marcia Rodriguez. Unless he had news from Ricky, he doubted he'd have the resolve to mention the issue, besides which, he needed more money and an extension to the cabin booking. He'd have to take his mother's medicine if she were going to provide more support.

Ricky didn't call that day, or the next. His mother did, placing multiple calls that went unanswered. Toby still had some money; certain he could get by until he'd spoken with the agent. He phoned him on the third day and asked him if the job had come up. Ricky was unabashed with his enthusiasm. *Whoa. That's amazing*, he gushed. *I was literally about to ring you, Tony. Unbe-fucking-lievable coincidence.* He had one mode of delivery, excitable. He made the news of the lost opportunity sound positive. He remained upbeat, effusive, certain that there would be other gigs. *It's inevitable with your talent, Tony. I just can't say when.* He urged Tony to keep in touch. *I'm here twenty-four seven, Man. I'll call you soon.* He promised to work tirelessly for Tony.

Toby hung up and went looking for a bar. He found one on Oxnard Street, Michael's Pub. The sign outside proclaimed Music, Darts and Pool, adopting North Hollywood's propensity for exaggeration by suggesting a cocktail bar. There were no windows, but he noted the happy hour between 4 and 7pm; he was keen to stretch his mother's money as far as he could. That promise was the building's only redemptive feature; it was otherwise grimy in keeping with the aesthetic of the street.

The only natural light in the bar came in through a door held open by a traffic cone. The absence of bright light was no bad thing, illumination would not improve the interior. Bank notes from countries that none of the regulars had visited festooned the ceiling above the bar. Few could claim exotic travel much beyond losing trips to Las Vegas. Behind the bar, shelves laden with spirits gave merit to the possibility of a cocktail; it was an unconvincing testimony.

There was no fluttering of saloon doors as Toby entered, yet the bar's occupants fell silent, pausing. The click of a pool ball greeted him as he crossed the threshold. The ball failed to find its intended hole. The player making the shot traced Toby's entry. Toby looked at him and his playing partner and felt in the presence of a ZZ Top tribute act. He couldn't see behind their glasses, but he was convinced the shades were concealing an accusatory look.

There were two others in the room, pot-bellied specimens perched on high stools at the bar. They swapped grunts as they watched a Dodgers game on a skittish plasma screen. The Dodgers trailed by the only run of the game, bottom of the ninth, bases loaded, no one out. Toby stood alongside them at a distance he judged to be beyond the range of a pudgy arm, watching the game, not daring to comment lest he wound whatever karma it was that governed proceedings, waiting for someone to serve him.

The next batter fouled four times, the first and fourth hits sailing deep into distant stands, the wrong side of either foul line, leading the commentators into a frenzy of superlative possibilities. A pitching coach entered the fray, an unheard discussion ensued beneath the commentators' barked mundanities.

TOBY – LOS ANGELES

The pause in play saw one of the bar dwellers nudge the other. It prompted the nudgee to look again at Toby. Toby could sense the contempt in the scrutiny. He wondered whether he should say something, thought better of it, settling instead for a cautious smile which earned him a grunt. Evidently the man had decided that Toby wasn't going to leave, irritated that a customer had interrupted his viewing. He waddled with a lack of urgency to the opposite side of the bar, putting his hands wide, leaning forward. He didn't smile. His posture implied a challenge rather than an invitation to order. Toby pointed at the only beer pump on the bar and mumbled, *Pint*, hoping that was the appropriate way to order a beer. He didn't add a *Please* or *Thank you*, he suspected that an economy of words was the accepted norm in Michael's Pub.

As if to confirm his thought, the barman took a pint from above the bar without comment, effecting a cursory introduction to the rinser, before filling the glass. The pump spat alternate belches of beer and foam, froth dominating the pour. Placing the head-heavy drink in front of Toby, he resumed his insolent pose, waiting for payment, not caring at the paucity of beer settling in the bottom. Toby took twenty dollars from his wallet but hesitated before handing the money across, instead using the note to point at the foamy mass, finding the temerity to ask for a top up, knowing that failure to assert himself would result in self-emasculation. He earned a scowl and the reluctant fill of his glass, froth slopping over the side into the drip tray below. Toby passed the note over, nodding *Thanks*, and fighting a grimace as his change settled in the dregs on the bar. Sliding the damp notes into his pocket, he escaped to a corner of the room where he thought he'd cause the least offence.

The prospect of Michael's Pub having the facility to support Toby's browsing needs seemed a thin prospect. With little hope of finding it, he scanned the room for a WiFi code, opting to use data when realising his doubts. He contemplated asking if a network was available, starting to rise, then settled again quickly as he earned another glare from the barman, who sensed further demands on his services and an extended delay to his baseball viewing. Subdued, Toby buried his enquiry, deciding it would be a push too far in the direction of vexation.

The barman heaved himself onto his stool to resume watching the game, flinging expletives at the screen as the Dodgers failed to convert their loaded bases into runs, vindicating Toby's assessment. The man next to him drained his beer and pushed his glass toward the barman, who took it rising, complaining that his team contained a bunch of useless mother fuckers. He rinsed the glass, filling it mostly froth-free to the top. The barman caught Toby watching him and pointed at the pump. Toby nodded and rose to collect his second beer, this one suitably poured. It seemed he was now an accepted addition to the room.

The bar filled as the evening progressed, while Toby filled himself with beer. He wondered whether Marcia Rodriguez ever strolled from the office and into Michael's, answering his own question by noting the complete absence of business attire. None of the new arrivals paid him much attention. He liked the solitude, enjoying the anonymity, musing about whether that was a good thing to enjoy if he was supposed to be a star.

It was dark when he left, shuffling sideways to avoid the smokers that had gathered for the curious solidarity that is a smokers' union, their collective approach to health destruction affording them the universal ability to congress. Smoking drinkers, Toby decided, were much more sociable than just drinkers. Most drinkers seemed only to have misery to share. Smokers managed to be cheerier when sharing their woes. Toby had never smoked but stopped at the Oxnard Liquor Market on his way home to pick up a six pack. Standing at the counter, waiting for service, he yielded to an impulse to buy a pack of Marlboro. *Might as well go full throttle*, he thought.

The little cabin greeted him with an oppressive hug when he returned, rousing him to move the table and chair outside. He put five of the beers in the fridge, sitting down with the sixth as he opened his cigarettes. He removed one, putting it to his lips before mimicking the tapping of pockets he'd seen others do, searching for a lighter that he knew he didn't have.

He shook his head at his stupidity and returned the cigarette to the pack.

In the early afternoon, when he woke the next day, there were six crushed cans in the sink that he didn't remember putting there. He opened his fridge to find something to eat, knowing it would be empty, feeling a sudden urge to try a Salvadorean tamale. He didn't bother to shower before walking the couple of blocks to Victory Boulevard, where he ordered take out and sat on a wooden dining chair, placed indiscriminately in front of the U-Haul centre next to the strip mall. After a greedy bite, tamales entered his register of great hangover foods. It was two o'clock and he swiped at his phone, leaving a greasy fingerprint on the screen, ignoring the missed calls from his mother, and noting the absence of calls from Ricky Stevens. *Fuck him*, he thought, *and fuck her*.

Wandering toward Rite Aid, he bought a disposable plastic lighter, discovering on leaving, that his leaden steps were taking him down Tujunga Ave toward Oxnard Street and Michael's Pub. Before turning right, he glanced toward the Actors' Equity Association, prompting thoughts that he might have more luck bumping into Marcia Rodriguez at this time of day. He fostered a plan to stroll a few circuits of the block so that a chance meeting would seem coincidental. By the time he reached the building, he'd walked far enough. Toby perched on a block wall opposite her building in front of the railings of New Tech Auto Care. A woman walking her dog skirted wide, using the fullest extent of the sidewalk to avoid him. He didn't like the look she cast him. It felt judgemental. *Fuck you*, flashed angrily in his head as he allowed the day's heat to drive the patience from him, ending his brief surveillance. *Marcia's out of luck today*, he thought. Michael's was beckoning.

When he was five beers in, he watched two women in impossibly tight leather pants leave the pub for a smoke. Getting up from what he now considered to be his seat, he joined them outside. Ignoring his newly acquired lighter, he waved an unlit cigarette with a docile swipe, a submissive need

A LITTLE SOMETHING TO HIDE

for help. A Zippo appeared, a fluid movement flicking open the cover to spark a flame. Leaning into her hand, searching for the authentic imitation of the practiced smoker, he revealed himself an imposter as he choked on his initial draw. He mumbled an unconvincing excuse, scurried away, embarrassed at his deceit, their giggles – humiliating.

To avoid discovery, he had furtive cigarette breaks until he was confident that his technique wouldn't undermine him. After a couple of days, conviction allowed him to sidle into a group and ask for a light. It was Billy who was first to offer him a flame, one of the two pool-playing men that he encountered on his first visit to Michael's. In his head, he had taken to calling them Billy Gibbons and Dusty Hill after the ZZ Top guitarists. Collectively he thought of them as The Toppers, but kept their monikers to himself, he wasn't yet part of the community, although his appearance now garnered acknowledgement and the occasional inclusion in fragmentary conversations. Billy became collegiate when he learned that Toby was from Albuquerque. *I'm from Phoenix,* he said. *We're practically neighbours.*

He invited Toby to play pool, promising not to hustle him because he was a regular. Toby routinely lost to Billy and Dusty, always bested, but he felt okay, he now had buddies.

He bought beer for his new friends, ignoring that they didn't buy two to each of his; they were a partnership when it came to their round. They drank more heavily than he did; he adapted quickly to their pace but couldn't go as long into the evening, earning him the *Pussy* sobriquet. He laughed it off, but said he wished he had their staying power. *I might have something that could help,* said Dusty. *And first time's free mi Amigo.*

They didn't go to the front of the building when they next went for a cigarette. Dusty and Billy ushered Toby past the toilets and down a short hallway to the back door. It opened onto a vacant lot reeking of putrefaction, waste spilling from overflowing trash. Neither Topper seemed troubled by the smell, Toby fought his nausea. Dusty pulled a plastic bag from inside his jacket, tapping it. *You done this before?*

TOBY – LOS ANGELES

Toby didn't know what *this* was, but didn't want to seem unworldly, so lied. Dusty let out the snort of a man who knows when he's hearing bullshit but didn't challenge him.

Reaching into a pocket, Billy withdrew a polished piece of ebony. Toby flinched when a five-inch blade appeared from the wood, the steel glinting as it captured the muted light of the back lot. Billy dipped it into Dusty's bag, deftly removing the excess with a grubby fingernail, leaving a thin thread of white powder on the dull edge of the blade which he drew across his top lip as he inhaled the cocaine.

Dipping into the bag again, he served the same to Toby, who copied Billy's action. His look of expectation caused the Toppers to laugh. *Give it ten minutes,* Dusty said, handing Toby a small plastic bag of the white powder. *This one's on me.* Toby tucked the cocaine in his pocket and followed his new friends inside.

The first thing Toby noticed was the beating of his heart, more pronounced, thumping beyond the centre of his chest; all pulses seeming to drum to a rapid beat. At his temples, constant blows pounded as though a tiny being was frantic to escape, hammering to break free. The beats were everywhere. Loud. Scanning the room, he searched to see who else was hearing his heart. No one was paying attention, he didn't know why they weren't staring, the noise was thunderous. One of the girls in leather looked at him, smiling. He asked if she could hear, then thought she was teasing when she said, *Hear what?*

Her name was Trudy and she guessed he'd been out with Dusty and Billy, making him wonder how long she'd been watching him, he thought he knew why, he was accustomed to lingering looks. *Did Dusty give you anymore?* she asked. Toby moved a protective hand over his pocket, unsure of her motive, answering with his action. *Be careful,* she said.

He didn't know what she meant. *I feel good*, he told her, repeatedly.

I can tell.

He thought Trudy lacked conviction. *No,* he said. *I feel **really** good.*

A LITTLE SOMETHING TO HIDE

He talked and talked until Trudy's friend, Meesha, tapped him on the shoulder, telling him they needed to go. He hadn't noticed the desperate glances Trudy was throwing at her friend, silently imploring the rescue that eventually came. He hoped the girls would ask him to go with them, they didn't, leaving him to return to the pool table where Billy was playing an interloper that Toby didn't recognise.

Billy missed a shot that Toby knew he could make easily. Hustling. Dusty wasn't anywhere. Billy motioned for Toby to buy the beers. Serf like, he went to the bar. The fat barman poured three beers, with no semblance of enthusiasm. *It's a great night,* Toby said.

The barman grunted.

Toby wondered if there was ever a man less suited to his profession. As he walked away, he couldn't help thinking he might have spoken the thought.

The barman wore his customary mask – pissed. The face said he might have heard, Toby couldn't tell, the face never changed.

He had meant for Dusty to have one of the beers, but the imposter took the third glass without asking. Billy nodded to let him know it was okay, the new guy was a friend. Toby didn't challenge the presumption. The more he got to know The Toppers, the more nervous they made him. They were superficially friendly, but there was always an underlying menace to their behaviour, like a mastiff at rest, contemplating an unprovoked mauling. It felt a good time to leave.

The girls in the leather pants were still at the bar when he left, puzzling him. He rationalised their presence in terms of his appeal, believing that the one he'd buttonholed had persuaded her friend not to leave, reflecting her attraction. She accepted the smile he gave, but to his disappointment, she failed to interpret it as the invitation he intended. Casting glances over his shoulder as he wandered home, he expected to see her following, but it was alone that he lay on his bed.

He couldn't sleep, the frantic whirring in his head stealing his slumber, stimulation overcoming weariness, rest yielding to narcotic. Bouncing from his bed, he entered the kitchen, peering into the fridge which cast an insipid glow, lending him a jaundiced complexion. It contained nothing by way of nourishment, nothing to slake a demanding thirst. He slid his head beneath the kitchen tap, greedily drinking the tepid water. His desire for beer eased, morphing into a different need. He returned to bed thinking about the packet that whispered from the pocket of his jeans.

He wasn't certain how to take it but had watched enough movies to guess. Using a knife from the drawer, he chopped the powder, forming an imperfect line on the little kitchen table, before taking a dollar bill from his wallet. Contemplating the note before rolling, he shook his head, urging himself to think bigger. Returning it, he swapped if for a twenty, it somehow felt more appropriate. He snorted the line, feeling the tickle of abrasion as it made its way into his nose. A thin sliver remained on the table which he hoovered with his twenty-dollar vacuum. He sniffed several times and waited.

A pulse thumped at his temples. He let out a whoop that only he would hear, it felt good, almost primal. Urges formed, the imprinted smile of the girl in the leather pants occupying his thoughts, his feet lurched, driving him inexorably toward the seedy bar. Cowpunk spilled into the road, drawing him back to Michael's. The girls weren't there, but The Toppers were still at the pool table, taking turns to beat whoever bet money against them. Dusty saw him at the doorway as Toby searched for the girls, catching his eye, signalling for him to follow. He slid down the narrow corridor, past the stinking toilets and out into the vacant lot.

Dusty had another bag pinched between two fingers when he turned to face Toby. They agreed the stuff was good and that Toby could have the gram for a hundred bucks. He had fifty dollars in his wallet.

You can pay the rest tomorrow, said Dusty.

Toby took the bag, leaving for home, where he was restless but fought the temptation to have more of the nose candy.

I'll share it with the girls later, he thought.

#

A LITTLE SOMETHING TO HIDE

In the morning, he faced the inevitability of a call with his mother, planning to tell her tales of call backs and nearly breaks, reassuring her that his agent was confident he'd land something soon, something big, all of it a prelude to asking for money.

Consider it a loan, Mom. I'll pay interest. Lots of it. It's just a matter of time.

Fabricating a bigger and better place to stay, one that was more appropriate to his image, he manipulated his mother's misplaced belief in his talents, appealing to her desire for his success, sure that she'd approve of his move. She didn't have any doubts; she knew he was destined for greatness.

Of course I'll wire the money, honey.

She was thrilled that he had a new place to stay, somewhere closer to the action. She hesitated when he said it was more expensive, but understood the importance, it was the next step in his career.

Do you think it's the right thing to do? he asked, already knowing her answer.

Absolutely. She couldn't deny him now, not when he was so close.

I need it for a deposit. Fifteen hundred. Could you send it now?

He tried to keep the desperation from his voice and mostly succeeded, promising his mother that he'd send address details on signing, adding a further reminder that he couldn't commit without the money.

The money travelled through the ether to Toby where, bit by bit, it moved from a tiny cabin in North Hollywood to the worn pockets of the Toppers' jeans.

The detours past the Actors' Equity Association ended as his obsession with Marcia Rodriguez waned. The longer journey kept him from his first beer of the day and the livelier liaison that awaited. Whether it was his looks and charm, or the white powder he was willing to share, he succeeded in getting the girl with the smile out of her tight leather pants.

Her friend endured his visits. The small plastic bags he shared, before disappearing for boisterous sex with Trudy,

TOBY – LOS ANGELES

made his presence in their cramped apartment tolerable. Meesha didn't like him, he loitered in the morning, parading in his boxers, his tan fading, unaware that the taut physique he brought to LA was showing signs of atrophy, the skin hanging looser now. It was obvious he thought there was something seductive in his appearance, not recognising the revulsion Meesha felt.

The deposit money for Toby's non-move didn't last. The Toppers extended credit for the first score after it had disappeared, they knew Toby well. They humoured him when he said he'd be good for four grams a week. When Toby didn't stump the money at the end of the week, Billy was accommodating, but firm. *You can have the eight ball now, but no more until you've paid.* He gave Toby seven days to settle his debt.

A smog-afflicted sun cast a murky light into his kitchen. Toby sat shuffling what remained of his cash across the surface of the small table, wondering what to do. He stared at his mother's number for as long as it took him to decide there was no alternative to calling. Unusually, she answered on the fifth ring. Normally she answered quickly with a chirruping greeting, today the joyous notes were missing. There was a reticence, a wariness, to her *Hello*. He was beyond pleasantries. Whatever etiquette his mother instilled in him had disappeared up his nasal cavities. He got to his point directly.

I need cash. Quickly.
Why?
I just do.
That's not a reason. She paused, causing thin tendrils of panic to wrap around his chest. *Your father thinks you should get a job. You need to start standing on your own.*

He caught the whimpering tone, her attempt to ingratiate. It troubled him that he exhibited some of her behaviours, reminding him of his pleas to Billy for more time to pay.

She demonstrated the worst of her traits, those she'd unsuccessfully hidden from Toby: divorcing herself from responsibility, blaming his father for the message she delivered, the wheedle that implied that it wasn't her fault, trying to stay in his favour so that he wouldn't despise her.

It was too late for that; she just didn't know it. Toby had long despised his mother; he didn't believe she was articulating his father's thoughts.

Hilary Ames had never listened to Toby's father; a transformation was unlikely now. *I'm sure you're disappointed, darling. I know you're close to making it, but maybe it's the right thing to do.* Another pause, this time waiting for Toby to speak. He didn't break; he owned elements of her character. *It will only be for a short while. I'm sure.*

He listened as she ascribed the lack of cash to his father, lamenting the cost of Toby's new apartment, reminding him to text the address so she could send him a care package. He almost said, *Fuck the care package, just send the money,* but the last vestiges of civility asserted themselves and he struck a conciliatory note.

I'm going back to the old place. To save a bit. But I need some help. Now.

*I'll send you something after the weekend. And your **regular** payment will follow soon.* She never missed the opportunity for a dig.

He wanted to argue, wanted to tell her that Monday was too late, but then he might have to explain. He ended the call, hanging up after a meek *Thanks,* and began planning his evasion.

He subconsciously fingered the small plastic bag in his pocket and decided he'd stop going to Michael's for a while. The prospect of seeing Billy before the cash arrived held no appeal.

It took Toby time to do the maths, the numbers wouldn't stick, but he calculated that the regular payment from his mother would arrive ten days after Billy's deadline. He could avoid him till then, pretend he'd gone back to New Mexico because his mother wasn't well. Yeah, that was a plan. That would work. Billy was his friend, he'd understand.

Ten days. Toby filled them with cans of Coors Light from Metros and ever thinner lines of coke. He didn't go near

TOBY – LOS ANGELES

Oxnard Street, even though the beer was cheaper at the Liquor Market. He didn't eat much, especially after the nose candy. *There's a meal in every line*, he giggled to himself. An observer would think him a little manic.

The next instalment of cash was just two days away when he came home from Mi Carbonero with a bag of pupusas, ninety-nine cents, the cheapest thing on the menu. He craved tamales, but they'd have to wait. He was still thinking about them when he entered the door of his cabin and found the seat in the kitchen occupied.

Billy had helped himself to a Coors Light. He sat whittling a stick that he'd broken from a young Acacia tree in the garden outside Toby's cabin, honing an already lethal shard with the knife Toby had seen in Michael's. Thin slivers of wood spiralled from the stake, falling at his feet.

Good to see you, Tobes.

Toby didn't quite agree. It felt anything but good.

Billy took a sip from his beer then stared at the can in disgust. He gave it a tambourine shake before dropping it on the table, a hollow *thunk* confirming it empty. *Grab a beer, Toby. And while you're at it, fetch your friend Billy another.*

Toby edged to the fridge, eyeing the Topper as he continued to whittle, before placing a beer on the small table, unable to disguise the tremor in his hand. Billy smiled, beatific, *Thank you*, he said as he opened the can, the grime under his nails still evident. Despite his fear, Toby flitted with the thought that The Toppers could improve their hygiene.

Billy didn't appear to be in a rush to explain his presence, not that Toby needed telling, they both knew why he was there. Toby wished Billy would get to the point quickly, but he ran his fingers slowly through his beard as he chatted breezily about The Toppers' latest hustle at Michael's Pub, some loser punk who was down in his cups and thought he could scam a few bucks from a couple of local idiots.

We local idiots showed him. He affected an incongruous primness, laughing at his attempt to sound proper.

A LITTLE SOMETHING TO HIDE

Toby didn't recognise the mimicry. He tried to speak, but each time he opened his mouth, Billy lifted a finger to quiet him. Toby stayed silent, less because of the finger and more because of the glistening knife held in the same hand.

Billy didn't seem to notice or care about Toby's rising anxiety. He complemented Toby on how well he looked, the pretension seemed set to stay, heightening Toby's discomfort. *You been making our powdery friend go a long way? That why you're looking so good?*

Toby started to answer but the finger halted him.

Haven't seen you at Michael's for a while. Trudy's missing you, Fella. You don't take care of her, she might start blowing someone else's pipes. With his feigned primness, the words fell mockingly.

I've been away.

Really? The pretence left him, the Arizonan burr returned. *That's not what the folks in Mi Carbonero are telling me.*

Toby felt his chest tightening, the express beat of his pulse thumping at his temples.

They tell me you love washing down their pupusas with a can of Metro's finest. He held up his beer, confirming his point.

I'm gonna be in Michael's on Friday, Toby blurted.

Well, that'd be a good thing my friend. The whole bar's missing you, and I know Dusty owes you a beer. Be smart if you collect it 'fore it disappears. Nobody likes things to disappear, do they?

I swear, I'll be there.

According to Billy, that was good.

Billy also reminded Toby just how much money he should consider bringing with him. It was a larger figure than Toby thought. Toby started to argue, but Billy's finger rose, along with the knife, silencing him. Billy cheerily explained the principle of compound interest and how, if a person weren't careful, it could run away on them.

The last thing anyone wants is something to run away on them.

It wasn't the first time Toby had been referred to as *something*. When Ricky Stevens had done it, it felt irksome, now it terrified him. Toby nodded his understanding of Billy's wisdom with a slow, cautious movement. He didn't want to move quickly in case it suggested aggression. He didn't need

TOBY – LOS ANGELES

The Topper to feel threatened, not that Toby was capable of threatening Billy. Billy looked at him for a time, measuring the impact of his lesson.

Good, he said, deciding the message landed. *I'll see you on Friday.*

He took the last of Toby's beers from the fridge and left, closing the door quietly, primly, behind him.

Toby fumbled for his phone and dialled his mother, hanging up before she answered. He was still holding the phone when she called back, but threw it on his bed as though the call had infused it with a powerful charge. She called again, twice, each time the phone sounded louder to him. He stared at the phone as though it was dangerous, something vicious, poised to strike. He steeled himself, ready to wrangle, breathed deeply, and took the call, trying to sound relaxed. For the first time in the four months that he had been in LA he was honest with her.

Mom, he said, *I'd like to come home.*

The Uber driver picked up a gaunt, sallow figure the next morning, one who was sixty pounds lighter than the young man who stepped onto Californian soil for the first time. He didn't know that his passenger was dancing at the edges of cold turkey, that the boy was craving another fix. The driver thought he seemed okay, if a little unkempt and harbouring an aroma that he knew would worsen as the day continued. He lowered the windows a fraction, a subtle gap that he hoped wouldn't reveal his revulsion. The action served to circulate the air in his car, occasional drifts of Toby's scent assailed him; he made a mental note to open the windows wide on the way to his next fare.

Cars queued as they negotiated their way onto Lankershim Boulevard, stalling the traffic on Tujunga Avenue. The driver studied an elegant woman walking towards them and was surprised when his passenger waved as she approached the Actors' Equity Association. The connection between the attractive woman and the filthy young man in the back of his car wasn't obvious.

A LITTLE SOMETHING TO HIDE

The woman noticed the flurry of hands and approached the car, peering in at the man waving to her, thinking it was a friend. She recoiled, disgust crossing her face at the sight of the vagrant in the rear seat. She admonished herself, irritated that she'd allowed the man to savour a cheap thrill. Her gullibility annoyed her intensely. She was smarter than that, she should have been more watchful. If he'd whistled, she would have treated him with contempt, belittling him for being a misogynistic arsehole. She took only mild satisfaction that her reaction had wiped the smile from his face. She'd seen hurt in his eyes – that softened her temper, as did a deeper memory that he seemed somewhat familiar. It wasn't a thought she carried beyond the door to her building.

The driver chuckled quietly at the kid's attempt to attract the woman, deciding that no connection existed; his passenger was just a horny dude aiming way above his league.

It hurt Toby that Marcia Rodriguez didn't recognise him. He was sure there had been a mutual attraction, just as there had been with the woman on the plane. His mother said he would have that effect on woman. It was one of her few claims that he'd chosen to believe. Marcia would disagree.

As the car pulled away, the driver began to get nervous, worrying that trouble approached, his passenger fidgeted notably. As their journey to the station continued, Toby searched the streets; scanning faces, head jerking left and right, his movements frenzied. A returned gaze, loitering too long, sent Toby wide-eyed, sliding in his seat to avoid detection, hiding below the window, *Fuck* exploding from him whenever he suspected discovery. *Hurry*, he whispered, urgently.

This is LA man, the driver thought without voicing the opinion. *Hurrying ain't an option.*

Toby gradually reappeared, like a child, peering above a sofa in a game of hide and seek, warily sitting up, before diving again, seeing another imagined adversary on the street. Toby spied the driver looking at him in the rear-view mirror.

Why are you looking at me?

TOBY – LOS ANGELES

No reason, he replied, returning his focus to the road, settling his passenger, diminishing the threat.

From the driver's perspective, the ride couldn't end soon enough, but an early termination worried him, he dare not risk the consequences of riling his passenger, he'd have to see this one through.

At the station, the painfully thin man exited the car, hoping for obscurity, but his movements were skittish, unnatural, attracting attention. Passers-by were alert to his actions. He thumped the back of the car, urging the Uber man to release his belongings. The driver usually retrieved his passengers' bags, but decided against the courtesy, preferring the confines of his car. He flicked a latch to open the trunk. *This one can take care of himself,* he thought. He didn't expect to get a tip and was thankful the app processed the journey's finances.

Toby ran from the car, leaving the trunk open. The driver's shout for him to close it went ignored. Toby couldn't give a fuck at the driver's irritation, he wanted to find his bus, and quickly. He didn't want exposure for longer than was necessary. The bus was already at its bay. Passengers from up the line were disembarking; fools stepping off, smelling the air, and believing that the stench of Los Angeles was the promise of hope.

Toby jiggled restlessly at the side as he watched them wander off. He fought the impulse to scream. *Run. Run away. Before they come for you.* When they had gone, he stashed his bags under the bus and joined the back of the shuffling queue, his eyes darting around the terminus, always searching, not knowing who he was searching for, but knowing they were out there, looking for him, *hunting* him, he knew they were coming.

He cast a final look, hoping that there was no one there to see him board the bus to Albuquerque, ruing the day he told The Toppers that was home. The thought that they'd know where to find him shortened his breath, he verged on hyperventilation. He tried to calm himself by taking a deep breath. It didn't help. The acrid diesel fumes spewing from the bus invaded his senses, another donor to the City's noxious smells. For Toby Ames, there was no scent of hope in that aroma, the only thing he could smell, was fear.

W WELLS ST / S LOVEKIN BLVD, BLYTHE

Arrivals
Time	From	Expected
15:08	Los Angeles	Expected: 16:00

Departures
Time	Destination	Expected
15:30	Phoenix	Delayed: 16:25

W WELLS ST / S LOVEKIN BLVD, BLYTHE

As the bus rumbles along the San Bernardino Freeway, through the endless housing that marks LA's eastern corridor, Toby Ames can feel the piercing stares from behind each pane of glass. From every house, hunters are seeking him, meaning him harm. He pulls the peak of his baseball cap over his face but doesn't cease his surreptitious glances beyond the windows of the bus, looking for those he must avoid.

Housing unfolds for miles until they reach Banning where it ceases, a landscape no longer of interest to developers, where the end of an airport runway signals the start of a barren panorama, the cerulean sea above drifting into the ragged parchment of the distant desert floor.

With no more houses to occupy his attention, Toby begins to worry about the other passengers, fuelling an internal fury at his lack of focus – his assailant could be on the bus. The fat hick wearing a permanent scowl, who sits across from the love-struck couple, looks likely. 'If he steps toward me,' thinks Toby, 'I'll be ready. That fucker'll be in for a nasty surprise.'

His fretting continues when they reach their next stop and nobody climbs off, prompting a concern about exchanges between Michael's Pub and Blythe; arrangements made for unwanted company and a razor-sharp blade. He need not worry, only one person joins the bus, and she doesn't look the type to carry a knife. With paranoia rising, answering the unbidden questions that plague him, Toby thinks, 'You can't be sure. Stay sharp.'

The newest traveller is incongruously chic. Her dress is a vibrant red, in stark contrast to the drab decor of the bus, an elegant Valentino sheath dress which screams its juxtaposition to the wicker basket she carries. Inside the basket are objects that Toby might consider lethal weapons, knitting needles and a small pair of dress-maker's scissors. Unlike Rosa Fernandez's needles, which beat an unremitting clackety-clack *rhythm, Gracie MacDonald doesn't intend for hers to shift a stitch, but they'll be suitably visible from her basket, enough for those that spot them to draw the conclusion that Gracie is a down-to-earth, Momsie type. They won't be quite right, she's now a* Grand-Momsie *type. Granny Mac. The thought almost fills her with warmth.*

She exchanges a nod of solidarity with Rosa but hopes to God the little Mexican woman doesn't want to talk about knitting. The basket and the knitting are devices to lend plausibility to her image. So are the supplies: sandwiches and snacks packed tightly into shabby Tupperware containers, a large flask of hot tea, and several skeins of cashmere wool.

There is an image she wants to preserve, the one that led her to choose the God-forsaken Briscola service for her travel arrangements. She doesn't think anyone else from Blythe will be on the bus, but she wants to be sure. She could have taken a private car, or better yet, chartered a flight, but that would reveal more about her than she wants her neighbours to know.

Wincing at the state of the seat she's chosen, she looks around to see whether another is available, but can't contemplate the idea of sitting next to a stranger. It's not that she couldn't entertain them, she could keep them spellbound for the duration of the trip; she's a storyteller with the ability to captivate.

Through her life she has told tales to entertain others and enrich herself. She's not concerned that she won't be interesting, rather, she worries that whoever sits next to her will be dull. The dull often feel compelled to participate, which is why she is grateful that there is an empty pair of seats, one for her and one for her oversized basket. The basket sits next to her, needles poking from the top, as menacing as she's able to make them appear, the basket a non-sentient guardian, an unequivocal fuck off *to anyone who thinks there's a welcome next to her.*

An ominous viscous smear covers one of the seats. The other has tears in the upholstery and the cushion sponge pokes through the wounds, wrangling to escape. She rests her bag on the armrest, muttering incandescently about the shitty bus company, searching the bag's interior, shuffling the contents until she unearths the item she seeks, exhaling with self-satisfaction as she pulls an anti-bacterial wipe from a tube she carries with her for when the world needs disinfecting. Having cleared the stain, she examines the wipe, concluding after forensic analysis that it reveals the remains of a child's lollipop. At least, she hopes that's what she's found, she doesn't want her over-active imagination to entertain the alternatives that a red smear might represent.

No one accompanies her. Archie, her husband, was declared missing-in-action forty-seven years earlier, when the oldest of their children was just three, and the youngest was still sucking the life from her tits. Three boys, a solid foundation to continue the family's legacy.

A LITTLE SOMETHING TO HIDE

GRANNY MAC – BLYTHE

Before Archie MacDonald went to Vietnam, Gracie and he raised hell for most of their time together. They drank beer, or liquor when they could afford it, smoked Marlboro; Regular for him, Lights for her, and whatever schedule I or II substances they could lay their hands on, getting hammered, both metaphorically and figuratively – they hammered the bottle and hammered each other. If they weren't arguing, they were screwing – banging their heads or just banging. It was a tempestuous life. Archie kept most of his bruises hidden.

When he first went to war, Gracie felt relief rather than anxiety that he was gone. She reckoned he felt the same, attributing his unvoiced feelings to his difficulty in living with a strong woman.

On the day she learnt that Archie was MIA, she gave up all vices; there was work to do. In his absence, she made him a promise that she would remain the picture of health until he returned, when all bets would be off, and they would celebrate wildly. To begin with, she mostly kept her word, she had a standing in the community to assert and she didn't need anyone questioning her actions or motives. She had three fine men to raise and a history to preserve.

In her baggage beneath the bus is a wardrobe's worth of knitted items for her first grandchild, a girl, Angus's daughter. Angus is her youngest, who traipsed to a college in New Mexico where he met a money-grubbing local girl while he was completing his postgrad studies, settling with her in Albuquerque. Gracie hates the whore for stealing her son and being incapable of producing a boy. It took them years to conceive, and a small fortune on IVF treatments, most of it Gracie's. *With all that fucking money, you'd've thought they'd order a boy.* Still, it was better than the luck of her older boys whose wives were barren. The possibility that the fertility of her sons might be the issue didn't feature in her thinking. Her boys would never fire blanks.

The knitwear will keep the child warm. At any time of the year in Albuquerque, the temperature during the day rarely dips below fifty, but that is irrelevant to Gracie MacDonald, she is determined that the child will never be cold, arguing that her views stem from the MacDonald's Scottish heritage, an inherent desire to fight against the cold – and the world.

The war in Vietnam appealed to Archie, she said. *His family could have taken the bullshit bone-spurs route if they'd chosen, but my husband wasn't chicken shit. He wanted to face the heat. He enjoys a fight.*

So did Gracie, knowing that her daughter-in-law would hate the woollens, but not as much as Gracie's insistence that the child wear them for the duration of her stay.

Scotland has never felt the soles of Gracie's feet on its soil, although she now proclaims it the mother country, doing everything to reinforce her claim. *With a family tree as rich as the MacDonalds*, she argues, *it would be remiss not to maintain the traditions*. Gracie insinuates a whiff of Scottish royalty with her assertions. If anyone asks, she's quick to explain. *It's only minor. You know, CLAN royalty.*

The wiser folk of Blythe know not to challenge her, knowing they might fall off the guest list to her annual St Andrew's Day celebrations, or never get an invite to the more exclusive *BNS,* the Burn's Night Supper. Worse still, she might take against them. Those that have known her longest know her stories are nebulous, but they also know that it's best not to argue with Gracie MacDonald.

According to Gracie, everyone knows that an invitation to a *BNS* is highly coveted. Whether guests like it or not, tartan is mandatory. If you're on the invitation list, appearing in even a scrap of the fabric is vital, failure to comply results in a miserable evening, she never tires of mentioning the slight.

Her subversive arrangements for importing haggis directly from Ramsay of Carluke is shared with relish, a covert operation choreographed to circumvent the 1971 ban on imports. Visitors are sworn to secrecy before she shares the intelligence, as though it's a consequential state secret. She knows no one is going to rat her out – if they know what's good for them.

Guests are treated to cock-a-leekie soup, the recipe a guarded family secret, maintained for centuries. To Gracie, it is irrelevant that no one asks for enlightenment. Most people leave intoxicated, pumped full of Glenmorangie whisky, bewildered by the evening's provisions, an affront to palates that are accustomed to more orthodox American fare.

Gracie never claims to be Scottish-American. To her, the addition of the American suffix diminishes her true heritage. She is just Scottish, although she acknowledges that her family's long history in the US means that her accent has suffered from Californication.

She is proud to have roots tied to the western Highlands, but equally proud to be in the strand of the family tree that ventured much further west. Hers were the earliest MacDonald settlers on US soil. They were tobacco farmers in Virginia, fought in the revolutionary war against the British, but avoided the civil war by already being out west, having got there by being in the Lewis and Clarke expedition of 1805.

Multiple-great-granddaddy Fraser MacDonald was a Sergeant Major in the Corps of Discovery, she says, a snippet everyone must hear. Having been integral to the party that travelled west, he earned an honourable discharge, becoming a merchant using his Army spoils, launching multiple commercial endeavours that led to the fortunes of subsequent generations.

The MacDonald's profited mightily during the gold rush, she claims. *They had trading posts everywhere. You go back far enough, you'll find most of the businesses around here had a MacDonald at the top.* If asked to elaborate, she'll brush the query away with, *Too many to mention*, before diverting attention to another aspect of the family's importance.

Her knowledge of the MacDonalds and their history on either side of the Atlantic is encyclopaedic, recounting tales of heroes and villains, delighting in both. Never lacking for an original story, family and friends are in awe of her chronicles. The MacDonald family history is extraordinary but for one inconvenient secret that she keeps from everyone. None of it is true.

Gracie isn't her first name, but she believes it's more Scottish than Emily Grace Barnard, the name given to her by her parents. They emigrated to Blythe from Wolverhampton in 1959, soon after Emily turned seven, discovering on arrival that their daughter had not only left her country behind, but also her name.

Before the move, her father worked as a hand on a sheep farm. The winters were drab affairs; most days beginning grey and moist, the soil heavy underfoot with winds delivering a chill that started at sunrise and remained in his bones until an evening in front of the open fire warmed him through. The fire stood in the kitchen, the only room benefitting from its heat, the remainder of the house an effective thief of the warmth it produced.

He loved the spring and the activity it brought; ewes delivering their offspring, the newness of life bringing promise for the months ahead, of better days and better weather.

The summers rarely delivered on the promises of spring, and with the hardships endured in the post-war years, tired of the bleakness of the rural Midlands, Emily's father packed his bags and his family, heading for California where he found work on a cattle farm in the Palo Verde Valley.

The blazing heat of Blythe's summers left him dry-mouthed and exhausted at the end of each day, but he never again experienced a cold so deep it would chill the marrow. Blythe was now his home.

The Barnard family arrived bearing asinine Black Country accents, not the Scottish lilt that Gracie's revised history implied. The intolerance that Blythe's residents showed toward the Barnard's brand of English manifested in a pretence of not understanding what the newest townsfolk were saying. To achieve acceptance, the Barnard's adapted. They were quick to exterminate the evidence of their origins, soon adopting local inflections. Gracie's accent was the first to go, swiftly developing the local nuances that concealed the roots she wanted hidden in favour of those she would later reveal.

From an early age she was inventive. The kids at her school knew she was different but didn't know anything of her background. The contrived back story of the Barnard family evolved with each telling, Gracie embellishing every shade of their life. The more accepting that others were of her tales, the more she exaggerated. Her teachers found it endearing, sharing the more outrageous accounts with her parents at Parent/Teacher evenings; her parents found their daughter amusing.

No one ever corrected the girl with the vivid imagination, they allowed the fictions to develop. Her peer group were more susceptible to her fantasies, accepting them as gospel. If a child should query Gracie's fables, concocted evidence of her story's authenticity dispelled their doubts.

The Barnards' humble background disappeared, replaced with a scandalous past – stories of family treason, of isolation and exile, of the contempt for her father's brilliance.

My father was a brilliant mathematician, Gracie said. *One of the best in the world. He invented the calculator and would have made millions, but my Uncle Casio stole the design. He had grandfather send Daddy to one of the family's estates to manage a sheep farm.*

As the tale gained acceptance, she'd elaborate, suggesting her father was too good-natured to challenge, allowing Uncle Casio and her grandfather to keep his money.

They sent him here out of guilt for what they did, a frown worn throughout the recollection, transforming to a beam as she considers the present. *He's so happy to raise cattle. He's biding his time to understand the American market before he buys an enormous ranch in Nebraska.*

In her earliest narratives, she painted a landscape of dreary Wolverhampton as a glorious riviera, rendering images of cirrus soaring above fertile valleys, the scents of lavender and camomile drifting on the breeze, prancing wildlife, imposing Renaissance architecture; the family seat being one of the finer examples, an imposing mansion drawing inspiration from French châteaux.

Later tellings saw the riviera yield to heather strewn moors, Wolverhampton morphed into the Highlands and the chateau became a crenelated castle, stoic and solid against the harsh conditions that shaped and strengthened her family.

She explains that her father is zen, karmic, and happy. The mathematician sacrificed his brilliance for contentment, waiving his rights to an enormous fortune so that he might find himself, tending to Brahman cattle, being at one with nature. She had answers for everything, and her friends continued to believe her, the teacher's continued to indulge, and her parents shook their heads bemused at how they could have fostered the ruminations of their daughter.

No one disabused Gracie of her more fanciful notions, allowing her to fabricate the life the family left behind. All went along with her; it was harmless fun.

A truth in Gracie's history was the meeting of Archie MacDonald at the Hob Theatre on Hobsonway when she was eighteen and he was sporting the stubble-coated head of a newly recruited Marine. Seated in the row behind her, he leaned forward during the movie to tell her that he was going to marry her. At the end of the film, he invited her to a nearby drugstore for a soda where she talked non-stop about who she was … or wasn't, as it more often transpired.

Archie liked her stories; Gracie liked his uniform. She especially liked it when he removed it and they could feel the closeness of each other. Within eight weeks she was expecting their first child and she made Archie keep his promise. They named their first son Reggie, after the earliest descendent that Gracie could find from the Clan Donald – Reginald, King of the Isles.

It was clear to her that by coincidence, both her and Archie's family were direct descendants, drawing up a family tree to prove her claim. No one disputed the sinuous strands of genealogical threads that cascaded down either side of the page and which circuitously co-joined at their sons, engineered by Gracie to deliver sufficient genetic diversity – she wasn't going to have anyone counting her boy's toes.

Reggie was just four-weeks old, and with less hair than his old man, when Archie set off on his first tour of Vietnam. He sent letters to Gracie every week, all on Corps issued letterhead; some with a dried bead of sweat that caused the tight scrawl of his writing to form a Rorschach's blot of undecipherable script. Gracie interpreted these to mean more than the distorted words might convey. Each letter came tucked into envelopes with red and blue diamond flashes around the edges announcing his missives. Bold lettering in the corner pronounced *FREE MAIL!*, the exclamation mark affirming his Scottish roots.

Archie wrote observational letters; of the country, its majesty, and its misery, for which he felt the Americans played a part. The letters spoke of the Vietnamese people, with their peculiar blend of warmth and hostility, but he never mentioned the conflict nor his love for her and Reggie.

He leaves that out for security reasons, she explained. Only she understood the depth of his feelings, qualifying that Archie was never one to be too emotional. *He saves that for when he's on leave.*

Ross's conception occurred when Archie returned a year later, shortly before the start of his second tour, where the tone of his letters changed, becoming darker, less buoyant, the optimism fading. On return, with Ross bouncing on his knee, Archie wore the haunted expression of one that has seen the life snuffed from children much like his own, from indiscriminate actions to which he contributed.

Later that night, Gracie set to bouncing on Archie in her attempt to lift his mood. It was the same night that their third son, Angus, began his journey to join the family. Angus never got to meet his father, nor was he mentioned in Archie's letters which were more sporadic, the content universally bleak. His third tour was his last.

She wore black for longer than others thought appropriate, scolding the stupid fucks who were dumb enough to express the sentiment, telling them that she was observing a Clan tradition, and they'd do well to mind their own fucking business. *It's customary*, she explained, *for widows of Clan chieftains to wear black for a full year after the death of their spouse.*

Folk soon learnt not to ask whether Gracie would hold a service to mark Archie's passing, experiencing an irascibility that they attributed to the trauma of losing her husband. In quiet they passed their judgement on her failure to honour her husband, but knew better than to express their views within her hearing. Others refrained from questioning his death, remembering her earlier MIA declarations, knowing it was prudent not to quiz her further.

Gracie was never comfortable unless she was dominating a situation. That was simple when relating her stories as a child, but as time progressed, and folks became more cynical about her truths, the defences she launched when challenged carried a spikier edge. Previously subdued anger began to colour her arguments. The sympathy she garnered started to wane, she could feel the community shifting, sensed her drift to the periphery from the centre. Gracie needed to soften.

The knitting needles were a device to recast her identity. Blythe was sweltering in the summer and a little chilly during the winter nights; it made Albuquerque look cold. During the second World War, Gracie's mother knitted socks for the troops. It didn't take much for Gracie to convert the story into one of sacrifice, her mother foregoing her aristocratic privilege for the cause of the war, the story evolving into lessons with her mother, teaching the young Gracie to knit, not through need, but in case the efforts for the fighting men required resurrection during a future war. Gracie's near constant knitting, she explained, was an act of preparedness.

In the sweltering summer sun, as the sleeve of another sweater emerged beneath the flying needles, her friends asked what she did with her knitting. She claimed her creations were shipped across the US. *My work goes to the children of the country's elite.* It was one of her lesser embellishments.

GRANNY MAC – BLYTHE

By necessity, Gracie MacDonald was entrepreneurial and industrious. As well as her publicly displayed needles, she had an undisclosed knitting machine in her bedroom. She worked day and night, the carriage of the machine flung left and right with a determination born from her husband's absence. Knitwear tumbled from the machine, items for babies and infants that she sent to independent mother and baby stores across the country. The knitting needles were mostly for show; the machine was her lifeline; it was her primary source of income.

Having spent a lifetime compiling stories of inherited wealth, Gracie undertook clandestine activities to sustain the façade. There was nothing illicit in what she did, although to her mind, the discovery of her effort, performed solely to maintain appearances, would be a more shameful admission than crime.

The secretive evening work allowed her to manage her boys' schedules, while appearing to be a woman of means, helping to maintain the lie. It suited her that Blythe sweltered, she didn't demean herself by producing knitwear for her neighbours.

When the boys were in school, she loved to take coffee with other mothers. She could talk, a lot, but was conscious of her audience's chafing at her inclination to dominate conversation. She needed allies, friendships she could manipulate and exploit. Although eager to occupy conversational voids, she let others fill them, pretending interest, mastering the art of subtle affirmation, buying the acceptance that she was desperate to gain, at the same time cultivating a wiser, more considered persona.

In the afternoons and evenings as the machine's carriage zipped along its needle bed, she allowed her mind to wander, to conjure the next story. Her roots in Scotland, and her lineage as a MacDonald, provided an endless source of stories and fascination for those inclined to listen.

Plausibility became a necessity. The playground accounts of her childhood, while entertaining, lacked credibility. The stakes were now too high for people not to believe her. She needed to be convincing, avoiding challenges from those who knew her better. Gently, and not so they noticed, she dropped her oldest friends. They slipped from invite lists to her parties, calls went unreturned, car-pooling ended; she allowed them to drift. It suited her plans.

She surrounded herself with new companions, evading those who could remember the pigtailed girl with a funny voice, entrenching herself as a MacDonald descendant. Subverting the realism of Wolverhampton and Blythe, she created a history of excitement and mystery. Her curated friends admired her, were in awe of the widowed warrior. Gracie became a woman resolved to fight, a model of how to live with courage and dignity in the face of heart-breaking loss.

She milked it, discovering another outlet for her creativity and entrepreneurialism. Founding a charity for the militarily bereaved, she organised regular fundraisers to allow the people of Blythe to give to the cause, appealing to their civic responsibility, discovering that Blythe's citizens were conscientious, yet frugal contributors. The donations proved insufficient to mask the amorphous mix of hers and the charity's expenses; she needed other sources of income.

When the opportunity presented itself, Gracie let people know she was an excellent mother. Her boys were active: football, baseball, soccer, track, basketball. Between them, they covered most high school sports, with their mother an active spectator, proclaiming a fervent desire to watch her boys play, while never missing an opportunity to rattle a charity jar at visiting supporters.

Many of the parents attending the games wore school colours, although Gracie observed the propensity for some to wear the shirts of their favourite franchises. Noting what she saw, she formulated a plan to raise more money while catering to their fanaticism.

The big leagues received letters; she tapped them all. Gracie's missives, alleging the agonies and hardships that the widows of Blythe and Riverside County endured, tumbled from the postbags of the Dodgers and the Lakers in LA; the Chargers and the Padres in San Diego; the Suns in Phoenix.

The letters were piteous affairs. Gracie wrote of the struggles facing the widows of Vietnam veterans, mourning a fatherless generation, emphasising the loss of male role models. Her letters carried the sacrifices of countless mothers, many of them raising children whose illegitimacy was unintentional, life plans redrawn by tragedy in a distant conflict. She drew upon her storytelling skills; the organisations responded to her pleas. Limited edition and signed merchandise flowed into the township of Blythe.

Previously modest charity events became banquets for the town's luminaries, where she auctioned the priceless memorabilia. Holding the gavel and encouraging liquor-fuelled guests to outbid each other, her charity's earnings started to flow. The auction dinners became a regular feature on the Blythe social calendar, it appeared that the teams she'd approached responded with staggering generosity.

While it was true that the teams provided items of value, their offerings had a remarkable ability to self-replicate. Gracie crossed county lines in her old Honda Civic to the nearest outlet mall, searching for matching replica shirts and balls. Once home, she diligently copied the signatures onto transfer sheets to reproduce the items she received. She developed a talent for duplicating certificates of authenticity, and sourced an out-of-town picture framer, who for generous cash compensation, recreated the displays housing the shirts. She kept the originals secure in a basement locker, waiting for the day when they would be worth considerably more than when she received them. When finished, only the most discerning eye could identify a forgery, and she didn't intend to invite such types to her fundraisers.

Unwitting participants at the auctions bid themselves into a frenzy to acquire their heroes' fake signatures. They gushed at Gracie's ability to extract so much from the franchises. She accepted the tributes, drowning in their unctuous praise, she painted an exalted picture of the contacts that she groomed, the strings that she tugged, and the depth of the connections that the MacDonalds enjoyed.

We've helped in the past, she said. *There are favours I can claim.*

Gracie MacDonald became synonymous with fundraising in Blythe. Schools, clubs, and other organisations solicited her help to generate the funds they needed to prosper. Her help was conditional; her War Widows Association required an even share of the proceeds. Desperate causes agreed. She cultivated relationships with the Palo Verde Valley Times, raising her profile, finding a platform for her invention and the mechanism to grow her network.

Blythe couldn't match her ambition. It was too small; she was too well known; *they* were too poor. The charity needed a broader base, a richer base from which to extract more money. Before long, Gracie was travelling the I-10, flitting between Blythe and Palm Springs, ferrying contraband mementos to events that drew wealthier patrons, patrons who advertised their money on bejewelled necklines and decorated wrists. The F250s and Toyota Corollas of Blythe's carparks gave way to sleek and stately European marques. The price of entry rose, Gracie's exuberant self-promotion brought a cachet to her dinners and an expectation that people would pay a premium. Ticket receipts and auction proceeds grew; her new benefactors were much more giving.

Gracie exercised absolute control of her evenings; every penny passed through her hands. She recruited staff directly, entertaining no external contractors; she had no desire to fund others' profitability. The knitting machine yielded to a laptop and an Excel spreadsheet. Meticulous in her record keeping, everything the charity earned was documented, some of it declared. The charity was legitimate, she made regular disbursements to the known war widows of Blythe. Despite no change to her husband's MIA status, Gracie counted herself among the widows, which is why there were occasional, more generous, disbursements.

At co-sponsored events, Gracie was dogmatic when it came to splitting the funds raised, insisting on an equal share. *Of course, that's after expenses,* she'd clarify, offering further lamentation on the cost of running a successful charity.

Sometimes it doesn't seem worthwhile running an event with the ratio of expenses so high. But it's more about giving something back to the community. It's a MacDonald tradition.

Co-beneficiaries often left disappointed.

As her income increased, Gracie MacDonald developed a reputation for elegance, if not of the mouth, then certainly in appearance. Newer friends commented on her developing chic. Older ones noticed that she was drawing closer to her pretended persona. Modest about her latest look, she attributed it to the connections she cultivated during her designer knitwear days. *It's my circle's way of giving back.*

The credulous learned of her friendship with Coco Chanel, and how Yves Saint Laurent was such a darling, both so *very* generous with their casual collections. Her friends, the real ones, tolerated her showiness, they were conscious that one day they might need her support. No one was quite sure what support they might need, but Gracie made everyone aware that she was *the* figure in town on whom they could rely. Notwithstanding, she never went as far as extending her offer to anyone in need.

Her paramours were a limited cohort in Blythe. None of them met her expectations, a measure she assessed by the car they drove or the watch they wore, she'd find ways to let them down gently, impressing upon them her need to preserve the memory of her husband. Having allowed her suitors to pay for meals and gifts, as they were attempting to impress their desires upon her, Gracie found it useful to draw on the ambiguity of Archie's absence.

Call me silly, but I still harbour hopes that one day they will find him.

She killed the ardour of those pursuing her by suggesting that Archie was like Hiroo Onoda, the Japanese soldier who continued fighting WWII until 1974. *While everyone else thinks he's dead, I think Archie's still out there, hunkering down, evading the enemy in the deepest jungles of Vietnam.* Knowing she was being fanciful, she insisted that she wouldn't entertain another relationship until she knew for sure.

That's what she said in Blythe. In Palm Springs, things were a little different. People didn't know her as well; it was easier to be discreet.

Her recruitment practices ensured there were always buff young men in the catering team. A minimum of two would find themselves assigned to her table, where she'd examine them during the evening, evaluating, selecting, making her choice, letting the chosen one know that she would like to make a generous contribution to his college savings.

Mostly they caught on, and if they didn't, a hand sliding across a thigh as the dessert plates disappeared was usually enough to focus their thoughts. *Even a widow has needs*, she argued, but only to herself.

Sometimes, if she were feeling frisky, those needs would see her make contributions to more than one college fund. With the right inducement, college boys could be so accommodating and experimental.

Other men were interested too; men that were better able to meet her fiscal, rather than her physical needs. Most were married, bored of their wives and arrogant enough to believe that a woman with no man in the house would be desperate for *companionship*.

Gracie was circumspect; she didn't want to upset the wives, limiting herself to outrageous flirting, stoking pride, loosening the men's wallets. Companionship from these men, with hair migrating from heads to uninviting cavities, she could do without, maintaining a belief that an evening in her company might induce heart-attacks in some of the stouter specimens.

Playing them was easy, she massaged egos, fuelled machismo, fostered competition by dropping hints about other men's boasts, rarely real, but selectively repeated around the room.

She invented petty jealousies between wives, exploiting their lust for trinkets, using it to arouse their alpha males. The silverbacks competed for supremacy, achieving it not through strength, but with the might of their finances.

It was easy to separate the men from their cash when two or more of the wives shared an interest in one of her lots. It led her to include antique jewellery at her auctions. Jewellery with history and intrigue. She was a master at creating both.

Drawing on her creativity, Gracie manufactured the hype surrounding her pieces. The pieces were genuine, the gilding lay in their history, weaving as she did stories with a scent of horror, the loss of provenance, untraceable items obtained by nefarious hands.

I found this in Europe, hidden in Berlin. It's from an ancient Austrian family, old money. They lost it during the war, along with their teeth.

Attending other auctions, Gracie snaffled the jewellery of little interest to others, providing that the metals were precious, and the gems were real. She also bought unremarkable pieces from second-hand stores and antique boutiques.

Finding a jeweller willing to act without question, Gracie commissioned alterations to her pieces, making unusual requests to adulterate the wear of the items she provided. If the jeweller wondered why his customer instructed him to age the items, he never asked, and she found it prudent not to volunteer the information. Always delighted, Gracie paid cash, made no demand for a receipt, and thanked him for his work with a promise to return. She was good to her word – again and again.

The ruse was risky, aware that her Palm Springs audience would be discerning enough to have their jewellery valued. The quality and value, or lack thereof, was easy to determine. She knew too that the concocted provenance of her pieces would crumble under scrutiny. What Gracie relied upon, and what her buyers obligingly felt, was profound embarrassment that they had paid extravagantly for items that were essentially worthless.

The argument, *'Well it's for charity I suppose'*, resounded in more than one Palm Springs jeweller. If confronted, Gracie was confident she could maintain her innocence, citing that she too was a victim of duplicity. It was a defence that she could only use once before losing legitimacy, signalling the end of her jewellery scheme. Despite the risks, she was able to maintain the scam for years. Embarrassment, it seemed, was a powerful inhibitor, and Gracie continued to deliver impressive returns for her charity.

Her activities went some way to plugging the gap created by Archie's absence. He was a big man, leaving a sizeable void. It suited Gracie to keep his memory distant, she was too busy with her work to lament his loss, but there was no avoiding the daily reminder of Archie that a look at her boys provoked. As they grew, so too did their resemblance to their father, intruding on her memory, stirring her anguish, exaggerating her loss.

The boys cherished what few pictures they had of their father, scattered images, secreted in battered storage boxes and fading Kodak sleeves. They encouraged their mother to tell them stories of their father, although the compulsive storyteller was oddly reticent to share. Inevitably, their perseverance prevailed, Gracie yielding to her proclivity for tales, launching into the fiction that affirmed their heritage, pronounced their nobility.

While the passing years diminished Gracie's hopes of his return, the boys were fervent in their belief that he would one day re-enter their lives, the head restored to the MacDonald clan. If Gracie ever slipped, voicing her doubts that he might not return, she'd face the inherited feistiness she had gifted her boys. They would not allow their mother to tolerate such thoughts; she had taught them never to give up.

The boys' respect for their mother ran deep. She made sure they were aware of just how much she had done for them, how the management of her life was all about enhancing theirs. They knew she had secrets, concealed to most, but to them, she confided the least important, the ones where a slip would prove harmless – or manageable.

Don't tell anyone about the knitting machine.
Don't tell people how hard Mommy works.
It's okay to let people think we have lots of money.

GRANNY MAC – BLYTHE

It made them co-conspirators. Gracie kept the details of her questionable actions hidden. She and her boys needed safeguarding; if her children didn't know anything, they couldn't incriminate her. By ensuring their ignorance about the worst of her behaviours, she maintained their innocence. Gracie thought she did well to conceal her darkest secrets; her boys were willing participants. She dangled promises: Air Jordans, Nintendo Gameboys, trinkets of value, trinkets of status. The bribery worked effectively; the boys maintained her mystery, the models of discretion. The local charity work and Gracie's labours on the knitting machine supported them until the boys went to college.

Although she spoiled them, she also worked them hard. The pretence that the MacDonald's were leaders meant that her boys had a legacy to fulfil. She drove them, unrelenting in her demand for exceptional performance. If they fell short, they felt her disappointment. Gracie's displeasure always resulted in pain for her boys, though not always physical; her irritation manifested in a variety of ways, her tongue capable of telling more than just fanciful tales.

Studying and training hard, they each earned scholarships from notable universities, their efforts underpinned by Gracie's remorseless pressure, offering no respite to her children, invoking the importance of their studies, while delivering them to sports fields for intensive coaching, believing that talent in the classroom, when combined with exceptional athleticism, would attract offers to ease her financial burden.

Her goals realised; the boys' colleges profited from Gracie's enthusiastic fundraising efforts; evenly split, naturally. She encouraged the alumni to excessive generosity.

Is that all you think of your alma mater?
Look at the start they gave you.
Surely the next generation deserves better.

She charmed and cajoled benefactors to ever greater levels of philanthropy.

A LITTLE SOMETHING TO HIDE

Ross's scholarship to play golf at Texas A&M proved to be especially lucrative. Oilmen had a propensity to show off their money. Gracie gave them the opportunity.

While Ross referred to what he did as *Swinging a few bats,* Grace adopted a more pretentious stance. *Ross's scholarship is an opportunity to learn the intricacies of an ancient Scottish artform.*

Either way, over the four years that Ross was improving his golf game, his mother made 1.6 million dollars from his college for her charitable foundation. In her best year of zigging and zagging sweaters from her old Singer machine, she made just $24,000, not that the US government was particularly aware of her earnings, it was still providing her with the same welfare cheques since Archie's disappearance.

As if in sacrifice to the additional prosperity, she gave up her assignations with college waiters – she didn't want her boys to hear scandalous stories about their mother from their peers.

To maintain her sons' complicity, Gracie equipped her boys with the toys they wanted. They kept schtum about their mother's ventures, mostly through ignorance, but also because driving a Dodge Camaro around campus made it easier to reinforce their mother's narrative. They were proud of her achievements and the renown that came from her account of the MacDonald legacy.

Gracie MacDonald finds it easy to fib. She never feels guilty about spinning yarns or taking money from people who should know better. Hers is a lifetime of invention, and as the half-truths and falsehoods slide from her tongue, they enter the realm of her reality. Once told, she finds it difficult to separate the two.

Her chronicles appear drawn from memory, genuine events that she experienced, or histories recorded. In the telling, the essence of her tales become her new truths, she finds it impossible to dissemble the myths. To her, they simply don't exist. The more depth she incorporates in her backstory, the more concrete it becomes. As one fact disappears, an invented one emerges. A practiced cross-examiner may find it impossible to detect her lies, so convinced is Gracie that what she says is real.

GRANNY MAC – BLYTHE

Only one thing causes her guilt. A secret that she keeps hidden from everyone, one that she cannot rewrite to make it vanish from existence; she has tried, repeatedly.

The lie is the one that everybody believes, her conviction to it is absolute, but she is the only person that she can't convince of her version of the truth. That lie is the outlier.

The evidence is in her wicker basket, it travels everywhere with her, gnawing at her, insisting on its presence. It is a secret that she shares with one other, but which she tells herself she must never reveal. Besides Gracie, Archie alone knows the unspeakable truth that she keeps from everyone but herself.

Now, as she sits on the bus on the way to meet baby Emily for the first time, she wonders whether it is time to come clean, to share with her boys just one more truth that she will beg them to keep. The thought blights her fugue as she watches the landscape slide by.

An unknown period passes while in her trance, surfacing to the surprise of knitting needles in her hands. The needles move, unbidden, operating independently of her thoughts, the metronomic clackety-clack, *quieter than Rosa's.*

A smile creeps upon her as she considers how wise Angus has been to name his daughter after Gracie, but a little sad that with Emily, the MacDonald name will disappear. Despite what she argues, Angus's genetics are to blame.

The quiet rage she felt towards her son for not allowing her to be at the birth of her granddaughter has stilled. He said that it would be more appropriate for his wife's mother and father to be at the hospital. Gracie wasn't happy about the arrangement and was planning to travel to Albuquerque early. She wanted to be there when little Emily arrived, intending to land on her son's doorstep unannounced, leaving Angus with no option but to take her to the hospital, but baby Emily had other plans, choosing to appear three weeks early.

Gracie considers it the first sign that having a girl is a troublesome addition to the family. Neither is she optimistic there will be another boy to add to the clan. Angus and his whore have the best chance, but the sands are close to running through on the bitch's biological hourglass.

If Reggie and Ross are to do the job, they will have to divorce and start again. Gracie believes that the vessels they chose as their wives are barren. Although separation in favour of younger editions seems unlikely, she will begin sowing those seeds when they come together to meet their new niece.

Her brow creases as she sets her needles down, pondering whether now is the right time to tell the boys her dark secret.

Returning the knitting to her basket, she digs inside, lifting a flap of material that conceals a compartment in which she has hidden a well-thumbed envelope. Diamonds of red and blue frame the edges, the writing on the front faded, the address, penned in the unmistakeable spidery crawl of her husband.

Taking the envelope from its nook, Gracie runs her hand over the writing, as if she can connect to the person who placed it there. She removes the Marine Corps letterhead it holds, unfolding it carefully, noting the Rorschach's blots that her tears made long ago. She doesn't need to see the words to recall them, she's read them before, hundreds of times. Each word is indelibly scribed on her heart; she can bring them to mind whenever she thinks of Archie.

She has never told her boys about the letter, she wants to wait until the time is right, when she deems that they can cope. That time is now. She has decided that with the newest generation entering the world, it is time to add to the family's legacy.

Sighing, she returns the letter to its envelope before hiding it again in her basket. She considers how she will break the news, mouthing each word in the letter, all 222 of them. She skips nothing, adds no embellishment. Every word falls from her mouth, plucked directly from the page. She has decided to be performative, delivering another of Granny Mac's famous stories. This one will be different though. Archie wrote this one, and this one is true.

PHOENIX BUS STATION

> **Arrivals**
> Time　　From　　　　　　　　　Expected
> 18:29　　Blythe　　　　　　　　Expected: 19:41

> **Departures**
> Time　　Destination　　　　　　Expected
> 19:00　　Flagstaff　　　　　　　Delayed: 20:11

PHOENIX BUS STATION

A mismatching palette colours the length of a Briscola coach. Azure blue melds into Californian orange, which in turn nestles against a scarlet-fever red. The visual assault continues, jaundiced yellow lightning bolts morph into the scheme's final hue, a scatological brown that wraps around the front of each vehicle.

A company logo overlays the garish pigments: an all-seeing eye which speaks of the mistrust the patriarch feels toward all. It lies alongside block capitals reading BRISCOLA COACH SERVICES in a font as dull as the designer who devised the vignette.

In an ill-advised attempt to preserve cash, Anthony Briscola commissioned his 43-year-old son to fashion something elemental. He failed in every regard unless he was seeking to create an elemental catastrophe. The impression it garners is a picture of a business in decay that neither the father nor the son recognises. The branding is a visual testimony to the company's culture. Incoherent, jarring, dated, and ugly. The branding provides credence to the cliché that money can't buy class. It is a cliché with which Anthony Briscola is unfamiliar. His psyche is such that he is unable to discern the difference between jocular humour and the sniggering that his corporate identity induces.

Passengers come and go on a Briscola coach, some stimulating subtle resentment from existing travellers, irritating with their inconsiderate shambling as they enter the bus, bags or body-parts colliding with those occupying aisle seats. The only person untroubled by such intrusions is Michael Williams, accustomed as he is to his legs proving an unavoidable obstacle.

A LITTLE SOMETHING TO HIDE

The uninhibited often share their conversations, barking down mobile phones at unseen protagonists, unperturbed at the ire that their too audible conversations draw from those around them.

Mostly, customers enter and exit the bus unremarked, engendering little interest from their travelling companions. Unconsciously content to be ignored, they traipse on and off as their journeys' deem, not so much forgotten by those they join or leave, just unnoticed.

There are exceptions, like the slight girl who steps aboard the bus in Phoenix. There is something other-worldly about her, a quality that defies description. A quiet embraces the interior of the coach as she climbs the stairs. Conversations cease. The infant George, previously grizzling, stills his whines. Muted treble notes escaping from headphones contaminate the airwaves above the emerging silence. The coach, beforehand idling with a dejected grumble, seems to adopt a winsome tone with her arrival.

Eyes rise from books. Rosa lowers needles to her lap, Michael fights a blush that steals upon him unbidden. All the passengers gaze at her as she climbs aboard, inexplicably feeling their moods lift as she passes them on the way to her seat. She smiles at those whose eyes she catches, draws smiles in return, including from Toby Ames, whose narcotic-fuelled anxieties have diminished in her presence. An artist might render her form in angelic brushstrokes.

Jeannie Roberts is looking forward to her trip as she steps onto the bus. She's identified a large plot of land alongside the Tijeras Arroyo Golf Course on the outskirts of Albuquerque, perfectly shaped to fit her plans.

She is exceptionally good at her work. The reception she receives on the coach hints at her magnetism. She radiates charm, empathy, and kindness; draws people to her. Almost universally, those that meet her will tell you what a privilege it is to know her, or they'll find accolades to highlight her remarkable talents.

When people seek comfort, she is the one to whom they turn. Her shoulders are slender, she is sylph-like, possessing a diaphanous quality, yet she bears the heaviest of emotional loads with ease, untroubled by the burden; she assuages the guilt of all who feel they have imposed.

Unlike most 24-year-olds that choose not to go to college after high-school, Jeannie has a sizeable savings account. She is not a social media sensation. She doesn't have a YouTube channel or a TikTok

PHOENIX BUS STATION

account, neither is she an influencer generating income from multiple sponsorship deals. Some might think she sits at the vanguard of film, music, or sport – a notion she would disabuse. The truth is more prosaic; she's a carer and a prodigious saver, of people and money, but most of all, she's a terribly lovely girl.

A LITTLE SOMETHING TO HIDE

JEANNIE – PHOENIX

Thomas Svenson, the careers counsellor at Thunderbird High School, was tired of making calls, bored of his profession. The delivery of his carefully crafted script lacked the vibrancy that followed its initial drafting six years earlier, written when flushed with zeal for his role, still fostering the belief that he could make a difference to the lives of Phoenix's teenagers. Now it contained a blend of unmerited optimism and barely concealed desperation. He no longer focused on enthusiastic delivery, yielding instead to the strain of keeping the mewling from his voice, as he sought to overcome his indifference to the prospects of so many of his charges.

As a prerequisite to placing the calls, he expected a list from each of his students which detailed the companies where they wished to work. Most gave responses that featured local businesses, reflecting either parental expectations or undeveloped ambition, making choices that stemmed from a mix of apathy and ignorance.

A weary sigh preceded each call he made, signalling Thomas's belief in another futile attempt to find a placement, another campaign to convince a dubious audience of his scheme's merits. He attempted to infuse his entreaties with benefits for the host company, while fighting the urge to beg for help. He knew that the picture he painted of youngsters adding value to a sponsor's organisation was discordant with their opinions, holding a certainty that the person on the other end of his call believed the student would be little more than a five-day burden.

It therefore came as a great surprise to Thomas that the first organisation on Jeannie Roberts' list expected his call. It was unusual for one of his calls to be welcome; excitement was unprecedented, yet that was exactly the reaction he got from

A LITTLE SOMETHING TO HIDE

the Executive Director of the Blazing Sun Residential Centre. Amanda Shearling could not have been keener to finalise the arrangements for Jeannie's placement. *We're so looking forward to Jeannie's week with us. I think our residents are going to love her.*

She was right.

The list Jeannie provided to Thomas included three companies, recorded in order of preference. Uniquely, it included the names, titles, and telephone numbers of those he should contact. Out of curiosity, Thomas Svenson telephoned the others on Jeannie's list and found himself consoling those whose names she'd provided. Expressing evident disappointment at not securing the services of Jeannie Roberts, both offered to act as standbys should her placement fall through. The counsellor thought he would press his advantage, asking if either would be willing to take another student. The reluctance that Thomas was accustomed to hearing re-emerged, if they couldn't have Jeannie, no one else would do.

Jeannie's impact at Blazing Sun was instant. Her smile rarely faded, disappearing only when circumstances demanded a more sober visage, attuned to the requirement for solemnity when it arose. At all other times, she wandered breezily, with the campaigning politician's ability to make everyone feel her undivided attention.

No subject was less than interesting to Jeannie. She treated trivialities as monumental, boredom or weariness never weighed on her features. She had time for everyone and never appeared impatient to be elsewhere, granting every request made of her, forgetting nothing and no one.

Those whose eyesight betrayed them welcomed the time that Jeannie spent reading aloud. Whether reading from a newspaper or a favourite novel, Jeannie could bring nuance to the words, she applied inflections to bring colour and life to lacklustre prose; she could animate a news report.

The melody of her voice matched the mellifluence of her words; a song was never far from her lips, her presence always announced by her perfect pitch as she strolled the corridors of the centre while carrying out her assignments. She made even the most mundane chores appear a celebration; embracing requests for help, singing her way through her work.

Her repertoire was inexhaustible and included every song beloved by the residents. Afternoons would pass with her fulfilling requests to sing another favourite. With an extraordinary range, no note seemed too challenging; she never missed a beat, and she provided harmony to those that wanted to indulge their own musical talents.

In quieter moments she'd sit on the opposite side of a board game, playing chess, checkers, scrabble, or whatever Parker Bros creation passed as entertainment to a resident. The games she played were always close encounters, with Jeannie possessing the skills required to be a deft and gracious loser.

Her effect on others encompassed more than just emotional fillips, her presence also had a physical impact. Slumped residents sat straighter in their chairs, as if improvements to their posture would earn the reward of her attention.

She never tired, her boundless energy served to stretch the hours available, creating time for everyone. Residents and co-workers marvelled at how much she achieved, demonstrating a maturity and compassion that belied her 17 years. If there was a way to make her more perfect, none knew what it might be. Jeannie was a phenomenon; an angel among us.

Her high school graduation signalled the end of her formal education. In the eyes of Amanda Shearling, she was already fully qualified and Blazing Sun was ready to accommodate a lack of conventional learning if it meant securing Jeannie's services. The residents also lobbied, quite unnecessarily, for her recruitment. Amanda had decided after just two days of Jeannie's placement that she wanted her on the team.

Jeannie planned a Nursing major to underpin her goal to be a carer, but Amanda argued that there was nothing a college could teach that Jeannie didn't already know. More importantly, Amanda didn't want to risk losing Jeannie to another institution; she had to have her on board. She offered her a full-time job at the end of the week's placement, promising Jeannie a position at any time.

A LITTLE SOMETHING TO HIDE

Jeannie didn't dwell on her decision, telling her parents she was taking the expedited path. The usual parental admonitions followed: a college education as a backup; the need to reflect on unspecified implications; avoiding a rush to decide; highlighting the years ahead of her. Jeannie was certain, deflecting her parents' concerns, she knew exactly what she wanted. They were as susceptible to her charms as everyone else. By the time she had finished calming their fears, they had agreed to her plan and promised their unwavering support, awed by her maturity, and proud that she was embarking on a career that would give so much to so many.

The Blazing Sun Residential Centre based its business model on long-term horizons. It didn't want its residents to arrive infirm, preferring instead that they segue into frailty, adopting the provision of care when time and circumstance required. Before then, Blazing Sun provided an experience more closely resembling the activities of a country club. Ill health or retirement weren't mandatory requirements to become a resident – a healthy bank balance guaranteed a place. If required, Blazing Sun provided care using a team of professionals that were available at all hours, all highly trained, or in Jeannie's case, exceptionally gifted.

The company's website defined the facility's setting as exquisite. Azaleas bloomed in the spring, manicured conifer woods provided pine-needle carpets, perfectly trimmed lawns, verdant year-round, defied the glare of the Arizona sun. Residents enjoyed state-of-the-art technology, leisure facilities, concierge services, plush surroundings. The centre in Phoenix was one of 15 it operated in the Southwest, catering to anyone with the ability to pay.

The starting price for a year in a spacious one-bedroom apartment at Blazing Sun was $300,000. More extensive accommodation was available – right up to 1.5 million dollars a year. In the inverse world of exceptional wealth, those suites were the most prized. Their annual rental bought the residents an electronic fob that would open the gates to the centre and the door to their apartments. Anything else cost extra, from the clean sheets on their beds to the food that entered their bellies.

The rental didn't cover a car parking space. That was another six thousand dollars a year, assuming you were content for your car's paintwork to fade in the glare of a Phoenix summer. Most residents were not. They preferred the twenty-five-thousand-dollar option of valet parking in the underground garage – for each of their cars.

The founders of Blazing Sun excelled at providing services to its residents and were even better at charging for them. Most residents gave away an annual slice of their net worth approaching a million dollars, and for the majority, that was just fine. Expense wasn't an issue.

Unlike the fifteen percent of Americans who thought they dwelt within the wealthiest one percent of the population, most occupants at a Blazing Sun Residential Centre had legitimacy to such a claim, not that they made it, it wasn't much of a boast, there was a reasonable likelihood a near-neighbour was wealthier; there weren't many residents that moved in with assets below the mid-ten figure region.

When they arrived, few of the residents either needed or wanted care. Pampering, yes. Care, no. The attraction lay in the country-club atmosphere and the comfort of mixing with an elite clique, swapping stories with the like-minded, and never having to be concerned with ulterior motives.

Michelin starred chefs and unabashed luxury contributed to guests' willingness to stay for the remainder of their days. The appeal of the place heightened with the knowledge that when their faculties waned, care would come to their apartments.

With tennis courts, swimming pools, fitness centres, and many on or next to golf courses, there were few places that people could live on a permanent basis that were grander than a Blazing Sun. No one entering a facility left it to find another home.

While most residents luxuriated in the splendour of the facilities for decades, the ravages of time eventually took their toll. When the inevitable decline in mental or physical health prevailed, the residents found themselves increasingly in the company of Jeannie Roberts.

Jeannie's presence was an elixir, a physical manifestation of the fountain of youth. Some considered her capable of prolonging their lives – in many ways she did, keeping everyone active and sharp. The curmudgeonly failed to keep smiles from their faces in Jeannie's company. She gave them experiences that a less attentive carer might not; she added happiness to their days. During the day she was an entertainer, in the evening, a carer, and in the lonely nights, a friend.

Family visits were a feature of life at Blazing Sun. There were few residents that didn't have at least one family member call each week. It was evident to Jeannie which residents loved the incursions and those that did not. It led her to categorise the family types.

There were those that chittered excitedly about forthcoming stays. The prospect of their sons and daughters, grandchildren and great-grandchildren coming to visit energised some, an opportunity to spend time with family, witnessing the growth and development of the newest members of their brood, to share and feel familial love. She called them the *Lovelies*.

Others contained their enthusiasm, almost begrudging the invasion of their offspring into their leisure time. They had never quite adapted to the company of their children; nannies and au pairs addressed the care of their offspring, while as parents they relentlessly pursued the wealth that now allowed them to live in splendour. To those residents, the weekly intrusion of their children was an inconvenience to their dotage. Receiving their offspring felt more like an obligation rather than an event they should welcome. Jeannie referred to them as the *So-sos*.

Even the name she adopted for the final category carried an air of geniality. The *Grumblies* consisted of those that hated the visits. It was clear to Jeannie that neither the residents nor their guests wanted to be with each other. Less kindly, in the staffroom and offices of the Blazing Sun Residential Centre, the team referred to these families as the sociopaths.

The patriarch of the family, and it was always a man, exhibited extreme narcissism. He invariably considered himself lord and master to whom all family members owed fealty. No love radiated from these families and self-worth was a fragile construct, one that rested on the whims of the father.

Accomplishments went unremarked, never celebrated, only compared, always falling short of some real or imagined feat of the patriarch. It was painful to witness the attempts of family members trying to win approval; they invariably failed, yet still they continued to come, either out of misplaced duty, or more likely an urge to remain connected to their legacy; there was always an eye on the money.

Whether that was true or not, Jeannie didn't know, but after the visits, when the families scurried from an increasingly irascible patron, carrying their bruises, hoping that the scars they gained would yield some future dividend, Jeannie would hear the diatribes of the family head, learn their thoughts, discover the belief that ungrateful offspring were hatching conspiracies. She would stem their fury, lead them from their darkness, skilfully changing the subject, lightening the mood.

Jeannie kept a mental note of everyone's relationships, quizzing people on their history, committing the details to memory. Reticence to discuss the past disappeared when Jeannie was the inquisitor, she could draw people into conversations to discuss their lives and encourage them to share their intimate thoughts and feelings.

Entrusting nothing to paper, she catalogued everything as memory, drawing upon the database in her head when necessary. She reminded residents of upcoming birthdays and anniversaries, remarking on gifts given in previous years and making suggestions for forthcoming presents. Her ideas were always stunning, the perfect gift, usually because a spouse either wittingly or unwittingly told her what they would love to receive, and she duly repackaged the hints. More than one former CEO now living at Blazing Sun expressed a wish that

A LITTLE SOMETHING TO HIDE

Jeannie had worked for them as an Executive Assistant during their careers.

Her encyclopaedic knowledge of the people she cared for was a talent that no one else shared; it made her everyone's favourite. The ability to make people feel special spread like contagion. Gentle hints and the nudging of others saw small kindnesses spread throughout the centre, quietly extending the care she gave through the actions of others.

Those that were the most infirm received special attention. On the night shift, when the porters played poker waiting for guests to call, the care team did their rounds, briefly checking on the residents' comfort. Her colleagues followed a process that consisted of cursory checks, which once done, would see them returning to the night desk to swipe at smart phones or gossip. The young woman with the unbreakable smile adopted a different practice.

If the residents were awake, most would tell their carers that they were fine. Jeannie's colleagues took them at their word, but she knew when they were not, challenging their answers.

Are you sure? she'd ask, while waiting silently at the door until they were honest. Her compassion opened them; with Jeannie they were willing to share. She'd glide into their rooms, making fruit teas before taking a seat on the sofa, and they would talk.

Other guests, those that needed the most care, would already be in their beds and she'd pull up a chair, sit next to them and take a hand. Often, they would ask Jeannie to read, comforting words from comforting books; Jojo Moyes, Mitch Albom, Joanne Harris, David Nicholls; bedtime stories for the fading, the sound of Jeannie's voice providing a balm. Sometimes they would chat, often they would ask about Jeannie, an excuse to savour more of her soothing cadences.

Jeannie spoke of a happy childhood, a family filled with love, both her parents teachers; her mother taught English, her father, Music, fuelling her love of learning and delight in the arts. She would share her favourite books, exchanging critiques with those that had read them, adding them to the reading lists of those that had not.

Some residents asked about her ambition, and she shared. It was simple, she wanted to care. It was a calling, the only thing she had ever considered. One day, she hoped, she would have enough money to start her own place. A modest venture, where she could be active and hands on, but where the care for guests was heartfelt.

She was careful not to be critical of her employer or her colleagues. She knew Blazing Sun was the best in the industry, it was why she sat them at the top of her work placement list, why they were the only place she wanted to work. She also believed that in every great company there was room for improvement. *My business will only make small adjustments to Blazing Sun's model.* When asked what she would change, her answer amplified her character.

Not much, she'd say. *I'll just add love.*

Jeannie loved the residents, and they loved her back.

Her aspirations went largely unmentioned, believing that voicing her ambition would undermine her employer. Anyone that cared to ask knew that she would be forever grateful to Amanda Shearling and the team at Blazing Sun. Jeannie had no intention of appearing disloyal. She was quick to espouse the brilliance of the organisation, only ever mentioning her dream to those that she spent time with on the night shift, as her words caressed them to sleep. Many had forgotten by the morning, some remembered, but didn't mention it again. She never told anybody twice, unless they asked, few did.

Maude Cleghorn was one of those that remembered and asked again. Maude had been at Blazing Sun for 32 years. She and her husband had moved there when he retired from his investment bank. He was a giant of a man, a Texan who moved to New York after he graduated from Stanford and charged to the top of his firm.

Brian Cleghorn epitomised his home state; rugged and weather-beaten, broad and powerful, an indomitable authority. He commanded a room when he entered, created a void when he left. He and Maude met in the Hamptons during a Thanksgiving weekend at a mutual friend's cottage. She was visiting from Savannah, Georgia and was most assuredly not looking for a husband, especially not one as pugnacious as Brian Cleghorn, but as Maude recounted many times over the years, he was a mightily persistent and determined fellow.

Brian could be relied upon to be gregarious, it earned him invitations everywhere. When he confirmed his attendance, ecstatic hosts spread the word, it guaranteed that others would follow. At the Hamptons, he spent little time focusing on other guests, even though they flocked to him for company. He entertained them but gave his attention to Maude. By the end of the weekend, he had convinced her that the loud-mouthed Long-horn and the erudite southern Belle would make a perfect team. He was right, their devotion was absolute.

Brian wasn't the only tenacious personality in the marriage. At forty-five, he retired, selling his stake in the bank for 280 million dollars and their houses on Park Avenue and Long Island for another twenty-five, yielding to Maude's insistence that they move closer to their children.

Their daughter, Dawn, lived in Phoenix and their son, David, in Las Vegas. Although commercial acumen and ruthless logic ruled his working life, Brian joked there was a danger of their inheritance vanishing if they moved to Vegas, deciding instead to award their proximity to Dawn.

The Cleghorns could have bought any house in Phoenix, and with it, the attendant aggravation of recruiting and managing the staff that attaches to a grand estate. Brian no longer shouted at people. He'd been doing so for 20 years and wanted to give his vocal cords a break. Besides, managing staff would take time away from the golf course.

Blazing Sun offered everything the Cleghorns were looking for. They had one of the larger suites; six bedrooms, a library that Maude filled with collectible first editions and original manuscripts, a home theatre, and private dining for sixteen. If the family grew as they hoped, there'd be plenty of space at

Thanksgiving. According to Jeannie, the Cleghorns were card carrying *Lovelies*.

The only thing that annoyed Brian about their new home was the inadequate nine-hole golf course. He hadn't finished his first round of golf before he was on the phone to Amanda Shearling asking for a course extension. She patiently explained to him that the business didn't own the course, there was nothing they could do.

Brian Cleghorn wasn't accustomed to people refusing his requests. By the end of the day, he had agreed terms for the course and the neighbouring 75 acres. Three weeks later, the earth moving equipment was preparing the back nine holes and the green keeper understood that nothing short of a championship quality course would be acceptable. Six months later, with the development complete, Brian handed the property deeds to Amanda, asking only that she allowed him preferential tee-times.

His passion for golf was all-consuming, but the absence from the boardroom left him with a shortage of playing partners, leading to incessant complaints that he didn't have enough people to play. To quiet his moaning, and without discussion, Maude obtained a set of clubs and joined him on the fairways. Any objection to his newest playing partner died when he spied the same determination that led to his retirement. Maude's plan prevailed; they spent the first four hours of every morning striding the fairways.

They never took breakfast in their home. Maude packed two bananas for her and a flask of coffee to share. Brian chugged peanuts for the first five holes, with each day's golf finishing with brunch in the clubhouse.

Brian usually won, but Maude enjoyed a quiet, subversive truth; that in all the years they'd played together, Brian had only hit one hole-in-one – Maude's count stood at nine. Whenever he boasted of his superior scorecards, she gently reminded him of her accuracy.

On the day he died, Brian still had fourteen holes to play. As he had done without difficulty on every day of the preceding 26 years, he upended a foil pack of Planters into his mouth at the par five, fifth tee. This time, he felt a chock of rogue nut lodging in his throat. The self-administered thump to his chest produced a deep hollow thud that carried across the still morning, serving only to accelerate his coughing. Maude watched in helpless alarm as the colour rose to his face, his golfer's ruddy complexion rising higher, crimson patches emerging at his cheeks before engulfing his face in an effort to win air.

Maude's understanding of the Heimlich manoeuvre came from dubious B-movie comedies. Wrapping ineffectual arms around her husband, she gave his stomach a squeeze, failing to displace the nut. He slipped between her arms and lay on the grass, clutching at his throat, trying to breathe.

The memory of Brian's eyes, panicked and pleading, before surrendering cognition, will never leave Maude. She wonders whether his final memory is of her kneeling beside him, inept, screaming for help as his bodily systems reacted to the absence of oxygen, blue lips adding another shade to his already puce face, nostrils flaring, the bullish man ebbing to an impassive form before her, ceasing to be a force. By the time the golfers on the hole behind had heard her screams and arrived where Brian lay, he was dead. Maude never swung a golf club again.

She was seventy-six on the day of Brian's death and fitter than most of the centre's residents, but with the abandonment of her daily golf game, Maude initiated the foundations for worsening health. The changes weren't sudden, emerging gradually, a leaching of her fitness, creaks entering once flexible joints, taut muscles losing their strength, tone dissolving.

For most of her adult life, Maude weighed close to 120 pounds. Variations were minor, a pound or two after Thanksgiving and Christmas, the excess gone by Valentine's Day. Before Easter, she made a conscious effort to lose a couple of pounds in anticipation of the chocolate binges that lay ahead.

After Brian's death, her tone strayed and her weight drifted, falling at first, as apathy gripped her when she saw meals as a chore. The Cleghorns enjoyed their food, loved that at the Blazing Sun the menu changed daily, and that Chef was accommodating to their requests. Wine accompanied all meals; Brian had brought his collection with him and paid for the necessary expansion to the centre's cellars. It was a significant extension.

He delighted in taking bottles into the kitchen and challenging Chef to create the perfect food match. He always took two, one for the following evening's meal, for serving to the Cleghorns with the latest culinary invention, the other to serve as Chef's inspiration and compensate him for his trouble. Chef treated Brian's 'trouble' agreeably, finding it easy to compromise his artistry when supping an eight-hundred-dollar Bordeaux with his favourite resident.

Maude didn't care to drink alone. With Brian gone, she continued to take wine to the kitchen, but only one bottle, and only for Chef. Brian's collection still contained over three thousand bottles and she didn't want to see it wasted. Chef and his team couldn't quite believe their luck, sharing the wine after service, while Maude chose to sip mineral water with her dinner. The absence of the man who had filled her with joy and vitality diminished her appetite, not just for food and drink, but also for life. Much that she had lived for was gone. Maude Cleghorn began to atrophy.

When Jeannie Roberts started at Blazing Sun, Maude, who stood at 5 feet 9 inches, was down to 105 pounds. Before Brian's death, her skin defied ageing, conspiring to obscure her years. Even the backs of her hands, which ordinarily convey a spiteful reality, remained taut and firm. Now it betrayed her, not only in her liver spotted hands, but as a cracked and wrinkled parchment that hung loosely; there was insufficient Maude to fill her skin.

She rarely left her suite and didn't participate in the activities the centre arranged. It was Brian who drove their life, entertained their friends, kept everyone laughing as he regaled them with his stories. Their friends supported her, both her fellow residents and those that visited, but the visits shortened, the time between them lengthened, and the arrangements diminished – Maude wasn't great company without her husband.

Dawn and David kept coming. Dawn every weekend, David at least once a month, flying himself in a plane that his father had bought him for his fortieth birthday. Dad was always their favourite, but they loved their mother, the slight woman always providing assurance and comfort with the firmness of her hugs. She had been the quiet one, holding the family together, planning holidays, keeping studies on track, guiding and nurturing.

It was impossible to arrest Maude's decline with their love. They watched as she faded, a tiredness creeping upon her, a pernicious thief stealing her vitality, causing them to experience a living grief for their mother. Their love for her had no place to go, it fell between them, lying unnoticed by Maude who seemed unwilling to receive the gift. There was nothing that they could say or do that would provoke her, to spark her back to life. They both kept coming, brought the grandchildren with them, and left feeling hollow and frayed from their unrequited efforts. It was taking its time, but Maude Cleghorn was slowly dying of a broken heart.

Jeannie Roberts saw the sadness in Maude the moment they met. Five years had passed since Brian's death, with the drift of every lonely day written on Maude's face. She could raise a smile whenever anyone greeted her, but they were fleeting, falling from her lips as quickly as they formed, designed to keep people from asking how she felt. Maude didn't want them to ask, the question caused her to lie. She didn't want to tell the truth, most wouldn't understand. Worse, she didn't want to see the look in the eyes of those that did, who understood Maude's belief, that life was getting in her way.

Jeannie's smiles were always genuine. She didn't knowingly moderate her smile for a situation, she never needed to wear a fake shine; the appropriate smile just appeared. Sometimes, they were beaming, her eyes alight. Other times she wore a knowing smile, painted with a softer brush, carrying a kindness that reflected an unbidden comprehension of a guessed-at truth. Maude got a knowing smile from Jeannie which lingered on the young girl's face. It caused Maude to wear her own smile for a moment longer than she might otherwise have done.

The first question that Jeannie asked was about the display of golf balls. Mounted above a wide sandstone fireplace were two identically sized frames of rich walnut, embedded with dark strips of mahogany enclosing a faded baize cloth. One contained a single ball in its centre, while the other housed nine, arranged in a diamond. Beneath every ball was a small brass plaque that recorded the date and hole for each of the aces. For the first time in a while, a smile lingered on Maude's face.

Every time I aced a hole, I had to bogie the next, said Maude. *My husband was a kind and generous man, but a horrible loser. If I didn't let him win the round, the evenings dragged on for a whole lot longer.*

Jeannie encouraged her to tell more. Soon, Maude was giggling as she recalled the exploits of her late husband. Two hours passed before she noticed the time, apologising to the young woman for keeping her, receiving the sweetest smile in return. For the first time in a long time, Maude slept soundly.

Dawn Cleghorn was leaving Blazing Sun a couple of weeks later as Jeannie parked her battered Subaru in the employee's car park. Dawn beckoned to Jeannie, who trotted to meet her, afraid of what she might learn when she encountered a tearful daughter. Wrapping her arms around the younger woman, Dawn pulled her close and smothered her with a hug, before letting out a mournful sob. *Thank you,* she cried.

When Dawn let her go, Jeannie waited while the older woman dabbed at her tears, discovering that her fears were unfounded, Maude was not only living, but in better form than the family had seen for years. She'd recounted her time with the sweet young girl, saying how happy she was to talk about Brian again. Dawn lathered praise upon Jeannie, and although embarrassed by the compliments, Jeannie acquiesced to her pleas, promising that she would spend time with Maude every evening.

A LITTLE SOMETHING TO HIDE

On their fifth evening together, Maude realised she didn't know a thing about the young girl sitting with her. Inviting Jeannie to speak, Maude was impressed with how assured she seemed and how beautifully she spoke.

There wasn't much that she shared that night, only that she had always wanted to be a carer and how much she loved her job. She soon turned the conversation away from herself and discovered a little more about the Cleghorn family, persuading the elderly lady to relive her memories.

Jeannie guided Maude back to her youth, where she recounted days of a privileged childhood living in old Savannah, hinting at dalliances to match Scarlett and Rhett's. Her eyes shone as she recalled the 60s, near scandals, pacts with friends and lovers to keep inappropriate liaisons from becoming the outrage of a disapproving older generation.

Gradually, Maude emerged from her lethargy, harbouring more enthusiasm for the visits from her son and daughter, and looking forward to the evenings when Jeannie would tap on the door to ask her how she was feeling.

On one of his stops, Maude's son suggested to his mother that she might be gaining weight. She scolded him for being rude, before chuckling that she might have slipped on a few pounds. She quickly dispelled his concerns, telling him there was nothing to worry about.

I'm just feeling better and eating a little more, she explained, defiantly. *Heck, I'm even having a glass or two of Daddy's best stuff.*

Maude asked Jeannie one evening whether she had a fancy man. Giggling at the phrase, Jeannie confirmed there was no room in her life for a partner; she was married to her job. It was the first time that Jeannie shared with Maude the dream of running her own facility.

That's a grand idea, said Maude. *But don't you go running off. I'd find it just peachy if you stuck around here until my time is up.*

I reckon that's a long way off, Mrs Cleghorn. Anyway, Jeannie added. *I'm not sure I'm going anywhere; I don't have nearly enough saved yet.*

Maude studied her, wondering if the youngster was trying to be shrewd, but all she saw was sweet innocence. After that,

JEANNIE – PHOENIX

they talked occasionally of Jeannie's goals. Maude promised that when she was gone, she would provide a little something to help Jeannie on her way.

Maude died in her sleep just a few weeks later. At the funeral, Jeannie stood apart from the family, allowing them the space to mourn. They insisted she join them, standing close, attributing Maude's revival to Jeannie, she was part of the family. David and Dawn were grateful for her care, convinced that Jeannie's presence prolonged their mother's life.

It was nothing. I'd do the same for anyone. She was speaking honestly, everyone at the Blazing Sun Residential Centre received Jeannie's love.

David called her about a month after they had buried his mother, asking Jeannie to join him at the offices of the family's lawyer. David and his sister stood to welcome her, greeting her with hugs as she entered an opulent space. Along one wall stood a large bookcase lined with gold-leafed tomes, bound in unblemished leather, seemingly untouched by hands, imposing titles designed to express knowledge and authority, instead announcing egotism and vulgarity.

The family's attorney sat behind a broad table, a model of tailored civility, striving to convey the learned air that justifies extortionate fees, holding a sheaf of papers that he shuffled and tapped to create square edges, impatient for the greetings to conclude.

He contemplated Jeannie with a degree of suspicion mixed with disapproval. If he was attempting to instil discomfort in her, he failed. She smiled in that Jeannie-perfect way and his mood softened. He understood immediately the Cleghorn's attraction.

Jeannie couldn't keep the surprise from her face as the attorney read the codicil that Maude added to her will. She knew the old lady was going to leave her something, she thought maybe a few hundred dollars, but to her astonishment, discovered that she was about to be two-hundred and fifty thousand dollars richer.

Expecting David and Dawn to be angry that their mother had deprived them of so much money, they instead greeted her with a hint of apprehension, combined with hopeful expectation, as though they were seeking Jeannie's approval of the gift – the family, after all, were *Lovelies*.

I don't think it's right that Mrs Cleghorn should leave me so much.

David exhaled his relief, failing to appreciate the contradiction when he confirmed that it was just a token. He was apologetic that his mother didn't make a larger bequest and hoped she was okay with what she was getting.

He didn't explain it to her, but Jeannie knew that David and Dawn would be splitting the best part of two hundred and fifty million dollars between them – they could have stood a little extra.

When Maude died, Jeannie cried at the loss of her friend, someone with whom she had shared her dreams, and who in turn, had shared her most intimate secrets. Only Jeannie knew that Maude Cleghorn had woken from her sleep shortly before her death, unable to breathe, suddenly robbed of air.

It was a subtly different oxygen deprivation to that of her husband, with Maude tense and pulling at the arms on either side of the pillow that covered her face, unable to free herself from the pressure – there was more strength than seemed possible in Jeannie's slender arms. For her part, Jeannie was glad that she couldn't see Maude's bulging eyes as she learnt of the treachery, or her expression as she discovered the betrayal of a person she loved.

Jeannie knew she was going to get a lot more than a few hundred dollars when Maude's time came, wishing now that she'd suggested more than a quarter of a million in her conversations with Maude about her start-up costs. If she'd known the old girl was going to give her that much, she might have pushed for a million.

Still, Maude wasn't her only hope. There were others.

Benjamin S. Spicer, Jr. was an archetypal *Grumbly*. His fortune came from real-estate and there weren't many that were fond of him or his practices. By comparison, the Briscola family's questionable activities appeared minor indiscretions.

His father started the family's empire by exploiting government grants to develop affordable housing after the war. Federal money flowed into the company to finance land acquisition and development. Spicer Sr. manipulated flabby regulations, unearthed corrupt officials, and abused cheap labour to construct residential projects that didn't always satisfy the Government's affordability criteria, and rarely complied with local building codes.

The younger Benjamin grew at his father's knee, learning how not to accept excuses from anyone unable to afford their rent. His father's mantra was simple. *If they can't pay, they can't stay.*

Benjamin sat in his father's office watching his father issue instructions to the hired muscle who would 'process' his evictions. In addition to his lawyer and accountant, the thugs were the only people that Benjamin's father paid on time and in full.

There are some people, his father would say, *who ya gotta pay on time. The ones that'll keep ya outta prison and the ones who might kill you. Everyone else can go fuck themselves. You gotta do to them first what they'd like to do to you.*

It was a philosophy the senior Spicer instilled in his son and which his son adopted with vigour. Nobody was going to fuck over Junior, not even when he was dead.

The young Benjamin worshipped his father, clinging to every word, mimicking him, pandering to his ego. The father delighted in trumpeting his boy's antics.

He's just like me, he would laugh when Ben Jr. did something to attract his approval. *Only, he's more of an asshole. You ask his brothers and sisters.*

There was no fondness for Benjamin from his siblings. Throughout his life he commandeered their belongings, diminished their achievements, played one off against the other. He manipulated them, and subsequently his father, to gain a greater share of the family's wealth. He positioned himself as the obvious successor to the company, using the knowledge and understanding he had garnered through a lifetime of shadowing the head of the family. It was only natural, he argued, that the family's holdings should sit in a trust that he would administer on their behalf.

Nobody noticed the progressive syphoning of assets into businesses for which Benjamin was the sole beneficiary. He kept the allowances trickling to his siblings without them realising that the wealth which underpinned it was no longer theirs to share.

When his older brother decided it was time to buy a new condo in Vail because Benjamin and his family were always using the existing place, he discovered that there was no money available. When he challenged his brother, Ben Jr. invited him to meet him in court.

Benjamin discarded three wives before deciding that a fourth wasn't worth the trouble. In his view, plenty of women were happy to whore themselves for the opportunity of becoming the next Mrs Spicer. Rather than making yet another nuptial commitment he wouldn't keep, Benjamin decided that occasional paid help would suffice to satisfy his diminishing libido.

There are five children that he concedes are his, several others that he won't acknowledge, from mothers whose names he can't quite remember. For each claim, Benjamin's attorney slid a non-disclosure agreement across the desk to his client's jilted lover, each with a cheque pinned to the corner, an incentive to develop the skills of a single parent. Benjamin calculates that those payments are cheaper than admitting paternity and the incumbent cost of raising an illegitimate child. If he grasped sooner how much his children were going to cost him, he might have spent a couple of bucks on condoms, although such action would be contrary to his opinion of masculinity.

Unabashed in his disdain for the family, he too shared his opinions with Jeannie. *My kids are assholes and their spouses are gold-diggers. They're money-grubbing fuckers who only visit when they need cash.*

Jeannie tried to convince him otherwise, but he wouldn't listen. She was gentle with her chiding as she adjusted the dialysis equipment that substituted for his ruined kidneys. The old man was a complete prick, but she didn't want to let him know her thoughts. She was cheery with her admonishments, which made him laugh. Jeannie was the only thing that made him laugh these days, that, and the thought that he was going to fuck over his children; now *that* was hilarious.

Delighting in his scheming, Benjamin changed his will, leaving his entire estate, over sixty million dollars, to Jeannie, telling her to expect a fight. He told her that she would lose it all in court, relishing his prophecy.

There's too much money for them to not come hard, he said. *You've got fuck-all chance of keeping it, but I wanna make those fuckers squirm.*

Although he was fond of Jeannie, he didn't care that she would confront the family's wrath and the turmoil that would take years to unravel. He was more excited about the pain that he would cause his family than worrying about Jeannie's potential anxiety. Not that she felt concern, she didn't plan to afford him any posthumous pleasure.

It was obvious to Jeannie that more than just Benjamin's five children would want to fight. Others would emerge, noses primed, sniffing for greenbacks: the ex-wives; those illegitimate children; stiffed contractors. Jeannie could do without the challenges, but she also had a plan, one that would see her compensated for being so ... *Jeannie*.

Benjamin S. Spicer, Jr was right – the family contested his will. He left specific instructions on who should attend the reading. In the cavernous lobby of the Craddock and Hall law firm, Jeannie stood alone, ignored by the huddles of family and friends, each party failing to remain solemn as they speculated about their winnings.

None of them liked Benjamin, but each of them was swallowing their sentiment, too superstitious to cast aspersions about the man, worrying they might jeopardise their reward for years of sycophancy. A hush fell at their summons to the board room for the reading of the will. No one took much notice of the diminutive stranger with the warm smile who followed them into the room.

Joseph Hall, Benjamin's personal attorney, sat at the head of the table with paralegals either side of him who were busily scratching notes onto yellow legal pads. The three children from Benjamin's first marriage sat closest to the attorney so they could commandeer the view over the Phoenix skyline. Opposite them, sat the two children from his second and third marriages, along with his third ex-wife. She demanded a seat by her son, the only minor of the five children, usurping the positions of the other two wives in the room. The wives sought separation from each other, while jockeying for a place that reflected the status they believed they deserved.

Those that weren't related or hadn't provided offspring to Benjamin Spicer stood around the walls, none of them bold enough to take a seat. Jeannie crowded herself into the corner nearest the door, competing with no one for the space behind a flip chart.

It took less than ninety seconds before the deceased's oldest son, Benjamin S. Spicer, III, interrupted Joseph Hall.

Who the fuck is Jeannie Roberts?

Joseph Hall looked over his shoulder to where Jeannie stood as she emerged from her partial obscurity, raising a hand in embarrassment.

I am, she said, barely above a whisper.

Everyone turned toward the voice. It was a mark of how divorced they were from their father and his care provision that none of them recognised her.

Who is she? said someone from the side of the room.

The attorney explained Jeannie's presence and why Ben Jr. was leaving everything to her. He hadn't finished speaking before Benjamin's oldest daughter mentioned legal challenges. Hall accepted the possibility. *But I don't think now is the time or place for such discussions,* he said.

JEANNIE – PHOENIX

Actually, I think it is, said Jeannie, inviting further scrutiny. *But just with the family,* looking around the room at the unrelated interlopers, taking in their stares, watching the realisation emerge that they were getting nothing and that their time in the room was over. Gradually they took their cue to leave. The paralegals busily scratched at their pads as people left the room. Eventually the children and the ex-wives were all that remained with Jeannie and the legal team.

Joseph Hall cleared his throat and suggested to Jeannie that it might be prudent for her to take legal advice before continuing.

That's okay, she said. *But what I've got to say is only for the family.*

She looked pointedly at each of the ex-wives, her implication clear. The attorney cut off the original Mrs Spicer before she could launch an offensive. Simultaneously, Benjamin's three former wives pouted in a moment of unwanted solidarity.

Can't Mom stay? said the youngest of Ben Junior's offspring.

Of course, said Hall, causing the former wife's pout to transform to a triumphant smile.

Jeannie didn't intend to fight, instead she flashed a Jeannie smile. In the circumstances, it didn't have its usual effect, but then she didn't expect it would, there was too much hostility in the room. The family, wrestling their impulses, granted her silence as she outlined her proposal.

Using oblique language to answer Jeannie's questions relating to potential legal costs, Joseph Hall employed a multitude of caveats and assumptions that allowed no one to calculate a definitive number, but his obfuscation left everyone in the room with the impression that the fees would be sizeable.

Jeannie's *Exactly*, was emphatic. She spoke as though they'd received a concrete number. Although no figures filled the air, everyone present was clear the costs would exceed their willingness to pay.

Benjamin Spicer's progeny let Jeannie finish her proposal uninterrupted.

Could you let us have some time? asked Benjamin III.

A LITTLE SOMETHING TO HIDE

In his office, Joseph chuckled at the deviousness. *Even from his grave he's a bastard,* he said. *Letting them think they'd have to fight. He didn't tell me about your part in this.*

Oh no, Jeannie explained. *He wanted them to fight. The proposal was my idea. I know he wouldn't be happy, but then he did say I would probably lose.*

This way, she continued, smiling a Jeannie smile, *they only lose two hundred thousand each.*

Joseph Hall had the feeling that the girl would go far.

A paralegal knocked at his door. *The Spicers are ready to see you, Sir.*

When they entered the room, they were more willing to tolerate the warmth in the young woman who was restoring all but a fraction of their fortune. Benjamin the third asked the attorney what he thought of the proposal.

Joseph provided a suitably ambiguous response, leaving them in no doubt that Jeannie was offering a great deal. Benjamin Junior's children hugged Jeannie as they stepped out of the lawyer's office, so did Joseph Hall.

Choosing not to inform them of the highly irregular adjustment she'd made to his dialysis machine a few weeks earlier, none of the people hugging her suspected that Jeannie Roberts had precipitated Benjamin Spicer's death.

Jeannie's ninth, and most recent victim, was Walter Rogers. His cancer was extremely advanced on the night he told Jeannie he had left her a little something to remember him.

Like the Cleghorns, his family were *Lovelies* and had agreed with Walter that he should add a codicil to his will favouring Jeannie. They felt it was the least they could do given the exceptional care that she provided.

Devastation engulfed the family when he died. Fewer than two weeks had passed since his doctor predicted he was entering his final three to four months. He went so quickly; they didn't have a proper chance to say goodbye. Comfort came from the knowledge that Jeannie cradled him at his end, they asked her whether he had said anything or known that he was going to die that night.

JEANNIE – PHOENIX

Jeannie assured them that he hadn't known and invented the words she knew they wanted to hear, rather than the words he spoke. For several days she had been halving his morphine dosage, steadily accumulating the withheld portion, building a stockpile that would remain undetected by the dispensary team. It saddened her that Walter would have to endure a little more pain than was necessary, but she did her best to comfort him as he held her hand on his final evening, telling her that she was an angel on earth.

His frailty was obvious, and Jeannie was certain that she had enough morphine to administer a final, lethal dose once he was asleep. She was confident that no one would notice an additional needle site in his already mottled arms.

When she told the family that he went peacefully in his sleep, her words were not entirely removed from the truth.

With his legacy payment warming her account, Walter's half-million-dollars takes her savings over the four million mark. She plans to transform the plot of land alongside the Tijeras Arroyo Golf Course into the *pre-eminent residential care facility, confident that she can pre-sell units to the wealthy individuals she's identified as potential victims.*

The database in her head stores more than the details of birthdays and anniversaries. Embedded in her memory is the name of every CEO, CFO or COO to appear in a Forbes magazine. She mulls its rich list, committing its denizens to memory, ranking them not by the measure of their wealth, but by their age, a metric much more valuable to Jeannie's interests.

Even though the cost of care is inconsequential to her future guests, Jeannie has already decided she is going to charge her clients much less than the Blazing Sun Residential Centre. After all, she has other ways of supplementing her income.

A LITTLE SOMETHING TO HIDE

FLAGSTAFF BUS STOP

Arrivals
Time	From	Expected
22:02	Phoenix	Expected: 23:26

Departures
Time	Destination	Expected
22:30	Gallup	Delayed: 23:56

FLAGSTAFF BUS STOP

Simon Carter is thankful for the mobility that comes with his job. It's not the instant mobility of a travelling salesperson, his moves require long-term planning, but he relies on instinct to know when the time is right. Every seven years or so, he packs his few possessions into an heirloom trunk he received as a present for his ordination and travels to somewhere new. It suits him, and his flock. He always knows when it's time for him to move on. It's immediately before his congregation draw the same conclusion.

He's climbed on the Briscola coach for the journey east. He doesn't drive; his work usually comes to him, and on those occasions when he needs to pay a visit, the trusty Schwinn that he rewarded himself when his mission began, is enough to get him to where he needs to go. As he watches it stowed haphazardly in the baggage hold by a sullen handler, he muses that the Briscolas have charged him more for the storage of his bike than its original cost.

Simon is leaving Flagstaff, Arizona which has been his home since 2013 and he's overdue a change. It's time to cross the state line and start afresh. He usually likes it when he crosses a state border, it gives him an opportunity to recharge, to reinvigorate, to resume his career from a point of anonymity, where no one knows him and, unless they delve, no one knows his past. He likes that arrangement. It's handy.

On his last birthday, he turned fifty-two and is feeling his years. The ageing process is not treating him with grace, the pace of change embitters him. Others his age seem unaffected, he resents that he's an outlier. Clean living doesn't seem to have done him any favours, age continued its stealthy pursuit, creeping upon him, launching an invidious assault. It's not the only thing that crept upon him. This is his fourth move in the past twenty-six years, but this time feels a little different.

The destination board on the front of the bus says 'ALBU⸍UER⸍UE.' He doesn't know why the Qs have revolted; a glitch in the board's software, maybe a failure of Briscola Coach Services to upgrade the technology. The almost revealed destination is where he intends to step off, but geography aside, he doesn't really know where he's going, only that new people are willing to accept him and all his imperfections. He too has something missing, a spiritual glitch, but it's best that the people he's travelling toward remain unaware.

On this occasion, Simon Carter is unsure whether he is pursuing something new or escaping from his past. It is one of many things that he no longer knows, a list that continues to lengthen the older he gets. Sometimes he feels that there is only one thing he knows for certain, that he can no longer perform his role with honesty.

The mechanics come naturally; they're embedded in muscle memory. The circadian rhythms of the Christian faith are hard coded into his spiritual DNA, the rituals tied rigidly to the Gregorian calendar, others linked to what he considers a schizophrenic lunar cycle. It unsettles him that Easter moves. The ceremonies are a procedure, and he is just a functionary in their performance, not a participant. It's why he feels he is no longer of use to his parishioners.

Father Simon has carried his wavering faith for years. The weakness didn't stem from a catalysing event. His was a gradual decline, seeping like helium from a balloon, at first, plump and full, floating, but anchored to the earth. His faith has gone now, withered, shrivelling to an empty vessel alongside its tether on the ground, lying as a reminder of what was once joyful, now lifeless and devoid of promise, ready for discarding.

If asked, he couldn't say when his faith started to diminish. He's not able to tie it to a moment or a situation that challenged his belief. It crept from him, like his health, slipping with age, where simple acts require adjustments: needing the gentle push of his hand when rising from a chair; his willingness to mow a lawn yielding to a call to a contractor; the cool slip of a cotton sheet against naked flesh, giving way to the warmth of pyjamas; or where niggling aches are no longer attributed to long-forgotten injuries, but portend of something more sinister – time's relentless pursuit of the body's decline.

SIMON – FLAGSTAFF

There was a time when Father Simon Carter believed with the certainty of the zealot, when every thought and sentiment was righteous, where proclamations were absolute. He provided others with the assurances that their doubts were trivialities to overcome, where fervour prevails over weakness. His faith provided a foundation for others, a safeguard against their wavering. People turned to him for comfort which he provided with a confidence born of belief. Now, he considers himself to be Simon Carter again; no longer Father Simon – he doesn't feel worthy of the prefix.

In a time now lost, he saw God's grace in creation; the beauty in the basic, the majesty of the mountains, the power of the seas, the wondrous vagaries of the seasons. The passage of a year provided an assurance of a life everlasting; the comfort of summer, followed by autumn's incline towards a death that winter confers, before that bitter season succumbs to spring's resurrection and the blossom of renewal.

Finding beauty in the world is now a struggle for him. From his modest apartment in Flagstaff, he sees an uninspiring landscape, the occasional hill in an otherwise drab interior town, five hundred miles from the nearest beach, with nothing uplifting to discover. He complains, but only to himself, about the seasons; the summer isn't as hot as he'd like, and the winters are too damn cold.

Once, he was an ardent proponent of the beauty of being. Being in a community, being in society, being a guide, a comforter, a spreader of the Word. Being available in a time of need, holding a hand, offering kindness, providing solace and care. The provision of those things remains a constant in his role, but their delivery lacks enthusiasm, his assurances are

A LITTLE SOMETHING TO HIDE

paler imitations of promises past. The fraud in his messaging, he hopes, goes undetected.

While their numbers have reduced, there are still things in which he recognises beauty. The melody carried in children's laughter; their sparkle as they discover the joy and wonder in their surroundings. He takes enjoyment from witnessing their discoveries.

Simon Carter loves children; he loves their innocence, their unshakeable faith and their unquestioning belief in the unknowable and their dogmatic defence of the unbelievable. He admires their certainty; it reminds him of something that he once shared.

Although succumbing to the inevitability of aging, Simon doesn't want to grow old, not in the way that society expects, or his profession demands; to be sombre, sober, steady, dull. That's not what he wants, he wants to be playful, carefree, happy and young.

When did the Church forget the importance of those things? he wonders, before acknowledging that he is experiencing their loss. Each morning, as he creaks from his bed, joints complaining of another day, he faces a reminder that youth is fast slipping from him, despite telling himself that he's not an old man. Demographics agree, but it's another thing he doesn't entirely believe.

Children preserve the last vestiges of Simon's faith. All children are beautiful in his eyes, experiencing the world through a prism of innocence, seeing life in all its glorious colour before the intrusion of reality tarnishes the view, removing the shine and staining the glory. Their purity is worthy of awe. He hopes that their naivety will sustain them and protect them from the cynical, but he knows that's a futile notion, it distresses him when he sees life's progression eroding their virtue. He thinks it's the loss of innocence that's destroying his faith.

Simon struggles with the ninth commandment; he's lied to himself for most of his life. His latest lie, that he can stave off aging, recurs often; it's a hope to which he clings. At night, with the blinds drawn and the glow of his laptop the only illumination in his sparsely furnished room, he studies what it means to be young.

Some might think that what he does is predatory. It is not an opinion that Father Simon shares. There is no malice in his actions. For him, it is an attempt to renew his soul, to stave off his doubts. He neither creates nor procures the images, they're widely available. A quick Google search reveals what he seeks, causing no one harm. There are parameters he follows for his curations which he considers unimpeachable.

Father Simon won't dwell on the picture of a child that looks troubled, he seeks only images of children that are happy. A happy child is a beautiful child. Their beauty sustains him. In his eyes, their perfection is a form of grace. They suffer no inhibitions, no shame. Theirs is an innocence laid bare.

Causing harm to a child is an idea he finds repugnant. Any suggestion that hurt might come to a child upon whom he gazes is abhorrent. He wants only to find children that feel loved, for that is what he feels towards them. There's a subverted word for what he feels, the individual Greek roots of which accurately describe him, and it angers him that it's attached to predators whose motives are anything but the love of children.

He is grateful that his role allows him to spend time in the company of youngsters entrusted to his care; they are safe with him, protected. The only time he touches a child is to give comfort. A fallen angel in need of a hug will feel his embrace. He will open his arms to the needy child, administer a healing cuddle, but never more. There are rules, boundaries to maintain, an order to observe. He knows too, that the simple act of hugging a child, providing comfort, breaks those rules.

Simon wishes that common sense would prevail. It grieves him that society has led us to the point where one cannot comfort a child in need, where to do so leads some to contemplate the reprehensible. Touching a child inappropriately is unforgiveable, heinous. No child has ever suggested wrongdoing, nor ever will. Of that, he is certain.

With Simon they are in the presence of love; he will keep them safe.

In the confines of his room, he only ever looks at still images and only of happy children. It is his rule, his qualification, his justification. They must never appear to be in harm's way. The children restore him.

Simon wonders whether his loss of faith began when he no longer considered pride a deadly sin, believing it misappropriated, a sin that is reasonable to ignore. He doesn't see the harm that comes from delighting in one's endeavours, taking pride in the work that he does with children. The children enjoy their time with him as he brings life to scripture and teaching, making it fun by enlivening the gospel stories for the youngest of minds. The congregation, especially the parents, are grateful to him for the spiritual guidance he provides. That, and the free childcare that comes with Sunday School provision.

Many of the parents are there for appearance, for the notional benefit that stems from others witnessing their presence. They believe they're good Christians, and because they don't suspect Simon's failing faith, they are unaware that the delivery of their children's religious education comes from a man whose belief wavers. With their children happy, the parents are free to refuel their spiritual tanks, like cars at a gas pump.

Father Simon doesn't suggest that they're hypocritical, that would be preaching what he practices, but he knows that after their Sunday fill, they will return to the demands of growing wealth and achieving the material comforts that dominate their lives. Christianity is such a useful badge for them to wear, however thinly it clings to them beyond the confines of the church.

Simon's heart gladdens when parents leave their children with him as they pretend to be good people. It means the children can be themselves. He loves to watch children grow, to see them develop. It is *the* privilege of his job. Infants progressing to young children, young children blossoming into adolescence, adolescents becoming young adults, although the last group always disappoints. Too often the innocence that he watches them carry through life vanishes. He suffers the curse of foresight; the knowledge of what they might become.

The blame, he believes, sits with the parents for the corruption they promote; Simon despises them. He prefers not to see the children grow to maturity; it breaks him. Parents corrupt. Life corrupts. That's why he likes the pictures of the young children that he views in the shadows of his room, with his face illuminated by the glow of his laptop, where he is alone with them and nothing else, and nothing but goodness can intrude.

A still image bestows immortality on a child, an idea he covets, their digitally-captured innocence preserved, enjoyable forever.

Simon cannot bear to see a child in pain, it weakens him, diluting what little faith he maintains, stealing his courage. What bravery he holds, clings to the coattails of his faith, and those two imposters are travelling companions, both moving beyond him, and he is unable to keep pace. He knows that in times of pain, an expectation exists that he shows strength, gives support and comfort; but when a child is hurting, he finds it difficult to meet those needs.

Cynthia Killalea looked to Simon Carter for that strength. While he does his best to conceal his weakness, he fears that when she peers deep into his soul, she will see the void, and discover that something is missing. She is a semi-lapsed parishioner, but still considers herself a good Catholic. Cynthia is not one of the token faithful, she remains God-fearing; the Killaleas don't have enough money to be otherwise – her faith, and their nine children, have prevented the accumulation of wealth.

Cynthia arranged the baptisms of all her children, each wearing the same christening gown that was handed down to her by her mother. The once bright white satin and lace has acquired the sepia-stained tiredness of a faded family heirloom.

The six oldest of her children have had their confirmations, always at Pentecost following their fourteenth birthday. Father Simon presided over five of them and knows the family well. She hasn't asked him yet, but he knows that Cynthia is considering an early confirmation for her nine-year-old, Niall, the youngest of her brood.

There is a hope that Cynthia holds, that Father Simon will understand and acquiesce, she sees his affinity with children, knows of his kindness. She's confident that he will make an exception for Niall. Niall won't make fourteen, he may not even make it to Pentecost. His treatment for the acute myeloid leukaemia he suffers isn't working.

Simon Carter will agree to an early confirmation for Niall, but his wavering faith leads him to believe that he'll be performing an altogether different ceremony for Niall before that day arrives.

Cynthia is tired from watching her child suffer; the effort of appearing positive exhausts her. Weariness, amplified by helplessness, accompany her whenever she nestles alongside Niall in the bathroom, his grip weak on the bowl as he loses the content of his stomach, his mother's hand stroking his back, unable to make the nausea pass or to stop the diarrhoea. Sometimes, when she strokes his hair, it comes away in her hand, testimony to the ravages of her baby boy's chemotherapy.

The other children are robust, the oldest argue and the youngest brawl, as siblings do, developing rivalries, seeking to dominate one another, feral in their interactions, but rabid in their defence of each other outside the home.

They're a tight unit, the Killaleas. No one moves against one without moving against the whole. They preserve and protect one another, but none of them can do a thing to save their baby brother, he's beyond their care, but not beyond their love. They love Niall, he's always been the gentlest, the most loved by each of the others, but they cannot help him – nobody can, and the family is helpless.

SIMON – FLAGSTAFF

That helplessness has asserted itself in Cynthia with a need to return to her faith, it is all that she has left. The Killaleas haven't entirely separated from the Church, but the family doesn't attend Mass as often as the Church elders would like, although Father Simon is an exception, he allows their lapses to go unremarked and unjudged.

They recognise the big dates, when her boys don shirts and ties, and the girls wear shiny patent leather shoes beneath below-knee length dresses suitable for worship.

At the Christmas Midnight Mass, her oldest will come steaming into the church along with her husband, Donal, after a night spent in their favourite bar, it adds gusto to their hymns. All but Donal will obediently sport charcoal crosses on Ash Wednesday. All the children, even the older ones, know not to leverage their father's shortcomings in an argument with their mother.

When you've left home, she tells them, *you're free to do what you want. But right now, you're sure as hell going to wear that cross and you'd better be thankful for it.*

When Easter arrives, the younger members of the family wipe the chocolate smudges from their faces before mass on Sunday; she's given up trying to get them to wait. They'll also be on their best behaviour on All Saints Day, when Cynthia is insistent that they pay their respects to their grandparents.

She considers her lapses only partial, convincing herself that on the occasions she and her family attend church, they are affirming their faith, not seeking its restoration. With Niall's sickness, Cynthia has become more ardent, more frequent in church, her petitions to God more fevered.

Simon witnesses her faith, her restive belief in a charitable deity. It grieves him to see her entreaties scorned, held aloft on the last vestiges of her hope. He cannot share his despair; the suspicion that her prayers are futile. Instead, he tries to give her the courage to continue and the succour that stems from the mutual faith that she believes they hold. In a thought he keeps to himself, he wonders whether she would still have hope if she knew his truth.

A LITTLE SOMETHING TO HIDE

On visits to their home, he sees the love the family has for their youngest. They're always maintaining a vigil, always waiting, always hoping. Simon stifles his winces at their hope, a parent or sibling is constantly at Niall's side, they might witness the betrayal.

The bedside table is laden with palliative potions to provide relief from his torment. The young man, despite the pain that is a constant companion, smiles every time Father Simon enters.

Although Niall is desperate to attend, he is still a year away from being able to join the youth club that Simon established to provide the youngsters of Flagstaff with an outlet to remain children, to avoid that kink in the road that leads to the inevitable.

Simon knows it does little more than delay the surge toward adolescence, when youth begins to embrace the reckless, but he hopes that his club may spare some, or limit the failings of others. He's stopped believing that he can ever save them. How can he, when he cannot save himself? Simon knows that the boy will never join the club, but the family hope that the priest might yet save their favourite son.

The priest's reputation as a man who cares for the youngest in the community is widespread, he has a way with children, can relate to them, is kind. Niall knows about the fun his siblings have on Friday nights at Father Simon's club, is eager to join, but he also knows that he never will.

It breaks Father Simon's heart to see that understanding on the child's face. It appears on the faces of all the family; he feels helpless to ease their hurt. To him, his words seem empty, inadequate, worthless. They thank him, his kindness means a lot, and he senses their desperation for his intervention, a desperation that sees them clinging to a belief that he might have a direct connection to the Almighty, one where he could intervene on their behalf to have their prayers answered.

SIMON – FLAGSTAFF

There is no connection, Simon doubts there ever was, or could be, and doubts that he could give them anything other than the falsest of hopes.

Every time he enters Niall's room, the boy's smile weakens Father Simon's soul. His heart falters at the hopelessness of the child's situation; sadness overwhelms him. From his bed, Niall lifts a hand in greeting as Father Simon crosses the room to sit beside him. The priest tries to return a smile, lips curling, revealing a sliver of coffee-stained enamel, but he fails with his effort. His eyes speak of sadness; the certainty of a loss to come and an inadequate comprehension of the unbearable pain that the boy's parents will feel at the passing of their child. This time he wonders whether Niall knows why he is there, the significance of the call.

Niall knows the reason for the priest's presence, knows that Father Simon will hold his hand, that he will hear whispered words granting absolution, that he will feel the silk of an oil cross drawn across his head.

The boy will take the tiniest morsel of wafer, dipped in wine, limiting the aggravation to his already troubled constitution. His mother has told him what will happen and the priest wonders if the boy really knows what it signifies. Taking a look at the child, he understands that the boy's knowledge is absolute. He's an intelligent soul, has a spirituality to him, a reassuring dignity, a calming disposition that belies his age. In the boy's eyes, Father Simon thinks he sees wisdom, an awareness of all that is to come, and a belief that all will be well. The priest senses the child's faith, and for the briefest of moments, feels pierced with an intense envy.

He is careful not to knock the canula that snakes from the back of Niall's hand to a drip standing sentinel at the bedside. The boy's hand, while warm, hints at a coolness that prophesises a foreshortened future. Father Simon squeezes gently, asking him how he is doing, feeling disgust with himself for posing such a facile enquiry and having nothing more profound to say. Niall takes the question, giving it more merit than Simon believes it deserves, painting a response that is coloured with gently intended mistruths.

He's a brave boy, thinks the priest.

Over his shoulder, he shares the thought with the boy's mother who is hovering, hoping to serve, ready to react to whatever call he might have. She acknowledges that Father Simon is correct in his observation.

I'd much prefer he didn't have to be, she says.

Simon can't tell whether there's an admonishment or a plea in her response, suspecting a bit of both. Not for the first time, a wave of shame rises to his cheeks, closely followed by a helplessness that he fails to keep from his eyes. It earns him a nod from Cynthia which he's unable to decipher. She rescues him from his discomfort.

I just want him to be an idiot like the others.

Niall's breathing is shallow, the D*BACKS logo on his chest gently rises and falls, highlighting a rhythm that the priest cannot but feel is a slowing drumbeat.

They find banalities to fill the air, exchanging thoughts about Spring Training; the boy lies when he tells the priest how much he is looking forward to it starting. Simon allows the falsehood to go unremarked, the cruelty is unnecessary. They exhaust their conversation, and the boy lies silent, the rise and fall of his chest, almost imperceptible, providing the evidence of his fading.

Father Simon can think of nothing to say that doesn't involve a non-existent future. He allows the silence to envelop them, grateful that they are comfortable in each other's company.

Eventually he asks Niall if he knows why he is there. The boy nods, smiling with a radiance that mangles the priest's heart and drives the air from Simon's lungs. He wants to scream at the Creator, highlight the unfairness, challenge Him on His cruelty, rail against the suffering that the child has endured, begging for it to end and for a restoration of Niall's health. He does none of that, knowing that his pleas will fall fallow, doubting that anyone or anything will hear.

He invites Cynthia to leave the room to allow Niall's final confession. She dutifully complies, the soft click of the door latch announcing that he and the child are alone. In a diminished voice, perhaps from the illness, perhaps with concerns for his sins, the boy begins an earnest plea.

The priest leans forward, offering an ear to better hear Niall and grant him the privacy of a quiet consultation. He turns his head so that their eyes do not lock. It means too, that the boy doesn't see the smile that the priest is unable to suppress – if only all such confessions were as light. Father Simon goes easy on the penance; absolution is uncomplicated in the face of such transgressions. They agree his mother can return.

Cynthia moves to the opposite side of the bed and wonders aloud whether the rest of the family should join them for the anointing and communion. Father Simon lets her choose. She consults with Niall, who despite his age and illness, displays an impatience that he inherited from his brothers and sisters. Simon sees it and thinks, *innocence slipping*. Cynthia sees it too, raising an eyebrow.

You may be the youngest, and you may be dying, but don't disrespect your mother, that eyebrow says.

Chastened, Niall defers, once more wholly obedient. *You decide, Mom.*

She looks at her son, sees his weakness, sees the ravages of his illness, and although she knows how brave he is, and that he wouldn't mind a room crowded with his family, she wants this occasion to be just for him – and for her.

For a moment, she considers inviting Niall's father, which causes a flash of anger that she manages to conceal. As a non-believer, Donal won't want to be in the room with the man in the black garb and his white plastic collar. Cynthia's anger isn't limited to her husband's impiety, his non-belief also embraces their son's illness. He's in denial that the end is near for their youngest child.

Donal's presence in the room would amount to a concession that he is unwilling to make. She knows that it will break them, but they will stay together, suffocating each other, with only the mutual regard for their eight other children to secure their marriage. *That*, she thinks, *and my fucking faith*.

Together, they form a triangle, arms extended, holding each other's hand as Simon offers a quiet prayer. He breaks the hold and begins his incantation. The words rise unbidden, delivered by rote.

Through this holy anointing may the Lord in his love and mercy help you with the grace of the Holy Spirit. May the Lord who frees you from sin save you and raise you up.

Another fragment of his faith falls away as he wonders why it is so easy for the Lord to save a child from sin, but not from pain.

Communion administered, they sit in quiet contemplation before he rises to leave. Simon hides his horror at how grateful Cynthia is for the visit, that he lowered himself for them. He feels dirty that the woman before him should feel it necessary to mewl, rendering herself pathetic with her thanks, when he knows that he is underserving.

It's nothing, he says. *It's my privilege to be here.*

It is more than nothing. What it is, he cannot admit. He cannot confess to the gradual breaking of his heart.

Outside, he tucks his right trouser leg into his sock. The early evening has given way to darkness and he notices how little illumination there is on the street where he has chained his bike. The cool of the night seeps through his coat and settles deeper into his soul. He thinks only of himself, of his need for cheer. Instead of climbing on the saddle, he walks, not yet ready to return to his darkened room and the glow of his laptop screen, although he suspects that he will no longer take joy from the results of his search. As he thinks about the boy that he has left, he is not sure that lifting his mood is possible. He wanted to leave, but he doesn't want to go home.

Two days later he is back at the boy's house, finding it awash with sorrow. Cycling past the cars that line the street, he chains his bike to a tree a block away. He needs the walk to compose himself, to draw on the cloak of his deception, to adjust to the weight of the heaviness in his heart as he nears the house containing one less light.

SIMON – FLAGSTAFF

The boy's father opens the door, his eyes red and swollen from tears wept in private, savaged by the reality that is no longer deniable. Ushering the priest in, he calls to his wife as Simon crosses the threshold. Father Simon offers his condolences which are too short to fill the interminable gap of silence that engulfs them while they wait for Cynthia.

She is thankful that he should come again and apologetic that it is so soon after his last call, as though there was something she could have done to prevent the need. The reason for his visit sits unspoken at the end of a sentence she's unable to finish. Embarrassed, she fumbles for words, settling for *He's in his room*, before scurrying down the passage with the priest in pursuit.

Standing over the boy, Father Simon Carter beholds Niall Killalea's pale face, infused with serenity, his anxieties now past, the pain gone – along with his hopes – consigned to history. He wipes a gnarled hand over the smooth dome of Niall's head, hairless, chemo-ravaged, and cold.

Simon Carter loves the immortality that a static image can bestow on a child, how it can capture the shine in their eyes, allowing him to imagine the melody of their laughter, which although unheard, he knows sits within the composition.

A happy child is a beautiful child, but nothing can compare with the beauty of the serene. A different image lies before him now. Niall Killalea is lifeless, unmoving, and indescribably beautiful. He is a still image, his innocence preserved, and he is agony to behold.

Every seven years or so, Simon Carter moves to somewhere new. Today he is climbing on the Briscola coach to leave the Catholic faithful of Flagstaff for good. They are sad to see him go, he has such a way with people, especially with children.

He never leaves because of shame or scandal; he leaves only because he senses that it is time to go, aware that with time, people begin to see his relationship with children through a different prism, one of their invention, one that may lead to the wagging of tongues, for no reason other than they believe it perverted in a man of his age.

'How,' they will ask, *'can any man be so understanding and loving of children without having something to hide?'*

Their poison distils from experience or belief – time doesn't just destroy innocence; it also corrupts the mind. Father Simon Carter has nothing to fear, but he understands people.

The move is different this time. Usually, he leaves just memories behind, of contribution to the community, of satisfaction, of reflection and of happiness. Ordinarily, he takes his few belongings and the hopeful expectation that he will create memories anew, that he will start afresh, like spring, with renewal and resurrection.

This time, he's leaving more behind, an essential element that he won't ever recover. He has lost his faith. Completely. The final traces escaped through his fingers as he felt the smooth, cool skin of the recently deceased Niall Killalea beneath his tired, gnarled hands.

He felt it disappear as he encountered the serenity forever preserved on the dead boy's face, a final still image etching itself forever into his memory, and with it a dawning realisation that he does, in the end, have something to hide, a secret to keep.

Finally, Simon Carter understands that he no longer believes in God.

GALLUP TRAVEL CENTER

Arrivals		
Time	From	Expected
01:59	Flagstaff	Expected: 03:43

Departures		
Time	Destination	Expected
02:30	Albuquerque	Delayed: 04:08

GALLUP TRAVEL CENTER

There are no new passengers joining the bus at its penultimate stop in Gallup, but one man is stepping off, Jimmy Lewis. He's the second driver and he calls Gallup home. His early departure from the bus reflects his character; he's a lazy sonofabitch.

You won't ever see him stepping forward to help a passenger unless there's a tight ass and a big ol' pair of tits that might need a bit of Jimmy love. Those girls will always get the treatment, but passengers struggling with luggage or offspring need not bother to seek assistance. He'll sit, perched in the driver's seat, watching impassively as young mothers wrestle with pushchairs and their children to get onto his bus. Sandra Mayhew can attest to his specialism of ignoring the imploring glance.

He's impervious to ill feeling and a lot finds its way to him, which as far as he's concerned, is just fine, he couldn't give two fucks. He's had to fend for himself for most of his life with an old man that only gave a shit when he had something nasty to say or a beating to deliver, so why should he do anyone a favour, let alone a stranger.

'Let 'em learn the hard way,' he thinks. 'I did.'

If he's impatient to get moving, he'll yell for his co-driver, Felipe, to shift their bags, which is more than they deserve, but at least it gets them going.

Jimmy Lewis doesn't like that he's partnered with an Hispanic. He remembers the Alamo, or at least that he needs to say he does. He has no idea when or what happened, just that Mexicans were involved, and it went better for them than it did for God-fearing Americans, leading him to hate Mexicans, a term he uses generically to describe anyone that originates south of the New Mexico frontier. Sometimes, he calls them spics, *it spits more easily from his mouth. It doesn't matter what title he uses, to him they're all the same.*

Whether someone comes from Colombia, Venezuela, or Nicaragua is immaterial to Jimmy. All he knows is that they've come to take American jobs, and the communist lefties let them roll across the border. Another thing of which he is certain – Donald J. Trump was right to start building his wall. The sooner he's back in the White House to finish it, the better.

Jimmy is one of The Base and is keen to tell folks that he's practically the foundation; *a Trump supporter who can't wait to see him MAKE AMERICA GREAT AGAIN again. He'll call BS on anyone who suggests that Trump doesn't care about the American people. 'Just look at what he did for Vets and taxes,' he'll say, and change the subject quickly if you ask him to elaborate, it saves him from having to face some uncomfortable truths about his lack of knowledge.*

When the Access Hollywood tape emerged, Jimmy decided to be impressed with Trump's choice of words. 'So what if he grabs 'em by the pussy. Any real man would do the same.' As for Stormy Daniels, Jimmy has looked her up, a lot. 'I'd bang her in a heartbeat,' he says, as though the likelihood is a probability.

Jimmy Lewis is smart enough to know that there are only four ways to attract a woman. You can be an athlete, an entertainer, or an asshole. He deliberately omits the fourth, it's part of his schtick, he cups the bottom of his drooping belly to limit his gut's jiggling, before laughing at himself, something only he's permitted to do. 'If you threw a cold at me, I couldn't catch it. I ain't no ball player.'

He's honest enough to know that he can't hold a note worth a dime, but he'll tell you straight, 'I'm a catch for plenty that should know better but can't help themselves. I'm mighty good at being an asshole,' he chuckles. 'There's a type of woman loves a man like me. I can sniff 'em out.'

The fourth way, and Jimmy can't believe that people even need to ask, is to be rich. He likes it when they do, he knows his earlier omission will draw the question and its asking fills him with a quiet surge of superiority. 'That's where all the good-looking whores end up, following the money. Ain't no other way to explain it.'

In Jimmy's opinion, being a rich athlete with more than a hint of the mongrel is absolute gold dust. 'Look at OJ Simpson. Stupid n__

was too dumb to know a good thing when he had it. If there was a man who could get laid for being rich, famous and a piece of shit, it was OJ. Hell, even white women were banging him.

'Good looking women can't help but fuck for money – ask Stormy. She took a hundred-thirty Gs of green from 45. Proves she's a whore. Still, he's got plenty, so why wuncha?'

Jimmy doesn't care that 45's a billionaire. 'I would be too if I was in the lucky sperm club.' Despite that, Jimmy knows that Trump's a man of the people, a living legend. In Jimmy's opinion, anyone that promises to drain the swamp and blow-up Washington has gotta be better than the corrupt assholes that are running the country. 'Just watch them trying to fuck us over,' he says. 'The pussies have already started with their second amendment bullshit.'

Anyone who cares to listen will hear Jimmy say that he would die to protect his rights and the rights of all Americans. It's why, in Jimmy's view, we need politicians like Trump who would do the same. 'Not that Trump's a politician,' he'll tell you. 'It's why he's better qualified to run the country. Trump's a businessman and a patriot.'

A true patriot, just like Jimmy.

Parler informs Jimmy's limited understanding of the Constitution, and he's quick to counter objections to his opinions. 'You try'n stop me ex'cising my freedom of expansion under the first 'mendment, I might remind you 'bout the second.' No one corrects the malapropism.

Despite a tortured relationship with his father, Jimmy's quick to chime that his old man fought in Vietnam to protect our rights. 'The Lewis men are a warrior class; you better believe it. Hell, if I wanna AK47 in my garage, I'm havin' an AK47.'

Not that he would, that's a Russian piece of gear.

Amongst his armoury, he's got a Colt AR-15 and delights in correcting the imbeciles who think the AR stands for assault rifle. As a firearms bore, if you mention AR and assault rifle in the same breath, he'll tell you you're wrong on two counts. 'According to the law,' he puffs, 'The AR-15 is not an assault rifle. Also, if you bothered to read your history, you'd know the name AR-15 comes from the original maker, ArmaLite. The AR,' he drones, 'comes from the company's name.'

Despite a lot of evidence to the contrary, Jimmy is a keen student of some aspects of history, relishing what little knowledge he possesses.

A LITTLE SOMETHING TO HIDE

Once started, he will happily launch into a tedious monologue of ArmaLite and the sale of its patents to Colt when the cash registers rang dry. Although it's tedious, most people listen when he ventures onto his favourite subject. By the time they've realised where he's heading, most astute listeners are wondering whether an unwanted interruption to his ramblings might just tempt him to break out the weapon, and not just for show.

When it comes to weapons, Jimmy knows his stuff. He likes to think it's a demonstration of learning that no classroom can teach, evidence of intelligence beyond a formal education. 'Don't gotta be book smart to be clever.'

He's proud of his family's roots in the working class, and carries the conviction that only Trump can prevent the decline in that great bedrock of America. Were his great-grandfather alive to witness his progeny's oratory, he would suggest that perhaps it was already too late.

In the past, Jimmy was a staunch advocate for the Democrats and what they once represented. 'My family's got a proud record of voting D. We voted blue before Woodrow Wilson was in shorts,' he says. He'll tell you too, albeit erroneously, that they've been union men since the Great Depression. Affecting mock desolation, he laments that those days are gone, elaborating with an incohesive narrative, attempting to explain that the socialists have corroded traditional Democrat values. It doesn't come out quite as Jimmy intends, so he adds a conclusion that emphasises his point. 'What more could you expect from a bunch of gay lesbian bisexuals?'

That's why he turned Republican – for Trump and guns. 'It's the real man's party. Trump's the guy we need. He bought jobs back from China, made America great again. Them socialist politicians only care 'bout handouts to n__s and spics. Trump looks out for real Americans.'

Jimmy knows there are wild conspiracy theories floating around the cyberverse, but he's smart enough to spot the truth among them, knowing with certainty that the Democrats are funding Antifa's bullshit and BLM, although he's a little sceptical about the deep state paedophile ring that's supposedly threatening our freedoms. 'But anything's possible with a Jew-boy like George Soros at the top,' he'll add, just in case someone doubts his commitment to the cause.

An influencer that Jimmy respects posted that Soros controls politicians, the media and Hollywood – making that particular piece of wisdom an irrefutable fact he's happy to regurgitate. 'That's why Trump's so good for the country. He's no politician and he's got too much money for anyone to control him.'

Jimmy can't wait for the Storm to blow through and the Great Awakening. It'll be just before the return of Trump, and Jimmy will have OAN or Newsmax on 24/7 for a ringside seat at the executions.

Controlling his vexation proved a challenge when he watched President (in name only) Biden's swearing in. 'Sleepy-Joe stole the election. He might be in Trump's bed right now, but it won't be forever. Donald's lawyers will get to the truth and his judges will throw them to the dogs. It's only a matter of time before Biden's back where he belongs; a know-nothing politician who should be in jail with his boy, Hunter.

'They paint Joe Biden as a saint, but I know better; he's a communist and he's gonna burn in '24. Trump's a serial winner and he'll beat the cabal and get back to building his wall.'

Jimmy's tired of seeing Mexicans cross through the gaps and into his backyard like the spic driver he shares his job with. 'The sooner they pay for the wall and keep their people in, the better.'

The only illegals that Jimmy thinks should stay are the ones that are useful, like Felipe. Although he hates having to share his job with him, Felipe can be useful to have around. 'Sometimes it's good to have an immigrant just where you want him.'

Jimmy got the measure of his co-worker early in their partnership. Felipe's furtive behaviour around anyone wearing a uniform signalled a fear of authority, a desire to avoid attention, an intent to slip through life leaving no crumbs, to dwell among the faceless.

Although Jimmy doesn't know why Felipe seeks anonymity, nor what great crime he wants to conceal, Jimmy is certain that some degree of larceny left its stamp on his co-worker's past, or maybe a deviancy. 'Kiddy-fiddling, most likely,' thinks Jimmy. Whatever his offences, Jimmy would wage Donald J. Trump's net worth on Felipe being an illegal. 'The only papers that boy carried across the border were for rolling weed.' Notwithstanding, he didn't care about what haunted Felipe, he knew only that whatever it was, he could take advantage of the man's fear.

A LITTLE SOMETHING TO HIDE

Jimmy knows that Felipe is on the clandestine payroll of the Briscolas. It doesn't surprise him, the Briscolas are only a couple of generations away from the ignorant guinea stock they fell from. 'They'll take on anyone if it can save them a nickel. Maybe when they've fallen far enough from the tree like my ancestors, they can start thinking of themselves as real Americans and stop employing illegals.' He doubts they'll ever be that honest. 'Once a thief, always a fuckin' thief.'

The contempt he harbours for his employer appears often. He hates that Briscola Coach Services employs spics and n__s. It led him toward forming a union to raise standards in the business. He knows there are plenty in the company that are like-minded. 'Damn dago owners killed it before it got started,' he complained. 'You can never trust an eye-tie.'

The knowledge that Felipe is desperate to avoid detection leads Jimmy to joke with him that he's only a phone call away from an ICE pick-up and a plane ride home. Jimmy repeats his wheeze whenever he wants Felipe to do something for him, or when he thinks the Mexican might be getting a bit lazy. 'I don't need the little fat fuck getting too comfortable, otherwise, what's the point of having him around?' Getting to climb on and off the bus at Gallup is a perk Jimmy worked hard to gain.

Felipe does everything that Jimmy asks him to do without complaining; he can't afford the risk that his colleague may be a bit nastier than just his sour shits and giggles suggest. It's why Felipe keeps his mouth shut about Jimmy's foreshortened journeys. Jimmy may not be the smartest person to step on a Briscola coach, but he's clever enough to know that silence about his behaviour is a price his co-worker is willing to pay to avoid discovery.

Not a month passes when he doesn't tell the boys of his Chapter a story of how he stiffs Felipe on their trips out West. He can't wait to tell them how he only did two four-hour stints at the wheel on this journey, and how he spent most of the time pretending to be asleep behind his aviator shades while he watched a young couple fingering each other. The boys will think he's talking horseshit, which is why he took a couple of sneaky pictures of a sly hand-job to show as evidence. Jimmy is never surprised by anything he sees on the bus. 'People will do all kinds of crazy when they think no one's watching.'

GALLUP TRAVEL CENTER

Jimmy keeps a close eye on the people that step onto his bus. Especially the aliens. *He can spot them a mile away. They're shifty and sly and they carry a foreigner's stench. Jimmy thinks about what he'd like to do to immigrants; fomenting plans which he'll share with the boys the next time they meet. The boys that he shares his time with are good guys; good and malleable, and not one of them would question an order from Jimmy. They're as loyal as they come.*

At weekends, when he's not traversing between 'Faggotsville, San Francisco' or 'Spicsville, Albuquerque,' he occasionally wears a tailored white number. He's especially proud of his brightly laundered, perfectly pressed uniform. The eyeholes of his pointed white hat are plenty wide enough to let him see how the socialists and n__s are ruining the greatest country in the world.

A LITTLE SOMETHING TO HIDE

JIMMY – GALLUP

Jimmy's favourite colour is white. If he could articulate why, he'd suggest it has a purity that elevates it above all others, although in the scatter ball that is Jimmy's mind, his musings aren't terribly profound.

When asked to elaborate, the light in his eyes falters, disclosing the gradual extinguishing of rationale thought, though he is no less sure of his conviction. In his head, everything that's good is white; the light, freshly fallen snow, mashed potato, Jesus, and the robes Jimmy wears to formal meetings and marches.

He thinks Hitler had it right with his views on the Aryan race, or *Airyin* as Jimmy pronounces it. *It's way superior*, as he lets his close acquaintances know. *My family came here ten generations ago. The best Germany had to offer. Settled in this shit heap the rest of the world calls Gallup, and set about building everything that is great about America – everything that's white, that is.*

While he's an advocate of white supremacy and reckons Adolf Hitler's approach to ethnic cleansing is overhyped, Jimmy doesn't know much about his heritage. He knows enough to affirm his credentials as a card-carrying American patriot; not that he has a passport, there isn't a country in the world that Jimmy wants to visit. He can't see the point when he already lives in the greatest country on the planet.

Jimmy's knowledge of his roots doesn't extend to knowing that his original family name was Lewandowski. Moreover, he's only three generations removed from a Polish-Jewish immigrant family that escaped Nazi Germany.

His great-grandfather, Joseph, with his wife Nina and their 16-year-old son, Abel, Jimmy's grandfather, arrived at Ellis Island on November 19th, 1942. Joseph was a student of

A LITTLE SOMETHING TO HIDE

Theoretical Physics at the University of Göttingen where he met Robert Oppenheimer. On arrival in America, he tracked down his old friend in the hope of rekindling their relationship and, more importantly for the penniless Lewandowskis, finding a job.

Oppenheimer, deep into the planning for the Manhattan Project, welcomed the call and nursed his friend through the suspicions of the government and military to have him engaged in the programme. Together they worked in secretive intimacy on the developments that led to the destruction of Hiroshima and Nagasaki in 1945.

Had Jimmy known about his great-grandfather's contribution to the allied war machine, he undoubtedly would have promoted the intelligence, boasting with unvarnished pride of such an estimable family connection. It might have caused him some challenges in reconciling a Jewish past with his preferred brand of racism, but Jimmy would find a way to skirt a track around the inconsistencies.

The reason for Jimmy's ignorance of the infamous role that his great-grandfather played in the blood-chilling conclusion to the second world war, was that Joseph's son, Abel, didn't approve of his father's science.

As a pacifist, Abel Lewandowski's disgust with his father's involvement in the atomic weapons programme led to an estrangement. The younger Lewandowski left the family home, changing his name to Andy Lewis to avoid association with his father. After the Japanese bombings, he never spoke to his father again, and like another of our travellers, invented a backstory, distancing himself from his father's genocidal inventions and the Jewish heritage that proceeded him.

That decision didn't stem from a newly developed anti-Semitism or an adopted irreligiosity. Instead, it served as a convenient mechanism for avoiding association to the Jewish contributors of the Manhattan Project. For the Jewish diaspora living in that corner of New Mexico at the time, the question inevitably arose, and for Andy Lewis, it was one he wanted to avoid.

JIMMY – GALLUP

To admit an abhorrence of conflict in post-war America, especially when the country classified his father as a hero, was tantamount to treason and an invitation to uncomfortable scrutiny. The Korean War, which Andy managed to side-step, only reinforced his views, but by then it was safer to be outspoken against an ideological war rather than a physical threat to the USA.

His pacifist advocacy wasn't enough to keep his son Frank, Jimmy's father, from the war in Vietnam. Both men developed a bitterness and enmity for the world around them, though for quite distinct reasons. Andy, for the needless destruction he felt impotent to do anything about, Frank for the curtailment of his liberty that military service foisted upon him. Together, they railed against authority, albeit from different perspectives which aligned only in a mistrust of the government and its institutions.

Jimmy was an effortless inheritor of their contempt, but a poor student. He didn't appreciate the nuanced arguments that embittered the older men, or understand the distinctions. Rather than attempt to comprehend them, Jimmy simply embraced their prejudices, along with others he developed uniquely, allowing him to adopt the family penchant for grousing.

The bitterness of his father and grandfather ran deep, but Jimmy didn't understand their motivations. As a child, he found his grandfather's arguments too difficult to follow, and his father's invective came laced with occasional violence borne by Jimmy and his mother; Jimmy's ears playing high notes from back-handed cuffs, while his mother conspired with Max Factor to conceal Frank Lewis's anger.

Frank's frustration was born of an altogether different kind of impotence to his father's, one where he was unable to displace the demons he bagged in Khe Sanh, which he combined with an unwillingness to allow others to help him purge the spectres.

The relationship between Jimmy's father and grandfather deteriorated, Andy unable to understand the trauma of his son, Frank further traumatised by having to listen to the old man's polemic. He didn't want to hear his father's arguments against a war that neither believed in, he thought it carried an unspoken condemnation of Frank's failure to exercise conscientious objection.

Their relationship became one of uncomfortable rage that neither was able to express adequately. Andy's arguments fell limp as he delivered them to a son fleeing the domestic battlefield, with Frank taking his fury to a bar where he steeped it in liquor before sharing it with his wife and child. The young Jimmy grew up dieting on the anger of his forebears, without understanding its cause, and decided that there must be merit in holding opinions that others considered toxic. Unmoderated by a father who might have cared if he'd noticed, Jimmy developed his own hatreds, including, without the faintest hint of irony, anti-Semitism.

Jimmy didn't reserve his prejudice for the Jewish, if anything, he was more tolerant toward them than anyone else he chose to dislike, possibly because of some preternatural awareness of his lineage, but more likely because, mostly, Jews were white.

To Jimmy's way of thinking, the Jews represent a lesser race, although they sit toward the bottom of his hierarchy of hate. Peak animosity is determined by skin pigmentation, the darker shades earning the greatest loathing.

National origin is next to assert, countries he doesn't know or can't pronounce wage low. He views predominantly white, English-speaking nations more favourably. He's a bit fuzzy about Europeans, should he find himself in debates regarding wars, allies, or French fries, he knows the ground's unstable beneath that particular pair of feet. Where Europe is concerned, there's a significant risk of exposing his ignorance if called upon to name sides – he'd rather take a quiet slug of beer than disappearing down that wormhole.

Any religion that's not his own is inferior, and if you're a woman, all you have to do is know your place. For those that dare question his misogyny, Jimmy's happy to offer a jocular clarification which is anything but funny. *If a woman don't know her place, all she gotta do is ask the nearest fella.*

JIMMY – GALLUP

If Jimmy found himself in the act of articulating his opinions, he'd allow a pause at this moment, reflecting on whether he's expressed the full extent of his pre-eminence. His views emerge as though from a checklist, rooted in his beliefs, piloted by the muscle memory of a lifetime of prejudice: white, conservative, Christian, male; the hallmarks of dominance in Jimmy's mind.

He knows something's missing, that he's forgetting a category, which is taunting him, sitting at the edge of his thinking, waiting to be grasped, another item in the list of traits to despise. The slurs have covered most of those that he aims to demean, he's almost ready to add the close that he uses to demonstrate his reasonableness, *Beyond that, everyone's pretty much okay*, but he knows he hasn't exhausted the list. He remembers, shakes his head as though disappointed at his omission before adding, *Unless they're into that LGBT shit*. Then, according to Jimmy, *they're unnatural faggots*.

In watching every passenger that climbed aboard, Jimmy holds a certainty that a couple have climbed onto his bus, but there's nothing he can do about it without getting into a world of trouble with the Briscolas. *Still*, he thinks. *If there are queers on my bus, I'll make sure they'll feel as welcome as a n__ at a Klan gathering*.

Jimmy supposes he's a Christian. It wasn't something his Pa encouraged, and his mother, unable to cope with the instability that her husband's PTSD provoked, had long since left them both. If there was a bible in the house, Jimmy reckons she took it. She didn't leave them with much of anything except their clothes and each other, and that wasn't much of a gift.

There are rare moments when Jimmy thinks that he occupied a kinder world, when his mother might have been a decent woman that went to church, but he doesn't remember going along for the ride. He'll tell you too, with an air of righteous indignation, that abandoning a baby boy to an abusive, alcoholic father, wasn't the most Christian thing she ever did. He could never understand how a mother could do that to a child, so he's pleased that someone as fucked up as

A LITTLE SOMETHING TO HIDE

her is out of his life. What he doesn't say, is that she waited until Jimmy was fourteen before she left, by which time she realised that her son bore an uncomfortably close resemblance to his father.

The only time his father took him to a place of worship was for his grandfather's funeral, when Jimmy was eight years old. He was too ignorant to know that they were inside a Synagogue, and he never asked to return. Jimmy doesn't put too much truck in the bible or organised religion. It's why his first thought when he saw Simon Carter's dog collar was *Paedo*.

Aren't they all? thinks Jimmy. *He's either that or a faggot, probably both.* He's confident enough to know that he is an excellent judge of character.

Jimmy doesn't think a black shirt and a white plastic strip constitutes a uniform, not a real one anyway. He likes a proper uniform, having spent two years in the military out of Fort Wingate and, like his daddy, he's a proud veteran – Jimmy rode along during the first Gulf War. His tales of heroism mostly omit that he spent his entire service holding either a potato peeler or a soup ladle, rather than serving with the *real* soldiers on the frontlines. He's proud of his military service but hates it when other soldiers are in the room. They know the truth.

Those soldiers never suggest that he's any less than they are. They're quick to point out that his role was critical in keeping the war effort going. *Without the contribution from the mess, the fighting units couldn't win*, they tell him. He feels their condescension, knows they're talking down to him and pretending to make him feel better.

He'd have been a hero on the frontline if he'd had the chance, but there's not much call for fighting as a 92G. Few that he knows are brave or clever enough to ask him what 92G means. If they do, his response is below their level of hearing, hoping that they don't feel compelled to repeat the question. *Army Culinary Specialist,* he mumbles.

These days, he doesn't meet his army buddies for drinks, he can do without the reminder that he spent the war in a kitchen. He knows what they're thinking. He prefers to drink his beers with non-serving men. They know to give him respect.

The service he gave to his country lends him a powerful voice at Chapter meetings; he's the only one attending who served, it earns him deference. The other members concede to his knowledge, believing that he knows what he's talking about, and Jimmy expects their admiration, which they duly deliver, he wouldn't tolerate anything less from the fine group of people with which he mixes.

Jimmy Lewis is a patriot. Two poles stand in his front yard and Jimmy is fastidious about the raising and lowering of flags at the start and finish of each day. Betsy Ross flies on the left and the Confederate Flag stands proudly alongside. In his world, they have equal importance. He's a patriot and a Southerner and proud of both. When the flags are flying, it means he's home; an implicit invitation for like-minded men to call by – so long as they bring a few cold ones.

There are rules for drinking beer with Jimmy. *It's gotta be American. Don't bring any of that Dutch or Belgium shit to my house.* He's partial to Budweiser – if the 7-Eleven has it on special, but a Miller or Coors will do fine if they're cheaper.

To attempt to educate Jimmy on the ownership structure of the companies that brew his favourite beers is to practise futility. He'd blink with beady eyes, trying to determine whether his interlocutor was a socialist, a communist or a faggot, before deciding they were all three, then begin harbouring thoughts about the best place to shove the barrel of his AR15. He lacks imagination, it's always the ass.

Jimmy is unlikely, however, to hear such debate from the company he keeps. The intricacies of a corporate entity elude most of his buddies. Any that might have an inkling will know Jimmy well enough not to remedy his understanding. What they all appreciate, is that if you're going to visit Jimmy Lewis and down a few beers, you had better have a convincing tale if you pitch up with a brew that bears a foreign stamp.

When the socialists elected a black man as President, Jimmy thought about leaving America. He could never grasp why Obama didn't lose the job for being African. He thought about it long and hard, for eight whole years. Not about having a *spook* as president – though that was bad enough – the part about leaving. In the end, he figured that no better place on earth existed, so he was staying put.

As far as Jimmy was concerned, the only good thing to come out of the Obama train wreck was that Chapter membership grew. As Treasurer, that meant there was a little more for him to skim. Jimmy was mighty pleased when the country came to its senses and put a God-fearing man back in the White House and not that jumped up strumpet Clinton. *Lord knows how bad shit would be if we let Lock-Her-Up run the country. Thank fuck for Trump. Won't be long before America wakes up and puts him back where he belongs.*

Jimmy was the first to put a Trump sign in his yard. He stuck it up way back in December 2015, long before Trump's name was at the top of the ticket and long before the President promised to MAKE AMERICA GREAT AGAIN. The first MAGA cap in town perched on Jimmy's head, and he made sure that everyone in the Chapter was wearing them when they were out on their business. He's still wearing it now, and no matter how sweat-stained it becomes, it will remain in place right through to 2024 and the four years beyond. Well before then, he'll be putting the yard sign back up, just as soon as the man says he's running again.

Fifty bucks goes from Jimmy's account to Trump's '24 campaign every month. He figures it's the least he can do, chuckling to himself, he reckons the boys would approve if they knew that's where some of their weekly fees were heading.

Soon after Trump's 2016 victory, Jimmy wrote to the White House and invited the President to join them at a Chapter meeting in Gallup. Chapter meetings take place in what he optimistically dubs his leisure complex. It's his garage, with unfinished sheetrock panelling on the walls, a few tattered lounge chairs, the biggest damn television the wall can stand, and a bar that always has at least one full bottle of Rebel Yell on the shelf. The fridge is full of the most reasonably priced American beer Jimmy can find, which is usually the remaining supplies his buddies have provided – why use his own hard-earned when others are willing to donate.

The response from the White House is on the wall behind the bar in a four-dollar frame he bought at Walmart. The President found the invitation flattering, but according to Jimmy, *He couldn't attend because he was too damn busy MAKING AMERICA GREAT AGAIN.* The President wished the fine people of Gallup well, adding that America needs its patriots.

Trump didn't sign the letter himself, but Jimmy was okay with that. It was on White House letterhead and Jimmy knew Trump was a busy man. Some guy named Miller signed it on his behalf. Jimmy figured that was the next best thing.

When Trump did a rally in Rio Rancho in September '19, Jimmy took the trip across to the Santa Ana Star Center to be front and centre. Trump pissed him off mightily when he said, *We Love The Hispanics*, but Jimmy Lewis gets politics. He knows that sometimes you need to say what people want to hear, even when you don't believe it. Jimmy will explain to anyone that needs to know, that Trump is a master of the little white lie. *White lies,* says Jimmy, *are another thing that proves that all good things are white.*

Jimmy believes that Trump is *the* master motivator, that he can rally anyone to his cause. He certainly proved that with the Proud Boys, a fine bunch of men who Jimmy met that day in Rio Rancho. He was mighty pleased he did; he signed up immediately. Jimmy likes the sound of the Proud Boys. He feels that the movement is more modern and open. *They're right out there, showing everyone what it is to be a true American.*

While he is proud of his Klan association, he has long felt that the Klan is losing its way, with views that are too narrow. It irritates Jimmy that most Klan operations occur in the shadows. Cogent thought is not one of Jimmy's strengths, but he believes he can infuse the Proud Boy's doctrine into the Klan's thinking, modernising it, making it more relevant. It also means he can get more guys involved, making his Chapter more active – more profitable.

On occasions, threats to Jimmy's leadership arise; there are factions within his group that consider the Chapter's actions too passive. Quick to quell the unrest, Jimmy argues that his military training justifies his control over the group's activities. *We need to be cal-cu-lated boys,* Jimmy says, emphasising the middle syllable, giving it a *k,* reminding them of their allegiance. *Leave the strategy to me. There'll be a time and a place...*

The unfinished sentence hangs over those at his meetings, a tacit promise that someday, he'll give them licence to unleash their testosterone-enhanced prejudice. He'll gently remind some of the more impetuous members of the Chapter that the secret to their success is control. A more realistic rendering of his view, is that Jimmy is a mite uneasy about his cohort's enthusiasm.

The work that Jimmy and his boys do is mostly persuasive. He likes to think of it as exerting influence. Mostly what they do consists of talk – and they're good at *talk*. It's the thing they do best; lacing their opinions with hate, finding contempt for those disinclined to agree, linking their contempt to some real or imagined event that they use as justification on which to hang their animosity.

A person showing the courtesy of holding a door open for a black woman will earn them a snowflake label and a place in Jimmy's heart of dark remembrances. Jimmy thinks that people show their weakness in all kinds of ways, and he demands a guard against such behaviours. He makes sure his boys know what's expected and they do just as he says. They're good like that. Good and loyal.

Jimmy needs loyalty, just like Trump. It must be absolute, and it must be evident. That's rule number one of his Chapter, closely followed by total fealty. He heard one of his new Proud Boy friends say *fealty* at the Trump rally and he nodded along. *Couldn't agree more*, he said, not knowing to what he was agreeing.

That he has no idea what the word means is irrelevant. His boys will also nod sagely, accepting the demand that they give it to him as their leader. No one is brave enough to ask what it means, that might induce the fury that Jimmy expresses when he hears a dumb-fuck question. Nobody wants to be the next person that he verbally reams. It's better to accept that

Jimmy is fuller of learning and hope they don't slip up in some way to light his fuse.

The next big rule is that you've got to pay your dues. He's been taking five dollars a week from each of his boys for the last six years, and with at least a dozen of them around his table once a week, he's more than covering his campaign contribution and Pornhub subscription. At the outset, he spun a yarn that he needs to send membership dues to headquarters. *How the fuck else do you think they fund the business of keeping America, American?* No one questions him. That's the loyalty he wants, though he has never sent a penny anywhere.

Some of Jimmy's boys dance on the fringe of lawlessness, a position he tolerates, knowing they're acting for all the right reasons. People need reminding where they're from, and a reminder of the rules for getting along in his country. That's what his Chapter is all about.

There are times when Jimmy's boys have caused injury – mostly unintentional – he doesn't want his associates to cause severe harm, he would never advocate a lynching, although he can see there's a place for them sometimes. He's sanguine that things can go wrong, and someone might get a little beat up along the way, but that's okay. He'd like to push his boys a bit harder, so that they can properly strike fear into the alien community, but he can't quite trust them to stem their behaviour before crossing the border into felony activity; he encourages a policy of passive intimidation. Jimmy isn't planning a stay in the cooler because one of his boys has more stupid than sense. His aim is to ensure that people know where they stand, that there are only true patriots and just one American Way.

Keeping his ear to the ground, Jimmy listens to local news for opportunities to advance his goals. He won't allow a dilution of the Way. Gallup needs to know that the commie faggots, with their cultural appropriation and tolerance for foreign bullshit, have no place in his backyard. Proud Americans like Jimmy and his family built the city, and he's determined that Gallup will remain all-American.

#

A LITTLE SOMETHING TO HIDE

When the Hispanic community arranged a *Cinco de Mayo* festival, Jimmy's crew gave the fair's generators a healthy dose of America's finest refined cane sugar. The lights went out early that evening, just after the day's light had inched over the horizon and the sparkle and crackle of the fair was beginning to fill Red Rock Park.

The organisers had no option but to halt the event. They tried to rally community spirit to see if they could keep it going, but Sherriff Hawley put their optimism to bed. Jimmy and his boys huddled at the fringes, not too far from the generators, watching the debate unfold. Sheriff Hawley was implacable. *I'm gonna have to shut you down for safety*, he told them, while Jimmy and his boys smiled on, stoking tension.

It was what Jimmy hoped would happen. He'd consider it a bonus if one of the wetbacks got het up enough to need arresting, quietly optimistic it might happen, knowing that if anyone could provoke that happy outcome, it was Cletus Hawley.

The city's future sheriff and Jimmy went to high school together, becoming the closest of buddies, calling the shots in school until Jimmy went away to Fort Wingate and Cletus followed his old man into the police department. He loved watching his friend at work. Cletus Hawley's job was to protect and serve, but he embraced enough of the bully to protect in a special way.

While they were waiting for the intransigence of Sheriff Hawley to overcome the remonstrations of the fair's organisers, a few of the Sheriff's deputies padded to where Jimmy and his boys gathered. They swapped jokes, enjoying communion with friends. When they weren't wearing the uniform of the City of Gallup Police Department, some of them took a beer in a converted garage, where they talked about donning an altogether different kind of uniform.

Jimmy and his boys made sure their banter and laughter drifted over the departing crowd, enough to ensure they would develop a suspicious inkling that Jimmy's crew were responsible for the end of the evening's festivities. There was no point in organising a little chaos if the quarry didn't know

JIMMY – GALLUP

it was the target. Expectations needed setting; they had to know who really ran the city. They also had to know that there wasn't going to be much that they could expect from Sherriff Hawley and his men by way of an investigation.

Jimmy knew he could rely on Cletus. *That poor schlub has a dumb-fuck name, but he stands by his friends. That's what a good man does, even if his parents were retarded when it came to naming their boy. Still,* Jimmy figured, irony continuing to linger around his thoughts, *you gotta live with the name ya given.*

The darkness that Jimmy's boys engineered induced a whiff of panic that pleased him. It meant that the crowd would more keenly feel what was to follow, maximising the impact of his message. The sudden gloom brought a strain to parents' voices as they raced to find missing children, grappling in the diminishing light to secure their offspring's safety.

Squeals of delight on the big wheel turned to shrill, fear-laced shrieks as the Meccano-like tower shuddered to a halt, light bulbs winking out, carriages stalling, adopting a pendulous swing, sinister in the night sky. The wheel's crew hastened to affect a manual rescue, each solid *lunk* of the cranking wheel slow and ominous as it eked each carriage lower to release tear-drenched children into relieved parents' arms.

The scent of fear among the crowd is the memory that Jimmy loves to savour. It speaks to him of a power that he can wield, the power to raise a darkness not only in the Gallup night, but also in the minds of those that were there, making them conscious that they are not in control, that Jimmy and his boys could come for them at any time if they stepped out of line. It doesn't matter to Jimmy that they wouldn't do anything more threatening than prematurely ending a carnival, or the thing they did next.

He smiles at the recollection of the speed with which his boys operated. He had drilled them well, practicing in a field behind Mikey Foley's barn. Mikey relied on many people at the fair to do the picking on his farm, but he didn't like the idea that he had to use foreign labour to harvest his crops. *You*

A LITTLE SOMETHING TO HIDE

cain't help, what you cain't help. I gotta do what I gotta do. Most of Mikey's sentences finished as they began.

All the boys sympathised with him when he said he had to use immigrant labour. Everyone agreed that Mikey would rather employ Americans, but economics just wouldn't allow. *My only choice is no choice. Bidness is bidness.*

The vague intrusion of this thought troubled Jimmy; the conflicting dilemmas were always difficult to reconcile. He put it aside. Mikey had loaned his field to the cause and was a staunch member of the Chapter, which was all that mattered. He'd done his bit, providing the land and the concealment they needed to practice their craft. The practice paid dividends on the night of the fair; Jimmy's boys operated with the speed of an Indianapolis pit crew. They worked fast; no one saw their actions in that first pitch of darkness.

A glow of satisfaction warms Jimmy as he thinks about the horror on the faces of the retreating guests as they went pass the only light illuminating the space. It stood ten feet high and six wide, held in place by four ropes, anchored by carnival tent pegs driven deep into the ground. The flames from the structure licked the ropes, eventually burning through to let the blazing cross collapse on the grass.

Jimmy suffered a hint of anxiety as the cross began to fall, thinking it might land among the fleeing families. He didn't want anyone hurt, not badly, especially as that might provoke a more in-depth enquiry into the origins of the cross. Jimmy's only interest was to scare the bejeezus out of the Hispanics. When he reflects, he is satisfied with his work, although the cross went close to landing on a teenage couple from the local high school, white kids, maybe even the kids of one of his friends. If it had hit them, even Cletus may have struggled to divert attention from the incident. *White kids' folks can prove a bit trickier to shake off than immigrants,* Jimmy thought.

At the time, he believed he saw something approaching exhilaration on the boy's face as the cross plummeted. It landed just far enough away not to be a real danger. The boy also knew he wasn't the target, excitement infused his reaction. *Hell*, Jimmy thought, *he'll probably share the experience with his dad over their first proper beer together*, a bonding moment to unify father and son, laughing at the wetbacks' fright.

Jimmy wished he could be with them when that happened; two patriots sharing a story about the effort it took to keep America great. What Jimmy could share, which the kid wouldn't have noticed, was the image he saw in the eyes of those fleeing, a miniature burning cross, searing itself into their hearts, creating a visceral terror in their panic. That tiny cross of flaming gold, branded on their fear-enlarged pupils, served to highlight that they are imposters in his country. That's what he wants them all to learn and to know; that this is not now, nor will it ever be, their home. It is Jimmy's job to keep reminding them of that fact.

The boys laughed about the fair for weeks, whooped and hollered when they remembered what they'd done. It was an especially proud moment for the youngest of their group, Jay Hawley, the son of Jimmy's best friend and the first of a new generation of members that would keep the movement flourishing. Jimmy had let him flick the Zippo that set the cross alight, a gesture to his father, and the act that concluded Jay's initiation. Jay was already showing signs of being a mean sonofabitch; he'd inherited a plentiful nasty streak from his old man, one that Jimmy had witnessed over many years as he and the kid's father fed each other's bullshit and bullying. Jimmy and Cletus were great friends; they'd always have each other's backs, which came with obligations. Jimmy would be the one to nurture Jay's meanness, while trying to control the boy's stronger impulses.

The kids that joined the Chapter sometimes knew no bounds of stupid, they needed an older head to piss on their dumber ideas. With no controls, chances were good that their actions would cause friendlier law enforcement officers to reconsider their disregard.

Scaring the shit out of someone so that they knew their place was one thing. Doing something properly criminal was another, and what Jimmy needed to avoid. *Just remember, if you do something stupid enough to make your dad care, you fucked up.*

A LITTLE SOMETHING TO HIDE

He owed it to Cletus to make sure the kid didn't become an embarrassment to his father. It was up to Jimmy to make sure that Sherriff Hawley's deputies had no interest in looking past their beer and donuts. It was easier now that Hawley's boy was one of them, but that posed dangers of its own. The kid was a firecracker.

Cletus and Jimmy agreed that they should stop when things went beyond being playful. Scaring someone into thinking that things could get a lot worse was just high jinks, they had to keep it that way. They had to curb the enthusiasm of the younger fellas who were too brainless to know that really hurting someone could bring a host of problems none of them wanted to face. Sherriff Cletus Hawley often asked the boys in Jimmy's converted garage not to add to his workload. *Let's try and stay on the right side of the law,* he would say, before slapping his son's head to remind the kid he was an idiot.

Jimmy never stopped finding that funny, although he didn't liked the look the kid got in his eyes when he thought his father wasn't looking. The boy looked just about ready to cause his father a mite of pain. Jimmy suspects that if Jay was fully juiced and Cletus reminded the boy he was a numb-nuts, his son might not be able to stop himself popping a cap in the back of his father's head.

The look that Jay Hawley directs to his father is similar to the one Felipe wears whenever Jimmy reminds him that ICE could knock on his door at any moment. Jimmy knows he's riling his partner, but is confident he doesn't have to worry about retribution. It pleases him mightily that his co-worker suffers the threat, but is too chicken-shit to do anything. It's a power that Jimmy wields, one that throws him an endorphin spike every time it's exercised.

Jimmy has no intention of calling the authorities – that is never going to happen, he'll lose the perks that come from keeping his Mexican friend wound tight. 'Hell,' Jimmy thinks, 'Why go an extra 140 miles to Albuquerque just to drive back when a stop in Gallup does the job?'

#

JIMMY – GALLUP

Yes, Jimmy Lewis is a lazy sonofabitch, amongst many, much worse things, but I am not one to judge. I feel nothing. If I could, I would want to feel regret. Regret that when the Briscola coach stopped in Gallup, Jimmy Lewis was able to step off before the bus reached its final destination.

Still, as he stepped by me, his liver felt the trace of an unseen finger.

A LITTLE SOMETHING TO HIDE

EL FUGITIVO

```
Arrivals
Time     From                        Expected
05:17    Gallup                      Expected: 07:01
```

EL FUGITIVO

Jimmy's gone and there's only one other to meet on the bus, the second driver, Felipe Alvarez. His full name is Felipe Oscar Alvarez Medina. He's not from Mexico as his co-worker would have everyone believe; he's from Colombia. He came to the United States when he was sixteen, not that the authorities here will find records of his arrival, nor much by way of his history; the remains of his past lie deeply buried, ossifying quietly. That's a situation with which he is content.

Felipe considers anonymity a satisfactory state. He does little to arouse curiosity. When he's not driving for the Briscolas, he enjoys a solitary existence, sprawling his 315-pound frame across his favourite chair, the remote control close, vying for space with his beer and snacks on a ratan side-table that he picked up at a yard sale, negotiating half the money off the ten-dollar sticker when he pointed out a tiny fissure in the glass inlay. He keeps the table close. He's five-feet, six inches tall with a corresponding wingspan and he doesn't like to move too far once he's settled.

He moved quickly once, a long time ago, when he left his homeland with the haste borne from an instinct to survive. He was lean then, wiry, alert, and keen to see his seventeenth birthday rather than lying in a pool of blood in a Medellín comuna.

Briscola Coach Services maintain the only records of Felipe that exist in the continental United States. Its custodians have no intention of sharing the detail with state or federal governments.

The information sits off-ledger in a secret file maintained by the firm's management accountant. The file contains more than just the details of undocumented employees; discovery of the file's contents would prove worse than inconvenient to those state officials who allow

A LITTLE SOMETHING TO HIDE

the Briscolas to flout their territory's regulatory frameworks, although the recipients of the Briscola sweeteners might relax if they knew that the file's disclosure would have catastrophic consequences for the family. It's why, after the Briscolas, the management accountant is the highest paid employee on their payroll; they invest in his silence.

Despite their willingness to subvert regulations, the Briscolas remain judicious about how many 'illegals' they have on their books, keeping their numbers close to twenty percent of total headcount, reasoning that a higher proportion might invite unwanted scrutiny from ICE or the IRS, but it's a risk they're prepared to take. The wages of their undocumented workers account for just four percent of their payroll costs. 'Gotta love the illegals,' laughs Anthony Briscola. 'They're like a rounding error in the books.'

The illegal workforce is another reason the Briscolas have a second driver on their coaches. In the event of a random inspection, one of them needs to be legitimate. Should the crimson-blue hues of law enforcement stop a bus, the legal employee enjoying the luxury of a snooze can expect an abrupt shake of the shoulder from their illegitimate counterpart.

For that reason, Jimmy Lewis would be quick to lose his job if the Briscolas discovered he was leaving Felipe to complete the journey alone, but he's oblivious to the risk he is posing to his employer, not that he'd care, he'd still say, 'Fuck 'em,' and continue to step off at Gallup; he despises the Briscolas.

Jimmy decided long ago that if they were stupid enough to fire him, he'd undertake a little data sharing of Felipe's employment status with the authorities that the Briscolas are so keen to avoid. He's confident he has the measure of the greaseballs, he's got leverage, as do they – they rely on each other not to use it. The implicit threat that surrounds them guarantees an uncomfortable impasse.

Jimmy likes the convenience of not having to travel all the way to Albuquerque. He doesn't believe he's paid enough to travel the final leg of the journey. Besides which, both he and Felipe know that Jimmy's premature departure means a smaller likelihood of ICE knocking on the Colombian's door.

Despite the inherent nervousness that comes with his presence in the country, Felipe has embraced the American way of life. He's a fan of the Texans, the Astros, and the Rockets, although he's never been to

EL FUGITIVO

Houston. He hasn't even crossed the border from New Mexico into Texas. He prefers not to stray too far from his home unless he's compelled to at the front of a Briscola coach. Notwithstanding, he couldn't afford the journey to Houston; the Briscolas don't pay him well and there are no discounted fares for employees. What he earns comes to him in cash on every third transit of LA. The amount and form are always the same, eighty used five-dollar bills tucked into a slim manilla envelope.

Seated behind a small table, in a room adjacent to the Customer Service desk, is the bespectacled management accountant. He's a bony creature with a translucent skin that always looks a little empty. What remnants of hair he possesses are the colour of a subway station mouse, thin wisps greased flat across the polished dome of his head. The bridge of his glasses sits above the nub end of his nose. He peers over them at people, and through them when busying himself at his laptop. He scrutinises the detail, cares less about the people.

Felipe doesn't know his name, he's not sure anyone in the queue in front of the accountant does. Those within the queue are mostly Hispanic, although they rarely hear their common language. They exchange looks, glances, nods of acknowledgement, but never stories. They all know it's best not to become familiar. It's safer that way.

The queue moves with surprising speed. The bony man is efficient. He glances up at each new face, saying one word, 'Name,' repeating it to each person. He hears muted responses, no one wants to volunteer information to those around them. They want only the bony man to hear their answers.

With each response, he traces a skeletal finger along a line in a spreadsheet that he annotates before reaching into a large wooden box beside him. The box is a solid piece of furniture, painted blue with imposing chrome latches and tumblers that the accountant sets to '0000' at the end of each day. Only he knows the combination. He lifts the lid minimally, opening its maw a fraction, allowing just enough space for his scrawny hand to enter and remove an unmarked envelope which he passes across, without comment, to each person whose name is on his list.

Riches sit within the box, dwindling, along with the queue. At the start of the day, it contains enough cash to pay for an Ivy League education, but no one considers snatching the box from the bony man. He appears incapable of defending himself, but he never travels alone. Loitering behind him, silent and brooding, stands his minder. He remains resolutely still, imposing, granite like, studying everyone.

He doesn't look quick, but no one is willing to test the theory. He can defend himself, and should the need arise, inflict all manner of pain. Felipe tries not to make eye-contact with either man; he doesn't want to reveal anything to them that a casual glance might convey. He knows they don't expect thanks, although he mumbles it quietly whenever he receives payment. The routine suits them all.

Felipe saved enough to buy a 65-inch television which dominates the only solid wall in his one bed apartment in Nob Hill, Albuquerque. At 410 square feet, it is palatial compared to the cabin that Toby Ames occupied in North Hollywood, and Felipe is happy to call it home. It is basic, but well appointed.

He got lucky with a landlord who was content not to ask questions in exchange for Felipe's silence regarding undeclared rent. They hold their mutual secrets securely. The landlord is a decent man, if not entirely law abiding. He ensures that his tenant has most home comforts. The appliances are cheap, but adequate.

Felipe has never stopped marvelling at how many conveniences North Americans enjoy. He can clean his dishes and his clothes without leaving his chair. It's a notable improvement from the comuna *that he left behind as a teenager.*

In Albuquerque he has more than just a lone moody gas ring for preparing his food, but he never cooks. He uses his microwave only to blast popcorn or reheat the remains of previous meals, although it is rare for him to leave scraps.

His rent eats up a third of his monthly earnings, but he's happy. The TV and a La-Z-Boy recliner rocker are his two most used possessions, closely followed by an old Nokia handset. He doesn't want to change it for a smartphone. He likes the simplicity of playing Snake; it's less complicated than modern games. Felipe likes to bypass complications.

He has programmed a handful of restaurants into speed-dial, eight of them, one fast-food chain for each day of the week and Ajiaco for his lunches. All of them deliver. He cycles through them when he's not on

EL FUGITIVO

the road. He likes a modest variety when choosing how best to narrow his arteries.

At the end of each trip, he finds himself sprawled over the surface of his chair. The TV is always on, the volume not too loud; he doesn't want to trouble the neighbours. It's important to avoid drawing attention to himself, although he doesn't stifle his yells when the Texans score, the neighbours, he knows, are fans too.

Like Toby, he likes tamales, but is fonder of empanadas which he has delivered every day from Ajiaco. He washes down his meals with several Rolling Rocks. He knows it's an indulgence, but he spends his money on little else.

The empanadas are the closest match he has found to an authentic taste of home. The taste of the street food in Medellín is the only thing he misses. He wishes Ajiaco would serve Chuzos o Pinchos; *he could kill for the greasy richness of those pork skewers. He doesn't miss the beer too much, although he will argue that a bottle of Aguila is better than the Rolling Rock that he drinks. Not that it's an argument he makes to anyone. There are few people he knows, and fewer that he meets for drinks.*

His choice of beer has less to do with taste and more to do with economics. It's his wallet that determines his preferred tipple rather than the taste. It's a sacrifice he's happy to make; it's not the first. Sacrifices have governed his life for as long as he has had to make them to survive.

A LITTLE SOMETHING TO HIDE

FELIPE – LOS ALPES

The people that Felipe escaped would make The Toppers piss their pants in fear. The bearded boys, with their wrap-around shades, pool room hustling, and part-time coke dealing, wouldn't have used a flashy blade as a threatening device where Felipe once lived. If a knife appeared, carotid arteries gushed before words; the luxury of a warning rarely offered. More often though, they avoided the messiness of a knife. A bullet to the head, the preferred method of justice, was swift and often arbitrary. Cartel trials were quick in the *comunas*; no legal counsel stood in garrulous defence.

Unlike their southern neighbours, Felipe found that US Americans loved to talk, to brag. He thought the former president was the worst. Donald Trump wouldn't have lasted beyond his morning dump on his gold-plated toilet in the *comunas*. They'd have seen him for what he was, a bullshitter and a conman, taking care of him quickly.

There were times when Felipe felt that Donald Trump deserved a bit of Colombian justice, figuring him for a man who would leave a pool of his own piss on the floor if he faced some of Felipe's experiences.

Felipe didn't believe a word the man said, but he hoped for some truth when the former president said the Border Patrol was sending home record numbers of bad *hombres* at the Southern Border. Felipe didn't want any of the *cabrones* that he knew from Colombia trekking through Central America and crossing into New Mexico, that was a terrifying prospect.

Felipe exists under a cloak of fear. For the last 26 years, he's feared discovery by ICE, the US Immigration and Customs Enforcement service, a preferred state of angst to the one from which he fled. He no longer fears the people he escaped. Too much time has passed for them to care, he knows they won't pursue him, believing that the effort to find and kill him outweighs the boost it would give to a cartel boss's reputation, although he can never return, he knows he would face a certain, pointless, death.

He suspects foreshortened lives awaited those he left behind, that his Colombian associates have long since perished in local disputes. They're probably dead, along with any personal risk to Felipe, but he doesn't want to explore that hypothesis; like money, memories can be inherited. Wisdom tells him to avoid the zealous kids seeking vengeance for ancient slights.

Those that he fears now are the people that he ran towards. When the Trump administration got into power, the thought of ICE knocking on his door and what they might do to him accounted for restless nights. Jimmy Lewis makes it worse when he steps off the bus with his gentle reminder of what he knows. Felipe knows that Lewis is a little unhinged and might one day pick up the phone to what he laughingly calls *Mr Frosty, Felipe's friendly ICEman*.

Felipe doesn't believe that ICE will physically harm him. He worries that if they find him, he will lose his liberty, that he knows too little to be of use to the Drug Enforcement Agency, with no prospects of negotiating a plea bargain to remain in the United States. He'd consider himself lucky if he found himself in a US penitentiary. There, he thinks, his hiding days would end; he could be himself again, his tensions disappearing, closely followed by relief.

It's the alternative that concerns him, the possibility of ICE not throwing him in jail, but out of the country, giving him a one-way economy seat on the first flight back to Medellín, where he might discover that the life expectancy of those he fears is longer than he believes, or that their unavenged legacy passed to the next generation. If that happens, he's likely to experience an extreme and excruciating pain, with his only hope that it will be brief. If memories of his betrayal remain, he knows he'll be dead within a month. While those he left behind viewed his action as betrayal, Felipe's perspective differs. He saw it as revenge.

FELIPE – LOS ALPES

He left without permission, not that he asked for it. It wasn't a case of raising a hand to the cartel and asking to leave the room. The cartel keeps its people or kills them. There is no middle ground. The risk is too great for alternatives. Those outside the circle could talk, so the cartel mitigates – the dead can't testify.

Felipe wasn't always obese. There was a time when he carried the frame of a waif, motivated by the hunger that stems from reedy meals. At the age of ten, with food cravings a near constant companion, he started a fateful relationship despite his mother's warnings, befriending Luis Martínez Correa. Luis always had food.

There were days when Felipe went to school and his mother couldn't put lunch in his bag. Always toward the end of the week, her paltry earnings from cleaning at the hospital unable to cover the cost of food. She cried when it happened, every time, knowing where it might lead. Felipe always told her not to worry, he would be okay, he would get something from a friend. While she knew goodness flowed through her child, his words frightened her. She knew why some of the children at his school had plenty. It terrified her to think her son might enter their circles.

Margarite Medina insisted that Felipe come home directly from school. She knew she couldn't control who he mixed with in the school yard, and the school would not intervene to keep him from the boys she didn't trust, but she could try to limit his contact with those she considered to be the vagabond children of the *comunas*, although vagabond implied a roguish cheek that masked a more sinister definition. Getting Felipe home each day was the best way she knew to limit his contact with Luis. She didn't want Felipe to mix with him. She wanted to keep him safe.

Luis's best friend was Sergio; they were inseparable. Sergio could make everyone laugh with his high falsetto voice that squealed like a long pull on a helium balloon. Whenever he opened his mouth to speak, Luis's raspy laugh soon followed.

A LITTLE SOMETHING TO HIDE

It made Luis sound as though forty cigarettes a day filled his lungs, but he didn't touch anything. His older brother said he'd kill him if he did. It was a threat Luis took seriously.

Luis and Sergio always had food, and they always had money. They never declared its source, but they were happy to share it with a hungry Felipe. Felipe earned it by doing Luis's homework. It was an arrangement that worked for them both. Sergio didn't do homework. He would whine about a dog dining on his algebra or a bandit stealing his spelling, always generating the laughter of his classmates. His teacher considered Sergio an idiot but concealed his contempt. Other children would face punishment for not completing assignments, but not Sergio. A Medellín teacher learns a wisdom that doesn't trouble other teachers. There are certain children they know not to punish.

Danger flowed through Medellín *comunas* irrespective of innocence or criminality. Local gangs put little store in the value of life. They peddled drugs, ran prostitutes, 'protected' shop owners and didn't care whether their customers lived or died. Territorial, they killed to preserve their patch, although boundaries were amorphous, constantly challenged. No one knew quite where they existed.

When Pablo Escobar died in 1993, his united Medellín disintegrated into factions, rival gangs clashed on the fringes; domains shifted in the victor's favour. It was another reason Margarite Medina wanted Felipe to come home. It was dangerous on the streets. At home she could protect him, wrap her arms around him, stop the world from seducing her son. She wanted to shield him from the dangers that surrounded them. She resolved to keep him safe despite their circumstances. Her resolve ended abruptly on another balmy evening shortly after her son's twelfth birthday.

She worked at the Belén Metrosalud on Calle 28, walking there and back each day, treading wearily alongside the endlessly drifting Quebrada Chocho. On the way home she turned onto Calle 21, trudging up the hill to her home, her mood becoming heavier with every step as she neared the dilapidated apartment above a salon offering manicures, pedicures, and makeovers. The prospect of crossing the threshold for pampering appealed to Margarite, indulging in the exchange of gossipy sweet nothings, ignoring the chemical pungency, trilling like the girl of her past. It was a luxury she couldn't afford.

The girls working in the salon wore heavy make-up, trowelled onto their faces, advertising in equal measure the services they provided and the hardships they disguised. They wore tight skirts and tottered on too-high heels, an imitation of refinement; the only thing distinguishing them from the girls that sauntered Candelaria's streets funding addiction and the gangs they served.

Seeing the girls in the salon left Margarite feeling the weight of her dowdiness and poverty. How she would love to escape the dreariness for a day, made up and dressed for an occasion that would allow her to be the person she wanted to be, rather than the woman she had become.

In their single-roomed apartment she helped Felipe with his homework, cooked their meals on an ancient Primus stove, and shared a rolled-up mattress that they unfurled each night and rolled away in the morning. The room suffered the drift of acetone from the salon below. On Friday nights, as the neighbourhood girls made their preparations for the weekend, the smell intensified, convincing her that those fumes would one day poison her and Felipe. She was wrong, the fumes weren't the thing that killed her.

In the *Comunas,* people lived on top of one another, shouting resounded from the houses, arguments were frequent and seldom private. On the street where she lived, Margarite knew of four families where the husband beat the wife, suspecting that her knowledge represented a fraction of the abuse occurring in the houses around her. She was grateful that the father of her child left them when Felipe was still a baby. It meant that she faced her hardships alone, but her hardships were easier to bear without the closed eyes that he occasionally gifted her.

In Los Alpes, young men loitered on street corners, tormenting passers-by, catcalling to girls with short skirts and legs that opened too readily. Their cacophony added to the soundscape that greeted Margarite in the dusk of an early October evening.

The taunts of the young men or the arguments that she heard were of no matter to her. She cared only to reach home, to find her boy studying, finding a way to escape their reality through education and hard work. He is a good boy, her Felipe. She knew that in time, Felipe would watch over her.

As she rounded the corner to her street, she was alert to an argument with a different pitch. There was a violence in the undertones, an extreme threat in what she heard. She wasn't listening to the words, everyone in Medellín knew not to hear too much. The realisation that she heard the language of death came too late. She knew that Death was near, that *I* was close, but what she didn't know, was that I was coming for her.

Margarite Medina could see fear on the face of the kid running towards her. He was older than her son, with a post-adolescent frame that lacked the bulk of manhood, yet he carried the strength of youth. She didn't know from what he was fleeing, but she knew that she was in his way.

He saw her too, not as a tired woman trudging home from a long day at work, but as a shield. His mind worked quickly, self-preservation separating him from humanity. He grabbed at her, spinning her behind him, a barrier between himself and the gunman that was chasing. His executioner didn't lower his weapon or alter his aim when the woman stood between him and the boy he was trying to shoot. He didn't care that he might hit an innocent bystander. The fleeing boy cheated him, earning his rage. Justice needed serving.

He fired at the fugitive, not caring that Margarite stood between them. He fired again, and again, and again. Seven shots in total before the youth had rounded the corner from which Margarite Medina emerged. None of the shots hit their intended target. Three of them caught Margarite before she hit the ground.

Her assailant walked nonchalantly toward her, unperturbed, peering at the near lifeless woman. He saw her desperation, mouth gaping in a silent pleading for help. Impassive eyes viewed Margarite, betraying nothing. He shrugged and walked on. It was, what it was. He'd get the guy another day.

Felipe Alvarez heard the gun shots from where he sat completing Luis's homework assignment. The noise carried down the street and through the open window of his apartment. It was a common sound during Felipe's childhood. No matter how much Margarite Medina wanted to protect her son, Medellín was not a safe place. He looked out the window for the briefest of moments and didn't think about the shots until later.

His mother would be home soon to cook their dinner, but he wasn't hungry. Luis had paid for his homework with hot *pinchos* from a street vendor. The meaty skewers were Felipe's favourite, he'd make sure Luis would get an A for this piece of work. He might have thought differently if he'd known at the time that Luis's older brother had just killed his mother.

It was dark before Felipe thought about the gunshots again. *Mamá* was late. She never took on a late shift at the hospital without telling him, even if they needed the money. It was one of their rules, the unbreakable promise that he would always know when to expect her. She would never leave him to worry.

When the slow meandering of the wall clock signalled that his mother was two hours late, his concerns grew. Felipe peered through the open window and into the night. The noise of Los Alpes hadn't yet diminished to its whispered late-night stirrings, the furtive exchanges for sex and drugs. The early evening chatter was still robust, lively, a safer sound than the quiet that follows.

Felipe closed his books before placing them in the corner where he kept his school things. The Alvarez Medinas were neat, dictated by an economy of space, everything tidied away once used; the need to find his mother did not break the habits she instilled in her son.

Taking his key from the hook by the side of the door, he pulled it closed behind him, waiting to hear the snick of closure before turning a lock that would provide little resistance to anyone determined to break into their tiny home, though no one would, their minuscule domain contained nothing of value. At the foot of the stairs, he stood on the threshold of the street, pausing before stepping into the evening. Instinct told him which way to go, he just wasn't sure he wanted to make the journey.

A small crowd gathered at the street corner ahead of him. An intermittent blue flashed against the ragged buildings that lined the street. The source of the light, a police bike, stood neglected to one side. A police officer, notebook in hand, half-heartedly took notes as he spoke to an elderly woman who gestured expansively up and down the street. The policeman hated that he would have a night of admin ahead of him, recording another killing, adding to the list of unsolved crimes in Medellín. He didn't know why they bothered.

A carelessly draped plastic sheet lay over an inert form on the ground. As Felipe approached, he could see that blood had spread from the body, forming viscous pools in the pock-marked street. A blue canvas espadrille protruded from the sheet; he recognised it as the shoe his mother wore to work.

Wrestling beneath the shoulders of bystanders to get nearer to where his mother lay, he broke through and lifted the sheet that covered her, alerting the police officer to his presence. Felipe recognised her just as a hand hauled him from where he knelt, the policeman tossing him against a building, admonishing his disrespect. Fighting his tears, he explained that the victim was his mother, receiving no compassion, only irritation.

Felipe stood alone, momentarily, before he felt the arms of a stranger wrap around him, pulling him into the protective embrace of someone kind enough to care. The police officer ignored him, returning to the gesticulating woman, but soon tired of her performance. Snapping his notebook closed, he returned to Felipe, asking perfunctory questions, the responses going unrecorded. The woman holding Felipe objected to his lack of notetaking. The policeman considered arguing but noted her glance at his officer's number. He removed the notebook from his pocket, took down Felipe's address and killed time by asking irrelevant questions which he hoped would irritate the woman.

The tightly wound streets of Los Alpes afforded limited access. Two paramedics arrived on foot, carrying a stretcher. The police officer lost interest in the boy, exchanging affable greetings with the new arrivals, sharing a joke; conduct that might have been familiar to visitors at a distant Gallup fair.

They were unconcerned about the dead woman or her child. There was a sense of futility to their work; no life for the paramedics to preserve; the policeman expected a cursory investigation. Instead, they conducted a gathering of old friends, a collegiate closeness developed over similar incidents. They shared a dark sense of humour; their ability to practice sympathy lost to the mundanity of their tasks.

The interest of the stranger holding Felipe also drifted. *¿Estás bien?*

He nodded through his tears, although he didn't know why. He was anything but okay. His mother was dead, he didn't know his father, he was alone.

Are you sure? she asked, looking for assurance and hoping to find resolve. She knew the streets of Los Alpes, to show too much sympathy might create a problem she didn't want to face. She got the same response, a feeble nod. Stifling her relief, she discharged herself from her self-imposed duty, ruffling Felipe's hair as she left him to face whatever the fates held.

The paramedics bundled Margarite onto a stretcher with robotic lethargy, carrying her into the night, leaving the crowd to thin and a lone child standing on a street corner. In time, the frightened boy returned to the box room that he and his mother called home. He unrolled their mattress, *his* mattress now, and climbed under the blanket they shared. Her smell lingered on the fabric, a trace of disinfectant, redolent of her hospital labours, providing no comfort to the newly ordained orphan.

In the morning he followed his routine, an automaton, searching in the box that functioned as their pantry, finding a half-filled pack of cereal. There was no milk; his mother always collected it on her way home, keeping it as close to fresh as they could without a refrigerator. He crunched his way through dried cornflakes and readied himself for school, gathering the books he needed, tucking them under his arm along with the assignment for Luis.

Luis and Sergio stood waiting. Felipe passed the homework over wordlessly, silent about his mother. He chose not to alert the boys or his school to her death. He didn't want to discover what might happen to him. It didn't occur to him to worry that the police might contact the school, albeit a pointless anxiety.

The day lagged and his teacher's lessons failed to register. Her words went unheeded as the day drifted slowly to its end. He hesitated in the school yard before going home, already breaking his mother's rules, it beat the alternative of being alone. Not yet. A life of solitude beckoned, but he wasn't yet ready for its call.

Luis and Sergio didn't object when he asked if he could join them. They walked the streets until the smell of greasy food drew them to a street vendor where Luis bought them *pinchos*. It was Felipe's first food since breakfast. They sat with their backs against a wall, seething humanity passing by, heedless of the street urchins, unaware of the tumult facing the newest of the group.

As ever, Sergio dominated conversation, inventing heroics, telling outrageous stories of missions and conquests drawn from his imagination. In a town where his friend, Felipe, would one day drive, Gracie MacDonald was doing the same. Luis laughed his gravelly laugh, each rasp encouraging Sergio to magnify his embellishments. Felipe could find no humour in his tales today. Neither of the other boys noticed.

At a pause in Sergio's storytelling, Luis adopted a conspiratorial lean, drawing the other boys toward him. He told them about the night before, of his brother's rage at the loss of twenty thousand pesos, cheated by an imp.

There's no place for the kid to hide. Jesús will cut off his balls and leave him to die like that stupid puta last night.

FELIPE – LOS ALPES

Luis cared only to burnish his older brother's reputation and failed to detect Felipe's shock at learning that it was Jesús Martínez Correa who ended his mother's life. As the story of her death unfolded, Felipe quashed the impulse to react, revealing nothing to his friends, not knowing what instinct prevented him from telling Luis that Jesús had killed his mother. He resisted defending her honour, chose not to highlight her innocence, or condemn the killing. A nascent faculty stirred within Felipe, inducing caution, urging silence even as Luis bragged about his murderer brother. He decided never to tell them that he knew the dead woman.

Luis bought more *pinchos* and the boys gnawed through them, each possessed of their own thoughts, quietly processing the news. For once, Sergio was quiet, not knowing whether to be reverent or funny where death intruded. Guarding his knowledge, Felipe rose to leave when he finished his food, making the excuse that their homework needed doing. They didn't protest his departure.

Sergio decided that the time for reverence had passed. As Felipe trudged down the street with a gait that was reminiscent of his mother's, he could once more hear Sergio's falsetto squeal and the grating rasp of Luis's laugh.

The box of cornflakes lasted two more days. Felipe joined the boys at the end of each day, letting Luis buy him food, maintaining his secret. Soon the street snacks were his only meal and he found himself peering into bins when alone, searching for something to supplement his diet. He grew thinner.

At the end of the week there was a knock on his door; his mother's landlord asking where she was hiding. *She's at work,* said Felipe.

The landlord peered over his shoulder, searching for Margarite before deciding the boy was telling the truth. He left, annoyed at her absence and his lack of rent. Felipe closed the door, wondering, deciding quickly.

The following day was Saturday; he went in search of Luis. He found him with Sergio, standing on a corner, doing nothing more than surveying the street. He told them he needed money, asking if they could help him to find a job.

Luis didn't question his motive, but looked hard at his friend, measuring him; Felipe's 12-year-old schoolfriend replaced by a streetwise cynic. Luis knew that if Felipe had come to him, there was only one job that he wanted.

Stay with us until we're finished, said Luis. *Then we'll see*.

It wasn't obvious to Felipe what they were doing, or when their nameless task might end. Occasionally, they recognised an older boy on a street corner and exchanged waves, which then led Luis and Sergio to scan the street until the boy disappeared. They repeated the behaviour whenever he returned.

Three hours later, two boys joined them that Felipe didn't know. Luis and Sergio high-fived them, declined their offer of cigarettes, and left with no further comment, gesturing for Felipe to follow.

Crisscrossing myriad streets, they passed ramshackle buildings where waste accumulated, providing lodging and sustenance for numberless vermin. The boys cast nervous glances behind as they followed a circuitous path, providing no commentary on who or what they were evading.

They reached an imposing black door in the side of a wall, solid steel but for a panel three-quarters of the way up, beneath which ran traces of oxidisation, like rusting icicles. Luis pounded his fist slowly against it three times, leaving an elongated pause before his fourth knock. The panel slid open, a pair of eyes with bloodshot notes peered through. Bolts *thunked* into their housings before the door opened outwards with a baritone whine announcing solidity and a thirst for oil.

The boys stepped into a darkened room, a pall of smoke drifting through, acrid and sweet. Small red tips glowed in pockets of the room as the occupants drew deeply on thickly rolled reefers. Felipe followed Luis to a table in a corner, around which three young men sat playing cards, sliding a bottle of *aguardiente* between them. A pile of money, haphazardly discarded, sat in the centre of the table, more money than Felipe had ever seen. As they approached, one of the men cackled, laid his cards down and swept the cash towards him. The chuckle had a similar timbre to Luis's laugh; Felipe knew he was in the presence of his mother's killer.

Luis stood silently at the side of the table, not wanting to interrupt proceedings, waiting for an invitation to speak. Jesús allowed a short passage of time to pass before deigning to acknowledge his sibling. They spoke in hushed tones, too low for Felipe to hear. The older brother looked past Luis to assess Felipe. He didn't say anything or invite him closer, just nodded, waving Luis away. Without knowing it, Felipe left the room as the cartel's newest recruit. He was now one of the *pequeños espías*, the little spies. As they were walking from the house, Luis confirmed that Felipe would be starting his job the next day, telling him to meet for *pinchos* at 7pm and that they would be working late.

After their supper, they sauntered to the spot where Felipe had found them the previous day. The boys that Luis and Sergio high-fived the day before were on the corner, leaning against the graffitied wall of an abandoned restaurant, attempting to look self-important. They left shortly after the exchange of greetings, allowing Luis, Sergio, and Felipe to slump as the new claimants to the wall. Felipe was about to ask what they were doing when Luis stiffened, alert to a lean figure in a black shirt and denim jeans who appeared from the laundromat on the opposite corner. *Javier,* Luis said, offering no further explanation, before looking up and down the streets leading to where the man stood.

Two men on a moped pulled alongside Javier, neither wearing helmets. As the rider drew the bike to a halt, the man on the back held out an envelope, which Javier took, swapping it for a larger bag. The moped wheezed in acceleration and Felipe watched the riders disappear down a side street. When he looked back to where Javier stood, the corner was empty.

Luis explained what happened and their role in the exchange. He taught Felipe the gestures they employed to signal safety, to warn of threat, or to abort a transaction. Felipe developed his familiarity with Jesús's operatives, the customers, the methods of exchange, how to recognise rivals, and how to spot the law, although little prospect existed of a visit from the authorities.

Most of the local police sat on Jesús's payroll and none of them was stupid enough to venture onto Los Alpes' streets unannounced. The police issued notice of patrols before they happened, it kept everybody safe.

At 3am, Luis announced that their shift was over. He pulled a wad of banknotes from his pocket, counting out twenty 2,000 pesos notes before passing them to Felipe. *There'll be more when you know what you're doing.* It was Felipe's first pay day. He didn't yet know if it was much, but it was twice the amount that had led to the death of his mother. As he folded the notes and tucked them into his pocket, he developed the first notion of how to avenge her.

Felipe paid his landlord, who again asked where his mother was hiding, not really caring about the answer, satisfied that she had left money with her son. He never again questioned her whereabouts, he was happy – the boy was paying, always on time and always in cash. The arrangement suited him perfectly.

Felipe's belief that the police wouldn't pursue his mother's killer proved correct. Maintaining perfect attendance at school, he kept the authorities from paying him a call. He planned to stay at school for as long as Luis remained a student, maintaining his patience for two more years.

Luis didn't graduate from school, but he graduated from their corner. Before long, he had taken Javier's place, relying on Sergio and Felipe to spot for him. The promotion marked an elevation in his brother's organisation. He became aloof towards Sergio and Felipe, no longer the kid paid to look for threats, now he had a real job. Although he relied on them, he now considered his friends beneath him.

They moved around the neighbourhood, from corner to corner, managing Jesús's petty trading. Jesús was ambitious, the local business meant little to his organisation, there were much bigger opportunities outside the *comunas*, but there were territorial rights to assert, a new cartel to establish, and law enforcement to corrupt.

FELIPE – LOS ALPES

Felipe began to think of Thursdays as bribery day. Every week, on corners around Los Alpes, one-way transactions occurred, the police in the pocket of the cartel collecting their payments. The routine never varied. One of Jesús's boys would lurk, surly in deportment, inviting investigation by the police, waiting for collaring and questioning. A charade followed, the officers demonstrating to casual observers that they controlled the streets, although witnesses to the event understood the lie. In the physicality of the exchange, envelopes slipped into shirts, as the loiterer got bundled away; diligent law enforcement purging the neighbourhood of the unsavoury.

Felipe watched it all. He noted the officers and studied the exchanges. Sometimes information passed, intelligence the police had uncovered of threats to Jesús's burgeoning cartel. The police didn't just turn blind eyes, they provided a form of protection. It was how they earned their payments.

The officer that attended his mother's murder was a Thursday regular, allowing Felipe to comprehend why they would never find her killer. The boys had nicknamed him *Bolitas*, Little Balls. He pretended to be tough, but they all knew he didn't have the *cojones* to follow through on his threats.

When Luis moved up in the cartel, Sergio took his place. Felipe remained a *pequeño espía*, taking the opportunity to discover more about the organisation, learning about its trade, its leader – and his brutality – discovering that Jesús was ruthless.

Jesús now had better control of the rage that led him to shoot an innocent woman, but he was no less brutal. He exercised vicious impulses that led others to fear him, although Felipe didn't care. It was one of the few times in his life when he felt he didn't have anything of which to be afraid. He was too busy planning how he would kill Jesús.

Information rarely passed down the organisation, the developing cartel's success relied on the direction of travel. Intelligence went up, orders came down. It was a protocol that

Sergio didn't always maintain, allowing his penchant for theatrics to lead to gossip. He was savvy enough not to speak outside the cartel but couldn't resist sharing what he knew with Felipe.

Luis was no longer interested in hearing from Sergio unless it was cartel business, he had moved beyond his friend's diversions. Felipe became Sergio's primary outlet for scandal, his stories infused with information about the cartel's plans.

As time passed, Felipe began to understand when intelligence sharing occurred. Watching *Bolitas* speaking earnestly with Sergio during a Thursday exchange, Felipe noted an absence of the officer's customary indifference. The policeman adopted a cagey set, scanning his surroundings nervously, demonstrating a wariness to exposure. Although the cartel had its *pequeños espías*, limiting the risk of discovery, *Bolitas* displayed obvious unease, more edgy than normal, indicating a greater level of import to the information he shared.

Ordinarily, Sergio would tell Felipe what was said before passing it to Luis. On this occasion, Sergio vanished from his corner the moment *Bolitas* was gone, returning later in the day. *Some heavy shit's going down, man,* he said to Felipe. *PNC. Gonna be fierce.*

Felipe knew what a visit from *Policía Nacional de Colombia* caused. Paranoia. Already heightened by indulgence in the cartel's product, it worsened when PNC threatened to call. It meant more *pequeños espías*, increased tension, greater expectations, volatile leadership – more danger.

Although Jesús's payments slipped into the jackets of many in the PNC, his influence wasn't yet deep enough for him to be comfortable that he could avoid trouble at the highest level of law enforcement; vigilance was paramount. Thanks to Sergio's indiscretion, Felipe knew a heavily armed PNC would be coming to visit. When the opportunity came, he wanted things to go wrong.

On the day of the raid, Felipe and Sergio found themselves on neighbouring corners, in the place where the PNC would likely enter Los Alpes. The boys could see each other along the narrow streets that ran off Parque De Los Alpes. With luck, Felipe hoped his plan would work.

Down the street before him, he witnessed the skulking of an advanced party, unrecognised PNC officers, crouching low, scurrying toward him. Behind them, local police trailed, ostensibly providing support, yet keen to avoid the front of the assault which could result in a death sentence. Their support was half-hearted; the cartel knew they were coming. It would be ready and undiscerning when the shooting started.

The job of the *pequeños espías* was to report advances to the centre, the compound where business happened, where Jesús sometimes stayed. Notification of the PNC's stealthy advance would alert the *sicarios* that waited there, hitmen loyal to Jesús, charged with the task of eliminating PNC officers before they could act; to assert the cartel's sovereignty in Medellín.

From the shadow of a doorway, Felipe watched as the PNC passed and pretended to make a call. He hurried to Sergio, intending to distract him, getting to him as the heavily armed officers were approaching and Sergio was raising his phone.

I've called already, said Felipe. *They know.*

Sergio smiled, he loved his friend's diligence, it meant cover if he ever made a mistake.

Bolitas was in the party that scurried past Felipe and Sergio. They exchanged glances, Felipe nodded; the cartel knows. *Bolitas* smiled at the thought of their appreciation, he looked forward to next Thursday.

I've got a surprise for you, thought Felipe, knowing that the *sicarios* and the PNC had surprises for each other.

When they heard explosions rather than gunfire, Sergio knew that something was wrong. The *sicarios* should be shooting first, their semi-automatic weapons cutting through the approaching assailants. The explosion meant an attack on the centre, entrances breached, disabling gases belching into the compound, panicking those within.

Controlled bursts of gunfire rang through the *comuna*, the sound of trained attackers rather than the frenetic shooting associated with a *sicario* assault. Sergio flashed Felipe a look, reaching for the handgun tucked in his jeans. Felipe stalled him, what good could a lone sixteen-year-old do? He liked Sergio and didn't want him hurt. Keeping him from joining the fray was the safest thing for them both.

Gunfire increased as the *sicarios* responded to the police attack. Felipe led Sergio to his small apartment where he switched on the radio, turning the volume up as loud as possible, masking the sound of the battle, and delaying a conversation with Sergio.

It was over sooner than he thought. Those cartel members still able to walk sported handcuffs, harried through the streets to waiting police wagons. Some left on stretchers, the bearers taking them to ambulances that idled on the edge of the *comuna*. Others had sheets draped over them for later attention; the living had priority.

Bolitas wasn't a priority. He'd been at the back, lingering, thinking he was safe, expecting to escape when the PNC advance began to drop, disappearing down one of the streets he knew so well. The absence of a warning from Felipe or Sergio, meant he was closer to the centre than planned, the likelihood of his participation in the skirmish growing the nearer he got to the compound. Though initially slow to respond, the *sicarios* reacted, deeming anyone in uniform a target. As *Bolitas* passed through the hole in the wall that had once held a solid steel door, the rattle of an AR-15 extinguished his final thoughts, bringing half of Felipe's plan to fruition.

Although the raid cost him his life, the intelligence *Bolitas* provided to Sergio had preserved those of Jesús and Luis. Jesús was prepared for his men to have a gunfight with the PNC, particularly given his belief in the advantage that came with foresight. He didn't care that there would be casualties. Most, he reasoned, would be on the side of the authorities, and serve as a demonstration of his growing power, providing the Police and the government something to consider, undermining the confidence that they were gaining control of the country.

Although he was prepared to see some of his men sacrificed, he saw no reason to put himself in the way of the offensive. The cartel needed its leader, he couldn't expose himself. No one dared question his rationale, either directly or in the quiet murmur of a hushed grievance. Secretly shared opinions often found their way to Jesús, leading the bearers to discover the folly of their views. Opinions that challenged Jesús's thinking were best left concealed.

While the PNC were killing and arresting his men, Jesús was playing cards with his brother at a luxury hillside villa, far from the decrepitude of the *comuna* compound. Felipe didn't know it at the time, but the man he most wanted to see dead, was taking deep relaxing draws on a Romeo y Julieta Churchill. For the moment, Jesús remained oblivious to the revision to his plans, believing himself indestructible, issuing orders to a servant to bring him another chilled Aguila.

On learning of the assault, his mood soured instantly, domestic staff slipped into the villa's recesses for fear of confronting their master. Only Luis remained in his company, wise enough to stay silent as his brother raged, upending chairs, flinging bottles, screaming obscenities.

In the *comunas*, life stalled for 48 hours, its inhabitants finding cause to remain in their houses, none wanting to risk an encounter with the cartel, its *sicarios* driven to violence by their crazed leader in the search for his betrayer. Jesús didn't care that the area remained flooded with PNC officers intent on hunting him down; his fury burned greater than his caution. While his men continued to disrupt the neighbourhood, his younger brother did his best to keep him from returning to the compound, urging him to wait for calm.

Luis was the only person whose counsel Jesús considered. Theirs was an uneasy relationship. Luis was never fully confident that his brother trusted him, relying on their familial bond for his safety. He didn't think his brother would hurt him; he was blood. Luis believed there was a sacred bond between siblings that not even his brother would breach. He persuaded Jesús to stay away from the *comunas* until the presence of the PNC diminished and the uneasy normality within Los Alpes returned. When it did, Felipe received a summons to the compound.

Jesús and Luis were waiting. Jesús sat behind a desk; a dictator scrutinising those in front of him. Luis stood to his left, a silent guardian. The *sicarios* that escaped the PNC lined the walls, trying to look threatening while trying equally hard not to do anything to draw Jesús's ire. In front of the desk were four other boys, *pequeños espías* like Felipe, Sergio included.

Felipe received a push towards his friend, trying to catch his eye, but Sergio was unmoving, implacable, all signs of his usual humour gone. Felipe nestled alongside, not daring to look again, wondering if Sergio had already shared his suspicions.

Once Felipe took his place, Jesús reached into a drawer and removed a Glock 45 which he placed on the desk. Opening another drawer, he took out a plastic bag, heavy with cocaine. Ignoring the boys in front of him, he tipped a portion of the powder onto the table's glass inlay. He tapped at the mound with a sliver of solid gold, the size of a credit card, engraved with the words *El banco de Jesús*, separating the cocaine into five identical lines and admired his work.

Slowly he counted those before him, enunciating each number clearly, repeating *Cinco*. He counted the lines of cocaine in the same manner. *Cinco*. A glass tube materialised in his hand, a conjuring trick that carried no amusement to those watching. He sniffed at one of the lines, it disappeared, leaving a thin crescent of white at the tip of his nose. He snorted, drawing his forearm across his face to remove the powder. He counted again, the powder first, then the boys. *Cuatro. Cinco*. He paused, bemused. *¿Quién va sin?* Who goes without?

No one answered.

Quietly, menace thick in his voice, he asked again.

Silence.

The third time, the question exploded into the room. It galvanised the first in line to leap forward and snatch at the glass straw, an angelic looking child, barely ten years old, sporting albino like hair with golden flecks. Before he could raise it to his nose, Jesús pinned his hand to the desk and lifted the Glock to the boy's forehead. The terrified boy stared into eyes from which all reason had vanished. The room held its collective breath, waiting to see what Jesús would do. His madness dissolved, replaced with an avuncular smile, disarming in its warmth. He released the boy's hand and pointed the gun at one of the lines on the table, inviting the boy to take the powder. Relieved, the boy did as instructed, smiling back with a confidence that belied his fear, before gingerly placing the glass tube back on the table.

Encouraged by the shift in mood, the second boy picked up the tube unchallenged, snorted deftly and returned to the line. The third, leaving Felipe and Sergio behind, stepped toward the desk. Another line of powder disappeared, smashing into already jangling synapses, leaving a single strand of cocaine.

Felipe and Sergio looked at each other, neither venturing forward, both knowing what it would mean.

Jesús waited.

Neither moved.

Pointing at each of them in turn, Jesús counted. *Uno. Dos.* Slowly, he lowered his gaze to the remaining strand of powder. *Uno.* Opening his arms to them, Jesús offered them the chance to step forward, to explain, to reveal the weakness in his organisation.

Sergio stepped forward, not the solemn, terrified boy of moments before, but the jovial idiot from their school days, arms waving, nervous energy driving his performance. He played to Jesús; his shrill falsetto now muted with advancing puberty. Jesús was unmoved. Sergio became increasingly outrageous, desperate, employing manic theatrics, attempting to diffuse the mood, to introduce levity where none existed. Words tumbled in a stream of conscious dialogue, anything to make Jesús laugh.

A smile crept to Jesús's face. Others noticed, and as Sergio performed, stifled laughs emerged around the room. He responded, becoming more animated. Giggles turned to laughter. The tension evaporated.

Relaxing, Sergio ended his performance with a flourish, yielding the white powder to Felipe with a bow and a sweep of his arm. Felipe didn't want it, he didn't touch drugs, but he approached the desk.

Jesús held up a hand to stop his advance. Felipe halted. Jesús turned to Sergio, who was still holding his pose, then slow clapped his performance, five staccato slaps of his hands. The atmosphere shifted instantly, palpably. Smiles vanished. He turned to look at his brother next to him. *¿Cuál?* he asked. Which one?

Luis pretended not to understand the question.

Jesús waited for an answer which wasn't forthcoming. *¿Cuál?*

A shake of the head. Neither.

Jesús's shoulders slumped, disappointed with his brother's response. He picked up the gun by its barrel and offered it to Luis. *Decidir.*

Luis took it from him, staring at the gun. The little boy that had once shared *pinchos* with his friends looked at his brother, toying with the idea of defiance. He wasn't yet the ruthless man his brother had become. A tear formed and traced a gradual path across his cheek, losing its momentum at his jaw. He conveyed a silent pleading to his brother.

Jesús was unflinching, there was no yielding in his gaze. He waited.

With only his eyes, Luis willed his brother to release him from the burden, to free them all from the sentence that awaited.

His expression conveyed nothing of his thoughts as he watched his younger brother return the weapon to the desk. He looked from the gun to Luis, then Sergio to Felipe, before surveying the rest of the room, discovering an unwillingness to meet his eyes.

Finding nothing to engage him, he picked up the glass tube that lay alongside the final line of cocaine, examined it carefully, turning it over in his fingers, seemingly oblivious to everyone present. The place was silent, save for the soft hum of a portable air-conditioning unit that did little to cool the room.

Jesús leaned forward and with an exaggerated sniff, cleared the table of the final line of powder. He lifted his head, closed his eyes, savoured the rush. The tiny crescent moon of cocaine reappeared on his nose. He didn't wipe it clear. He leaned back in his chair; eyes shut. No one spoke.

Moments passed, stretching out. The boys, still in their line, shifted uncomfortably. Jesús opened his eyes, regarded each of them, weighing a decision. He picked up the Glock, nodded to himself, resolute.

Levelling the weapon at the first boy who had stepped from the line, he allowed the shadow of a smile to warm his features, gently shook his head, then pointed the gun at the next in line. He replicated his action, moving to the third, repeated the process, then held the gun at Felipe. He lingered for longer, waiting to see how Felipe would react.

Jesús might have been surprised if he knew how calm Felipe felt. Profoundly still, unafraid of his fate, Felipe had reconciled that death was near. He waited for the end. If Jesús had an insight into Felipe's thoughts, he would have pulled the trigger, the boy's calmness signalling his guilt. Instead, he shook his head in the same gentle manner and moved the gun onto Sergio.

A tumult fell from him, a semi-coherent babble: pleading, denial, meagre defiance. Jesús lifted the weapon to his lips to hush the mewling boy. The effect was like hitting a mute button. Sergio fell quiet, although his lips kept moving, an actor in a silent movie, eyes bright with panic, the mournful hum of the defective air-conditioner providing the only sound.

Luis step forward, imploring Jesús not to shoot his friend.

Jesús held up a hand. *Silencio.* A quiet threat.

Luis started to speak, causing a flicker of rage from Jesús.

Silencio. Louder, but still a whisper. Jesús pointed the gun at Sergio again, returning his gaze to him. Time and heart beats ticked.

A LITTLE SOMETHING TO HIDE

Jesús, no. It was barely audible, coming from his left, from Luis.

Jesús closed his eyes in frustration. His brother really didn't know when to shut the fuck up. He lowered the gun, keeping it beneath his hand, and grinned. An uneasy relief spread through the room at the possibility that Luis had prevailed.

Gracias, said Luis. It was the last word he uttered before his brother pointed the Glock at him and blew a hole in his chest.

Standing, Jesús cast a glance at the slumped form of his brother, then looked around the room seeking challengers. Most of those present found something of interest on the floor, only Felipe held his gaze. He had no fear of Jesús and didn't care if the man knew that he wanted him dead.

In that moment, Jesús knew his betrayer and contemplated a second execution. Instead, he tucked the gun in his waistband and smiled at Felipe, nodded knowingly, and left the room. He didn't need to kill again today. His brother's death would reinforce his position at the head of the organisation, no one would challenge a man who could kill one of his own. The *gilipollas*, Felipe, could stew in his own shit for a while before he had him killed.

Felipe didn't stop to speak before he left the compound, ignoring Sergio's shouts to wait as he raced to his apartment. Knowing the layout exactly, those precise places where he and his mother stored what little they owned, he kept the room dark when he got there, avoiding the light that might alert someone to his presence.

Finding the cereal box where he hid his money, he dumped the contents into his ragged school bag, before adding a change of clothes, making sure to conceal the fourteen million pesos he had slowly accumulated while working for the cartel. He looked around; the familiarity of the shadows taunted him. He wouldn't miss them; they had never provided comfort.

As he left, he pulled the door closed, locking it out of habit, though he would never be back. His feet scattered whispers of dust on the stairs as he slid from the building. It was quiet out, the street seemed to pose no threat, but still he shrunk into his hoodie, attempting to anonymise his appearance. He hadn't gone far when a figure emerged from a doorway. Sergio stepped into the illumination of a streetlamp. *I've been told to kill you.*

Felipe held his breath as Sergio reached into the pocket of his jacket. In the dim light, he couldn't discern what he held, but he expected the end to come quickly. Sergio stepped toward him, close enough to touch, bringing his arm up, holding it out to Felipe. *¡Vamos!*

Felipe looked at his friend, confused. He expected him to be holding a gun, but instead Sergio offered him a greasy bag. He recognised the familiar smell of their favourite street food as he took *pinchos* from his friend for the final time. *I'll tell him you were already gone.*

With no passport and no one to help him, escaping Colombia was daunting. Felipe caught a bus that night from Medellín, wandering the streets away from the terminus, hiding from anyone that might be searching, until it was time to leave for Cartagena where he headed for the docks, and an opportunity to sneak onto a ship that would take him anywhere. Slithering through the port, he clung to the sides of containers as he flittered unseen down the looming corridors they created.

The dock seemed to bray, the noise providing a form of security, solace even. Throughout the day and in the recesses of the night, the port dispensed activity. Trucks growled, warning signals grated, fork-lifts whirred, chains thundered against concrete and steel, stevedores barked instructions and insults at each other, all of it drowning out the slapping of worn shoes on the dockside as a young man scurried up an unmanned ramp, not knowing to where his feet were taking him.

To Veracruz. Mexico.

After two days at sea, his supply of food and water depleted, he revealed himself to an angry crew member who marched him to the ship's captain. The wily sailor took pity on him, for a price, relieving him of two-million pesos in exchange for feeding him for the rest of the journey and guiding Felipe to safety when they made landfall.

Felipe spent his first night on foreign soil in an empty boxcar tucked into a railway siding. In the morning he skulked around the area, less concerned about discovery, the anxiety of his escape diminishing, replaced by concerns that were less paralysing, almost exciting; optimistic thoughts of what his future might hold.

His instinct was to travel north, as far as he could, where he believed dreamers were welcome. He had confidence he could find his way, the people he met were untroubled by a kid with only a ragged backpack and false hopes. No one challenged his purpose, they indulged him, letting him pass through their lives, a memory which faded as quickly as the time it took to form.

Two weeks after arriving in Mexico, his supply of money dwindling, he sat in the shade of a derelict restaurant, forty miles from Berrendo and the US border, waiting for the chicken man to arrive.

A weathered man, as battered as the vehicle he drove, drew his truck to a stop in front of the restaurant. Rheumy eyes peered at Felipe from beneath a sweat-soaked Fedora. *Felipe*, he said, somewhere between a question and a statement. Felipe nodded, climbing into the cab alongside the old man. As he closed the door, the driver shugged the truck into gear and rumbled back onto the road.

Sitting quietly, watching the barren landscape of dried scrub and distant hills rolling past, Felipe didn't feel the need to share his tale with the driver, nor did the old man feel compelled to ask. He knew the boy's story, having heard it many times before – the hopes and woes of the folk he carried were always the same.

The two-hundred-dollar fee that he and Felipe agreed was his only concern. He knew it wouldn't be enough to suborn anyone on either side of the border, but he wasn't worried. No one cared about the contents of a refrigerated truck. If they did, he'd claim the boy climbed in when he wasn't looking, adding that anyone dumb enough to risk freezing their balls off was going to find a way into the country anyway.

He stopped the truck five miles from the turnoff to Berrendo, ushering Felipe into the back, holding out a hand for the last of his money. Felipe passed it over and climbed into the chilled interior. The chicken man put a finger to his lips, demanding silence, an action that reminded Felipe of why he was making the journey.

At Antelope Wells, Felipe heard a muffled conversation between the driver and a crossing guard. He subconsciously held his breath as the doors swung open for inspection. Commercial traffic didn't pass through this part of the border, but the old guy had ignored protestations for years with his truckful of chicken pieces. The guard decided an inspection was in order today, a quiet reminder to the driver that he couldn't always do as he pleased.

The frigid air and the smell of vacuum-packed poultry overwhelmed the guard's enthusiasm and rigour. His nose wrinkled; he threw a cursory glance inside the dimly lit truck. If his inspection had been deeper, he might have seen a pair of hazel eyes peering at him through a gap in the crates, wide-eyed with fear, but he didn't; he hated his job and the isolation of the Godforsaken outpost, it didn't warrant an heroic effort on his part. He lifted a couple of packs of chicken from one of the trays, ignoring the mock protest of the driver, waving him on as the doors clattered closed. Felipe breathed again.

Discerning improvements in the road's surface, Felipe knew they were safely in the United States. Twenty minutes later, the driver freed him from the chilled container to ride shotgun with him until they reached Deming, where they stopped at Pepper's Supermarket. He regarded Felipe for a moment, then without expression, said *Buena suerte*. Besides his name and the muted conversations at the border, it was the only thing Felipe had heard him say. He climbed from the cab to face his first day alone in his adopted country. The truck rumbled on.

A LITTLE SOMETHING TO HIDE

Felipe stood at the side of the road with his eyes closed, face turned to the sun, allowing its warmth to swallow him. Los Alpes was nearly 3,000 miles behind him, he had no money, and yet he felt a sense of calm that he hadn't known since before his mother's death. He took his first steps in his new country, direction unknown. He wondered if he would keep moving; safety lay in motion; it made him more difficult to find.

The dumpsters at the local McDonald's and Taco Bell provided him with sustenance for the next two days and a place for him to hide. On the third morning, he heard the familiar babble of his native tongue coming from a flat-bed pick-up in the carpark; migrant workers gathering for the day ahead.

Felipe approached nervously, improbably fearing identification, his escape ruined. He found a woman who looked tired, but had soft, understanding eyes, just like his mother's. He asked if they had work. She leaned across to the man opposite, tapping him on his knee before gesturing to Felipe. The man considered the boy in front of him, total comprehension crossing his face. He shuffled along the makeshift bench, creating a space, patting the seat next to him, providing Felipe with the chance he needed.

While the Briscola family was never generous with its employees' salaries, every three years or so, it increased the size of the monthly payments that nestled within the bony man's solid blue box with its imposing chrome latches. The increases never stemmed from benevolence, rather an acknowledgement that staff numbers were dwindling, that it was time to adjust payments in order to maintain its preferred ratio of undocumented workers.

Like many of the long-term employees of the company, Felipe was expecting to see an increase in the amount he collected each month. The 'or so' portion of their wait had extended to 18 months. In that time, Felipe's rent had increased twice and the cost of an empanada from Ajiaco had also headed north, his living expenses were consuming a greater proportion of his disposable income.

FELIPE – LOS ALPES

He had suffered the pressure on his finances for more than a year, maintaining silence on the subject, but when reviewing his latest payment and discovering that yet another month would pass with no swelling of his income, Felipe experienced an uncharacteristic triggering, finding himself once more at the front of the queue, contention poised on his lips. He didn't dwell on preamble. 'When are we going to get a raise?'

The bony man, in all other circumstances scrupulous, appeared surprised. 'Pardon me?'

'When are we going to get a raise?' Felipe repeated.

The management accountant peered over his shoulder to check that his minder was present. The be-suited beast nodded, acknowledging that he was alert to trouble.

'Name?'

'Felipe Alvarez.'

'Well, well, well,' said the bony man, standing to address the waiting queue. His quiet demeanour vanished, replaced with an assertive bearing, his voice finding a volume never before experienced by those in the line. 'It seems that Felipe Alvarez here, is unhappy with what we're paying him. Does anyone else share Mr Alvarez's opinion?'

Most eyes found the floor, the walls, or the ceiling. No one offered a response.

'I thought not. It seems the market is not yet ready for a correction, Mr Alvarez. Be assured that when it is, you will benefit along with your colleagues. No one will miss out.'

Felipe felt cowed, his rebellion crushed. He'd emerged from obscurity to challenge the bony man and exposed himself to humiliation. He'd also exposed himself to a new arrival, a young man not long in the country, harbouring a story similar to Felipe's.

It would have terrified Felipe to know that the young man was from Los Alpes, and that he too had stood in the same room Felipe had occupied 26 years earlier, had also born witness to indiscriminate executions.

The executioner's methods were little changed from a quarter-century before. Now though, no one he suspected of betrayal left the room alive. Every person he killed, and all those that stood in the room to witness, knew that he would never again make the mistake he made with Felipe Oscar Alvarez Medina. With every execution, he cursed *his name and added $50,000 to the reward for anyone who could find him.*

The young man in the queue contemplated the risks to his own life. He hadn't done anything to betray Jesús, he simply found himself unnerved at the prospect of becoming a sicario, *morally ill-equipped for the prospect of pulling a trigger. His morals withered though with the prospect of earning 1.9 million dollars for the discovery of Felipe Alvarez.*

He was thinking about the risks as he watched the small fat Colombian leave the building, thought more while he waited in line to collect his four-hundred dollars, and more still while he walked outside into the warm Californian day. The sky seemed unusually clear; the haze of Los Angeles wallowed elsewhere. It felt like a lovely day. No, it seemed a great day. A perfect day in fact, to make a call.

He dialled the number of his closest friend back home, the only one he thought he could trust. 'Mi amigo,' he said when the phone was answered. 'I think I can make us some money.'

```
Arrivals
Time    From              Expected
05:17   Gallup            Cancelled
```

NEARING ALBUQUERQUE

As Jimmy stepped from the bus in Gallup, a fair-haired man climbed onto the coach to occupy a seat near the front, as close as he could get to riding shot-gun. Despite his hair, which shines white with hints of gold, he sports a honeyed complexion, maple in tone, his skin smooth, still bearing the unblemished traits of youth. His eyes are a warm hazel, just like Felipe's, but remain hidden behind designer lenses that mask what thoughts he carries. He stands close to six-feet, weighs 180 pounds and bears a physique that speaks of power and strength. His clothing, casual, yet expensively tailored, adds to his appearance, the detailing of a handsome man. He is accustomed to admiration, both for how he looks and for what he does. He is good at his job, never failing an assignment. In his native land, they refer to him as 'El Muñeco de Nieve Bebe', *The Baby Snowman, it's an appellation he enjoys. It speaks of a pleasantness that belies his reputation.*

Most that meet him for the first time would place him in his early twenties, yet he is closer to forty, just a few years younger than the driver of the bus. He boasts a warm smile, it puts people at ease, garnering congeniality. He displays his best for Felipe who smiles in return, acknowledging his presence, not recognising the man who once stood on a street corner in Los Alpes as a pequeños espías *on the day the PNC came to town.*

The Baby Snowman was approaching ten-years old when he took his first and last snort of cocaine. He remembers it well, remembers the grip of the man who pointed a gun at his head when he was the first to step forward, a step that witnessed the start of his rise.

In the pitiless world of a Colombian drug cartel, life is cheap. The cliché is never better employed than when considering the cartel's practices. Its trade, reliant on the perpetuation of addiction, leads to the cartel's fortunes, is ruinous to its benefactors.

It is natural, therefore, that the loss of lives from the pursuit of its aims and the protection of its practices is viewed coolly, it's a cost of doing business. Unlike most costs a business incurs, a drug cartel has little inclination to reduce such expenditure, death is a by-product of its trade.

Unless the business of death yields intelligence, for which a cartel adopts lingering methods of extraction, expeditious endings best serve its needs. Justice, sentencing and execution are swift, the right of appeal, non-existent.

When Jesús killed his brother Luis, he not only ended the life of his one living relative, he also extinguished the last remnant of his humanity. Luis was the only person to whom Jesús held any affection, in killing him, he killed the last of his compassion. In the days that followed Luis's death, Jesús's rage grew with the failure to find Felipe. He railed against him, blaming Felipe for his brother's death, building a characterisation, creating a myth that Felipe bore responsibility for the loss of Luis. Jesús sought vengeance, reasoning awhile that Felipe's death was inadequate compensation. Felipe must suffer for his transgression. He wanted him found, returned to Los Alpes, where he would be confined and made to suffer daily, experiencing an unbearable pain that would leech the life from him until he was able to bear it no more. His suffering would be long and explicably painful.

When the call from LA was relayed, Jesús called for his most trusted lieutenant. 'Bebé Muñeco de Nieve. I want you to do something for me.'

It took Felipe several years to stop worrying about the cartel. He doesn't harbour Toby's paranoia; he no longer worries that a cartel sicario will track him down. He reserves his concerns for the folks from ICE; he doesn't ever want them to find him. Felipe's life is dull, a state he finds to be better than peachy, he's happy to keep it that way – driving, empanadas and beer are perfectly okay from his point of view.

As a combination, they've served to alter his form. When he entered the United States at Antelope Wells, crouching behind crates of chicken pieces, shivering, and wondering if he'd survive the cold, he was a *skinny kid weighing just 105 pounds. He is three times that weight now and not a lot of him resembles the waif of the past.*

At first, he enjoyed the weight gain. He considered it a sign that he was leading a better life. When he topped two hundred pounds, and every item in his wardrobe felt uncomfortable, he started to think he had a problem, not that he did anything to address the issue. Instead, he consoled himself with comparisons to many of the passengers that stepped onto his Briscola coach, assuring himself that he remained on the slimmer side of obese.

Felipe didn't plan to change his diet or begin exercising. His American dream meant he could dine on every variation of fast food when he was on the road, switching it up to favoured feasts from Ajiaco when he was home. His waistline grew as his arteries narrowed.

The Briscola coach passengers are bored with the unrelenting monotony of the landscape as the bus traverses the wide expanses between Gallup and Albuquerque. It is wearying to witness so much that is dull, although Felipe is accustomed to driving when he's tired. It's a feature of his journey that he overcomes with fantasies of inflicting harm on Jimmy Lewis. It has been a long journey, and he knows that the bastardo *Jimmy Lewis has done less of the driving than usual.*

His violent fantasy includes calling Lewis a 'goddamn motherfucker' as he punches him, imagining the cartilage of the gringos *nose crunching beneath his fist, blood spattering Jimmy's face. He'd love to stand over his prone body and spit on him, although he will never get that opportunity.*

The desolation of the landscape gives way to a burgeoning city, the I-40, the old Route-66, morphs into the Coronado Freeway as Felipe draws closer to his journey's end, to his home. His concentration heightens as he nears the Rio Grande, perpetually snaking south, its waters a fluid chocolate, rich with alluvial pigments.

Felipe both loves and hates reaching this point in the road. He loves that his journey is almost complete, that he'll soon be lying back in his La-Z-Boy watching the Astros with a chilled Rock in his hand. He hates it because his anxiety rises.

His partner has gone and he's entering urban territory once again. The probability of police is more likely, and he never knows when one of Albuquerque's finest might fancy a random inspection of a dilapidated Briscola coach. On this part of the freeway, the speed limit is sixty-five miles per hour. Felipe never exceeds sixty. He will do nothing to risk attention.

His anxiety reveals differently today. Today he feels a tightness in his chest. It's mild and uncomfortable at first, he thinks it's just another dash of the heartburn that he so often suffers. A thin bead of moisture breaks across his forehead, he drags an arm across to dry his brow. The perspiration is quick to come these days, he attributes it to his weight, idly thinking that he needs to start doing something. The thought dissolves as he considers how warm he's feeling, cursing the Briscolas for their failure to maintain the air conditioning.

Felipe tugs at his collar where there should be a tie. The garment's absence is a sackable offence, but most drivers remove them when they clear departure termini, replacing them before reaching LA or their destination. The ties are cheap, static polyester with elasticated bands that cut into the expanse of Felipe's neck.

It feels as though he's wearing a tie now, although his sits in a cup holder, neatly rolled, alongside a neighbouring holder which contains the third 30-ounce Coca-Cola that he's consumed on the trip. He glances at the tie as if needing confirmation that it isn't clutching his throat. He is developing a growing awareness that something is profoundly wrong.

The Baby Snowman notices the change in the driver, notices the approaching river and the distant skyline of the city beyond, deciding it is time to make himself known, to focus the mind of the man driving the coach. He steps toward Felipe, placing a firm hand on his shoulder.

'Please sir,' manages Felipe, 'You must sit down.'

The reply comes in Spanish, a Colombian variant, a voice he's heard before. 'Ha pasado mucho tiempo mi viejo amigo.' It's been a long time my old friend.

Felipe risks taking his eyes from the road to better see the man beside him. A dull thud of recognition punches a gasp from him, causing a further tightening in his chest.

'I've come to take you home,' says The Baby Snowman.

Felipe knows instantly what that means, the pain that it represents. It is a pain that he thinks he might prefer to the invisible band now wrapping itself around his chest, constricting him. His breathing becomes more laboured, as though the air doesn't want to enter his lungs. He tries to breathe deeply, but there feels a barrier that his breath cannot surmount, a wall for it to scale before it can enter and ease the pressure that is building.

The contraction worsens, a monumental pressure, crushing him with its force. The pain is acute, his concentration flees. He sees nothing, blinded by the intense burn. He fights, arching against the pain, recovering some semblance of vision, dimly aware that his bus is veering from its lane. They are travelling faster too, his foot weighing heavier on the accelerator. He knows this but is unable to respond. He cannot move his leg to slow the bus.

Thinking Felipe is trying to unbalance him, The Baby Snowman draws his Glock to persuade Felipe to behave, but the weapon is beyond being a useful tool to influence the coach's driver, nothing will persuade him now, he has moved past the point where he can respond to external stimuli.

From somewhere behind comes a shriek, the first passenger alert to the trouble: Gracie MacDonald. Gracie is aware of everything. Her squeal breaks the torpor of the other passengers whose minds have drifted with the miles. They look up to see that Felipe's correction has them heading toward the concrete barrier at the roadside.

Felipe realises it too. With an effort that feels colossal, he lifts his foot across to the brake, hitting it hard to avert the danger. There should be tension beneath his foot, resistance to the force applied. The pedal yields to the excess pressure, collapsing into its well. The bus continues its course with no change in pace. 'Fucking Briscolas,' thinks Felipe, before another burst of pain causes him to slump across the steering wheel, revealing a vision long forgotten that makes him forget The Baby Snowman, provides him with comfort in his final moments. He sighs, contented, 'Voy a casa mamá.' He is leaving his passengers; his time is short.

The barrier at the side of the road is the only thing that can save the passengers now, Felipe is beyond bringing them to a stop. The Baby Snowman realises that his countryman is incapable of action, he attempts to push him from his seat, but his weight is too great, the Snowman's efforts fruitless. He cannot change the course of the bus; his first failure is his last.

A LITTLE SOMETHING TO HIDE

The bus cuts an angle across the road, narrowly missing cars on the inside lane. It crashes into the barrier, throwing all on board forward, most heads crack against the seats in front, three do not. The window at the front of the coach provides no resistance as Jesús's sicario is thrown against it. Rather than shattering, it pops free, the Colombian assassin flies through the opening and is rendered rag-doll, battered between the bus and the road.

Sandra's ending is faster, no chair sits before her, only the railing that leads down to the buses' toilet. She sails over this, catching her head on the corner of the bathroom unit, which buries itself deeply into her eye socket before momentum causes her cheek to shatter, a fragment piercing her brain.

Baby George's car seat, unsecured alongside her, becomes a projectile. He flies, buckled in his unanchored chair, still alive, unaware that the underside of his seat has sliced through the elevated head of Michael Williams, removing the six inches of his height that his mother had once joked she would take from him if he ever stooped to consider a bribe. The faintest breath of time elapsed between the deaths of Sandra and Michael.

After removing the top of Michael's head, the car seat continued its trajectory, passing through an already fractured window before the bus plunged into the Rio Grande. A state trooper, the first on the scene, found the seat nestling on the bank above the river, its occupant quiet, his wailing and tears exhausted, wearing wounds that will mark his features for life, an innocent spared. In a conspicuous twist of fate, the man who once abandoned the boy and his mother will graciously accept the responsibility to raise and love his son.

Although decelerating, the buses' momentum takes it through the barrier, a metallic howl signalling a deep gouge along its length. Had the Baby Snowman approached Felipe anywhere in the proceeding fifty miles, perhaps inducing his heart attack sooner, the bus might have rolled to a halt on a flat expanse of desert, but not here, not now. The Rio Grande roils below, a short fall away.

It is perhaps not as far as the metaphoric fall that awaits the Briscolas in the months to come, with Felipe's death inviting closer scrutiny of their employment practices. They will discover that the sums they paid to their management accountant proved insufficient to guarantee his silence.

NEARING ALBUQUERQUE

For now though, there is no dramatic teetering on a cliff for the bus, no cinematic pause on a precipice that yields to a climactic rescue, it plummets into the river below with little time passing between the death of the first and the death of the last. Felipe Alvarez's heart attack led to the accident, but it is the plunge into the waters of the Rio Grande that represents the terminal act.

And so, here I am, subverting humanity, brooking no luxury for discernment. As arbitrary as the cartel seems, I am more so. There is no measure of goodness that prevents me from exacting my toll, no preference I gift to the kind, no penalty for the wicked. If I did, Jimmy Lewis would have felt more than just the chill trace of my hand drawing a lingering line across his stomach. His death will follow in time. It will be slow, insufferable. He deserves what is coming to him.

Although Jimmy escaped with his life, he will lose his job when the Briscola's learn that he wasn't on the bus. The leverage he holds over the Briscolas is about to disappear into the river below. The family will encourage a spurious prosecution against him, citing the human trafficking of an unnamed Colombian national. They'll be unsuccessful, but they'll ruin him on their way down.

While Jimmy Lewis is pouring himself a coffee in Gallup, adding Half & Half because he couldn't possibly drink anything black, I passed unnoticed through the Albuquerque bound coach, brushing a finger across each of the passengers, arms splayed as though passing through a field of tall grass, the susurrations too low to hear.

The lightness of my touch goes unnoticed, although Toby Ames, his senses distorted by the lasting effects of nose candy, reacts to the touch with a jerk but can see nothing more than his demons. Baby George issues a single strangled squawk that alarms his mother, but she cannot find the source of her child's disturbance. Perhaps he registered the brush of my finger on her cheek and understood what it represents. He will live – for now.

Some of the passengers are strangers, some have been in my presence before. I know Jeannie Roberts, having felt the pressure beneath her hands each time she stole an elderly life. Sometimes she sang, other times she whispered gentle nothings, always with a smile, always, she told herself, with love.

A LITTLE SOMETHING TO HIDE

While Amy and Mary-Beth held Antonio's hands, I cradled him in my arms as Robert Jamieson stood by deciding that it was finally time to speak his truth. Robert will die a man in love, utterly content with his choices. His parents will never know of his love for Peter or that their sometime doleful boy had found his nirvana, that he was truly, blissfully, happy.

I bore witness to the heavy breathing of Rosa Fernandez as she stood at the top of the stairs after pushing Jorge with all her strength. I knelt beside her husband, waiting to take him home, while he bled, his head twisted at an impossible angle, an incongruous rictus smile painted on his face.

Tim and Briony's previous pleasures didn't warrant my company. They were living out their fantasies when Felipe's heart gave way, Tim holding her to him, the pleasure divorcing him from the impending danger. When the emergency services recovered their bodies, a substantial piece of Tim's anatomy remained in Briony's mouth, they could have matched it to a picture on her phone. They found the rest of Tim elsewhere.

The darkest secrets of those on board travelled with them into the abyss; secrets they kept hidden from the world and sometimes from themselves. Their deceits died that day, along with their truths.

Like the truth that the MacDonald boys will never discover, that in a quiet corner of Vietnam, Archie MacDonald spoons into the back of his wife, Linh, when they go to bed each night. Linh doesn't know, or care, about the great heritage of the MacDonald clan, and Archie has long forgotten Granny Mac's lies. Archie and Linh's life needs no embellishment. Theirs is a love that has endured from the day he wrote the letter to Gracie and the boys, asking for their forgiveness, telling them that he was never coming home. He will never learn of his ex-wife's death, nor will his boys learn of their father's happiness.

Toby Ames' mother will glory in a life that could have been. For once, her acquaintances will indulge her fantasies. They will agree around their kitchen tables, to which she is never invited, that it's not right to be critical of a woman who has lost her only child.

With the exception of Baby George, all will die on the coach. The last to go will be Father Simon. He will be alive when the bus hits the water, issuing a fervent prayer, his need for God's help suddenly profound, as though his faith is fully restored. He will know little of what is happening to him as the river forces the last of the air from his lungs. He will be unconscious as he drowns in the flowing waters of the Rio Grande, the place where he will finally learn whether or not God exists.

A LITTLE SOMETHING TO HIDE

ACKNOWLEDGEMENTS

During the early stages of writing this novel, I entertained the idea of travelling the route by way of research, however, the Covid pandemic served to scupper my plans to research the journey. I guess therefore, some kudos should go to Google Maps and Google Earth. If things don't sound right about the places within or the landscape, that's my fault. Google did its best.

There are many people to thank for supporting me on an altogether different journey that has led me to this point. To my dear friend, Reverend Paul Cowan, thanks for providing me with guidance and kindness and for a faith that shines brighter than Simon Carter's.

To the fabulous folks who agreed to be early readers, the insights provided not only helped to improve the book, but more importantly, gave me the confidence to pull on my big-boy pants and send it out into the world. So, huge thanks to Rodney Strong, Nic Veltman, Jean St John, Mel Eeles, Suzy Grogan, Fiona Horsfall, Hela Giddings, Emily and Richard Langdon, Moira Dean, Rachel Page, Justine Whitfield, Paul and Hannah Cowan, Lisa Richardson, Phil Wright, Sacha Emery, Simon Pook, Niamh Cole, Andrew Buchanan, Nimmi Menon, Kate Phillips, Chris Brown, James Walsh, Martin Warriner, Alison Rideal, Eimear Noone, Carol Turner, and Alison Davies – thank you, thank you, thank you. You helped me over the hurdles that my fear put in the way.

To the group at West Berkshire Writers, where I was slow to be brave, thanks to Michael (Jack) Diamond and John Clay who happened to be sitting closest to me when I was throwing around a copy of the manuscript.

As I was working my way toward publication, I had the opportunity to work with some industry professionals, each of whom helped me to advance along the way. So, cheers too, to

Hayley Webster for your editorial insights and for the proposed structural changes that made this a better book, Amanda Preston who suggested the name change that took me away from my beloved 'Nearing Albuquerque' and convinced me to find something more pointed, Matt Shaw, who at the Bournemouth Festival of Writing, provided the epiphany that led to the serialisation of this book, Bo Sullivan who corrected my misplaced Americana, the immensely talented Jason Heffer of Disrupt Media, who took my scattered thoughts on cover design and transformed them into the glorious rendering that you hold in your hands, and David Gaughran, whose freely available resources provide much needed practical advice and the stepping stones to follow to get this out into the world.

Thanks too, to my wonderful sister, Susan, and the best children a man could hope for in Jamie and Pippa. I truly felt the love in your labours.

There's one early reader above all others who deserves a special mention. The first, as ever, who suffers more dodgy drafts than most, my gorgeous love, Alex. Thank you for being there, for indulging me when cricket served as the ultimate procrastination, and for providing the love and support needed when the black smudges didn't quite cohere to the ideas. You made the first awkward efforts better and kept the fire burning.

A LITTLE SOMETHING TO HIDE

If you enjoyed reading *A Little Something To Hide*, please leave a review.

To keep up to date with the work of Craig Brown, sign up to his mailing list at craigbrownauthor.com or follow on socials:
Socials: @GOMinTraining – Facebook / Threads / BlueSky / Twitter/X / Instagram

And finally ...
I'm often asked what inspired the characters in *A Little Something To Hide*. The truth is that each came from a different place. Mostly, the dog and I discussed them on our walks in the morning, imagining the worlds that they inhabit. I have included a short essay on the thinking behind each character in each of the serialised volumes. If you wanted to read the entire series of essays, with a bonus essay on the conception of *A Little Something To Hide*, you can find them in a single volume, *Nothing Left To Hide: The Origin Series*, by scanning the QR codes overleaf.

Craig
Newbury, June 2024

A LITTLE SOMETHING TO HIDE

UK

USA

Australia

India

Canada